THE
SCANDALOUS
Sabbatinis

Three sensational, passionate novels from
bestselling Mills & Boon® author

MELANIE MILBURNE

Scandalous Dynasties

June 2013
THE SCANDALOUS KOLOVSKYS
Carol Marinelli

July 2013
THE SCANDALOUS ORSINIS
Sandra Marton

August 2013
THE SCANDALOUS WAREHAMS
Penny Jordan

September 2013
THE SCANDALOUS SABBATINIS
Melanie Milburne

THE SCANDALOUS
Sabbatinis

MELANIE MILBURNE

Published in Great Britain 2013
by Mills & Boon, an imprint of Harlequin (UK) Limited, Eton House,
18-24 Paradise Road, Richmond, Surrey TW9 1SR

THE SCANDALOUS SABBATINIS
© Harlequin Enterprises II B.V./S.à.r.l. 2013

Scandal: Unclaimed Love-Child © Melanie Milburne 2010
Shock: One-Night Heir © Melanie Milburne 2010
The Wedding Charade © Melanie Milburne 2011

ISBN: 978 0 263 90729 2

009-0913

Harlequin (UK) policy is to use papers that are natural, renewable and recyclable products and made from wood grown in sustainable forests. The logging and manufacturing processes conform to the legal environmental regulations of the country of origin.

Printed and bound by
CPI Group (UK) Ltd, Croydon, CR0 4YY

SCANDAL: UNCLAIMED LOVE-CHILD

MELANIE MILBURNE

Melanie Milburne says: 'I am married to a surgeon, Steve, and have two gorgeous sons, Paul and Phil. I live in Hobart, Tasmania, where I enjoy an active life as a long-distance runner and a nationally ranked top ten Master's swimmer. I also have a Master's Degree in Education, but my children totally turned me off the idea of teaching! When not running or swimming I write and, when I'm not doing all of the above, I'm reading. And if someone could invent a way for me to read during a four-kilometre swim I'd be even happier!'

To Carey and Laura Denholm,
such wonderful friends and fabulous company.
Thanks for being there for us when we needed it most
and thanks too for all the side-splitting jokes! XX

CHAPTER ONE

BRONTE was doing a hamstring stretch at the barre when she heard the studio door open. She looked in the wall-to-ceiling mirror, her heart screeching to a halt when she saw a tall dark figure come in behind her. Her eyes flared in shock, her hands instantly dampening where they clung to the barre. Her heart started up again, but this time with a staccato beat which seemed to mimic the frantic jumble of her thoughts.

It couldn't be.

She must be imagining it.

Of course she was imagining it!

It couldn't be Luca.

Her mind was playing tricks. It always did when she was tired or stressed. And she was both.

She curled her fingers around the barre, opening and closing her eyes to clear her head. She opened them again and her heart gave another almighty stumble.

It just couldn't possibly be Luca Sabbatini. There were hundreds, no, possibly thousands of stunningly handsome dark-haired men who might just by chance wander into her studio and—

'Hello, Bronte.'

Oh, dear God, it was him.

Bronte took a slow deep breath and straightened her shoulders as she turned and faced him. 'Luca,' she said with cool politeness. 'I hope you're not thinking of booking in for the first class of the afternoon. It's full.'

His dark eyes roamed over her close-fitting dance wear–clad body slowly, lingering for a heart-stopping moment on her mouth, before meshing his gaze with hers. 'You look as beautiful and as graceful as ever,' he said as if she hadn't spoken.

Bronte felt a frisson of emotion rush through her at the sound of his voice: rich and dark and deep and smoky with its unmistakable and beautifully cultured Italian accent. He looked the same as the last time she had seen him, although perhaps a little leaner if anything. Well over six feet tall, with glossy black hair that was neither short nor long, neither straight nor curly, and with the darkest brown eyes she had ever seen, he towered over her five feet seven, making her feel as dainty and tiny as a ballerina on a child's music box.

'You've got rather a cheek to come here,' she said with a flash of her gaze. 'I thought you said all that needed to be said two years ago in London.'

Behind his eyes it looked as if a small light had gone on and off like a pen-sized flashlight. It was a tiny movement and she would not have seen it at all if she hadn't been glaring at him so heatedly. 'I am here on business,' he said, his voice sounding a little rusty. 'I thought it might be a good chance to meet up again.'

'Meet up and do what exactly?' she asked with a lift of her chin. 'Talk about old times? Forget about it, Luca. Time and distance has done the trick. I am finally over you.'

She turned and walked back to the barre. 'I have a class starting in five minutes,' she addressed him in the mirror. 'Unless you want to be surrounded by twenty little girls in tights and leotards, I suggest you leave.'

'Why are you teaching instead of dancing?' he asked as his gaze held hers steady in the mirror.

Bronte rolled her eyes impatiently and turned back to face him. She placed one hand on her hip, her top lip going up in a what-would-you-care curl. 'I was unable to make the audition at the last minute, that's why.'

A small frown pulled at his brow. 'Were you injured?'

Bronte suppressed an embittered smile. Heartbroken and pregnant sort of qualified for injury, didn't it? 'You could say that,' she said, sending him a cutting look. 'Teaching was the next best option. Back home in Melbourne seemed the best place to set up to do it.'

His dark gaze swept over the old warehouse Bronte and her business partner Rachel Brougham had fashioned into a dance studio. 'How much rent do you pay on this place?' he asked.

A feather of suspicion started to dust its way up Bronte's spine. 'Why do you ask?'

One of his broad shoulders rose and fell in a noncommittal shrug. 'It's a sound investment opportunity,' he said. 'I'm always in the market for good commercial property.'

She frowned as she studied his inscrutable expression. 'I thought you worked in hotel management for your family?'

Luca smiled a ghost of a smile. 'I've diversified quite a bit since I saw you last. I have several other interests now. Commercial property is a sure bet; it often gives much better returns than the domestic property market.'

Bronte pressed her lips together as she worked on controlling her emotions. Seeing him like this, unannounced and unexpected, had thrown her completely. It was so hard to maintain a cool unaffected pose when inside she felt as if she had been scraped raw. 'I am sure if you contact the landlords they will tell you the place is not for sale,' she said after a short pause.

'I have contacted them.'

She felt her spine slowly turn to ice as her eyes climbed all the way back up to his. 'A…and?'

His half-smile gave him a rakish look. It was one of the things that had jump-started her heart the first time she had met him in a bookshop in London. Her heart was doing a similar thing now, for all her brave talk of having got over him.

'I have made them an offer,' he said. 'That's one of the reasons I am here in Australia. The Sabbatini Hotel Corporation is expanding more and more globally. We have plans to build a luxury hotel in Melbourne and Sydney and another on the Gold Coast of Queensland. Perhaps you have heard about it in the newspapers.'

Bronte wondered how she could have missed it. In spite of her animosity towards him, from time to time she couldn't stop herself trawling the papers and gossip magazines for a mention of him or his family. Only a few months ago she had heard of the separation of his older brother Giorgio and his wife Maya. She had also heard something about his younger brother Nicoló winning an obscene amount of money playing poker in a Las Vegas casino. But she had heard nothing of Luca.

It was as if for the last two years he had completely disappeared off the news media radar.

'No, but then again I have better things to do with my time,' she said with a disparaging look.

His dark eyes continued to hold hers in a stare-down Bronte was determined to win. She tried to keep her expression masked but even so his presence was having an intense effect on her. She could feel her skin tightening all over, her heart was racing again and her stomach was fluttering with a frenzied flock of razor-sharp wings. Seeing him again was something she had never allowed herself to think about. On a cold, miserable, grey day in November almost two years ago he had brought their six-month affair to an abrupt and bitter end. Her love for him had over time cooled down until it was now like a chunk of sharp-edged ice stuck right in the middle of her chest. What sort of naïve fool had she been to have loved such a heartless man? He had not once returned any of her calls or emails. In fact she suspected he had switched addresses and numbers in order to get her out of his life.

And now he was back as if nothing had happened.

'Why are you here?' she asked with a pointed glare. 'Why are you *really* here?'

He continued to look down at her from his towering height, but something about his expression had softened slightly. His dark eyes reminded her of melted chocolate, his mouth a temptation equally irresistible. She could almost feel those sculptured lips pressing down on hers. Her lips tingled with the memory and, as she thought of how he had made her feel in his arms, her chest felt as if someone was slowly pulling scratchy pieces of string from all four chambers of her heart.

Bronte felt her guard lowering and hastily pulled up the drawbridge on her emotions, standing stiffly before him, her arms folded across her middle, her mouth tight with renewed resolve.

'I wanted to see you again, Bronte,' he said. 'I wanted to make sure you are all right.'

She blew out a breath of disgust. 'All right? Why wouldn't I be all right?' she asked. 'Your ego must be far bigger than I realised if you think I would be still pining over you after all this time. It's been nearly two years, Luca. Twenty-two months and fourteen days, to be exact. I've well and truly moved on with my life.'

'Are you seeing anyone?' he asked, still watching her in that rock-steady hawk-like way of his.

Bronte pushed up her chin. 'Yes, as a matter of fact I am.'

He gave no outward sign of the news affecting him but she sensed an inner tension in him that hadn't been there before. 'Would your current partner mind if I stole you for dinner this evening?' he asked.

'I am not going out with you, Luca,' she said with deliberate firmness. 'Not tonight, not tomorrow night, not ever.'

He moved a step closer, his hand coming down on one of her arms to stop her from moving away from him. Bronte looked down at his long, dark, tanned fingers on her creamy bare skin within touching distance of her breasts, and felt her body shiver all over. It felt as if her blood was being heated to boiling point from that simple touch. She felt the drum roll of her heart and the deep quiver of her belly as his fingers subtly tightened. 'Is one night so very much to ask?' he said.

She pushed at his hand but he brought his other one

over the top and held her firm. He was too close. She could feel his warm minty breath on her face. She could smell his lemon-based aftershave. She could feel her body responding as if on autopilot. 'Don't do this, Luca,' she said in a cracked whisper.

'Don't do what?' he asked, holding her gaze steady with his as his thumb slowly, mesmerisingly stroked along the back of her hand.

She swallowed a lump of anguish. 'I think you know,' she said. 'This is a game to you. You're here in Australia and you want a playmate. And who better than someone you already know who is going to go away when it's over without too much fuss.'

A corner of his mouth lifted in a rueful smile. 'Your opinion of me is a lot worse than I expected. Didn't I give you enough compensation for bringing an end to our affair?'

More than you know, Bronte thought. 'I sent the opal pendant back,' she said with a defiant glare. 'They're supposed to be bad luck. I kind of figured I had already had my fair share in meeting you.'

A tight spot appeared beside his mouth, like a pulse of restrained anger beating beneath his skin. 'It was very mean-spirited of you to return it in that state,' he said. 'It was an expensive piece. How did you smash it? Did you back over it with an earth mover or something?'

She pushed her chin a little higher. 'I used a hammer. It was immensely satisfying.'

'It was an appalling waste of a rare black opal,' he said. 'If I had known you were going to be so petulant about it I would have given you diamonds instead. They, at least, are unbreakable.'

'I am sure I would have found a way,' she said tightly.

He smiled then, a rare show of perfect white teeth, the movement of his lips triggering the creasing of the fine lines about his eyes. 'Yes, I am sure you would have, *cara*.'

Bronte felt that quivery feeling again and tried desperately to suppress it. What was it about this man that made her so weak and needy? His mere presence made her remember every moment they had spent together. Her body seemed to wake up from a long sleep and leap to fervent life. All her senses were switched to hyper vigilant mode, each and every one of her nerves twitching beneath her skin to be subjected again to the exquisite mastery of his touch.

He had been the most amazing lover. Her *only* lover. She had been romantically and perhaps somewhat foolishly saving herself for the right man. She hadn't wanted to repeat the mistakes her mother had made in falling for a wastrel and then being left holding the baby. Bronte had instead fallen for a billionaire and the baby she had been left holding he still knew nothing about.

And, given how appallingly he had treated her, she planned to keep it that way.

'I have to ask you to leave, Luca,' she said. 'I have a class in a few minutes and I—'

'I want to see you tonight, Bronte,' he stated implacably. 'No is not a word I will tolerate as an answer.'

She pulled out of his hold with a surge of strength that was fuelled by anger. 'You can't force me to do anything, Luca Sabbatini,' she said. 'I am not under any obligation to see you, have dinner with you or even look at you. Now, if you don't leave immediately, I will call the police.'

His dark eyes hardened to black ice. 'How much rent did you say you were paying on this place?' he asked.

Bronte felt a lead-booted foot of apprehension press down on her chest until she could barely breathe. 'I didn't say and I am not going to.'

His smile had a hint of cruelty about it. He reached into the inside breast pocket of his suit jacket and handed her a silver embossed vellum business card. 'My contact details,' he said. 'I will expect you at eight this evening at my hotel. I have written the name and address on the back. I am staying in the penthouse suite.'

'I won't be there,' she warned him as he turned to leave.

He stopped at the door of the studio and turned to look at her. 'Perhaps you had better speak to your previous landlords before you make your final decision,' he said.

'Previous?' Bronte's eyes flared as the realisation dawned. 'You mean you bought the building?' Her heart gave a stutter like an old lawnmower refusing to start. 'Y…you're my new landlord?'

He gave her a self-satisfied smile. 'Dinner at eight, Bronte, otherwise you might find the sudden rise in rent too much to handle.'

Bronte felt anger rise up like lava inside an ancient volcano. Her whole body was shaking with it. Her hands were so tightly fisted her fingers ached, and her blood was pounding so hard in her veins she could hear a roaring in her ears. 'You're *blackmailing* me?' she choked.

He met her excoriating look with equanimity. 'I am

asking you on a date, *tesore mio*,' he said. 'You know you want to say yes. The only reason you are making all this fuss is because you are still angry with me.'

'You're damn right I'm still angry with you,' she spat.

'I thought you said you were over me,' he returned with an indolent smile.

Bronte wanted to slap that smile right off his face and only a smidgen of self-discipline and common sense stopped her. 'There is a part of me that will always hate you, Luca,' she said. 'You played with me and then tossed me aside like a toy that no longer interested you. You didn't even have the decency to meet with me face to face to discuss what had gone wrong.'

The hot spot of tension was beating beside his mouth again but Bronte continued regardless. 'What sort of man are you to send one of your lackeys to do your dirty work for you?'

His eyes darkened as he held her burning gaze. 'I thought it would be less complicated that way,' he said. 'I don't like deliberately upsetting people. Believe me, Bronte, meeting you in person would have been much harder on both of us.'

Bronte rolled her eyes again. 'That is *such* an arrogant thing to say. As if for a moment you had any feelings. You're a heartless, cruel bastard, Luca Sabbatini, and I wish I had never met you.'

The studio door opened again. 'Sorry I'm late. You would not believe the traff— Oh, oops…sorry,' Rachel Brougham said. 'I didn't realise you had company.'

Bronte walked stiffly to the reception desk, using it as a barricade. 'Mr Sabbatini is just leaving,' she said with a pointed glare at Luca.

Rachel's gaze went back and forth like someone at a Wimbledon final. 'You're not one of the parents, are you?' she asked Luca.

'No,' he said with a crooked smile. 'I have not had the pleasure as yet of becoming a father.'

Bronte couldn't look at him. Her face felt like a furnace as she silently prayed Rachel wouldn't mention Ella.

'So…' Rachel smiled widely, her grey eyes twinkling with interest. 'You know Bronte, huh?'

'Yes,' he said. 'We met a couple of years ago in London. My name is Luca Sabbatini.' He held out his hand to Rachel.

Please, God, please don't let her join the dots, Bronte begged silently.

'Rachel Brougham,' Rachel said, taking his hand and shaking it enthusiastically. 'Hey, I think I read something about you in the paper a couple of weeks ago. You're in hotels, right?'

'That's right,' Luca said. 'I have some business here and thought it would be a good opportunity to catch up again with Bronte. We're planning to have dinner tonight.'

'Actually, I have something on to—' Bronte began.

'She'd love to come,' Rachel said quickly, giving Bronte an are-you-nuts-to-turn-him-down look. 'She hardly ever goes out. I was only telling her the other day how she needs to get a life.'

Bronte sent her friend a look that would have stopped a charging bull in its tracks. Rachel just smiled benignly and turned back to look at Luca. 'So how long are you in Melbourne?' she asked, leaning her elbows on the reception counter as if she was settling in for a good old natter, her expression rapt with interest.

'A month to start with,' he said. 'I will use Melbourne as a base as I have some distant relatives here. I will also be spending a bit of time in Sydney and the Gold Coast.'

Bronte hadn't realised Luca had family here. Although, now that she thought about it, Melbourne had a huge Italian community so it was not all that unlikely he would have cousins or second cousins, even perhaps uncles and aunts. They hadn't really talked too much about their backgrounds when they were involved. Bronte had always found his reticence about his family one of the most intriguing things about him. It was as if he wanted to forget he was from wealth and privilege. He rarely mentioned his work and, although they had dated for six months, he had never flashed his money around as some rich men would have done. They had eaten in nice restaurants, certainly, and, apart from that hideously expensive parting gift delivered by one of his minions, she had never received anything off him other than the occasional bunch of flowers. But then hadn't he unknowingly given her the most priceless gift of all?

'Well, I am sure you'll have a fabulous time while you're in Australia,' Rachel went on, just shy of gushing. 'You speak fabulous English. Have you been here before?'

'Thank you,' Luca said. 'I was educated in England during my teens and have spent the last few years travelling between my homes in Milan and London. I haven't so far had the chance to travel to Australia but both of my brothers have. My older brother's wife is Australian, although they met abroad.'

The first of the afternoon class began to arrive. Bronte watched as Luca turned to look at the group of small children who filed in with their mothers or, in a couple of cases, with their nannies. He smiled softly at them and several mothers did double takes; even the girls beamed up at him as if he was some sort of god or well known celebrity.

'If you'll excuse me,' Bronte said to him stiffly as she moved from behind the reception desk, 'I have a class to conduct.'

'I will see you this evening,' he said, locking gazes with her. 'I have a hire car so I can pick you up if you give me your address.'

Bronte thought of the modest little granny flat she and Ella lived in at the back of her mother's house. She thought too of all the baby paraphernalia that would require an explanation if he was to insist on coming inside. She was not ready to explain anything to him after what he had done. He'd had his chance to find out about his baby and he'd callously thrown it away. 'No, thank you,' she said. 'I can make it on my own.'

He gave her a gleaming smile. 'So you've made up your mind to come after all?'

She gave him a beady look in return. 'It's not as if I have much choice in the matter. You're hanging the threat of charging me an exorbitant rent if I don't comply with your wishes.'

He reached out and trailed the point of his finger down the curve of her cheek, the action setting off a riot of sensation beneath her skin. 'You have no idea what my wishes are, *cara*,' he said softly and, before she could say a word in return, he had turned and left.

CHAPTER TWO

'OF COURSE I'll mind Ella for you,' Tina Bennett said to Bronte later that evening. 'She'll be tucked up in bed in any case by then. Are you going out with Rachel's brother David again? I know he's not exactly your type but he seems a rather sincere sort of chap.'

Bronte cuddled her fourteen-month-old daughter on her lap, breathing in her freshly bathed smell. 'No,' she said, meeting her mother's gaze. 'It's someone I met while I was in London. He's in Melbourne for a few weeks and decided to look me up.'

Tina's slim eyebrows moved together in a worried frown. 'Bronte, darling, is it him? Is it Ella's father?'

Bronte nodded grimly. 'I stupidly thought this day would never come. When he broke off our relationship the message I got was he never wanted to see me again. "A clean break," he said. Now he's suddenly changed the rules.'

'You don't have to see him if you don't want to, darling,' Tina said. 'It's not as if he knows about Ella. Anyway, after the way he treated you, I don't think you are under any obligation to tell him.'

Bronte's long heavy sigh stirred the soft feathery dark brown hair on the top of her baby daughter's head.

'Mum, I've always worried about the timing of it all. He broke things off before I knew I was pregnant. If I had found out just a week earlier it might have changed everything. Perhaps if he had known he might not have been so...so adamant about never seeing me again.'

'Darling, what was a week either side going to do?' her mother asked. 'He had clearly already made up his mind. He wouldn't even agree to talk to you on the phone let alone see you face to face. What were you supposed to do? Tell him via a third party?'

Bronte bit her lip as she looked at her mother. 'Maybe that's what I should have done,' she said. 'Perhaps then he would have agreed to see me again. We could have at least discussed options.'

Tina Bennett gave her daughter a streetwise look. 'And what options might those have been? It's my guess he would have marched you straight off for a termination. A man with that sort of lifestyle would not want a love-child to support. It wouldn't suit his lifestyle.'

'I would never have agreed to that,' Bronte said, holding Ella even closer to her body. 'I would never have allowed anyone to talk me into getting rid of my baby.'

'Darling, you were young and madly in love,' Tina said. 'I know plenty of young women who have done things they later regretted just because the man they loved insisted on it.'

Bronte looked down at her little daughter, who was now snuggling against her chest, her dark blue eyes struggling to stay open as she fought against sleep. It worried Bronte that there might be some truth in what her mother had said. She *had* been young and madly in love. She would have done almost anything to keep Luca by her side. As it was, she had made a pathetic fool of herself chasing after him like a lovesick teenager, leaving countless 'call me' messages and texts on his phone, not to mention pleading emails that made her cringe to think about now.

'You're not going to tell him about Ella, are you, love?' her mother asked.

Bronte gently brushed the soft hair off her sleeping baby's face. 'When he came into the studio unannounced like that today, all I could think was how much I hated him.' She looked up at her mother. 'But one day Ella is going to be old enough to realise she doesn't have a father. She's going to want to know who he is and why he isn't a part of her life. What am I supposed to say? How will I explain it to her?'

'You'll explain it the way I did to you,' her mother said. 'That the man you thought would stay by you deserted you. Remember, Bronte: a father is as a father does. As far as I see it, Luca Sabbatini was nothing more than a sperm donor. One day you'll meet some nice man who will love you and Ella. He will be a far better father to her than a man who cut you from his life without a backward glance. What's to say he does it again if not sooner rather than later? He won't be just hurting you this time, but Ella too.'

'I guess you're right,' Bronte said on a sigh as she rose to her feet, carefully cradling Ella in her arms. 'But there's a part of me that thinks he has a right to know he fathered a child.'

'Men like him don't even like children,' Tina said matter-of-factly. 'They see them as too much responsibility. Believe me, I know the type.'

A small frown tugged at Bronte's brow. 'When my junior class arrived at the studio this afternoon he looked at them…I don't know…almost wistfully, as if he was imagining being a parent one day.'

'Bronte—' her mother's voice sounded stern '—think carefully about this before you do something you might regret. He's a very rich man. A very rich and powerful man. He might take it upon himself to pay you back for not telling him about his child. He could take you to court. You'd have no hope of fighting him and, even if you did, you'd have the burden of paying for the legal work. And, don't forget, given his pedigree background, he would have the best of lawyers at his disposal. The family court is much more accommodating when it comes to fathers these days, especially well-to-do ones. Even if he got partial custody, it would mean Ella would have to fly back and forth to Italy or wherever he currently lives. You might not see her for months on end, and then one day when she's older she might decide not to come back to you at all.'

Bronte felt her heart contract in fear at such an outcome. Luca came from such a powerful dynasty. The Sabbatini clan would be the very worst sort of enemy to take on. Their power and influence reached all over the world. She hadn't a hope in taking Luca on in a custody battle, let alone his family.

The bitter irony was she had never intended to keep Ella's existence a secret. In spite of Luca's insistence that he never wanted to see her again, as soon as Bronte had found out she was pregnant she had tried to contact him. After a couple of fruitless weeks of not getting through to him, she had eventually flown to his villa in Milan but the household staff had refused her entry. The housekeeper had told her rather bluntly that Luca was in America with a new lover.

The news had hit Bronte like a fist in the face. It had devastated her that he had moved on so quickly. She even wondered if he had had his American mistress the whole time he had been seeing her in London. After all, he had never once stayed the full night with her at her flat and he had never allowed her to spend the night with him at his luxurious London home. He had never taken her away for a weekend; she had never even stayed in a hotel with him. He had always insisted on driving her home, his excuse being he was an extremely early riser and didn't want to disturb her. In hindsight, she realised she had been so naïve in accepting his explanation. How gullible of her to have never questioned why he would not spend a single night with her after making love. What sort of lovers didn't spend the night entwined in each other's arms? Street workers and the men who paid them, that was who, Bronte thought bitterly. Luca had treated her like a whore and she had been too blind to see it. But this time she would not be making the same mistake. She would meet him and that would be that. It would be a form of closure for her, something she had longed for when their affair had ended so abruptly. Saying goodbye and meaning it would be very satis-fying. She would be finally free of the man who had caused her so much heartache and bitterness, and then and only then would she be able to move on with her life.

Bronte caught a cab to the city rather than worry about parking. She wanted to be able to make a quick escape if things got tricky. She reasoned that an anonymous cab was a much safer exit plan than her battered car with its baby seat full of crumbs and juice stains in the back.

She had dressed for the occasion with deliberate care. Although not exactly destitute, she didn't have the sort of money to throw around that allowed her to fill her wardrobe with designer clothes. But she had a few select items she had bought on sale that made her feel feminine and elegant without being overdressed or too showy.

The hotel was one of the premier ones in the Southbank Complex along the Yarra River. The luxurious marble foyer with a sweeping two-sided staircase with a fountain as its centrepiece gave the hotel more than a touch of Hollywood glamour. Bronte felt like a movie star arriving for a glamorous event as one of the uniformed doormen opened the doors for her with a flourish.

The staircase led to a classy bar area with deep leather sofas placed in intimate formations to give privacy to guests as they socialised over a drink. Bronte saw Luca rise the moment she stepped into the bar. She felt a flutter in her chest as he came towards her and she noted that practically every female head turned to look at him as he moved across the carpeted floor.

He was dressed in a charcoal-grey suit, teamed with a snow-white business shirt and wearing a tie that was red with stripes of silver. He seemed even taller than he had in the studio earlier that day, even though Bronte was now wearing heels.

She felt his gaze move over her, taking in her little black dress, cinched in at the waist with a black patent leather belt which matched her four-inch heels and clutch purse. She was glad she had taken some extra time with her make-up. She had dusted her skin with mineral powder and blush and had made her eyes smoky with eye-shadow and kohl pencil, and her lips ripe and full

with a glossy pink lipstick. Her dark brown hair she had
smoothed back into a chignon that gave her an added
air of sophistication. *Let him look and regret what he
threw away,* she thought with a gleam of satisfaction as
his pupils flared with male appraisal.

'You are looking quite stunning, *cara*,' he said as he
came to stand in front of her, his eyes running over her
asssessingly.

She gave him a tight formal smile. 'Let's get this over
with, shall we?'

He drew in a breath that pulled at the edges of his
mouth. 'Bronte, there is no need to be so prickly,' he
said. 'We are just two old friends catching up, *sì*?'

Bronte's fingers dug into her clutch purse. 'You are
no friend of mine, Luca,' she said. 'I think of you as a
stupid mistake I made. Something I would like to forget
about. I don't like reminding myself of failure.'

His forehead furrowed as he looked down at her. 'It
was not you that failed, Bronte. It was my problem. My
issues. It was never about you.'

Bronte blinked up at him in surprise. Was that some
sort of apology? Or was it part of the softening up process? She was well aware of the Sabbatini charm. It
was a lethal potion that could bewitch any unsuspecting
woman. And she had not just been unsuspecting but
naïve and innocent with it. She had fallen for him so
easily. It embarrassed her now to think of how easily.
One look, one smile and that bottomless dark chocolate
gaze locking on hers had done it. 'So you are prepared
to admit you handled things rather callously, are you?'
she asked in a wary tone.

He gave her a rueful movement of his lips that fell
just short of a smile. 'I have regrets over a lot of things,

Bronte. But the past is not something any of us can change. However, I would like to compensate for the hurt I caused you in ending our affair so abruptly and without proper explanation.'

She gave him an embittered look. 'How are you going to compensate me? By blackmailing me into seeing you? It's not working, Luca. You can blackmail me all you like but it won't make me fall in love with you again.'

His dark eyes flickered for a pico-second, a fleeting shadow of something she couldn't identify or understand. 'I realise that is rather a lot to ask after all this time,' he said. 'I would be happy to take it one day at a time, for now.'

Bronte set her mouth. 'You have one evening, Luca, and this is it. I am not doing this again. Say what you have to say and let's leave it at that.'

An arm in arm couple moved past them, the female half turning back to look at Luca. She whispered something to her partner and then he too stopped and stared.

Luca smiled politely but stiffly at the couple and then took Bronte's elbow in the cup of his palm, saying in an undertone, 'Let's get away from the eyes of the public. Before we know it, the press will be tipped off.'

Bronte couldn't bear the thought of being alone with him in his hotel room, but neither could she bear the thought of having her image splashed with his over tomorrow's papers. She could almost imagine the headlines: *Italian hotel tycoon dates ballet teacher single mother*. She would never hear the end of it from the parents of her students, let alone Rachel and her mother.

She followed him to the bank of lifts and silently stepped in beside him as one opened. The doors whooshed closed and she felt as if the air had been cut off along with the background noise of the hotel. It was like being in a capsule with him. The lift was large but it felt like a matchbox with him standing within touching distance. Her stomach gave a nervous quiver. She hadn't been alone with a man since...well, since him. Her one recent date with Rachel's newly divorced older brother had been in a crowded public restaurant. David Brougham hadn't even touched her the whole time they'd worked their way through an eight course degustation menu. *Note to self,* she thought. Never go to a fine dining restaurant with a morose, newly divorced man. Bronte had listened patiently as he had relayed his angst about his marriage breakup and the custodial arrangements for his children, and silently prayed for the evening to be over.

As the lift soared to the penthouse floor Bronte looked at Luca from beneath her lowered lashes. He had a frown of concentration on his forehead and there were twin lines of tension running either side of his mouth. His arms were hanging by his sides, but she saw him clench and unclench his hands as if he was mentally preparing himself for something.

'I thought you would be used to the intrusion of the media by now,' she said into the humming silence.

He turned his head to look at her. 'Believe me, Bronte, you never get used to it. Do you know what it's like having every moment of your life documented? The lack of privacy is unbelievable. There are times when I cannot even have a cup of coffee without someone wanting to take a picture. It drives me completely crazy.'

'I guess it's the price of success,' she said. 'You were

born into an extremely wealthy family. The public are fascinated by how the other half lives.'

He gave her a quirky smile as the lift stopped at his floor. 'Are *you* fascinated, *cara*?'

She pursed her lips and stepped past him, holding her head at a proud angle. 'You and your family hold no fascination for me whatsoever. I have too much to do in my own life to be keeping track of someone else's.'

As they came to the correct number he inserted his key card into the penthouse suite door and held it open for her to precede him. 'So you haven't kept yourself up to date on all my affairs over the last two years?' he asked.

Bronte spoke without thinking. 'There's been hardly anything about you in the papers and magazines. It always seems to be about your brothers. It's as if you disappeared off the face of the earth the first year after we broke up.'

He gave her a long thoughtful look as he closed the door behind him. 'For a time that's exactly what I wanted to do,' he said, leading the way through to the large lounge. 'What would you like to drink?' he asked over his shoulder.

Bronte was still thinking about why he'd wanted to disappear without trace. There had been something in his tone that seemed tinged with regret and a part of her wondered if it had something to do with her.

Of course not! she chided herself crossly. He was a playboy who had had numerous affairs before she had come along. The only thing that might have set her apart was her innocence and naivety. He had obviously found that a novelty and was hoping for a rerun. She could see it in the dark depths of his eyes every time they meshed with hers. She felt the rush of her blood too, which reminded her rather timely that she was not quite as immune to him as she would have liked.

'Bronte?' he prompted, holding up a bottle of champagne.

'Oh…yes, thanks,' she said, feeling gauche and awkward.

After a moment he handed her a fizzing glass of French champagne, the price of which, Bronte noted, would have paid her last electricity bill, not just for her granny flat but most probably the studio as well.

'To us,' he said, touching his glass against hers.

Bronte hesitated before she took a sip. Luca watched her quizzically, one brow slightly elevated. 'Not to your taste, Bronte?' he asked.

'The champagne, I am sure, is lovely,' she said. 'It's what we're toasting to that is not palatable.'

He held her flinty look with consummate ease. 'You choose, then,' he suggested, holding his glass just in reach of hers. 'What shall we drink to?'

Bronte raised her glass and clinked it against his. 'To moving on.'

His brow went up a little higher this time. 'Interesting,' he said musingly. 'Does this mean the man you are seeing is a permanent fixture in your life?'

Bronte wished she could say yes. And if it was anyone but David Brougham she might well have done so. She felt she needed an excuse, a good excuse, not to see Luca again. It was just too dangerous; not because of Ella, but because of how he made Bronte feel. She could feel emotions bubbling under the surface even now. Dangerous emotions: needs that ached to be fulfilled, longings that wouldn't be suppressed, no matter how hard she tried.

She was supposed to hate him.

She *did* hate him.

He had abandoned her, leaving her when she was so vulnerable and alone. And yet one meeting with him and her mind was filling with images of them together: him kissing her, his lips sealing hers with such passion, his arms around her body, holding her against the surging heat and potency of his. How could she forget how he made her feel? Would there ever be a time when she would not feel her heart twist and ache when she heard his name mentioned or saw it in print? Would she ever be able to forgive him for not loving her, for not even respecting her enough to say goodbye face to face?

'You seem to be taking rather a long time to answer my question,' Luca observed. 'Which can only mean one thing: you are not seriously involved with him. If you were madly in love with someone, surely you would have no hesitation in telling me.'

Bronte drank some of her champagne, stalling for time, for courage, for anything. 'It seems to me it wouldn't matter to you how I answered. You have your own agenda. That's what this little tête à tête is all about, isn't it?'

He wandered over to one of the massive leather sofas and indicated for her to sit down. He waited until she was perched on the edge of one of the cushions before he spoke. 'I want to see you, Bronte. Not just tonight. Not even just now and again.' He waited a beat, his eyes intense and unwavering on hers. 'I want to see you as much as possible while I am here. I want you back.'

Bronte's hand trembled as she held the champagne glass. She tried to hold it steady by cradling it with both of her hands, her heart beating like an out of time pendulum. 'I…you…I…I'm afraid that's not possible…' she faltered.

He came to sit beside her, his hand removing the glass from her shaking ones. 'I mean it, *cara*,' he said and took both of her hands in his warm, dry ones. 'I have never forgotten you.'

Bronte felt anger come to her rescue. She wrenched out of his hold and jumped to her feet. 'I am not some stupid plaything you can pick up and put down when you feel like it,' she said. 'You were the one to end things. You wanted a clean break and you got one. Coming back after all this time and telling me you've changed your mind is not just arrogant, it's downright insulting.'

Luca rose to his feet and pushed a hand through his hair. 'Bronte, I wasn't ready for a relationship two years ago. You came along at the wrong time. God, how I wish I could have met you just a year later. Even six months later. Everything would have been so different then.'

She glowered at him and he felt a spike go through his chest. He had not expected her to hate him quite so much. This was going to be a little harder than he'd expected but he was prepared to work hard for what he wanted. If there were obstacles in the way he would remove them. If there was a way of winning her back to him he would do it, even if he had to resort to ruth-less means. He had hoped he would not have to apply any sort of pressure. The rent thing was an insurance scheme on his part to get this far. First base was to see her again in private. He hadn't even thought as far as second and third. He had just so desperately wanted to see her again.

Bronte was still sending him looks with daggers and

spears attached. 'So what brought about this sudden change, Luca?' she asked.

Should he tell her? Luca wondered. He had told no one; not even his mother or brothers or elderly grandfather had known the truth about his trip to America until the deed was over and he was safely on the other side. He hadn't wanted his family to go through the agonising heartache of knowing they could lose him or, even worse, have him come back to them damaged beyond recognition. He had seen his father propped up in a semi-conscious state in the last weeks before he'd finally died from the injuries he had sustained in a head-on collision. That had decided it for him. He had wanted to spare his mother and brothers from witnessing anything as gut-wrenching as that.

Luca hated talking about that time, now that it was over. He liked to push it to the back of his mind, inside a locked compartment inside his brain. In the weeks and months afterwards he would creak it open almost daily, marvelling that he was still here, functioning and breathing and talking. Now he just wanted to forget it had ever happened. The shame of his body letting him down so cruelly was something he no longer wanted to mull over. Telling Bronte about it would only make it come back to haunt him. It was too personal and too private and there was no way he could risk anything being leaked to the press if she wanted to try her hand at a payback. It was better she didn't know. He just wanted his life to begin again from now. He was ready to move on and he wanted to do so with a clean slate.

'I am at a time of life when I am looking for more stability,' he said. 'What we had was good, Bronte.

Some of the happiest times of my life were those I spent with you.'

Her slate-blue eyes were dark with suspicion. 'Were those good times just with me, Luca? Or are you getting me mixed up with someone else?'

'I never betrayed you, *cara*,' he said. 'There was only you during that time. No one else.'

Her eyes rolled upwards as she swung away from him, her arms doing that barricade thing across her slim body, warning him off, shutting him out. 'You betrayed me by ending our relationship without a single explanation as to why,' she said in an embittered tone.

Luca took a deep breath, holding it for a few seconds before he slowly released it. 'I never intended to hurt you the way I did, Bronte. I accept full responsibility for it. I know it's hard for you to understand, but I had no choice. It was not the time for us. We met too soon.'

She turned back to look at him, her expression so scathing it actually hurt him to maintain eye contact. 'So, now you've sown all your wild oats, you want what, exactly?' she asked. 'You're not proposing marriage, are you?'

Luca was not going to offer something that would be thrown back in his face, or at least not yet. There were other ways to bring about what he wanted. More subtle ways. 'No,' he said. 'I am not proposing anything long-term at this stage. I am here in your country and I would like to see if what we had before can be resurrected.'

Her lips pressed so tightly together they went white. After a tense moment she expelled her held breath on a whoosh. 'You are unbelievable,' she said. 'You think you can just pick up where you left off, all things forgiven?

What planet did you just drop down from? As if I would agree to being involved with you again. *As if!*'

It was the tone of her 'As if' that did it. Luca felt his temper snap to attention like an elastic band stretched to the limit. 'You might not have any choice in the matter,' he said.

Her eyes flared as his words hit home. 'You wouldn't dare...' She almost breathed rather than said the words.

He pushed his jaw forward, his eyes locked on hers. 'I want you back in my bed, Bronte. If you don't agree then there is nothing more to be said between us. You will have one week to vacate the premises of your studio. If you don't vacate in one week the rent will increase substantially.'

Her soft mouth fell open, her eyes still as wide as saucers. 'You can't mean that...' she swallowed and then swallowed again, her voice coming out even scratchier '...y...you can't possibly mean that...'

Luca came over to her and stood just within touching distance, his eyes pinning hers. 'The decision is yours, Bronte,' he said, running a hand down her upper arm from shoulder to elbow, each and every pore of her flesh rising in shivery goosebumps under his touch. 'Which is it to be?'

CHAPTER THREE

BRONTE couldn't think. Her mind was whirling like a fairground ride that had been set at too fast a speed. He wanted her to sleep with him. He wanted to resume their affair. He didn't want anything permanent. He was going to use her and discard her like he did before. Round and round the thoughts went until she felt dizzy and sick and heartsore. How could he do this to her? He was the one who had walked away. It wasn't as if she had done anything to hurt him. He had broken her heart, he had all but ruined her life and yet here he was acting as if she owed him!

She stepped back from him, biting the inside of her mouth until she tasted blood. She turned on her heel and began pacing the floor. She had to think of a way out of this. *Was* there a way out of this?

'Come here.'

Bronte felt his two word command like hammer blows to her heart. How ruthless he sounded! She was nothing but a chattel, a possession he had bartered for. She stopped pacing and stood her ground, her chin high, with her eyes flashing their hatred at him. 'If you want me then you'll have to drag me kicking and screaming for I will not come willingly.'

His lips slowly curved upwards in a sexy smile. 'Are you absolutely sure about that, *tesore mio*?' he asked in a low husky drawl.

Now that you mention it, Bronte thought in panic as she recalled his warm electrifying touch on her arm just moments ago. He had set spot fires all throughout her body with that one stroke of his hand along her upper arm. He had awakened every nerve of her skin, made her heart beat twice its pace and made a hole open up deep inside her, a hollow ache she knew from experience could only be filled by him.

He came back to where she was standing; actually, shaking was probably a more accurate description. He placed a broad fingertip beneath her rigid chin and slowly but surely lifted it until her eyes had nowhere to go but meet his. 'It's still there, isn't it, *cara*?' he said. 'The chemistry between us. I felt it the moment I walked into the studio this afternoon. I can feel it now. You can too. I can see it in your eyes. I can feel it when I touch you. You tremble all over.'

Bronte stopped breathing when he brought his mouth to the corner of hers. He brushed his lips against her skin, a feather-light touch that made her quiver in reaction, fulfilling every word he had just spoken about her response to him. Her body was her betrayer; she had no hope of disguising how he affected her. His warm hint-of-mint breath skated over her lips before touching down on the other side of her mouth, the same soft brush of lips on sensitive skin evoking the same heady rush of feeling inside her body. She heard a soft whimper and realised with a little jolt it had come from her mouth. Her lips had softly fallen open, her mouth an open invitation for the plunder of his.

But he didn't do it.

He smiled that lazy smile as he met her bewildered, uncertain gaze and then he slowly pressed a soft barely-there kiss to each of her eyebrows. 'You have the most amazing blue eyes,' he said, low and deep like a bolt of satin dragged across gravel. 'Like the heart of a flame, dark and fiery. They burn one minute and the next they shine like the surface of a deep ocean.'

She trembled all over as he ran his hands down both of her arms, his fingers encircling her wrists like handcuffs. She felt the soft tug that brought her flat against his body, her belly coming into contact with his arousal. Heat exploded inside her, pooling between her thighs, hot and fragrant with need. How could she still want him when she hated him so much? It didn't seem fair that her body would betray her so shamelessly. She hated herself for being so weak. She hated him for making her want him. She hated that she wanted to lean into him and offer her mouth and body to his to pleasure. The pressure of want was building deep inside her: an ache, a pulse, a drumbeat that would not be ignored.

'Beautiful, sweet Bronte,' he said just above her mouth. 'Do you have any idea how much I still want you?'

Bronte felt the proud probe of his hot hard flesh and felt an answering quake of want in her inner core. It was like a hungry beast growling for satiation inside her. Her body stepped up its demand for assuagement, torturing her with tiny exquisite reminders of the pleasure she had felt with him in the past. Her mind was full of images of them locked in erotic poses: his body pinning her from above, from below, from behind or up against the nearest wall or even on the kitchen counter, his body pounding into hers, her arms locked around his neck or waist, her body coming apart time and time again.

'Tell me you feel it too,' he said just above her mouth, his warm breath a caress, a temptation, a torture. 'Tell me you remember how it was between us.'

Bronte was beyond speech. She just wanted to feel his mouth on hers, even if it was for the last time. Surely it wasn't wrong to want that? Just a taste, a reminder of how it felt to have him kiss her senseless. She pulled her hands out of the loose grasp of his and linked them around his neck. She looked him in the eyes, drowning all over again in their dark brown depths. And then she rose up on tiptoe and pressed her mouth to his, somehow knowing that in doing so she was passing a point of no return.

It was like fire meeting fuel. A burn of longing that flickered and then roared, consuming everything in its path. Her mouth opened at the first searing, searching thrust of his tongue, her tongue dancing with his, darting away shyly at first and then flirting with his outrageously, boldly, wantonly. He groaned deeply as he deepened the kiss, his hands guiding her body as he backed her up against the nearest wall, his mouth increasing its pressure, its heat and its passion until she felt as if she was being sucked into a whirlpool of clawing, desperate need.

With the wall at her back, his body had more leverage against hers. She felt the hard ridge of him against her belly, the pounding heat of his blood surging through his veins in primal response to his need to mate. She felt the urge too. It was beating inside her like a primitive tribal drum, the walls of her feminine core quivering in anticipation of the delicious friction of his commanding possession.

His mouth was like a naked flame against hers. His kiss was scorching her but she returned it with matching heat, her tongue darting and diving in a cat and mouse game with his. His hands slid up her body and cupped her breasts, gently but possessively, his thumbs claiming her erect nipples as his own to pleasure, to caress and to tease into submission.

Bronte arched up against him shamelessly. She wished she could rip her clothes off in one movement to feel his warm masculine hands on her bare skin. She tugged at his shirt, pulling it free of his trousers, sliding her hands up his chest, her fingers exploring the hard musculature that had delighted her so much in the past. She felt the hard, flat nubs of his nipples and the scratchy dusting of masculine hair over his chest. He was in every way possible a man: strong and capable, lean but hard muscled, fit and virile, potent and irresistibly sexy.

His mouth moved from hers to her breast; the hot moist feel of him caressing her made her spine turn to liquid. She made a soft sound in the back of her throat, something between a whimper and a gasp.

'I have dreamed of doing this,' Luca said throatily. 'Touching you, feeling you respond to me. No one else has ever turned me on quite like you do.'

It was just the reminder Bronte needed that she was not the only one he had been with and she was certainly not going to be the last. He had worked his way through a glamorous array of women since he was a teenager. She had known of his playboy reputation when she first met him but somehow hadn't been able to resist his seductive charm. She was older and wiser now. And she had responsibilities. Ella was her most important one. There was nothing she would not do to protect her baby girl. Denying herself this was a sacrifice she had to make. For now, at least, until she could find a way out of the honey trap Luca had lured her into.

She let her hands drop from around his neck, her eyes meeting his. 'I can't do this, Luca,' she said. 'Not here. Not like this. It's…it's too soon.'

His eyes seared hers for an endless moment, a muscle working in his jaw as he fought to control his rampant desire. 'Remember our deal,' he said.

Bronte slipped out from his arms where they were propped against the wall either side of her head and put a little distance between their bodies. She struggled to get her breathing to steady, difficult when her pulse was fluttering like a hummingbird inside her veins.

'Deal?' she asked with a scornful look. 'Don't you mean the bribe you put on the table, Luca? Money for sex.'

'That is rather a crude way of putting it,' he said.

'It's the truth, though, isn't it?' she asked. 'You want to turn me into a whore. You open your wallet; I open my legs. That's the so-called deal, isn't it?'

A nerve ticked like a pulse at the side of his mouth. 'Don't cheapen yourself like that, Bronte.'

Bronte gave a choked laugh that was just shy of hysteria. 'You tell me not to cheapen myself when you have insulted me more than any other person I know.'

He drew in a breath and moved across the room, standing at the windows that overlooked the shimmering lights of the city below. Bronte saw the stiff set to his broad shoulders, the straight spine and the long legs standing slightly apart.

She longed to go to him and wrap her arms around him, to take whatever he was offering, but she knew in the end it would only lead to further heartbreak. How could she ever trust he wouldn't walk out on her again? She would not survive it a second time. It had nearly done her in the first time. It had only been the responsibility of Ella that had made her come to her senses and grow up—and grow up fast. But, even so, it was tempting. Oh, dear God, it was tempting. To feel his arms around her one more time, to have him hold her as if she was the most precious thing in the entire world. How she had dreamed and longed for one more time with him over the last two years.

'Fine,' he said after a long moment, his voice sounding hollow and empty. 'You are free to go.'

Bronte felt her heart give a little start. 'But I thought—'

He turned, his dark eyes hitting hers. 'Go, Bronte. Before I change my mind.'

She swallowed and took a hesitant step towards the door, but then she remembered her clutch purse was sitting on the sofa. She glanced at it but, before she could move, he stepped forward and picked it up.

He came over to where she was standing and handed it to her. 'This is all wrong, isn't it?' he said.

She rolled her lips against each other, not sure if he wanted an answer or not. Of course it was wrong. It was wrong for her to still want him, no matter what terms he laid down. It was shameless of her, needy and pathetic and desperate, but that was what he reduced her to. No man had ever made her feel so desperately in need. No man had made her heart ache with an indescribable longing. No man had made her want to throw herself at him in spite of everything.

She had to leave.

She had to leave *now*, before he saw how close she was to offering herself for further hurt. She had to leave before these minutes alone turned into an hour or two of stolen pleasure that, just like in the past, would trick her too-trusting, too-romantic mind into thinking they had any sort of future.

'I have handled this all wrong,' he said again with a rueful tilt to his mouth. 'I should have called you first, given you some warning, perhaps. Maybe then you would not be so wary of me. You would have been better prepared, *si*?'

'Why didn't you?' she asked in a scratchy voice.

One of his broad shoulders rose and fell. 'I wanted to see your instinctive response to me, not a rehearsed one.'

Bronte gave him a disdainful look. 'You make it sound like some sort of social experiment.'

His eyes stayed on hers: dark, tempting, fathomless. 'I would like to see you again, *cara*,' he said. 'Tomorrow night. No strings this time. No threats or bribes or blackmail, just two people having dinner together. If you like, we can pretend we have met for the first time.'

Bronte chewed at her lip, torn between temptation and uncertainty. Was this some sort of set-up? What if he still wanted to pull the financial rug from under her feet? 'The rent thing...' she said. 'I don't have that sort of money. I think you know that.'

'Forget about the rent,' he said. 'I don't want you in my bed because you have no choice in the matter. I know you will come to me, Bronte. It is inevitable. I knew that as soon as I walked into the studio.'

Had she been that transparent? Bronte wondered. 'You are deluding yourself, Luca,' she said with a proud hitch of her chin. 'You mistook surprise for something else.'

His knowing half-smile travelled all the way to his eyes. 'So beautiful,' he said, trailing a slow-moving finger down the curve of her cheek. 'So very beautiful.'

Bronte flinched in case she betrayed herself completely. His touch was like a feather and yet it set every nerve screaming for more. 'What's going on, Luca?' she asked, rubbing at her cheek as if he had tainted her.

His expression was like a blank stone wall. 'What do you mean?'

'This…' She waved her arm to encompass the suite. 'You. Me. Us. I'm not sure what's really going on. I get the feeling there is far more to this than you're telling me.'

He gave her a small twisted smile. 'Is it so hard for you to understand I wanted to see you again? Would it not have seemed strange for me to travel all this way, knowing you lived in the same city where I would be based and not at least try and make contact with you?'

Bronte's mouth tightened with cynicism. 'Do you make contact with *all* your ex-lovers wherever you travel in the world? If so, I am sure by now your little black book would be classified as overweight luggage.'

His smile lingered for a moment as if he found the thought amusing. 'There have not been as many lovers as you might think,' he said. 'I have been busy with… other things.'

Bronte wondered what *other things* had taken up his time. She knew he worked hard in the family business but he had found plenty of time in the past to play hard too. If he wasn't squiring yet another wannabe model or Hollywood starlet like his equally single younger brother Nicoló, what had he been doing?

'Did you drive here or catch a cab?' Luca asked.

'I caught a cab,' she said. 'I didn't want to have to worry about parking.'

He reached for a set of car keys on a nearby sideboard. 'I'll drive you home.'

Bronte felt a frisson of fear run through her like a trickle of ice-cold water. 'You don't have to do that,' she said quickly. 'I mean…it's no trouble getting a cab. I would prefer it, actually…'

His eyes narrowed just a fraction. 'What is the problem, Bronte? You surely trust me to get you home safely? I do know which side of the road to drive on here.'

'It's not that,' she said. 'I would prefer to make my own arrangements.'

'Is there someone waiting for you at home?' he asked.

'My private life has nothing to do with you, Luca,' she said. 'Not any more.'

He continued to watch her, his eyes dark and inscrutable. He didn't speak, which made the silence open up like a chasm between them.

'Look,' Bronte finally said, moving from foot to foot with impatience, 'I have to work tomorrow. And I don't want my mother to worry.'

'Your mother?' A deep frown appeared between his brows. 'You live with your mother?'

She straightened her spine. 'What's wrong with

that?' she asked. 'Property is horrendously expensive in Melbourne. I can't afford the studio rent and a mortgage. I'm just starting out.'

'How long have you been teaching at the studio?' he asked, still frowning.

'About a year,' Bronte said. 'Rachel and I trained at the same academy together. She broke her ankle in a car accident a couple of years ago and had to give up dancing. We decided to set up our own ballet school.'

Another silence passed but to Bronte it felt like hours. Each second seemed weighted; even the air seemed heavy and too thick for her to breathe.

'The audition you said you missed,' he said, watching her steadily. 'Did that by any chance have anything to do with me?'

Bronte felt her heart trip and carefully avoided his gaze. 'W…why do you ask that?'

'We broke up, what, about four weeks before you were due to audition, right?'

She gave a could-mean-anything shrug and fiddled with the catch on her clutch purse. 'I didn't see the point in trying for the company when my heart wasn't in staying in London,' she said. She brought her gaze back up to his. 'It was time for me to go home, Luca. There was nothing in London for me. The competition was tough, in any case. I didn't have a hope of making the shortlist. The audition would have been yet another rejection I just wasn't up to facing.'

'So you preferred to not show up at all rather than to fail.' It was not a question but a rather good summation of what she had been feeling at the time.

Bronte hadn't realised he had known her quite so well. She hadn't spoken to him of her doubts about making the grade. Their relationship hadn't been the sort for heart-to-heart confessions. She had always felt as if he was holding himself at a distance, not just physically but emotionally, so she had done the same. 'Yes,' she said, deliberately holding his gaze. 'I did, however, speak to the head of auditions in person and explain I was withdrawing my application. I had at least the common decency to do that.'

There was another long drawn-out silence.

'I know you took it hard, Bronte,' he said in a husky tone. 'I didn't want to hurt you but I am afraid it was unavoidable. I had to end it. I had no other choice.'

Bronte blinked back the smarting of tears. She was *not* going to cry in front of him. She had cried all the tears she was ever going to cry over him two years ago. 'Was there someone else the whole time?' she asked in a cool crisp tone. 'You can be honest with me, Luca. I am a big girl now. I can take it. I wasn't enough to satisfy you, was I? I wasn't worldly enough for your sophisticated tastes.'

He gave her a brooding frown. 'Is that what you thought?'

She flattened her mouth. 'It's what I know,' she said. 'I was a novelty for you at first but it must have become annoying after a while. I was good enough to have sex with but not good enough for you to take on any of your trips abroad. But no doubt you had plenty of women to step into my place.'

He continued to frown at her. 'That is not the way it was, Bronte.' He raked one of his hands through his hair, making it look as if he had just tumbled out of bed. 'I've always preferred to travel alone. It's less complicated.'

Bronte bit the inside of her mouth to control her

spiralling emotions. Why hadn't she left five minutes ago before it had got to this? 'We went out for close to six months,' she said. 'Not once did you spend a whole night with me. Not once, Luca. You never even took me for a weekend away. Not even into the country. I was your city mistress. The easy girl you could bed any time you liked. You only had to pick up the phone and I was available.'

Luca came over and captured Bronte's flailing hands, holding them firmly in his grasp. 'Stop it, Bronte,' he said. 'You were no such thing. Not to me.'

She looked at him with tears shining in her eyes. 'You used me, Luca. You can't deny it. You used me and when you got tired of me you let me go.'

Luca looked down at her hands, struggling to get away from his. His hands were so olive-skinned and dark and big compared to her slim, small creamy ones. Her hands reminded him of small doves fluttering to get away. Her body was so slight. Everything about her was so dainty and elegant. Her dancer's body, the way she carried herself, the way her eyes looked so big and dark in the perfect oval of her face.

He looked into those big dark eyes and wondered how he could repair the damage he had done. He could see the pain his rejection had caused. It glimmered there amongst the sheen of tears she was so determined not to shed in front of him.

She was so unlike any other woman he had been with in the past. He had loved the fact he was her first lover. She had seemed embarrassed about it but he had secretly delighted in it. He wondered if that was why he could not forget her. She had touched him in a way no one else had ever done. There was a place deep inside of him no one had ever been able to reach and yet he had felt as if she had come so very close. He had not wanted to fall in love with anyone, not with his health the way it had been back then. But with Bronte he had come close. Too close. That was why he'd had to back off before he was in so deep he wouldn't be able to think rationally. The more time he'd spent with her, the more he'd realised how unfair it would be on her to tie her to him when there was no guarantee he could give her anything in return.

Luca released one of her hands so he could put his other hand in the small of her back, bringing her up against him again. He loved the feel of her body flush against his. She fitted against him as if she had been made for him. He felt his body stirring and wished he could show her what he found so hard to say out loud. But it would only scare her away. It was too soon. He had to take things slowly and carefully this time. She was like a shy fawn with an innate sense of danger. She needed time and careful handling. He had the patience for the careful handling, but time was something he didn't have at his disposal. A month was all he had to get her to come back to him, to see if the magic was still there so they could build some sort of future together. Would it be enough?

'Don't fight me, Bronte,' he said softly. 'You are angry at me and I know I deserve it, but we still have something between us. You know we do.'

Her eyes flared like a cornered animal facing a dangerous predator. 'W...we share nothing,' she stammered. 'I don't want to see you. I don't want to be your sex slave. I don't want to be your...your anything.'

He brought her other hand to his mouth, kissing each

of her stiff fingertips until he felt them tremble against his lips. He kept his eyes trained on hers, watching as the point of her tongue darted out nervously to anoint her lips. 'I am not asking you to be anything but my partner for dinner tomorrow evening,' he said.

She swallowed tightly. 'And...and after that?'

He kissed the backs of her bent knuckles, still holding her gaze. 'If you don't want to see me again I will have to accept it,' he said.

Her eyes narrowed in suspicion. 'You'll let me go? Just like that?'

Luca stroked away the frown that had appeared between her brows. 'If you frown all the time you will get wrinkles.'

She arched her head away from his touch. 'You didn't answer my question, Luca.'

Luca let out a sigh as he dropped his hand back by his side. 'I didn't have to blackmail you into my bed in the past,' he said. 'I don't see why I should need to do so now.'

Her chin came up and her eyes flashed blue fire at him. 'So you think I'll just dive in head first then, do you?'

He examined her taut expression for a moment or two. 'I think what will happen will happen, *cara*,' he said. 'We should leave things to fate, *sì*?'

She continued to regard him warily. 'Fate, huh? Like it's fate that you're suddenly my landlord.'

'You're not in any danger of being kicked out on the street,' Luca said.

'Can I have that in writing?' she asked.

He stood looking down at her for a long moment, breathing in her scent, that hint of honeysuckle and sun-warmed sweet peas that unfurled inside his nostrils, making them flare to take more of her in. 'You really don't trust me, do you?'

She folded her arms across her chest. 'No, strange as it may seem, I don't trust you. I don't like you and I can't wait to see the last of you.'

Luca felt his spine tighten with irritation. Did she have to keep reminding him of how much she hated him? Did she think it would make him want her less? If anything, it made him want her more. Or was that her intention? Was she playing hard to get to teach him a lesson, or to get more out of the relationship this time around? Maybe the last couple of years had toughened her up. Maybe she had enrolled in the academy of gold-diggers and now knew how to use men to serve her own ends. Either way, it didn't matter. He wanted her any way he could get her. If she had changed, well, so had he. He was not the same person he had been two years ago. How could he be? Too much had happened.

He went over to where he had put their champagne glasses down before. He picked up her glass and brought it back to where she was standing. 'It would be a shame to let such good champagne go to waste,' he said, offering it to her. 'Why not stay a few minutes more and help me finish it?'

She looked at the glass as if he was handing her a poisoned chalice.

'It's just champagne, Bronte,' he said. 'Let's finish our drink and catch up on the last two years.' He took a sip from his glass, hoping she would follow suit. Anything to prolong the time he had with her in case she didn't show up tomorrow. 'Tell me about your teaching. Do you enjoy it?'

She took a tiny sip of her champagne and then held the glass with both of her hands around the stem. 'I do, yes,' she said. 'The children are lovely.'

He patted the sofa, indicating for her to sit down. She sat on the edge of the seat again, ready for instant flight. 'How many students do you have?' he asked, trying to put her at ease.

'We have sixty at the moment but I would like to see it go to about two hundred,' she said. 'I have plans for extension of classes. I would like to hire a couple more teachers for jazz and tap, and I want to incorporate some adult classes.'

Luca took a sip of his champagne. 'You teach adults?' he asked. 'Isn't it too late for an adult to learn? I thought ballet was something you had to learn at a very young age, the younger the better.'

'That's true, but there are lots of women and some men, when it comes to that, who have studied dance in the past and have let it slip,' she said. 'Doing a weekly or twice weekly class with other adults is a good way of keeping in shape.'

Luca let his eyes run over her slim form. 'Yes, well, it certainly hasn't done you any harm,' he said with a crooked smile. 'You're as slim as ever. How often do you practice?'

A light blush shaded her cheeks and she looked down at the contents of her glass again. 'A couple of hours a day,' she said. 'I would like to do more but with El…' She stopped mid-sentence and sank her teeth in her lip before continuing falteringly, '…I mean with every-thing there is to do around here I…I haven't got a lot of time.'

Luca watched as her colour deepened even further.

She reminded him of a shy schoolgirl, nervous, timid, not sure of herself in spite of all of her talent. It was so endearing he felt as if a large hand was pressing down on his heart. He thought of all the streetwise women who had thrown themselves at him in the past. They had used their looks and glamour and wily ways to get his attention. Bronte, on the other hand, had done nothing of the sort. She had always been reserved and held a lot of herself back. It made him all the more determined to draw her out of herself. She was such a rare find, so pure and unblemished. Like a rare diamond.

She got up from the sofa and put the glass down. 'I'm sorry, Luca, but I have to go.'

'What's the hurry?' he asked, rising to his feet.

She turned and faced him, her gaze quickly falling away from his as she searched again for her clutch purse. 'My mother will be wondering what's keeping me. I said I was only going out for a quick drink.'

'Bronte, you are twenty-five years old,' he pointed out. 'Do you really have to check in and out with your mother as if you were fifteen?'

Her eyes gave him a hard little glare. 'My mother has been very good to me. She has stood by me and supported me unconditionally. I don't have to answer to her, but I choose to out of respect for all the sacrifices she has made for me.'

'Surely she won't begrudge you a night out,' he said. And then, after a beat, added with a curl of his lip, 'Or has it more to do with this other man you're seeing?'

She sent him a challenging look. 'What if it does?'

Luca felt a rush of jealousy hit him like a tsunami. His stomach clenched as he thought of her with another man. His skin broke out in a sickening sweat as he imagined them together. He felt nauseous thinking about it. He didn't want to think about it. He *wouldn't* think about it. 'What is his name?' he asked in a cool unaffected tone when inside his guts were churning.

Her small chin rose. 'I don't have to tell you.'

Luca put his glass down before he snapped the fragile stem. He surreptitiously clenched and unclenched his hands, fighting for control. She was deliberately goading him, dangling her lover in front of him like a red rag to a raging bull. 'Are you sleeping with him?' he asked, not wanting to know but asking anyway.

'That is none of your business.'

He watched as she snatched up her purse, which had slipped down between the loose cushions of the sofa. She clipped it shut and stalked to the door, throwing over her shoulder, 'Thank you for the drink. Goodbye.'

'We have a date for tomorrow,' he reminded her.

She stiffened as if she had been snap-frozen from head to foot. 'I won't be able to make it,' she said, not bothering to turn around and face him.

'Damn it, Bronte, I am only asking for one night,' he said in rising frustration. 'Is that so very much to ask?'

She turned then, slowly, meeting his eyes with a glare of deep, bottomless blue anger in her own. 'Yes, Luca, it is too much to ask. You never gave me a single night of your time the whole time we were together.'

Luca felt his jaw snap together like a steel trap. His teeth ached with the pressure of forming the words to speak. 'So this is payback, is it?'

'No, Luca,' she said, opening the door. 'This is justice.'

And then she shut the door in his face.

CHAPTER FOUR

LUCA didn't find the mobile phone until an hour after Bronte had gone. He had paced the floor in anger for half an hour before he stopped to pour himself another drink from the barely touched bottle of champagne.

He took the bottle and his glass over to the sofa where Bronte had been sitting earlier. He tossed the first glass down and then poured himself another, barely tasting it before he swallowed. Right at this moment he didn't care if he got drunk. It would certainly be preferable to this.

He swore viciously and pushed his hair back off his forehead. He had hoped the night would have turned out differently but he had obviously been fooling himself. Bronte was well and truly over him. She had walked out and made it clear she wasn't coming back. He had hoped she still felt something for him. It was a wild hope, a vain, perhaps even an arrogant hope, but a hope all the same.

She had taken a long time to admit to loving him but when she had finally said it he knew she had meant it. Back then he hadn't been entirely sure if what he felt for her was love; all he knew was he felt different when he was with her, unlike he had ever felt before. But at that time he hadn't been sure he had a future to offer her. So he had kept his feelings to himself. He knew he had often come across as cold emotionally. He was often irritable and short-tempered with her on the days after he had been unwell and, while he knew it had confused her and made her feel insecure, he had never told her why he was feeling out of sorts. He hadn't wanted her to feel obligated towards him. She was the sort of person who would sacrifice herself and he hadn't been prepared for her to do that. It was his burden, his cross to bear and he had borne it and finally, thank God, got rid of it.

He reached forward to pour himself another glass of champagne, when something hard pressed against his thigh. He looked down and saw a slimline black mobile phone poking up through the cushions.

He smiled a slow smile as he pulled it out. It was the same model as his, only his was the newer upgraded one. He turned it over in his hand, pressing the silent switch on the side to ringtone. It immediately buzzed with messages; one by one they came up on the screen. It was impossible not to read them, even if his conscience told him it was an invasion of privacy.

How did it go?

What's he like?

Did you tell him about you know who?

Call me!!!!!

Luca scrolled past the other icons, but his finger stilled on the photo gallery one. He hesitated for a fraction of a moment before he pressed it to open it. There were a lot of pictures of a baby girl. He couldn't determine the age but he thought she was under one year old. She was small, like a doll, with dark brown hair and big blue eyes.

His gut seized and his hand shook as he scrolled through a couple more photos. She was a miniature version of Bronte. She was still in nappies; it looked as if she had only just started to walk. Luca felt a pain like a thick metal skewer go through the middle of his heart. He hadn't been expecting this. He hadn't seen it coming. He felt a fool for not realising. No wonder she didn't want anything more to do with him. Bronte had well and truly moved on with her life.

She'd had a baby.

She'd had another man's child.

The knowledge was too painful. His chest cavity felt too tight, suddenly too small to accommodate his organs. He couldn't breathe without pain. Each breath was like a knife between his ribs. His lungs felt as if they were going to explode.

He couldn't bear to look at any more pictures. He couldn't trust himself not to smash the phone if he came across the child's father in one of them. He didn't want to know who it was or what he looked like. No doubt it was some solidly dependable suburban type who had swept Bronte off her feet and offered her the security she longed for. Luca hadn't noticed a wedding ring on her finger but having a child with someone these days often came first. She had said she lived with her mother but did her lover and the father of her child live there too? No wonder she hadn't wanted him to pick her up or even know where she lived. *Dio*, he couldn't bear the thought of her going home to lie in someone else's arms. Even now she could be making love with the father of her child, perhaps conceiving another one with him right at this very moment.

His fingers clenched around the phone as he laid his

head back against the sofa cushions. He closed his eyes tightly, almost painfully, trying to block out the taunting images his brain concocted, thinking instead of how a few months could have changed everything.

The phone began to vibrate in his hand.

Luca opened his eyes and looked down at the screen. He slid the answer arrow across and held the phone up to his ear. 'Hello.'

There was a short silence marked by some rapid breathing.

'Luca?'

'Bronte,' Luca drawled, idly crossing one ankle over his thigh. 'How nice of you to call.'

Another tight silence.

'You have my phone.' The words came out like small, hard pellets. 'It must have slipped out of my purse or something.'

'Yes, it must have,' he said. 'You want to come and get it or shall I bring it to dinner tomorrow night?'

'I...'

'Or I could bring it around to your place now,' he said.

'No!'

Luca curled his lip, trying to ignore the pain in his gut. 'It would be no trouble, Bronte. Where do you live?'

'I don't want you to come here, Luca,' she said stiffly.

'Lover boy wouldn't like it?' he asked.

The silence this time crackled with tension.

'I need my phone,' she said. 'I will come and get it now...if that's all right? I mean if it's not too late or anything.'

Luca glanced at his watch and smiled. 'I'll be waiting for you.'

The call ended and he tapped his fingers against the phone where it rested on his thigh, his smile disappearing as a heavy frown pulled at his forehead.

Bronte pulled into the hotel's arrival bay and reluctantly left the keys with the valet parking attendant. She had tried to explain she wouldn't be long but hotel policy forbade parking out the front, even for short intervals. The tense exchange of words with the attendant on duty hadn't improved her already overstretched nerves. The moment of panic when she'd realised she had left her phone behind had practically sent her heart into a fibrillation. A heart attack at twenty-five was unlikely but Bronte felt as if she was going to go very close.

Had Luca looked at the photos of Ella? There were literally dozens of them. Fortunately there were none of Ella's firstborn ones or any from the first few months of her life. Bronte had transferred all her photos only a couple of weeks ago so she only had more recent photos on it.

But even so…

Would Luca see the likeness? Her mother had assured her it was unlikely. Ella was small for her age and had the same hair colour as Bronte and the same slate-blue eyes, dainty features and creamy skin.

Bronte wasn't so sure her mother was right, however. At times she could see a lot of Luca in her daughter. When Ella was concentrating over a puzzle or a toy she couldn't quite figure out, she frowned just like Luca frowned. And just lately, as Ella grew more and more adventurous now she was finally walking, she often gave Bronte a look of gleaming satisfaction that was Luca through and through.

Ever since she had realised she had left her phone behind Bronte had berated herself. Why hadn't she noticed the clasp on her purse was faulty? She should never have agreed to see him. What was she thinking? What good could come of it? It was perfectly clear he was after a quick affair. She had seen the intention in his dark, smouldering eyes. He wanted her. And that kiss! What had she been doing, responding to him like that? What madness had overtaken her? He was testing the waters and they were as hot as he had arrogantly expected.

Fool, fool, fool! Why had she fallen for it? She should have been more determined, more strident, more… more…in control of herself.

She rested her hot forehead on the wall of the lift, trying to get her breathing to calm down. All she had to do was pick up her phone and leave. Simple. Just take it and leave. Don't talk, don't linger and for God's sake don't look at him too long in case he saw more than she wanted him to see.

The lift seemed to take ages to climb to the penthouse floor, or perhaps that was because Bronte was sweating out each heart-stopping second in a rising state of panic.

Finally the lift arrived and she walked on legs that felt as spindly and unstable as a newborn colt's. Her brief knock on Luca's door was answered by him after an annoyingly lengthy interval. She wondered if it had been deliberate.

'Come in,' he said, holding the door wide open.

'No, thank you,' she said tightly. 'I'll just take my phone and leave.'

He folded his arms across his broad chest, rocking back on his heels in an indolent manner. 'Since you've driven all this way back here, why not stay a while and chat?'

Bronte held out her hand. 'My phone.'

Luca took her hand and tugged her into the suite, closing the door with a sharp click behind her. He smiled mockingly at her shocked and outraged expression. 'My way, Bronte, or you won't get your phone back at all.'

She glared at him with eyes as narrow as that of an embroidery needle. 'That's theft, you bastard.'

'You can have your phone after we've had a little talk,' he said, leading her into the suite.

She tugged at his hold to no avail. 'I don't want to talk to you, Luca.'

'Would you like a drink?' he asked, pointedly ignoring her attempts to pull away. 'I'm afraid there's not much champagne left. But I could always open another bottle.'

'I am not here to socialise,' she said through clenched teeth. 'I just want to get my phone and go home.'

He held her in front of him, looking down at her flushed features and tightly pursed lips. 'Why didn't you tell me about your child?' he asked. 'I'm assuming it's yours? She looks the image of you.'

Her face paled and her eyes looked stricken. 'You looked at my photos?' she asked in a hoarse-sounding whisper.

'There was nothing too incriminating there, I can assure you,' Luca said. 'No boudoir scenes, for instance.'

Her face regained some of its colour, two hot spots on each cheek. 'You had no right to touch my phone.'

'On the contrary, Bronte, it was on my sofa and it rang while I was holding it,' he said. 'Did you want me to ignore your call?'

She gave him an icy glare. 'That's what you would have done in the past, wasn't it?'

Luca had to admit she had won that round. He could hardly tell her now how hard it had been to see his phone ringing with her number showing on the screen and having to restrain himself from picking it up just to hear her voice one more time. In the end he had changed phones and numbers so in a weak moment he would not be tempted. And there had been many weak moments over the following months. 'How seriously involved are you with the father of your child?' he asked. 'You're not wearing a wedding ring so I am assuming you're not married.'

She looked at him for a long moment, her eyes flickering with something he couldn't quite identify. Her teeth caught at her bottom lip, pulling at it until he was sure she was going to draw blood. 'No, I'm not married...I... The thing is...' She winced as if she found the subject painful to talk about.

'You're no longer together, is that it?' he said.

She gave her lip another gnaw and finally released it. 'Yes...something like that...'

'Well, then,' Luca said. 'At least we've cleared up that little detail. There is a lot I would do to get you back into my bed, but taking on a jealous husband is not one of them.'

'I am not going to—'

Luca put a finger against her lips. 'Don't speak so soon, *cara*,' he warned.

Her eyes flared as he brushed his finger along her

lips. The softness of her mouth had always amazed him. She had a classically bee-stung mouth, irresistibly kiss-able. He bent his head and gently brushed his mouth over her lips, tasting her sweetness, wanting more, but holding back to give her time to reveal how much he affected her. Her lashes came down over her eyes, her tongue darting out and depositing a light sheen of moisture over her lips before disappearing again. He felt her breathe, in and out, a ragged sort of sound that seemed to catch inside her chest.

He bent his head again, hesitating just above her mouth, waiting for her to meet him halfway. 'Go on, *cara*,' he whispered against her lips. 'You know you want to.'

'I don't want to...' Her eyes met his briefly before falling away again. 'I don't want to see you. I don't think this is a good idea...you know...rehashing the past. It never works.'

He brought up her chin again, holding her gaze with his. 'We could make it work. Just you and me. No one else needs to know.'

She pushed against his chest and slipped out of his hold, crossing her arms over her body, turning away from him. 'There's not just the two of us to consider any more,' she said. 'I have a child. I have to consider her. She is my first priority. She will always be my first priority.'

Luca raked a hand through his hair. He didn't want to think about her love-child. It wasn't that he didn't love kids; he did and had always hoped he would have a family of his own one day. He just couldn't get used to the idea of Bronte being a mother to someone else's baby.

Had she had the child as a result of a rebound affair?

That somehow made it so much worse. If things had been different, he would have loved to have married Bronte and had the family he knew she wanted. She had hinted at it once or twice but he had deliberately avoided picking up the bait. It had been too painful back then to think about the life he wanted and the life he had been given. The bond of a child was a big deal. What if she still felt something for this guy? The kid was adorable. How could Bronte not feel something for the father of her little baby girl?

Luca had a bigger fight on his hands than he had thought. If he was to somehow convince her to get involved with him again he would have to learn how to be a stepparent. And it was not the easiest of relationships either. He had several friends who had never got on with their parents' partners. It had caused numerous arguments and resentments, some of which went on over years. Bronte's little girl was very young, but nothing could change the fact that Luca was not her real father. Circumstances had prevented him from having that privilege and there was nothing that he could do to change that now.

'How old is she?' he asked.

Bronte pushed a strand of hair back behind her ear and almost but not quite met his gaze. 'She recently turned one.' *Recently, as in two months ago,* she silently added.

His forehead creased as he did the numbers in his head. 'So you hooked up with her father what…a couple of months after you came back to Melbourne?'

Bronte hated lying outright but what else could she do? She hadn't had time to think this through. Everything had happened so quickly. Luca suddenly turning up at the studio—was it only that afternoon? And this evening's awkward meeting and the careless loss of her phone had not given her time to get her head around everything. 'Is that so wrong?' she asked, taking an evasive approach. 'You would have moved on just as, if not more quickly.'

'But to get pregnant to some guy you hardly knew—'

'Don't preach at me, Luca,' Bronte said in irritation. 'I did know him. I thought I knew him well. It just didn't work out.'

'Do you still see him?' he asked. 'Does he have contact with the child?'

Bronte realised now how many lies it took after you told one to keep the others in place. There was going to be no way out of this other than more and more lies. She hated herself at that moment. It seemed so wrong to lie to him and yet the alternative was too terrifying. Maybe she could work up the courage over time. Maybe there would be a right time to tell him. Maybe they could become friends first and then she could tell him he was Ella's father. Yeah, right, maybe she was kidding herself. She looked at his brooding frown and inwardly gulped. Yep, she was definitely kidding herself. 'No,' she said.

'What? You mean he doesn't want contact with his own flesh and blood?' he asked with an incredulous look.

'Look, Luca, I'd rather not talk about it,' she said. 'If I could just take my phone and—'

'So how do you manage?' Luca asked. 'Does the father contribute financially to the child's upbringing?'

The child. How impersonal he made it sound, Bronte

thought. 'Her name is Ella,' she said. 'And I manage perfectly fine without help from anyone.'

'How do you work and look after a little child?' he asked, still frowning darkly.

'The same way thousands of other working single mums do,' she said, 'juggling, compromise and guilt.'

'So that's why you live with your mother.'

'Yes,' she said. 'It works out for both of us. She works part-time and I work on her days off so she can mind Ella.'

He continued to look at her with a frown pulling at his forehead. His hands were thrust in his trouser pockets, the sound of his change and keys rattling the only sound breaking the heavy silence.

'I really should get going,' Bronte said. 'Mum stays in the granny flat with Ella. She can't go to bed back at her house until I get home.'

'If I hadn't ended things with you the way I did, do you think you would be in this situation now?' Luca asked, looking at her intently.

Bronte felt the pull of his magnetic gaze, her heart stumbling like a long-legged horse stepping into a deep pothole. 'There's no point in discussing it,' she said. 'Life happens. It's not as planned as we would like to think it is.'

'Did you plan to get pregnant?'

'No, that was an accident,' she said. 'But it's not one I regret. Ella's the best thing that's ever happened to me.'

Luca took the phone out of his pocket and handed it to her. 'I guess you will need this,' he said. 'She's very cute by the way. She looks exactly like you.'

Bronte felt a thick lump lodge in her throat. 'Th…

thank you.' She clutched the phone to her thumping chest, blinking back tears of relief, regret and deep self-loathing.

He stepped closer and cupped her cheek, holding her face so tenderly more tears came to her eyes. 'Why are you crying, *cara*?' he said softly.

She swallowed and gulped back a sob. 'It could have been so different...' She blinked a couple of times but the tears still fell. 'I wanted it to be so different...but now it's too late...'

He brought her head against his chest, his fingers splayed in her hair, the deep rumble of his voice as he spoke tearing Bronte's heart in two. 'I know, but that is my fault, *mio piccolo*. I wasn't ready. I was in a bad place in my life. I wasn't able to give you what you wanted. But then I wasn't even able to give myself what I wanted. It was just not our time.'

Bronte stood in the circle of his arms, wishing she could stay there for ever. But after a moment he stepped back from her. His expression was hard to read. He was smiling but it wasn't a smile that reached anywhere near his eyes. There were shadows there instead, flickering shadows that gave no hint of what he was feeling.

'I should let you get home to your little girl,' he said, sliding his hands down her arms to her wrists, holding them loosely with his long fingers.

A pain deep inside her chest made it almost impossible for Bronte to speak. 'It was...it was nice to see you again, Luca.'

He brought one of her hands up to his mouth, pressing his lips to her bent fingers. 'I hope one day you will forgive me for how I ended things,' he said.

'It's OK,' Bronte said. 'I should have accepted

your decision. I think I made a terrible fool of myself. Actually, I *know* I made a terrible fool of myself. I practically stalked you. I was so desperate to tell you I was…' She stopped and quickly regrouped. 'I mean…I was so desperate to know if there was something I had done to upset you. I should have realised our relationship had run its course. You had never offered anything permanent and I was a fool to hope and dream you would. I was caught up in the whole romance of my first real love affair. I was too immature to see it. Perhaps I didn't want to see it.'

'Don't beat yourself up about it, Bronte,' he said. 'We have this chance now to see if we can make a better go of it.'

Bronte felt her heart give a flutter like a startled pigeon. 'Y-you want to… I mean you still want to… I can't, Luca. I can't see you. I told you that.'

His jaw took on an uncompromising set. 'You told me yourself there is no one else in your life. What's to stop us revisiting our relationship if it's what we both want?'

'It's what you want,' she said. 'It's not what I want at all.'

'I don't believe that,' he said, tightening his hold on her wrists as she tried to get away. 'The way you kissed me earlier told me how much you still want me.'

'You made me kiss you,' she argued.

'Don't split hairs, Bronte,' he said. 'We were kissing each other. We want each other just as much as we ever did.'

'I can't have a casual affair with you,' she said. 'I

have responsibilities now. I haven't got room in my life for you.'

'Make room,' he said and, tugging her close, brought his mouth down on hers.

CHAPTER FIVE

'GOSH, you look like you didn't get any sleep at all last night,' Rachel said as Bronte came into the studio the next day. 'Was it your hot date or your darling daughter who kept you up all hours?'

Bronte gave her a don't-speak-to-me-about-it look.

'Come on, Bronte,' Rachel pleaded. 'You didn't even return any of my texts. What happened? Did you tell him about Ella?'

Bronte blew out a sigh. 'No, I didn't get around to it.'

Rachel's brows went up. 'What *did* you get around to?' She leaned closer and peered at Bronte's chin. 'Hey, is that what I think it is?'

Bronte put her hand up to the reddened patch on her chin where Luca's evening stubble had left its mark. 'It's nothing,' she said.

Rachel folded her arms in a you-can't-fool-me pose. 'Beard rash only happens when you get up close and personal,' she said. 'So the spark is still there, huh?'

Bronte pulled her hair back into a high ponytail, all the while trying to avoid her friend's eyes. She felt so conflicted about last night. That final kiss had burned her like fire. The stubble rash on her chin was nothing to what she felt inside. She was still smouldering with want, a hot needy craving for more of Luca's touch. He had ended the kiss and sent her on her way, only after he had extracted a promise to meet him for dinner this evening. She had practically stumbled back to her car, her emotions on a roller coaster ride as she thought of the danger she was dancing with.

She had spent most of the night once she got home arguing with herself over whether she should have told him from the get-go about Ella. But then the counter argument was always the same: how could she trust him not to take Ella away from her? After all, he had left her in London without a single explanation as to why their affair was over. What was to stop him doing the same thing again, but this time taking Ella with him? It was just too risky. She had to protect her daughter. She had to protect herself.

'So are you seeing him again?' Rachel asked.

'Yes,' Bronte said, slipping out of her street shoes to begin her stretches. 'Dinner tonight. I don't know why I agreed to it. I know it's only asking for trouble. He wants to resume our relationship as if nothing happened.'

'That's men for you,' Rachel said, rolling her eyes. 'So did he tell you why he broke things off before?'

'Not really,' Bronte said, frowning. 'Just that it was a bad time for him or something.'

'You think there was someone else?'

Bronte let out another long breath. 'I don't know what to think. When I spoke to the housekeeper at his place in Milan she was adamant he was involved with someone in LA.'

'But?'

Bronte met her friend's grey gaze. 'I get the feeling

Luca is not being totally straight with me. I don't trust him. I don't think I will ever trust him after what he did. He could have a woman in every country for all I know.'

'You said he wants to resume his relationship with you,' Rachel said. 'But how are you going to do that without telling him about Ella?'

'He knows about Ella,' Bronte said. 'He just doesn't know she's his. I left my phone behind and he saw some of the pictures I'd taken of her lately. I let him assume she was someone else's child.'

Rachel frowned. 'How'd you do that?'

Bronte gave her a sheepish look. 'I sort of lied about her age.'

Rachel shook her head in disapproval. 'That could come back to bite you, Bronte. You should have told him. It will only make things much worse the longer you leave it.'

'I can't tell him,' Bronte said, pressing a hand to her aching head. 'He could take her off me. You don't know what the Sabbatinis are like, Rachel. They're one of the most powerful dynasties, not just in Italy but all over Europe. They're practically royalty. They have money and prestige and power beyond belief. I spent a bit of time on the Net last night when I couldn't sleep, looking them up. His father died about three years before I met Luca, but Giancarlo and Giovanna Sabbatini brought their three sons up with more silver spoons than you could possibly count. Luca's grandfather, Salvatore, is reputed to be one of the richest men in the whole of Europe. Luca told me very little of his background when we were involved. I'm not sure why, maybe because so many women were attracted to him and his brothers because of their wealth. I didn't even know who he was when we met. He thought that was highly amusing. I think it might have been one of the reasons he let our relationship continue as long as it did as it was such a refreshing change from what he was used to. He was sick of people fawning over him. He once said to me it is hard to really know who your friends are when you have money.'

'You do realise that Ella is by birth entitled to some of that money, don't you?' Rachel said. 'She's got Sabbatini blood in her veins. And, according to what I read in the papers about Luca's older brother's marriage breaking up without an heir, Ella is so far the only grandchild.'

Bronte pressed her lips together. She hadn't thought of it quite like that. She hadn't thought about Ella's rights and entitlements as a Sabbatini heir. What if some time in the future her daughter resented her for not allowing her to get to know her father and his family?

'Look, Bronte,' Rachel went on. 'I know Luca hurt you and you don't trust him not to hurt you again, but you can't keep his own flesh and blood a secret from him for ever. For all you know, he might be surprisingly good about it. After all, he was the one who cut you from his life. You did your best to contact him so if anyone's to blame for him not being a part of Ella's first year and a bit, it's him.'

Bronte's shoulders sagged. 'I know I have to tell him some time. It's just finding the right time to do it.'

'There's probably never going to be a perfect time to drop that sort of news into the conversation,' Rachel said. 'But it's better he hears it from you rather than from someone else or, worse, stumbles across the truth himself. Photos are not the same as seeing someone face to face. As soon as Luca walked in here yesterday I realised who he was. That's why I kept my mouth shut. Ella might favour you primarily, but no one could ever question she wasn't his daughter. Once he sees her in the flesh, he's going to see it for himself.'

Bronte tried to put her fears aside as she got on with her day but it was impossible to ignore the prospect of the evening ahead. She got home early enough to feed Ella her dinner and bathe her and have some play time before putting her to bed. Ella was a little grizzly and out of sorts and kept gnawing on her fingers, which made Bronte feel uneasy about leaving her.

'I think she might be teething again,' Bronte's mother said as she came into the granny flat to babysit. 'She was a bit grumpy yesterday too.'

Bronte placed her hand on her daughter's forehead, frowning as she felt its clammy heat. 'I'd better check her temperature. She feels hot.'

Tina produced the rapid test ear thermometer and handed it to Bronte. The reading was normal but still Bronte felt in two minds about leaving her daughter in such an unsettled state. 'Maybe I should ring Luca and cancel,' she said. 'He gave me his contact details. Or I could just leave a message with the concierge at the hotel.'

Tina plucked the whining child from Bronte's arms and cuddled her close. 'Get it over with, love,' she said. 'Have dinner with him and then say goodbye and leave it at that. He'll soon get the message you're not interested. I know Rachel thinks you should tell him about Ella but I think you'd be better to let this particular sleeping dog lie.'

Bronte knew why her mother was so adamant about keeping Ella's paternity a secret from Luca. Tina was frightened her little granddaughter would be taken to live far away in another country. Apart from Bronte and Ella, Tina had very little in her life. A single mother herself from a young age, all she had was her work at a machinery parts factory, which could hardly be called a fulfilling career. Bronte and now little Ella were the entire focus of her life. She had never dated, rarely socialised and had few hobbies. Rachel had warned Bronte many times that her mother was living her life vicariously through Bronte but it had been too hard for Bronte to do anything about it. She had needed her mother, just as much if not more than her mother needed her.

'If she doesn't settle, promise you'll ring me,' Bronte said as she rummaged through her wardrobe for something to wear.

'She'll be fine,' Tina assured her. 'I'll nurse her for a while until she drops off.' She looked down at the infant in her arms and continued wistfully, 'I love watching her sleep. It reminds me of when you were a baby. It was just you and me in those days. I don't know what I would have done if anything had happened to you. You were my whole world.'

Bronte smiled and leant down to kiss her mother and her little daughter. 'I won't be late,' she said softly. 'And thanks, Mum, for everything.'

Tina smiled back but Bronte could see there was a tinge of worry in her eyes as she watched her leave.

Luca straightened his tie and shook down his shirt cuffs, freeing them of his dinner jacket. He had had meetings all day and his head was buzzing with all the things he had to do over the next month. This trip to Melbourne was proving to be one of the best decisions of his career in the family corporation. He had begun the negotiation for plans for a boutique hotel development in the city as well as two more commercial property investments: a large office block in the CBD and a parking lot with the potential for expansion.

And then there was Bronte. He had found it hard to sleep last night once she had left. He still couldn't believe he had let her leave. He had been so close to pulling her back towards his bed and solving the issues over the past by doing what they had always done best. The trouble was he wanted her to come to him willingly. Seduction was easy; working on a relationship was harder. He didn't want to end up like his brother Giorgio with a bitter estrangement from his wife and very likely a costly and acrimonious divorce pending. Luca wanted to get it right this time. He wanted to start again, put the past aside and work on his future—the future he hadn't been sure he would have. Life for him now was about living. Taking each day as a blessing and moving forward with renewed purpose. Bronte was his stumbling block to moving on. He had to know if he had a chance to make things right with her. To see if what they'd had was still there.

The issue of her child was something he found challenging but it wasn't the child's fault and he knew he would learn to love her as his own once he spent some time with her. His family might not see it quite that way but he would deal with them if and when the time came. The pressure for the acquisition of a Sabbatini heir had already caused the breakdown of his brother's marriage.

Giorgio and Maya, in spite of several gruelling IVF attempts, had failed to produce the grandchild and great-grandchild his mother and rapidly ageing grandfather longed for.

There was a tentative knock at the door and Luca gave his hair one last finger-comb before he went to answer it. He had wanted to pick Bronte up but she had insisted on meeting him here. The restaurant was only a short walk along the Southbank complex so he had agreed, knowing that pressuring her too much would only bring her back up. It wasn't his intention to antagonise her. His intention was to get her back into his life and into his bed as quickly as possible, to reawaken the feelings he hoped she still had for him. It was a gamble but he couldn't rest until he knew for sure. He saw the way her eyes flared when they met his, and the way she sent the tip of her tongue out over her lips as if anticipating his next kiss. He felt the tension in the air, the way the invisible current of energy drew them together, as it had always done in the past. She might have slept with another man since, but he felt sure she still wanted him.

He opened the door and she was standing there in a cocktail dress of an intriguing shade of blue. The colour made the dark blue of her eyes look like fathomless lakes. She smelt divine: a mixture of orange blossom and ginger this time, spicy and fragrant and intensely alluring. Her straight dark brown hair was loose about her shoulders, glossy as silk, held back from her face with a slim black headband. Teamed with the cocktail dress, it gave her a child-woman look that was amazingly sexy. She was wearing heels but she still had to crane her neck to meet his eyes. Her mouth was soft and shiny with lipgloss, but in those first few moments he noticed how her teeth nibbled at the inside of her mouth, as if she was nervous.

'Bronte,' he said, leading her into the suite. 'How do you manage to always look so beautiful and elegant?'

She gave him a tentative smile but it was so fleeting he wondered if he had imagined it. 'I picked this up at a second-hand clothing store. At ten dollars it was a steal. I don't have too many fancy clothes.'

Luca wondered if she was deliberately reminding him of the different worlds they lived in. He had always found it amazing how money had never impressed her. She found pleasure in the simplest things. He had learned a lot from the short time he had been with her. He had learned that money could bring comfort to your life and privileges but it didn't necessarily bring happiness and fulfilment and it certainly didn't guarantee good health.

He led the way to the lounge area and, once she was seated, he handed her a gift-wrapped package.

She looked up at him with rounded eyes. 'What is this for?'

'Open it,' he said. 'I thought after last night it might come in useful.'

She unpeeled the satin ribbon tied around the package and then carefully peeled back the layers of tissue to reveal the designer clutch purse he had bought in between meetings earlier that day. He watched as she ran her index finger over the designer emblem, before lifting her gaze to his. 'It's beautiful...thank you...but you shouldn't have spent so much money.'

'You'd better check to see if the catch works,' he said with a wry smile.

She bit down on her lip and she opened and closed the purse with a snap that sounded like a gunshot. He saw her slim throat rise and fall over a tight swallow and the way her fingers trembled slightly as she refolded the tissue around the purse. A small frown had lined her smooth forehead and when she looked up at him again he saw a shadow of uncertainty in her eyes. 'Luca...' She moistened her lips and started again. 'There's something we need to discuss...I should have told you last night but there didn't seem to be—'

Luca moved to where she was sitting and placed his hand on her shoulder. 'If you're going to make a fuss about me buying you things, then don't,' he said. 'I know you can't be bought with money. I shouldn't have pulled that stunt over the rent. I admire your independence. But this time just accept this in the spirit in which it is given.'

She rolled her lips together and looked down at the purse lying on her lap. 'It's very kind of you. I really needed a new purse. Thank you.'

He held out a hand. 'Come on,' he said. 'Let's get going to the restaurant. I made an early booking as I figured you would probably need to get home at a reasonable hour to your little girl.'

Her eyes darted away from his. 'Yes...yes, I will.'

Luca took her hand as they walked down to the restaurant. Her small fingers interlaced with his, but he sensed tension in them, a fluttering nervousness that made him wonder if she was having second thoughts about this evening. He had told her no strings, just dinner, but the pulse of electricity that already charged between their bodies was a heady reminder of all they had experienced together in the past. Was she thinking of how many times dinner together had led to mind-blowing sex soon after? His body twitched in memory, his blood surging to his groin as he walked his mind back through the images he had stored of them together. He had clung to those memories during his darkest hours. They had been a powerful motivation for him to fight his demons, to wrestle them to the ground so he could finally reclaim his life.

The restaurant overlooked the Yarra River and the city beyond. There were clouds in the night sky, brooding clusters of tension that crackled in the eerily still air.

'Do you think there is going to be a storm?' Luca asked, pointing to a particularly furious-looking cloud bank in the distance. 'It certainly feels like it, don't you think?'

'I heard something about it in the weather report in the taxi,' she said.

Luca stopped to frown down at her. 'I thought you were going to drive in. I would have picked you up. Why didn't you call me and tell me you'd changed your mind?'

She turned her gaze to the grumbling clouds. 'I was running late. Ella was a bit unsettled. I wasn't sure I'd find a parking spot.'

Luca waited until they had resumed walking before he asked, 'Is that why you're so tense this evening? Are you worried about being away from her?'

'It's hard not to worry at times,' she said, not looking his way, nor at the view but at the ground at her feet. 'It's part of being a parent. You never stop worrying from the moment they are born.'

'I guess you're right,' Luca said. 'My brothers and I

are all in our thirties but my mother is always worrying about something or other to do with one or all of us. Mind you, I think there have been times when she has had good cause to be worried. The three of us have had our fair share of mishaps, and then, of course, there was the death of our sister when she was a baby that really did the damage.'

Bronte stopped in her tracks and looked up at him in shock. 'You never told me you had a sister.'

He gave a shrug. 'It was a long time ago. I hardly even remember her, or only vaguely. She died when I was three and Nic was eighteen months old. He doesn't remember her at all. Giorgio remembers her the most clearly. He was six at the time. It really affected him. He won't talk about it, even after all these years.'

'What happened?' Bronte asked.

'Sudden Infant Death Syndrome,' he said. 'Or cot death, as it was called back then. My parents went through a terrible time, my mother especially. There wasn't the knowledge about the cause of it then. My mother felt everyone blamed her. The truth is, she blamed herself. The police who came to the villa after Chiara died didn't help matters. It was a long time before my mother got over it, although, at times, I wonder if she really ever did get over it. She's completely obsessed about having grandchildren, my grandfather too, especially after my father died. It's made things extremely difficult for Giorgio and his wife. I am sure it's one of the reasons they have separated. Maya couldn't take the pressure of not being able to conceive.'

Bronte felt a hammer blow of guilt assail her. She even stumbled slightly, as if the blow was physical.

Luca's hand tightened on hers as he steadied her, his brow creasing as he looked down at her.

'Careful,' he said. 'I don't want you to break an ankle on our first date.'

She gave him a strained smile and continued walking. 'I'm sorry about your family's loss,' she said after a moment. 'I'm sorry too about your brother and his wife. It must be a very difficult time for both of them.'

'It is,' Luca said. 'As much as I'd like to knock both their heads together at what they are throwing away, I've had to stay out of it. Giorgio can be very stubborn and once his mind is made up, that's it. He's too proud for his own good. But then, who I am to criticize?'

Bronte mulled over that while he led her into the restaurant. It was a while before they were alone again. The waiter brought drinks and discussed the menu and the day's specials and then reappeared with warmed olives and freshly baked bread and a tiny dish of extra virgin olive oil and balsamic vinegar, before discreetly moving away to leave them in their intimate corner.

Luca raised his glass to Bronte. 'Here's to new beginnings.'

Bronte's hand shook as she touched her glass against his. 'To...to new beginnings.'

The silence fell like a thick suffocating blanket.

Bronte could barely breathe as each second passed. The restaurant noise of dishes and cutlery and glassware faded and her ears filled with a roaring sound of impending doom. Outside, a loud crack of thunder sounded, making her flinch and almost spill her glass of wine.

'Hey.' Luca took her free hand and gave it a gentle

squeeze. 'Are you OK? Is the storm bothering you? Are you frightened of them?'

Bronte shook her head. 'No, not really.'

He studied her for a moment. 'You seem really on edge, *cara*. You don't need to be. Just relax. We're just two friends having dinner, remember? I'm not going to put the hard word on you at the end of the evening. We can take things as they go. No pressure, OK?'

Bronte felt sick with nerves. There was no easy way to say what she had to say. She had only made things worse by leaving it this late. She should have told him as soon as he saw the photos of Ella. Why had she made it so hard for herself by dragging it out so torturously? She took a large sip of wine to garner her flagging courage. The crisp dry wine moistened her dry throat but the shot of alcohol did nothing to settle her frazzled and frayed nerves. 'Luca,' she began, 'I have something to tell you.'

'Don't say you don't want to see me again,' he said before she could continue. 'We both know that is not the case. I know I stuffed things up before but I want to make it up to you. I think we have something special, Bronte. I think it could work if we just give it a try.'

Bronte toyed with the stem of her wine glass. 'Are you saying you…you have feelings for me?'

His small smile was enigmatic. 'You wouldn't be sitting here with me now if I didn't feel something. As to exactly what it is, well, isn't it a bit early to be talking about that?'

She ran her finger around the base of her glass this time, her eyes falling away from his. 'I'm not sure how to tell you this, Luca. I never thought I would be in this situation.' Her heart felt as if it was weighted. It ached with a bittersweet pain that made her want to break down and cry for how unfair life was. She had longed for him to give her some clue of his feelings in the past and yet, now he had, she was about to destroy them, she was sure.

She looked up and met his gaze across the table. 'When you left me in London I was devastated. I know you never promised me anything. I know I was much more in love with you than you were ever going to be with me. You never said what you felt. I know a lot of men are like that. Most of my friends experienced the same frustration of never knowing what the man they were dating felt about them. To be frank, sometimes I thought you didn't even like me, that you were just there for the sex. You seemed to give me so many mixed signals. We were all set for a date and then you would suddenly cancel half an hour before. And then you were grumpy and difficult one day and yet charming and attentive the next. I never knew where I stood with you, but I tried to be patient because I loved you so much.'

Luca reached for her hand again, lacing his fingers with hers. 'Back then, I wasn't in the position to offer you the sort of commitment you wanted, Bronte. I know that's not much of an explanation but I'd rather not go into the reasons why I acted the way I did. It's not relevant to here and now. All that matters is we are together again and both committed to working at what we had before. We've been given a second chance. Let's not blow it. Let's work on getting to know who we each are now, not who we were back then.'

Bronte looked down at their joined hands and let a few more seconds thrum pass. It was like waiting for a bomb to go off, watching the timer countdown second by agonising second and being able to do nothing to stop it. She knew once she said the words nothing would ever be the same. She slowly raised her eyes to his, her aching throat going up and down over a convulsive swallow.

'Bronte!' A female voice spoke from behind her in the restaurant.

Bronte pulled her hand out of Luca's and turned in her seat as one of the young mothers from the studio approached the table, her husband in tow. It took Bronte a moment to gather herself and she worried that her smile might not have seemed wholly genuine. 'Hi, Judy…hi, Dan.'

Judy waggled her brows expressively as she glanced at Luca before returning her gaze to Bronte's. 'So… who's your date?'

'Um…sorry,' Bronte said. 'Judy, Dan, this is Luca Sabbatini. Luca, Judy and Dan's daughter Matilda does ballet at the studio.'

Luca rose and politely shook the couple's hands. 'I'm delighted to meet you both,' he said, smiling that killer smile.

Bronte saw the way Judy's knees practically buckled. 'Lovely to meet you, Luca,' Judy said. 'Wow, Bronte's been keeping you a big secret. How long have you known her?'

'We met a couple of years ago in London,' Luca said.

'You're here for work, aren't you?' Judy's husband Dan asked. 'I'm an architect. The firm I work for are bidding for the contract for your hotel development.'

'Give me your business card,' Luca said, reaching into his jacket pocket for one of his own and handing it to Dan. 'I would be happy to look over your proposal with you. I have a temporary office in the city. My secretary will tee up a time for you to come in and have a chat.'

'That's very good of you, Luca,' Dan said, beaming.

'Does your daughter enjoy her ballet dancing?' Luca asked after a tiny silence.

'Oh, yes,' Judy gushed. 'She's mad about it, has been since she was Ruby's age. That's our other daughter, the baby. Well, not so much a baby now but we always call her that. They seem to grow up so fast. She's the same age as Ella. That's how Bronte and I met. It was in hospital having our babies, wasn't it, Bronte?'

Bronte nodded, barely able to get her voice to work. 'Um...yes.'

Judy prattled on, 'Ella and Ruby have the same birthday. They were born at exactly the same hour. Isn't that the most amazing coincidence?'

There was a split second as Bronte watched helplessly as the pin was finally pulled out of the grenade.

Judy said, 'They were both born on the fourth of July last year, Independence Day. And at fourteen months old they are both headstrong and independent, aren't they, Bronte?'

CHAPTER SIX

'Y-YES,' Bronte said lamely. 'They are...'

Judy smiled up at her husband. 'I guess we should get going to our table. It's our anniversary.' She turned back to Bronte and Luca, who hadn't said a word, nor moved a muscle. 'Lovely to meet you, Luca. I hope we'll be seeing more of you.'

'I am very sure you will,' Luca said, shaking both of their hands once more.

'And thanks for that offer,' Dan chipped in. 'That's amazingly generous of you.'

'Not at all.' Luca brushed Dan's thanks aside.

The couple moved on and Luca remained standing.

Bronte was looking down at her place setting, her slim shoulders rolled forward, with her teeth gnawing at her bottom lip.

'We're leaving,' he clipped out, throwing some money down on the table to cover their ordered meal.

She looked up at him with a pinched look. 'But...but people will wonder what's—'

Luca snatched at her hand and pulled her to her feet. 'I don't give a flying you-know-what for what people think,' he bit out savagely. 'I am not going to discuss this in a public restaurant.'

Bronte stumbled out of the restaurant with him, desperately hoping Judy and Dan wouldn't notice from their seats towards the back of the room. The tension in Luca's hand as he held hers was almost brutal. His fingers were like savage teeth biting into hers as he pulled her along beside him, his mouth set in a hard flat line. His dark eyes were dangerously brooding, his frown equally so. Once they were outside, every step he took pounded the pavement with his fury. The storm that had been brewing earlier was now in full force, as if it had sided with Luca. The flashing lightning and booming thunder mimicked the expression on his face, the electrifying hatred in his gaze zapping her like lightning each time he looked at her.

Bronte ran her tongue over her dry lips. 'Luca...I was trying to tell you when Dan and Judy arrived...'

His hand tightened like a vice as he swung her to face him. 'You were trying to tell me what?' he asked. 'That you deliberately *lied* to me from the moment you saw me yesterday? You told me the child was one year old. I did the calculations and you knew I would, didn't you? That's why you cut a couple of months off so I wouldn't suspect she was mine.'

Bronte hung her head. 'I'm sorry...'

He wrenched her back along the pavement. 'It's a bit late for an apology, damn it. You have a hell of a lot of explaining to do. I am so angry at this moment you should be thanking God we are in a public place. But you just wait until we get back to my hotel. You had better have your excuses handy.'

Each of his words was like a blow to Bronte's chest. She had known he wouldn't take the news well, but to have heard it the way he did had made it so much worse. He was shocked and angry and rightly so. He had missed out on the most precious first months of his child's life. Even though he had refused to see her after he ended their relationship, Bronte knew she'd had a responsibility to tell him, even if it had to have been in a letter addressed to his villa or house in London. He would have got it eventually. But her hurt at his rejection had made her act in a passive aggressive way. She could see it now. How she had secretly relished the fact he didn't know about Ella. It was her little payback for the heartbreak he had caused her. It was an appalling thing to do and she was deeply ashamed.

She couldn't give back what she had stolen from him. Each day of the fourteen months of Ella's life was irreplaceable. Sure, she had photos documenting every little milestone, but how could that compensate for the real thing? Even if he had not wanted a part in his child's life, he should at least have had the right to choose. She had denied him that right and now he was after revenge. She just knew it. Luca Sabbatini was not the sort of man to walk away from something like this with a shrug of his shoulders. He would want her to pay for what she had done and pay dearly.

The lift journey up to Luca's penthouse felt to Bronte as if she was being led to the gallows. As each floor number flashed past, her heartbeat escalated. She felt sick with anguish, guilt and nerves. Her stomach was curdled with the fear he would take Ella away from her. He'd already said how much his mother longed for a grandchild. And what could be more perfect than a little girl to replace the one she had lost in babyhood? The odds were stacked against Bronte keeping custody. How could she afford to contest such a case? She earned too much to qualify for legal aid and too little to take on the Sabbatini dynasty. But she was not going to give up without a fight. She would do anything to stop him from taking her little girl away from her.

Absolutely anything.

Luca activated the swipe card and practically frog-marched Bronte into the suite. He shut the door with a bang that reverberated like a cannon boom. 'Why the hell didn't you tell me you were pregnant?' he asked.

She looked at him with stricken features. 'I tried to contact you time and time again but you refused to meet me face to face.'

Luca felt a knife jab of guilt but he pushed it aside to make room for his burgeoning anger. 'How did it happen? You told me you were on the Pill and, in any case, I always used protection.'

'I don't know how it happened,' she said. 'I must have missed a dose or something. And then there was that time when the condom broke.'

Luca remembered that time as if it had happened yesterday. He had been so eager to see her after being away on a business trip. He had barely got the condom on in time and then it had broken. 'When did you find out you were pregnant?'

'A week after you told me our relationship was over.' She bit into her lip again and another flick knife of guilt caught him off guard.

Luca took a breath but it felt as if he was breathing through barbed wire. His throat felt raw and his chest so tight it ached unbearably. He scored his hair with his fingers, not surprised to see how unsteady his hand was. He could feel the tremors of rage rolling through him. Rage and remorse, a juxtaposition of emotions that made it hard for him to think clearly.

He had a child.

A little girl.

Fourteen months old and he had not shared a second of it. He had not seen her growing in Bronte's womb; he had not been at the birth. He knew nothing about the birth, how long the labour was, whether she had given birth naturally or by Caesarean. He didn't know whether she had fed the child herself or given her a bottle. He knew nothing about his daughter: the sound of her voice, the feel of her baby skin, the softness of her hair or the touch of her little hands. How could he ever get that time back? How could he forgive Bronte for stealing it from him? It had already poisoned what he felt for her. He had come back with such hope at resuming their relationship. But now he felt as if he didn't know Bronte at all. She had changed. She was a scheming little thief, and his loathing of what she had done made him want to cut her from his life all over again. But he couldn't because of his little daughter. His heart tightened again at the thought of that little girl in the photos he had seen.

His daughter.

'I wanted to tell you in person,' Bronte said in a small voice. 'But you didn't return my calls or emails. I went to your villa in Milan but I was turned away at the door. Your housekeeper said you were with your mistress in the US.'

Luca felt an avalanche of guilt come down on him. He had made it impossible for her to contact him. He had covered his tracks so well, not even his family had been aware of where he was and what he had been doing. He had spun them the same tale: a whirlwind affair in the

States. And it had worked, perhaps rather too well. 'You could have sent a letter,' he said, still not quite ready to take the whole blame.

'Is that how you wanted to hear you had fathered a child?' she asked.

'It would be a damn better way than finding out in a restaurant in front of complete strangers,' he shot back.

She lowered her gaze and did that thing with her bottom lip again. 'I told you, I was about to tell you when they arrived...'

'When?' he asked. 'Between the main course and dessert? How were you going to slip it into the conversation? "By the way, I had your child fourteen months ago; I thought you might like to know now that you're here in Melbourne." For God's sake, Bronte, what the hell were you thinking?'

She looked at up at him with tears shining in her eyes. 'I didn't expect to ever see you again. You made it so clear our relationship was over.'

'So you punished me by keeping my child a secret,' he said. 'Is that it? Is that why you didn't try harder to get the message to me?'

Guilt flooded her cheeks a cherry-red. 'I didn't want any of this to happen...'

'Meaning you never intended for me to find out,' he said heavily. 'Well, I've got news for you, Bronte Bennett. I want my child. You have got one hell of a fight on your hands if you think you're going to keep me away from her.'

Bronte felt a rod of anger straighten her spine. 'You can't take her from me, Luca. I won't allow it. She's my child. I'll fight you until my dying breath.'

'You and whose legal team?' he asked with a malevolent look. 'You do realise who you are up against here, don't you? You haven't got a hope of winning this, Bronte. Not a hope.'

Bronte hated herself for doing it but right at that moment her temper got the better of her. 'First you have to prove she is yours,' she said with a jut of her chin. 'Have you thought about that, Luca? How do you know she isn't another man's child? You only saw me two or three times a week when we were together, sometimes even less. I had plenty of time to play around behind your back.'

His expression went as dark as the thunderous sky outside. His hands went to tight fists, his breath hissing out from between clenched teeth. 'A paternity test will soon sort out that. I will apply for one in the morning. If you don't agree, expect to hear from my lawyer.'

Instead of feeling she had won that round, Bronte felt as if she had lost much more than a few verbal points. She had lost his respect. She could see it in his eyes, the way they had stripped her bare. It was one thing for him to have the freedom to see who he liked when he liked but quite another for her to do the same. She had been his possession, his little plaything on the side, and it would infuriate him to think she had given herself to someone else while involved with him.

'Who was it?' he asked through tight lips. 'Anyone I knew at the time?'

Bronte turned away. 'I don't have to explain myself to you. You certainly gave me no explanation for what you got up to when you weren't with me.'

He grabbed her arm and spun her around to face him,

his expression still as menacing as the storm raging outside. 'Who the hell were you seeing?' he asked.

Bronte tugged at his hold, squirming at the bite of his fingers. 'Stop it, Luca. You're hurting me.'

His hold loosened, but not by much. 'Tell me who you were seeing, damn it.'

She felt tears approaching and fought them back valiantly. 'Tell me who you were with in LA,' she said. 'What was her name? Was it someone famous or someone married so you had to keep it a big secret?'

His eyes flickered for a moment, his mouth pulled so tight it was white-tipped at the corners.

'Was she very beautiful?' Bronte asked, struggling now to keep her voice from cracking. 'Did she love you? Did you love her?'

He dropped his hand from her arm and stepped away. He rubbed the back of his neck as if trying to soothe a knot of tension there. He didn't speak. He just stood in front of the bank of windows and looked at the last of the storm's activity outside. His back was like a fortress, a thick impenetrable wall she had no hope of scaling. In spite of his hostility, she wanted to go to him, to put her arms around his waist, to hold him, to breathe in the aching familiarity of his scent.

'Luca?'

He turned to face her, his expression rigid with determination. 'I want to see her,' he said. 'I want to see my child.'

Bronte took a little step backwards. 'You mean… now?'

'Of course I mean now,' he said, scooping up his car keys from the coffee table.

'But she's asleep,' Bronte said. 'And…and my mother's there and—'

'Then it's time your mother met the father of her grandchild,' he said. 'She's going to have to get used to me being a part of the child's life.'

'"The child",' Bronte said, throwing her hands out wide. 'Can you please use her name? It's Ella.'

'Does she have a middle name?' he asked, his eyes hard and black with contempt as they pinned hers.

Bronte compressed her lips. 'Her full name is Ella Lucia Bennett.'

He blinked and the strong column of his throat moved up and down over a swallow. 'You named her… for me?'

She let out a small sigh. 'I wanted her to have something of you, even if it turned out she never met you. I felt I owed you that. I felt I owed her that.'

A little muscle in his jaw worked for a long moment. 'I want my name on her birth certificate,' he said. 'I don't suppose it's there?'

She shook her head. 'No, I didn't see the point at the time.'

'Did you tell anyone I was the father?'

'Not until recently,' she answered. 'My mother eventually pried it out of me. Rachel figured it out when you came to the studio yesterday.'

There was a small tense silence.

'I'm starting to think a paternity test is going to be a waste of time,' he said. 'You didn't cheat on me, did you, Bronte?'

She shook her head. 'No. There's been no one but you.'

Luca curled his fingers around his keys until the

cold hard metal cut into his palm. He needed time to process everything. His head was still reeling with the knowledge he was a father. He felt as if he had been pummelled all over. He ached with a pain he couldn't describe. It was worse than anything he had ever experienced. He couldn't imagine how he was going to sort out the mess his life had suddenly become. Things were going to get a whole lot more complicated when it came down to the practicalities. He lived between Milan and London. Bronte lived in Melbourne. Thousands of kilometres separated him from his daughter. That was one of the first things that had to change. 'Let's get going,' he said, moving across to hold the door open for her.

'Luca…wouldn't it be better to do this tomorrow when we've both had some time to think about things?' she asked. 'To cool down a bit, think things through in a more rational state of mind?'

'What is there to think about?' he asked. 'I want to see my daughter. I haven't seen her once and she's fourteen months old. I am not prepared to wait another hour, let alone another day.'

She moved past him with her head down, her expression shadowed with worry. Luca wanted her to be worried. He wanted her to be aware of what she had done. He wanted her to feel something of what he was feeling, how cheated he felt, how completely devastating it felt to have your world turned upside down without warning.

After asking for directions to her home, Luca retreated into a brooding silence. He couldn't hope to keep something as big as this silent for long. The press would very likely get in on the news. He had to call his mother and brothers and his grandfather. He didn't want them to read it in the press rather than hear it from him. And then there were legal things to see to, such as changing his will to make sure Ella was well provided for in the event of his death.

And then, of course, there was the issue of where to go from here with Bronte. He glanced at her, sitting with her head bowed, her eyes on her knotted hands in her lap. A sharp little pang caught him off guard when he thought of her trying to contact him with the news of her pregnancy. He wondered what she must have been feeling, alone and abandoned, far away from her family and friends. He thought too of the audition she'd had her heart set on. A once in a lifetime opportunity she had relinquished in order to have his baby. So many women would have chosen another option but she hadn't. She had soldiered on, giving up her dream to give life to his daughter.

'Tell me about the pregnancy,' he said. 'Were you well throughout?'

She lifted her head to glance at him. 'I was sick a lot in the beginning,' she said softly. 'I lost a lot of weight in the first three months but after that things settled down a bit.'

Luca felt another jab of guilt. 'What about the birth? Did you have someone with you?'

'My mother was with me.'

He gripped the steering wheel tighter, thinking of what he had missed out on. That first glimpse of new life, hearing the miracle of that first spluttering cry. 'Was it a natural birth?' he asked once he got his voice into working order.

'Yes. I think the fact that I was fit and well helped a lot. I had a relatively short labour. It was painful but I wanted to do things as naturally as possible.'

'Were you able to breastfeed her?'

'Yes, but it took a while to get things established,' she said. 'For something so natural it's harder than you think to get things right. I weaned her a couple of months ago, just before her first birthday.'

Luca let silence build a wall between them. He wasn't quite ready to let her off the hook. He knew he hadn't made things easy for her by being so adamant about ending their relationship, but he still felt she could have tried harder, *should* have tried harder.

The closer he got to Bronte's mother's house, the more nervous he felt. His stomach was a hive of restless activity. It seemed like a flock of sharp-winged insects was inside him trying desperately to find a way out.

He was about to see his baby daughter for the first time. He would be able to touch her, to hold her in his arms, to feel her petite little body nestled up against him.

He already loved her.

That had surprised him. He thought he would have to meet her first, but no, as soon as he knew she was alive he felt something switch on inside him. The urge to protect and provide for her was so strong he couldn't think about anything else. He was determined to give her everything money could buy, to give her the sort of childhood that would give her every opportunity to blossom and grow into a beautiful young lady, well educated, compassionate and ready to take on the world.

'It's the third house on the left,' Bronte said. 'The one without a fence.'

Luca parked in front of the small weatherboard house. As far as he could see, it was neat but in no way luxurious. Humble was probably a more appropriate word. There wasn't much of a garden, just a lawn and a few azaleas and camellias that lined the boundary of the block. The contrast with his family's villa, his childhood homes in Milan and Rome and the holiday villa at Bellagio couldn't be more apparent. He knew for certain there wouldn't be any household staff opening the door as they approached, nor would there be a team of gardeners to tend the block, nor a driver at the ready to run errands.

Bronte's car—he assumed it was hers as it had a baby seat in the back—was parked in the driveway. There was no carport or garage. The car was at least fifteen years old and looked as if it needed new tyres. The thought of his child being ferried about in that accident-waiting-to-happen appalled him but he decided to keep that conversation for another time.

The walk to the back of the block where a small granny flat was situated was conducted in a stiff silence. Luca could feel Bronte's apprehension coming off her in waves. One of the curtains twitched aside and he saw a woman whom he assumed was Bronte's mother staring at him with wide, nervous-looking eyes.

Bronte opened the door and led Luca inside. Her mother came towards them, her expression cold and unfriendly.

'You must be Luca,' she said, pointedly ignoring Luca's proffered hand.

'That is correct,' he said, dropping his hand back by his side.

'Mum…' Bronte gave her mother a pained look. 'Do you mind if—?'

Tina Bennett ignored her daughter and addressed Luca. 'What you did to Bronte was unforgivable. You left her pregnant and alone. She was only twenty-three years old. She had her whole life ahead of her and you ruined it.'

'Mum, please—'

Tina continued her attack undaunted. 'Did you ever think what had become of her after you threw her out of your life? Or did you simply move on to the next floozy, someone who was more your type?'

Luca seemed very tall as he stood looking down at her mother, Bronte thought. He contained himself well. He showed no sign of being angry at the way her mother was speaking to him. 'Mrs Bennett—' he began.

'It's Miss,' Tina snapped. 'Like mother, like daughter, Mr Sabbatini. I too was abandoned by the man I loved when I was carrying her. I have never married. Being a single mother makes it hard to find someone who is prepared to love your child as their own. You can ask Bronte about that. She's had one date, one boring, going nowhere date that was really only a favour for her friend Rachel.'

'Mum,' Bronte spoke with firmness, 'I want to be alone with Luca. There are things we need to discuss in private. Thank you for minding Ella for me.'

Tina tightened her mouth as she gave Luca a mother lion protecting her cub look. 'I won't let you hurt her again,' she said. 'You can be sure of that, Mr Sabbatini. Bronte and Ella are all I've got. I'm not going to stand by and watch some rich, spoilt playboy take either of them away from me.'

'It is not my intention to hurt anyone,' Luca said coolly and calmly. 'I am here to see my daughter. That is my priority at this point. Bronte and I haven't yet got around to discussing where we go from here but, as soon as we do, you will be the first to know.'

Tina looked as if she was about to say something else but, after another pleading look from Bronte, she turned on her heel and left.

CHAPTER SEVEN

Luca turned his gaze to Bronte's, his expression rueful. 'Something tells me I didn't make such a great first impression.'

'I would have liked to have warned her you were coming,' Bronte said with a note of reproach in her voice.

'Don't talk to me about warnings,' he threw back. 'Yesterday I was a single man with no responsibilities apart from my work. Now I find I am the father of a fourteen-month-old toddler.'

Bronte worked hard at holding his accusing gaze. 'I know this must be a shock. And I'm sorry about Mum but she's just being a mum. She's frightened and uncertain about what happens next.'

'So she should be,' he said with a brooding frown.

Bronte felt a quake of unease rumble through her stomach. 'Wh…what do you mean?' she asked.

His eyes held hers for a tense moment, bitterness, anger and vengefulness all reflected there. 'Look at this place,' he said, waving his hand to encompass the small room and simple furnishings. 'This is not the place where I want any child of mine to be brought up. There isn't even a front fence, for God's sake. What if

Ella was to walk out on the road? Have you thought of that?'

Bronte summoned her pride. 'There is nothing wrong with this place,' she said. 'The fence is going up as soon as we can afford it. And, anyway, Ella is only just walking and she is never left alone. Not for a minute.'

'That is not the point,' he argued. 'She deserves much better and I am going to make sure she gets it. Now, please lead me to her. I want to see her.'

Bronte clamped her lips down on her response and silently led him to the small bedroom next to hers. The blue angel night light was on, casting a soft luminous glow over the room. Ella was lying on her back, arms flung either side of her head, her rosebud mouth slightly open, the covers kicked off her tiny body. Bronte gently pulled the covers back up, conscious of Luca standing next to her, his eyes looking down at the sleeping infant.

The only sound in the silence was Ella's soft snuffling breathing.

Luca looked at the angelic face of his child and felt a seismic shift inside his chest. He was totally overcome by emotion. Feelings surged through him, knocking him sideways. He swallowed against the lump in his throat, surprised to feel the burn of tears at the backs of his eyes. He blinked them back and, with a hand that was not quite steady, he reached down and brushed his fingertip across the velvet softness of Ella's tiny cheek. She made a little noise, something between a snuffle and a murmur, as if she were dreaming, before settling back down with a little sigh.

Luca picked up one of her tiny hands. It reminded him of a starfish, the little splay of fingers with their perfect fingernails so small in comparison to his. Her fingers curled around one of his, the tiny dimples on her knuckles appearing as she tightened her hold, as if subconsciously recognising she belonged to him. He could not explain how it felt. It was totally overwhelming. He longed to hold on to this moment, to keep it forever in his memory.

How would it feel as the years went by, holding this little trusting hand in his? Walking her into school for the first day, holding her steady as he taught her to ride a bike, her holding on his arm as he led her one day way off in the future to the man who would one day be her husband? It was too much to absorb all at once. Other men had nine months to prepare for it. He had been cheated of that. He was in catch up mode and it hurt—it hurt so much he could barely breathe.

'You can pick her up if you want to,' Bronte whispered at his side. 'She usually sleeps pretty soundly.'

'Can I?' he asked, looking at Bronte for reassurance.

She gave him a tight little movement of her lips, her eyes suspiciously moist. 'Of course,' she said, reaching past him to ease back the covers.

Luca wasn't sure how to do it but was too proud to ask for help. He had bounced the occasional friend's baby on his knee but he had never picked up a sleeping baby before. Wasn't there something about their neck you had to be aware of?

'Just gather her underneath her shoulders and knees,' Bronte offered in the silence, as if she had sensed his hesitancy.

'Ri-ght...' He did as she said and his little daughter

nestled against him as he lifted her out of the cot with another soft murmur.

'There's a chair over here.' Bronte pushed it forward and he sat down, cradling Ella against his chest.

Luca couldn't take his eyes off her. The perfection of her amazed him. She had the most beautiful face, like an angel. She favoured her mother, but now that he had her up close he could see traces of his own mother and even his long-dead baby sister. She smelt so sweet, a combination of talcum powder and baby that was indescribably beautiful. He traced a gentle fingertip over each of her tiny eyebrows and then the up-tilted button nose that was so like Bronte's. Love flowed through him like a torrent. It filled him completely; there wasn't a space inside him that wasn't consumed with love for this child.

'Would you like some time alone with her?' Bronte asked after a long silence.

'It's all right,' Luca said, carefully getting to his feet and carrying Ella back to the cot. He laid her down gently and pulled the covers back over her, tucking them in either side of her. 'I don't want to wake her. She might feel frightened at not knowing who I am if she should suddenly wake up.'

He stood back from the cot and took a steadying breath before turning to Bronte. 'We need to talk.'

She nodded resignedly and led the way out of the room.

The kitchen–living room combined was on the small side but with Luca there it made it shrink to the size of a doll's house. There was nowhere in the room that kept her more than two metres away from him. It was intimidating to say the least. One step from him and a reach with one of those long arms of his and she would be snared. The most bewildering thing was, she wasn't entirely sure she would try to move away if he did reach out and touch her.

Bronte was so moved by watching him with Ella. She hadn't been sure what to expect but seeing the love on his face for his child had made her all the more certain he was not going to walk away from his little daughter. He would want to be an active father. He came from a strongly connected family background, a rich heritage that Ella was entitled to be a part of as a Sabbatini. The only trouble was, where did Bronte fit into it all according to his plans for the future?

'Would you like a cup of tea or something?' she asked to fill the silence.

'No tea,' he said.

She gestured to the one and only sofa. 'Would you like to sit down?'

'No, but you had better do so,' he said ominously.

Bronte sat down on the chain store sofa and pressed her knees against her hands to keep them from trembling. 'Don't take her off me, Luca, please, I beg you,' she said, the words tumbling out of her mouth in an agonised stream. 'I love her so much. I would do anything to make it up to you. I know it was wrong not to try harder to tell you. I realise it now. I couldn't bear it if you…' She couldn't continue as the tears began to fall. She bowed her head and stifled a sob.

'Tears are not going to work with me, Bronte,' he said through tight lips. 'I have lost more than a year of my child's life. Do you have any idea of what that feels like?'

She looked up at him with red-rimmed eyes. 'I know how upset you must be—'

'You don't know the half of it,' he ground out. 'I look at Ella and every day I have missed is like a punch to my guts.'

'I have photos and some home videos to show you—'

'For God's sake, Bronte, a child's life is not like a movie I've missed when it came to the local cinema,' he said, raking a hand through his hair. 'I can *never* have that time back. I can never tell her when she is older what it was like to see her born. I can never tell her what it felt like to hold my hand over your belly to feel her wriggling in there. I can't tell her when she took her first step or when she first smiled.'

'She's still so young,' Bronte said. 'She won't even remember you weren't a part of her life in the beginning. Children don't really remember anything until they are about three years old. You have plenty of time to make up for what you've lost.'

'And how do you suggest I do that?' he asked. 'Aren't you forgetting something?'

Bronte pressed her lips together. She knew what was coming and took a breath to prepare herself for it.

'You live in Australia,' he said. 'I spend half my time in Italy and the other half in London.'

'I…I know…' Her voice was a thready whisper.

'Which means one of us has to move.'

Her eyes rounded, her mouth going completely dry. 'You'd do that? You'd consider moving here to be closer to Ella?' she asked.

His expression was derisive. 'Not me, Bronte,' he said, 'you.'

'Me?' The word came out like a squeak.

'Of course you,' he said. 'I can't run a corporation the size of mine from this distance. You can teach ballet anywhere.'

Bronte got to her feet in one agitated movement. 'Are you out of your mind? I can't move to Italy or wherever you want me to. I'm building up my career. It's just getting to the stage where I can expand and take on more teachers. And I have my mother and friends here. My support network is very important to me.'

His mouth took on a stubborn line. 'You move or you lose Ella,' he said. 'I am not going to have her travelling back and forth in planes on access visits. I want to be fully involved in her life. I am not prepared to negotiate on this.'

Bronte opened and closed her mouth, trying to think of some way to make him see reason. She couldn't believe his obstinacy. Did he really think she should uproot everything at his bidding? What role was she to play in his life? Was she just to be the mother of his child or was he expecting something more?

'I want my family to meet Ella as soon as possible,' he said. 'And it goes without saying we will have to get married as soon as it can be arranged.'

Bronte stared at him in stupefaction. 'Are you crazy?'

'I am not going to be drawn into an argument about this, Bronte,' he said. 'Ella is a Sabbatini. She has certain rights and privileges as a grandchild and heir. I will have no one refer to her as a love-child. I want her to have my name.'

'She can have your name without you having to

marry me,' Bronte said. 'I can have it put on the birth certificate.'

'Bronte, let me make something very clear,' he said with an intractable set to his mouth. 'We have a responsibility towards our child. She needs a mother and a father. The only way to see that she gets what she needs is for us to marry and stay married.'

'But I don't love you any more.' Bronte said it even though she wasn't sure if it was true. She didn't know what she felt towards him. She felt so confused about him. He had barged back into her life and was threatening everything she had clung to for security. The hurt over his rejection was like a wound that had been re-opened. It ached deep inside her and she was terrified of being hurt all over again.

'I do not require your love,' he said. 'There are plenty of very successful marriages which exist on mutual respect and common interests. We will start with that and see where it takes us.'

Bronte sent him a defiant glare. 'I hope you're not expecting me to sleep with you because I'm not going to. If I have to marry you, it will be in name only.'

His eyes were like glittering black diamonds as they held hers. 'You are not the one dictating the terms here, Bronte,' he said. 'You will be my wife in every sense of the word.'

Bronte's heart gave a nervous flutter as his implacable statement hit home. She could see the fiery intent in his eyes. He wanted her and he was not going to settle for a sterile hands-off arrangement. The thought of sleeping with him was all the more terrifying because she was sure she would fall in love with him all over again. She couldn't dissociate the intimate act like some of her peers seemed able to do. She felt the emotional connection deeply. In the past she hadn't just loved him with her heart and soul, but her body as well. 'You seem to have it all worked out,' she said, trying to keep the wobble out of her voice.

'It's for the best, Bronte,' he said. 'In time, you will see that. I know it is a lot to ask of you to relocate, but your mother can visit any time she likes. And you can fly back for visits. You will not be under lock and key.'

She turned and paced what little space she had. 'I need some time to think about this,' she said, pressing her hand to her temple where a cluster of tension was gathering.

'There isn't time,' he said. 'We have to get moving on this. We have a wedding to arrange. I want it to be a proper one, not some hole in the corner affair.'

Bronte swung back to face him. 'I haven't said I will marry you, Luca. Don't rush me. I told you I need some time to think about this.'

He came over to where she was standing, his expression so in control, so commanding, so indomitable, it sent a tremor of unease through her. 'If you say no to our marriage, you are never going to see your daughter again,' he said. 'Have I made myself clear enough?'

Bronte bristled with outrage. 'You bastard,' she said in a snarling hiss. 'You arrogant, cruel, heartless bastard.'

His eyes glinted as they roamed her furious features, his body so close now she could feel the male heat of him. She had nowhere to escape. She was backed up against the wall, her heart going like a jackhammer in her chest as he planted his hands either side of her head, his strongly muscled arms making a cage around her quaking body. She sent the tip of her tongue out over her lips, a rush of unruly desire gushing through her like a flash flood.

His eyes went to her mouth, his lashes lowering in a smouldering manner. She held her breath as he came closer, the soft waft of his breath over the surface of her lips making her heart kick-start in reaction. When he finally touched down on her lips she felt an explosion of desire in her body. It roared like petrol thrown on a fire. Leaping flames of need rose up and consumed her. She opened her mouth to the possessive thrust of his tongue, a hollow pit opening in her stomach as it mated erotically with hers. This was no poignant tender kiss of a revisited relationship. This was a kiss of anger and out of control needs. Bronte tasted Luca's anger and frustration and gave plenty of her own back. She used her teeth on his lower lip, not the tender teasing little nips of the past, but savage wildcat bites that drew blood. He took control of the kiss, pushing her further back against the wall, his aroused body hot, hard and urgent against hers.

It shocked her how much he wanted her.

It shocked her how much she wanted him.

Her body had superseded any counter argument her mind tried to throw up to resist him. The simple truth was she wanted him to make love to her, to reclaim her body, to imprint it with the potency of his.

His mouth was still locked on hers as his hands lifted her cocktail dress, searching for the slick wet heart of her. He cupped her first through the lacy barrier of her knickers, which were already damp with want. She arched her spine as he pushed the lace aside to slide one finger into her. The sensations rippled through her, making her want more and more of his touch. She whimpered against the crushing heat of his mouth as his hand left her moist heat to unzip his trousers. She blindly assisted him, her fingers stroking along his steely length, delighting in the feel of him so aroused. It was something to cling to, this need he had for her. He might not love her, he might never find it in himself to forgive her for denying him knowledge of his child, but he wanted her with a fervency that secretly thrilled her.

She could have pulled away. She could have stopped things before they went any further but she didn't. She dug her fingers into the tautness of his buttocks and urged him on.

He thrust into her with a deep bone-melting thrust that sent her head thudding against the wall behind her. He set a furious pace but she matched it. It didn't matter that they were still fully clothed; it didn't matter that no one had mentioned protection.

The friction of his thickened body brought her undone within seconds. She had never been able to come without added stimulation before but this time her body shattered into a thousand pieces, the convulsions of her inner core setting off his equally powerful release. She felt the pumping of his body as he emptied himself.

His breathing was still uneven as he stepped back from her and re-zipped his trousers. 'That should never have happened,' he said grimly. 'I hope I didn't hurt you.'

Bronte smoothed down her dress. 'I thought that was your intention—to hurt me as much as possible for keeping Ella a secret from you.'

His expression was contorted with regret. 'Anger is

a dangerous emotion when it's out of control,' he said. 'I had no right to take it out on you in such a way. I'm sorry. It won't happen again.'

Bronte felt a little sideswiped by his sudden mood change. She wasn't sure how to deal with her own feelings, let alone his. Her body was still humming with the aftershocks of his lovemaking. She could still feel his presence inside her even now, the twinge of unused muscles and the damp heat of him reminding her of how much passion simmered between them. Those out of control needs were satiated for now, but how long was that going to last? If she were to marry him and live with him there would be no way of ignoring the sexual tension that crackled like a current of electricity between them. She stepped away from the wall and wasn't quite able to disguise a little wince as her body protested at the movement.

Luca's frown deepened. 'I did hurt you, didn't I?'

Bronte felt her cheeks heat up. 'I'm fine. It's just been a long time…well, you know…'

There was an awkward little silence.

'It's been a long while for me too,' he said, rubbing the back of his neck again.

Bronte looked at him, wondering whether to believe him or not. When she'd met him he had a reputation as a playboy. What he wanted, he got. No woman could resist him. She couldn't quite see him adhering to a celibate lifestyle for longer than a week or two. He was too full of life, too full blooded, too intensely and potently male.

He looked at her with a wry expression. 'You don't believe me, do you?'

'Why should I?' she asked. 'You've told me practically nothing of your life over the past two years. For all I know, you've probably had numerous affairs, one after the other. A long time between lovers for you might mean a couple of days.'

He held her look for a long moment before shifting his gaze. 'It's not been like you think, Bronte. I've had other things going on in my life. There has been no one of any significance for quite some time.'

'How very restrained of you,' she said with an attempt at sarcasm.

He ignored her comment and wandered over to the small bookcase and picked up a photograph of Ella. 'You mentioned you had photos and DVDs of her. I would like to have copies made, if you don't mind.'

'Of course I don't mind,' Bronte said. 'I'll get them together for you. I'll have to bring them to your hotel tomorrow, however. Mum has most of them at her house. There's not much storage space here.'

He turned and looked at her. 'Why do you live here instead of in the main house with your mother?'

'I thought it was important to maintain some element of independence for me and for Ella,' she said. 'My mother—as you saw—is rather protective. She means well but at times she can be quite smothering. I make allowances for her because she's been alone for so long. Living here is a sort of compromise. Mum is close by to help me with Ella but there is enough distance, small as it is, to establish some boundaries.'

'How do you think she will take the news of our marriage?'

'The same way I am taking it,' she answered. 'With a great deal of apprehension.'

Luca came back over to her and ran a fingertip down her cheek. She didn't veer away, but he saw the way her eyes flickered with wariness. Her mouth was swollen from his kisses, puffy and pink and all too tempting to kiss again. 'There is no other way to do this, Bronte,' he said. 'You do realise that, don't you?'

She snatched in a breath that seemed to catch in her throat. 'You're blackmailing me, Luca, can't you see that?'

He steeled his resolve. 'I admit it was not the most polished proposal, but the end justifies the means. I want my child. I want to provide for her. I want her to be a part of my extended family. I want her to embrace her Italian heritage, to learn my language. I can't give her that at a distance and you can't do it on your own.'

'But a loveless marriage…' Her eyes communicated her anguish. 'Ella's just a baby now but it won't be long before she's old enough to see things are not quite right between her parents. No amount of money can compensate for that. Surely you see that?'

Luca placed his hands on her shoulders, holding her gaze with his. 'We will work at our relationship. There is no doubt of the attraction that still exists between us. That is a good enough basis to start from.'

'You're asking me to give up everything,' she said, still with that worried look in her slate-blue eyes. 'I have so much more to lose than you. I will be alone in Italy. I don't speak the language, or at least only a few words here and there. What if your family doesn't take to me? Have you thought of that? I have never met them. They will no doubt be just as angry as you are about Ella being kept a secret all this time.'

Luca dropped his hands from her shoulders. 'It won't be easy. I am the first to admit that. I will do what I can to make things go as smoothly as possible. My family will accept you. I will make sure of that. They will adore Ella and in time may come to adore you too. It will take time. You will have to be patient.'

He put some distance between them before he spoke again. 'I will compensate you handsomely for marrying me. I will have an agreement set up by my financial and legal people. That should help dissolve some of your current doubts.'

Bronte screwed up her forehead in a frown. 'You think you can pay me to be your wife? You think I can be *bought*?'

The look he gave her was cynical. 'One thing I have learned through business is that everyone has a price. I am sure you have one too.'

She glared back at him furiously. 'You think you can afford me?' she asked, not caring if she was goading him too far.

His top lip curled upwards with the same cynicism she saw reflected in his gaze. 'Name your price,' he said.

Bronte threw a figure at him, an astonishingly ex-orbitant sum that would have made most men flinch in response. Luca's expression was mask-like. It showed no emotion. It was as if they were discussing a business transaction.

'Fine,' he said. 'I will make sure the funds are deposited in your bank account as soon as possible. You will need to give me your banking details, unless you would like me to write you a cheque here and now.'

Bronte scribbled her details down on a piece of paper, a war going on inside her over what she had just done. She had sold herself. Her future was now in his hands. She handed him the note, her eyes not quite able to hold his. 'I will need to give the parents of my students some notice,' she said.

'I am sure your business partner will be able to see to everything,' he said. 'I want us to be in Italy at the end of the month. I want our marriage to be conducted at the family hotel in Milan. That way, all of my relatives can be there. It is too far for my elderly grandfather to travel all the way to Australia.'

Bronte's eyes flew back to his. 'Are you out of your mind? I can't possibly tie up everything here in less than three weeks!'

'I am a busy man, Bronte,' he said. 'I have commitments here that will now have to be put on hold until we get back.'

She frowned again. 'So you're expecting me to follow you back and forth across the globe?'

His eyes challenged her to defy him. 'That is what most loving wives would do, is it not?'

It took Bronte a moment to catch on. 'You...you want me to pretend our marriage is normal?'

'But of course,' he said.

She folded her arms crossly. 'That's out of the question. I won't do it.'

'It is not negotiable, Bronte,' he said. 'I will not be made an object of ridicule the world over for having a wife who hates the sight of me. You will at all times and in all places maintain the guise of a devoted wife.'

Bronte fumed as she stood facing him. 'Is this marriage going to be an exclusive arrangement or are you going to continue with your philandering ways?'

He held her gaze for an interminable pause. 'That, *cara*, will depend entirely on you,' he said. 'Why would I stray if all my needs are being met at home?'

'And what about my needs?' she asked, giving him a glowering look.

He picked up his car keys and made his way to the door before he answered. 'I think I showed you only a few minutes ago how effectively I can meet your needs.' His dark eyes ran over her from head to foot, undressing her, caressing her, tempting her all over again. 'As my wife, Bronte, you will want for nothing.'

He closed the door on his exit and Bronte finally let out the breath she hadn't even realised she had been holding.

You will want for nothing, he had said. But what about what she wanted most of all? No amount of money was going to buy her the love she so desperately craved.

CHAPTER EIGHT

BRONTE decided to take Ella with her to Luca's hotel the next day, not just so he could spend time with his daughter if he happened to be there, but more to protect herself from falling into his arms as she had done last night.

Her body was still quivering with aftershocks, her flesh still tender from where he had possessed her so thoroughly. She felt ashamed of how she had fallen into his arms so quickly. Her actions had cancelled out every word of protest she had made to him about resuming their relationship. It would give him all the more power over her. He had always had the advantage. Wasn't it true that the person who had the most power in a relationship was the one who loved less? By loving Luca in the past, she had become the most at risk of being hurt, and that was exactly what had happened. But this time the risk was much higher because Ella was part of the equation.

As soon as Bronte got out of the car a swarm of paparazzi came towards her, seemingly from nowhere. 'Miss Bennett?' A journalist held a microphone in her face. 'Is it true your daughter is the secret love-child of Luca Sabbatini, the hotel tycoon?'

Bronte tried to stop the cameras flashing in little Ella's face. 'Do you mind?' she snapped. 'Keep away from her.'

Several camera shutters went off like a round of air rifle bullets. Ella started to cry and Bronte opened the back door of the car and fished her out of her seat, holding her close against her chest as she walked into the hotel with the bag containing Ella's baby DVDs and photos banging painfully against her hip.

The press followed like a pack of hungry dogs snapping at her heels. She bolted towards the reception counter and, trying to soothe Ella as well as ignore the camera flashes, she handed the bag over to the concierge. 'Could you please put this aside for Luca Sabbatini?' she asked. 'He's staying in the penthouse.'

The concierge smiled and placed a swipe key in front of her. 'Signor Sabbatini asked for you to be given this. If you give me your keys, I will get the valet parking attendant to take care of your car for you. If there is anything we can do to be of assistance with the little one, please don't hesitate to ask. We have cots and baby food and a babysitting service if you should require it.'

'Er... I'm not staying here,' Bronte said quickly. 'I'm just dropping off the bag with...er... I'm just leaving this for him.' She pointed to the bag perched on the counter.

The concierge gave her an urbane smile. 'Signor Sabbatini expressly asked for you to be given full access to his suite. He is not here at the moment but should be back shortly. He would like for you to wait until he returns.'

Bronte ground her teeth. She had two choices: turn

around and put Ella through the drama of facing the press again, or go up to Luca's suite and kill some time until the paparazzi left, hopefully before Luca returned. She let out a breath of resignation and picked up the swipe card and the bag of DVDs and photos. 'Thank you,' she said. 'We'll wait for him.'

The suite was blessedly quiet and Bronte was finally able to settle Ella, who had come close to becoming hysterical over the fuss downstairs. Her little face was bright red and her eyes still streaming, and tiny heart-wrenching hiccups were rattling intermittently in her chest. 'Don't cry, darling,' Bronte said softly, rocking her gently from side to side. 'Shh, it's all right. They've all gone away now.'

But for how long? she wondered. And how on earth had they found out about Ella being Luca's child? Had Luca made some sort of announcement without telling her? It was a frightening thought that this was what she and Ella might have to live with: the constant intrusion of the press which Luca had described previously. How would she ever cope with it? How could she protect Ella? She didn't want her daughter terrified every time they went outside. Was this *really* how celebrities and royalty lived? If so, it was absolutely unbearable.

Ella gave one last little hiccup and laid her head on Bronte's shoulder, her dark lashes falling down over her eyes. Bronte carried her through to Luca's bedroom, her stomach giving a little flutter as her eyes went to the bed that looked the size of a football field. She thought of herself lying there in Luca's arms, not in anger or out of control passion but in mutual longing and need.

And love...

No, she checked herself sternly. You don't love him

any more. He killed everything you felt for him by shutting you so ruthlessly and mercilessly out of his life.

But still…

The smell of him was in the room, the musk and hint of citrus that she could not, even after two years, get out of her senses.

She laid Ella gently down on the middle of the bed and placed a bank of pillows either side of her to keep her from falling off. She couldn't help a little flare of her nostrils as she held a spare pillow up to her face, breathing in the scent of Luca, a host of memories flooding her brain.

Not one night, she reminded herself as she tossed the pillow to the floor in a fit of pique. He couldn't even stay with you one full night. How on earth do you think he is going to settle down to being married with a child? He wanted custody and he was going about getting it. Bronte was superfluous. She would be dispensed with as soon as the lust he felt for her died down. He didn't know how to run a relationship. He was too selfish, too closed off, too focused on his career. He didn't know how to make sacrifices for other people. He didn't know how to love.

And yet he seemed to love Ella…

Bronte strode out of the bedroom to get away from her traitorous thoughts but they followed her, just as the paparazzi had done earlier. Click, click, click went the shutters of her brain, bringing up the touching moment when Luca had seen Ella for the first time the night before.

Bronte had always found Luca to be so emotionally distant, but last night she had seen a side to him she had never glimpsed before. He had looked down at the child in his arms, his eyes so full of wonder and amazement that she was his. Bronte had thought she had seen a hint of moisture when he'd turned and faced her, but in a blink it had gone so she didn't know if she had imagined it.

The door of the penthouse suddenly opened and Luca came in carrying a briefcase and a toy shop bag bulging with toys. 'Bronte,' he said, frowning. 'The concierge told me there was a bit of scene with the press outside the hotel. Is Ella all right?'

Bronte folded her arms across her chest. 'She was terrified. It took ages to calm her down. She's sleeping on your bed.'

He put the briefcase and toys down and reached up to loosen his tie. 'I should have warned you,' he said. 'I'm not sure how they found out. I was going to make an announcement once I had informed my family.'

'Have you told your family?'

He shrugged himself out of his jacket and laid it over the back of one of the plush sofas. 'Yes,' he said. 'They were shocked, as you can imagine, but pleased, especially my mother. She can't wait to meet Ella. I have promised to email some photos. Did you bring them with you?'

Bronte gestured to the bag on the floor near the sound system. 'I've brought everything I could find. I even have a lock of her baby hair in a matchbox. I found another one this morning and divided the lock in two. I thought you might like one of your own.'

He picked up the bag and found the matchbox. He set the bag back on the floor and looked at the commonplace box for a moment. Bronte watched as his long tanned fingers opened it, his dark eyes homing in on the tiny curl of silky hair. He touched it and smiled, but there was sadness in it.

She swallowed and moved forward, taking the bag off the floor to ferret out the first album of pictures of Ella. 'I haven't had time to make copies of everything. I thought you might like to have it done professionally or something. This one is of the first few months of her life.'

Luca took the album and sat down on the sofa. Bronte didn't know what to do with herself. She wasn't sure if she should go and sit beside him or leave him alone to view the photos by himself. 'Um…I think I'll go and check on Ella,' she said and darted out.

When she finally came back in, Luca was sitting with his eyes glued to the huge flat screen TV where he had put in one of the DVDs. The sound of Ella's tinkling laughter as Bronte lifted her high in the air filled the room. The next clip was of Ella having her first swimming lesson at the age of six months. They were tears and screams and then happy splashes as she gradually got used to the water on her face during the mother and baby class.

Luca looked up and pressed the mute button on the remote control. 'I can't find a DVD with Ella as a newborn. Do you have one?' he asked.

Bronte went through the bag, feeling self-conscious about how disorganised this was making her appear. Was he criticising her for being a bad mother? Was he thinking a devoted mother would have everything filed in neat, beautifully scrapbooked albums, or DVD cases in chronological order, not stashed haphazardly in a green shopping bag? No doubt his mother would have her sons' locks of hair in priceless heirloom velvet boxes with the family name inscribed on the outside, not in a run-of-the-mill matchbox. She chewed at her lip as she hunted through the bag, the stretching silence shredding at her already overwrought nerves.

'Can't find it?' he asked.

She sat back on her heels. 'I must have missed it when I gathered the others up from Mum's place.'

'I would like to see it,' he said. 'I will come around and get it tomorrow, that is if you can find it by then.'

Bronte got to her feet and glared at him. 'I know what you are implying, so why don't you come right out and say it?'

He didn't rise from the sofa; instead, he sat back and returned her look with the elevation of one of his midnight-black brows. 'And what would I be implying?' he asked.

She hissed out a breath. 'You think I'm doing a bad job of being Ella's mother. I can see it in your eyes. You think because I haven't got all this stuff organised properly I can't possibly be a good mother to her.'

This time he did rise from where he was sitting. His increase in height made the room shrink, irrespective of its commodious proportions. 'I think you are project-ing your own insecurities on to me,' he said. 'You are the one who thinks you are an inadequate mother, not me.'

Bronte felt her back come up at his too close to the truth summation of what she felt a lot of the time. 'You don't know anything about parenting,' she threw back. 'You don't know what it's like trying to earn a living and bring up a baby. You don't know what it's like to be so tired at the end of the day or sick and overwrought and still have to get up half the night, if not all the night, to see to a baby's needs. You live in a cotton wool world, Luca, you always have. You don't even have to make your own bed, for God's sake.'

His mouth tensed as if he was holding back a stinging retort, the silence going on and on and on until the air felt thick and too heavy to breathe.

Bronte wondered if she had revealed a little too much of her struggles and if he would go on to use it against her in a custody battle. She was making things so much worse by losing control of her emotions. Like last night, falling so readily into his arms, demonstrating so conclusively how much she still wanted him. She bit her lip and moved to the other side of the room, staring down at the view below rather than see the light of victory shining in his dark eyes. She needed to get away to garner her self-control. She needed to regroup. Her feelings were getting the better of her. Next thing, she would be on her knees begging him to take her back, marriage or no marriage.

'I admit I have a lot to learn,' Luca said. 'But at least I am willing to do so. A lot of men simply walk away from their responsibilities. But I will not. I want to be involved in every way possible with Ella.'

Bronte spun around. 'Well, why don't you start right here and now?'

He frowned as she stalked towards the door, only stopping long enough to take out her purse from the change bag she had brought for Ella. She practically shoved the bag against his abdomen, her eyes flashing at him in frustration and fury. 'Have the rest of the evening with her,' she said. 'You can feed her and change her and try and settle her when she won't be settled. I will be back in a couple of hours.'

Luca flinched as the door swung shut on her exit. He let out a long breath and sent his hand through his hair. He heard a little whimper coming from his bedroom and went through to see if Ella was waking.

She was sitting up in the middle of his bed, surrounded by pillows, two big fat tears rolling down her cheeks. 'Mummy?' She scrubbed at her blue eyes and looked so forlorn Luca felt his heart tighten to the point of pain. 'Mummy gone?'

'Mummy's gone out for a while, *mio piccolo*,' he said and gently lifted her off the bed. 'But *Papà* is here. *Papà* is always going to be here. You will never be alone, my little one.'

Ella smiled at him through her tears and batted at his face with a dimpled hand. *'Papà.'*

Luca cuddled her close, her little legs wrapping around him like a monkey's. She smelt…actually, she didn't smell so good. He looked at the wet patch on his bed and grimaced as he felt the dampness soaking through her candy-pink leggings to his hands. 'I don't suppose you can give me any hints on this process,' he said wryly as he carried her out to the lounge area where the change bag was. He picked it up with his spare hand and took Ella to the bathroom. He put her on her feet on the floor but, before he could even unzip the bag or remove her leggings, she was off. 'Ella, wait,' he said, missing her by millimetres as she giggled and toddled out, her sodden and loaded nappy seeming to mock him as she went.

Luca went in pursuit and captured her just as she knocked an ornament off one of the coffee tables in her effort to hide beneath it. Thankfully, the ornament just thudded to the carpeted floor without breaking and without hurting her. 'You little minx,' he said with a smile as he tugged her gently out by the ankles before he scooped her up in his arms.

Ella giggled and patted his face again. '*Papà* finded me.'

Luca smiled, even though his chest ached at the irony of his little girl's words. 'Yes, Ella, *Papà* found you.'

He took her back to the bathroom and this time held on to her with one hand while he tried to open the change bag with the other. Ella wriggled and squirmed but somehow he managed to get a new nappy out as well as a change of clothes.

He decided upon inspection that it was a bath job, not a simple change of nappy. He ran a warm bath, carefully checking the temperature before he put Ella in. She laughed and kicked her legs under the water, splashing him in the process. He wished he had thought to buy some bath toys. He remembered having a rubber duck as a child and some little cups and a jug to play with. He made a mental note to get some the next day, as well as some baby bath instead of the heavily perfumed hotel bath foam in case it was too strong for her skin.

He thought of all the times Bronte must have done this, bathed and changed Ella, while juggling all the other things she had to do. No wonder she hadn't had time to sort out photos and albums.

'Out now?' Ella said, holding her arms up.

'Er… Right,' Luca said, reaching for a fluffy white towel. He wrapped it around her and lifted her out and carefully dried her. She fussed over getting dressed again, seeming to want to run around naked, but he somehow managed to convince her to wear a new nappy and another pair of leggings and matching dress.

'I'm hungry,' Ella announced matter-of-factly.

Luca wondered if room service catered for kids this young. What did kids of this age eat, anyway? He knew she had teeth; he had seen them shining like little pearls when she grinned so cheekily at him. He just hoped she didn't have any allergies he should know about. But surely Bronte would have told him. Mind you, Bronte hadn't told him much. She had stormed out and left him to it, no doubt to drive home her point about him knowing zilch about being a parent. It annoyed him that she was right. He didn't have a clue and was still running on instinct and doing a pretty poor job of it if the current position of Ella's nappy was any indication.

He adjusted it as well as he could and carried her back to the lounge. She sat on the floor and played with his phone while he used the hotel phone to dial room service. Within a very short time indeed a waiter came up to the suite with a suitable meal for a toddler, which Luca then proceeded to offer to Ella.

More food ended up on the floor than in her mouth, and he seriously considered giving her another bath as she had smeared yoghurt all over the front of her dress, not to mention her face and hands.

Luca wondered what to do next. Was she too young to be read to? Not that he had any children's books. He made another mental note about getting some tomorrow.

He sat her on his knee and made up a story to keep her occupied. She looked up at him with a big smile and then settled her dark little head against his chest, right where his heart was beating. One of her thumbs crept up into her bee-stung mouth but he decided against pulling it out. He continued with his story until she finally fell asleep in his arms.

He held her for a long time, just sitting there feeling her slight weight on his lap, wishing he had been there for her birth, for every single moment of her life. How could he make it up to her? How could he make it up to Bronte? Would Bronte ever forgive him for cutting her from his life the way he had? He had thought he was doing the right thing at the time, but now he had to face the fact that a simple phone call would have changed everything. If anyone was to blame, it was him, not Bronte. She had done what she could do to reach him but he had made it impossible for her to get through. Even if she had written to him, he knew he would not have opened it. He had made a pact with himself and it had come back to bite him in the most devastating way.

Ella sighed and gave her tiny thumb another couple of substantial sucks before she settled back down to a deep and peaceful slumber.

Luca stroked his hand over her little silky head, his eyes misting as he thought of how much he had missed. He would do whatever it took to put things as right as they could be.

Whatever it took…

Bronte came back to the hotel feeling a little foolish for her outburst. She had worried the whole time she was away, thinking of Ella waking up disoriented and confused. What had she been thinking, rushing off in a tantrum like that? It surely wouldn't help Luca see her as a responsible and sensible young mother.

She got to the penthouse floor and, rather than use

the swipe key, gave the door a soft knock so as not to wake Ella if she happened to still be asleep.

There was no answer.

She waited for another minute and then used the key. She walked into the lounge area to see Luca soundly asleep, with Ella, also out for the count, snuggled up against his chest. The penthouse looked as if a whirlwind had gone through it. There were toys and clothes strewn about the place and the remains of Ella's supper were still on one of the coffee tables.

Luca suddenly opened his eyes and, with his free hand, he quickly rubbed his face. 'How long have you been back?' he asked.

'Not long,' Bronte said, shifting her weight. 'Look, I'm sorry about storming out like that.'

He gave her a crooked smile. 'You did me a favour, Bronte. It's what I believe they call quality time, *si*?'

She chewed at her bottom lip as she looked at what seemed to be smears of yoghurt all over the front of his designer business shirt. 'I hope it wasn't too steep a learning curve,' she said. 'Ella can have a mind of her own at times.'

'She's a Sabbatini,' he said with the same lopsided smile. 'We're all a little bit stubborn about getting our own way.'

'Yes, well, I'm not going to argue with you about that,' Bronte said, folding her arms.

Luca looked down at the sleeping child. 'She's a great little kid,' he said. 'I just wish I could have known about her from the start.'

'It was your choice to cut all contact.'

He raised his gaze back to hers. 'Yes, it was and I take full responsibility for it.'

Bronte frowned at him. 'So you're…you're apologising?'

He gave a small shrug. 'Would it help if I did?'

She drew in a tight little breath. 'Maybe, maybe not.'

Luca gently eased Ella off his lap and settled her onto the sofa, bunching up a couple of scatter cushions to keep her from rolling off the edge. Then he rose to his feet and came over to where Bronte was standing. 'About last night—' he began.

Bronte felt hot colour shoot to her cheeks. 'I'd rather not talk about it,' she said and took a step backwards but he caught her by the arm and held her in place.

'I think we do need to talk about it,' he said.

'It doesn't mean anything, you know,' she said, throwing him a cutting look. 'It was just sex.'

His eyes smouldered darkly as his thumb began to gently caress the underside of her wrist where her pulse was skyrocketing. 'It is never just sex with you, Bronte.'

She put her chin up. 'Maybe I've changed in the time we've been apart.'

He brought her wrist up to his mouth, pressing a soft kiss to the sensitive skin, his eyes holding hers mesmerised. 'Then if you have changed you will have no problem with our marriage being a real one,' he said. 'It will just be sex, nothing more, nothing less.'

Bronte felt the discomfort of being hoisted on one's own petard. 'I know what you're trying to do,' she said, pulling her hand away. 'You're trying to make me fall in love with you again.'

'I am trying to make you see how we can have a wonderful life together,' he said. 'I know there are hurts to deal with. I know you don't trust me not to walk out on you again. But, Bronte, I am not the same man I was two years ago.'

She rolled her eyes. 'People don't change that much, Luca. You'll have to do a whole lot more than talk if you want me to consider staying with you.'

A flinty look came into his eyes. 'Don't forget who you are dealing with, Bronte,' he said. 'I can still make things very difficult for you if you don't agree to marry me and move to Italy.'

Ella chose that moment to whimper. Bronte went to her and picked her up from the sofa, holding her close, as if daring Luca to take her from him. 'You can make me marry you, Luca,' she said bitterly. 'You can even make me live in a foreign country and make me play the role of the devoted wife. But you need to remember one thing: you can't—no matter what you do or say—make me love you again.'

Luca watched as she gathered Ella's things together, her stiff angry movements communicating her hatred of him. 'I would like to see Ella each day until we leave,' he said through tight lips.

'Fine,' she said, throwing him a filthy look over her shoulder as she stalked to the door.

'Bronte?'

She drew in a harsh breath and faced him with an irritated look on her face. 'Yes?'

His eyes bored into hers. 'Last night wasn't just sex. Not for me.'

Her expression faltered for a moment, her small perfect white teeth sinking into her full bottom lip. But just as quickly she reset her features into a tight little mask of indifference. 'I bet you say that to all your lovers,' she said and, without another word, left him with just the lingering fragrance of her perfume for company.

CHAPTER NINE

THE next three weeks passed in a blur of activity. Bronte's head was still spinning from the arguments she'd had with her mother over her acceptance of Luca's proposal. But in the end Bronte had refused to budge, knowing that if she said no to Luca she would not see Ella again.

He had made it perfectly clear: she was to marry him or suffer the consequences. It wasn't much of a choice, but then a secret part of her couldn't help but think of what life would be like married to him. That passionate interlude, which had left her body still smouldering in its wake all this time later, made her realise their marriage was not going to be the sterile paper agreement she had first thought. Even that evening at his hotel, even though he had only pressed his mouth to her wrist, she had felt every sensory nerve in her body stirring to throbbing, aching life.

However, since that night Luca had kept his distance physically. He kept their conversations brief and businesslike. He didn't touch Bronte once, not even to give her a kiss of greeting or goodbye. With Ella he was tender and attentive. He spent what time he could with her between appointments while Bronte watched in the background. It made her heart tighten every time she saw Ella's big blue eyes looking up at Luca so trustingly. His relationship with her was developing so rapidly, making Bronte feel as if Ella preferred her father now to her. Her little hands reached up to touch his stubbly face and her tinkling bell-like giggles brought a smile to his face, softening his features so much it made Bronte feel all the more wretched about how she had handled things.

Luca had organised an account at a high street wedding designer. Within moments of stepping into the smart boutique, Bronte found herself zipped into an exquisite gown that didn't just cost the earth but quite possibly half of the universe too. Other things were delivered to the studio or the granny flat: designer clothes, lacy lingerie, toys and clothes for Ella.

Two days before they were due to leave, Luca arranged to come to the flat for dinner. He wanted to be there in time to bathe and feed Ella, as he had done the night at the hotel, as he had been unable to do since due to business commitments.

He arrived just as Bronte's mother was leaving. Tina gave him a death stare as she began to pass by him on the doorstep but he stalled her by holding out an envelope to her.

'What is this?' Tina asked suspiciously.

'It is an all expenses paid trip to Italy for your daughter's wedding,' Luca said. 'I hope it will be the first of many visits to my homeland.'

Tina's mouth pursed, her gaze eyeing the envelope as if it was going to burst into flames as soon as she touched it.

'I want you to continue to be involved in Ella's life,'

Luca said. 'You are her maternal grandmother. You have been a big influence in her life so far. I don't want that to change.'

Bronte watched from the sidelines as her mother's eyes moistened. Tina took the envelope with a grudging murmur of thanks and left.

Luca closed the door and turned to face Bronte. 'Do you think she will come?'

Bronte tucked a strand of loose hair back behind her ear. 'I've talked to her about it. She has a passport but she's never used it. She had planned to go on a trip to visit me in London but I came home before she could get there.'

A frown pulled at his brow, making his features darken. 'You can't resist reminding me of how I let you down, can you?' he asked.

'I wasn't doing any such thing,' she said. 'I simply told you—'

'*Papà!*' Ella toddled over, carrying the teddy bear Luca had given her, which was almost as tall as she was. '*Papà!*'

Luca smiled and scooped her up into his arms. '*Mio piccolo,*' he crooned. 'How is my baby girl?'

'She's been saying *Papà* a lot,' Bronte said. 'Especially when she sees the toys you bought her.'

He smiled and kissed Ella's button nose. 'I intend to give her everything money can buy,' he said.

Bronte unwound her twisted hands. 'Luca...I don't think it's wise to spoil her with too much too soon. She's very young. I don't want her to feel entitled to everything she sees. She needs to learn to appreciate things by learning to wait for them.'

He turned his black-brown gaze on her. It was hard,

not soft and tender, and his smile had gone, leaving his mouth tight-lipped. 'Do not tell me what I can and cannot do with my very own child,' he said in a clipped tone.

Bronte raised her chin. 'She's a baby, Luca. She's not even two. She doesn't need a lot of expensive clothes and toys. She needs love and attention and security.'

'She will get that and more,' he said, putting the wriggling child back down on the floor to play with her toys.

'I am not sure how she is going to feel secure with us locked in a loveless, passionless marriage,' Bronte said, folding her arms across her middle.

Luca's eyes met hers, their smoky black depths sending a tingling feeling down her spine. 'You think our marriage will be without passion?' he asked.

Bronte felt her face crawl with colour. 'I'm not sure what to think. You've organised everything at breakneck speed. You've demanded I pack up my life here but I don't know what is expected of me on the other end.'

After a long moment he released a long sigh. 'I know this is hard for you, Bronte,' he said. 'It is hard for everyone. I feel for your mother, I really do. I feel for my mother and brothers and grandfather, who have missed out on all of Ella's babyhood so far. But you are Ella's mother and I am her father. There is no other way to do this.'

Bronte felt the sting of tears but fought them back. 'You want everything your way. You want control. I understand that, but it's hard for me. I've worked so hard for my career. But now I am expected to give it all up for what? A marriage that is doomed to fail.'

'It will not fail if we both work at it,' he said. 'I

understand how important your career is to you. I am making arrangements for you to teach in Milan.'

'I don't speak the language,' Bronte said glumly. 'I'm not going to get very far without that.'

'You can take lessons,' he said. 'I want Ella to speak my language. It is important that she learns both English and Italian while she is young. It will help her if you speak both to her. I can organise a private tutor for you.'

'It seems to me you can organise just about anything,' she said, scowling.

'Not everything,' he said, raking a hand through his hair. 'There are some things money will never be able to buy.'

Bronte watched him crouch down to help Ella with a toy. He ruffled Ella's soft fluffy hair, his smile tender but touched with sadness at the same time. There were times when she thought he was locking her out. A mask would come down over his face, like a shutter on his emotions, leaving her wondering what it would take for him to trust her enough to tell her what he was really feeling.

Luca rose from the floor with Ella in his arms. 'I think she needs changing.'

'I'll do it.'

'I can manage,' he said. 'I got through it the last time. I need the practice, in any case.'

Bronte led him through to the small bathroom and handed him the baby bath solution she used to protect Ella's skin. 'I'll set out her night wear and a new nappy in the nursery for you,' she said.

When she came back Luca had Ella splashing in the bath. He was playing with a yellow duck, making quacking noises, to Ella's delight. It was a typical bath time scene, a loving father and a happy, contented infant having fun together. But Bronte felt shunted aside. She could imagine over time how Ella would no longer look to her for anything. It would all be about Luca. She understood how he wanted to make up for the time he had lost, but still she couldn't quell the feelings of insecurity that were plaguing her incessantly.

After Ella was dried and changed Bronte left Luca to read a story to Ella before tucking her into bed. She noticed it was an Italian one, the melodic-sounding words reminding her of how soon she would be locked out by language as well as Ella's burgeoning love for her father.

After checking on the casserole she had in the slow cooker, she waited for him in the living room, blindly leafing through a magazine for the want of something to do other than chew her nails.

Luca came out after a few minutes. 'She went to sleep like an angel,' he said.

'She's usually pretty good about going to sleep,' Bronte said. 'I guess I've been lucky that way. I'm not sure how I would have coped with a really difficult baby. It's been hard enough with her being so spirited and energetic.'

His mouth tightened. 'There you go again, playing the blame game. Painting yourself as the victim. We were both victims, Bronte. When are you going to see that?'

Bronte shot to her feet. 'When are you going to see that you can't just pick up where you left off? You broke my heart, Luca. You shattered my self-confidence. I don't want to get hurt again. I *won't* get hurt by you again.'

'Do you hate me that much?'

Bronte opened her mouth but then shut it, turning away so he couldn't see the glisten of tears in her eyes.

A taut silence beat for a moment or two.

'Bronte?'

'I think you already know the answer to that,' she said, still with her back to him.

The hairs on the back of her neck lifted long before his hands settled on her shoulders. How had her body known he was so close? A shiver went down her spine as she felt his strong tall body just behind her. If she leant backwards she would touch him, she would feel his heat and potency.

And she would be lost.

His warm breath skated over the sensitive skin of her neck as he spoke low and huskily near her ear. 'You don't really hate me, *cara*. You hate that you still want me.'

Bronte spoke through stiff lips. 'I don't want you. I loathe you.'

He gave a soft chuckle and slid his hands down the length of her arms, his fingers making a bracelet of steel around her wrists. 'Why don't you show me how much you loathe me?' he said, brushing up against her from behind.

She squeezed her eyes shut, trying to resist the temptation. She could feel his body responding to her closeness, his arrant maleness and the musky scent of his arousal. Her body crawled with desire, every nerve ending dancing with the need for more of his touch. Her breasts felt tight and achy, looking for the caress of his mouth and hands. Her inner core pulsed with need, a liquid hot need that had never really died down. It had smouldered like coals damped down in a fire, just waiting for the moment to spring back into leaping life.

'Go on,' he said, nibbling on her earlobe with the soft playful bite of his strong white teeth. 'Show me. I dare you.'

Bronte shivered again and her head fell to one side as his mouth moved over her neck before going to the top of her shoulder. She felt every movement of his lips, the soft brushes, the little nips, the slow drag and the sexy slide of his tongue. She was crumbling with need. She could feel her legs giving way...

He turned her in his arms and locked his eyes on hers. 'Double dare you,' he said softly, tauntingly, irresistibly.

Bronte felt her lashes go down as his head came down. She felt the breeze of his breath but he went no further. He hovered above her mouth, waiting for her to come to him. She held off for as long as she could but it was a battle she was never going to win. She wondered if that was why he had kept his hands off her for the last three weeks, to prove how little she could resist him when he turned on the charm.

Well, he was right. She couldn't resist him. She couldn't fight it any longer. With a soft sigh of surrender she reached up and pressed her lips against his.

It was a slow kiss at first, soft and sensual but leisurely. Bronte wasn't sure when it changed or who had changed it. But suddenly there was nothing soft about it any more. There was hard urgency and heat and fiery purpose as his mouth commandeered hers. His tongue stroked for entry and slipped in when she gave it, teasing hers into an erotic mimic of what was to come.

Her body went wild with want. She snaked her arms around his neck, holding him closer, her pelvis rubbing up against the rock-hardness of his. Her breasts flattened against his chest, the tight nipples driving into him as he kissed her hotly and deeply.

She kissed him back with just as much urgency. She used her teeth to bite and nip, teasing him, leading him on until her body was screaming for release. She heard him groan deep in the back of his throat as her tongue darted and dived out of reach of his, only to come back to tease and taunt him with hot moist licks.

He swung her around, away from the wall and pressed her to the floor at their feet. Clothes were discarded piece by piece but there was no order to it. Bronte heard something rip but disregarded it. All she could think about was being pinned by his strong powerful body and being taken to paradise.

His hands were everywhere. One minute he was cupping her face, the next her breasts, his thumbs rolling over the pert nipples until she was gasping with soft little breaths of pleasure. His mouth took over from his hands, the hot moist caresses curling her toes and melting her spine.

She could feel the rough carpet on the tender skin of her back but she was beyond caring. She reached for him once he had shucked himself out of his trousers and underwear.

'If you are about to do what I think you are, I should warn you that you might get more than you bargained for,' he said in a voice that signalled how close he was to going over the edge.

Bronte sent him a sultry look from beneath her lashes. 'I'm sure you will recover quickly from the experience.'

'Don't do it, Bronte,' he bit out, his muscles clenching harder. 'Don't do it...*ahhh*...'

Bronte smiled to herself as he shuddered through his release. He might have kept his distance for the last three weeks but he was no less immune to her than she was to him.

He pushed her back down to the floor, leaning over her with his weight, his mouth starting to work its way down her body. 'My turn, I think,' he growled playfully.

Bronte felt a shiver rush down her body as his mouth closed over her breast. He sucked on her tantalisingly, drawing from her a whimpering cry. He went lower, down over her sternum, dipping his tongue into the tiny cave of her belly button before going deliciously, dangerously lower.

She drew in a sharp breath as his fingers gently opened her. She gripped his shoulders as his tongue brushed against her most sensitive point. A shudder went through her and then another as he repeated the caress again and again, picking up her internal rhythm, leading her step by inexorable step into the whirlpool of release. Her whole body shook with the explosion of pleasure that rippled through her. It was shameless, it was erotic, and it was primitive and unstoppable.

Bronte fell back but he wasn't finished with her. He moved back up her body, leaving her in no doubt of his rapid recovery. He was rock-hard and ready to go all over again. She gasped as he thrust into her deeply, the tight clutch of her inner muscles urging him on and on.

She dug her fingers into his buttocks, holding him tight as he went harder. She felt every movement of his body in hers. Delight coursed through her, lifting her skin in delicate goosebumps of pleasure. It had always been this way between them: a roller coaster ride of passion and pleasure that knew no bounds.

'Tell me to slow down,' he said against her neck.

'Go faster,' she whispered back shamelessly.

He brought his mouth down hard on hers, kissing her as his body continued its passionate pounding within hers. She lifted her hips for each downward thrust, urging him on as her need for him climbed higher and higher.

The final lift-off was cataclysmic. It shook her from head to foot, every convulsion of her body sending shockwaves through his. Bursts of colour exploded in her head like a crazy kaleidoscope. Pleasure shot through her like a powerful drug, leaving her limbless and useless in his arms.

She felt him plunge into oblivion moments later, the quick, hard final thrusts pumping the life force from him until he collapsed against her.

As soon as it was over Bronte felt ashamed. Their coupling was about lust, not love. It was the same as in the past. She was a convenience, a plaything to entertain him. He didn't want anything else from her. He didn't love her. He was incapable of loving her. He was only marrying her to get his child.

'You are very quiet,' Luca said, raising himself up on his elbows to look down at her.

'Please get off me,' she said, pushing against him with her arms.

He controlled her flailing hands in one of his. 'Stop, damn it. What's the matter with you?'

She rolled her eyes. 'How can you ask that?'

'Bronte, we had consensual sex,' he said. 'You're surely not suggesting anything else?'

She glowered at him. 'This is all a game to you. You don't really want me as your wife. I'm just a means to an end. You get Ella with me thrown in for free. How convenient, a willing bed partner to entertain you whenever you feel like it.'

Luca studied her face for a moment. 'This is about the last three weeks, isn't it?'

She turned her head away so she couldn't look at him. He turned her head back, anchoring her chin so she wouldn't pull away. 'Look at me, Bronte,' he said. 'I've kept my distance to give you some space to think about the future. I had a lot on my mind, in any case. I had to cram six weeks of business into three. This is not all about you.'

'It's never been about me, has it?' she tossed back bitterly. 'Right from the start, our relationship has always been about you. What you want, what you were prepared to give or not give, to do or not do. It was never about what I wanted.'

This time when she pushed at him he let her go. She snatched up her clothes and disappeared into her room, shutting the door behind her.

Luca rolled onto his back and rubbed his hand down over his face. She was right, of course. He had never allowed her to dictate the terms of their previous relationship. He had always been the one to state the way things were going to be. He couldn't have handled her turning up unannounced at his London home. He couldn't have handled spending the night with her, or with anyone. He had never spent the night with anyone. It wasn't something he could have trusted himself to do until recently.

He got to his feet and pulled on his clothes. He used the bathroom and then checked on Ella. He stood, looking down at her sleeping angelic face, his heart feeling as if two large fingers had it in a hard pinch.

He heard a sound at the door and turned to see Bronte standing there. 'Is she all right?' she asked in a whisper.

'She's fine,' he said. 'I was just checking on her.'

She turned and went back to the kitchen. Luca heard her opening a cupboard and turning on a tap and then the hiss of the kettle as it came to a boil. He pressed a kiss to his fingertips and laid it gently on Ella's cheek before he left the room.

When he came into the kitchen Bronte's face was still looking stormy. She banged a cup down on the bench and then a tin of instant coffee, sending him a fiery look. 'Dinner's not quite ready but if you want a cup of coffee while you wait then this is all I've got. I don't have any wine.'

'Bronte, let's get something straight right from the start,' he said. 'I am not for a moment suggesting you haven't done a brilliant job of bringing up Ella to this point.'

She stood in a huffy silence, her slate-blue eyes wary as they held his.

'Ella is a contented and happy toddler,' he continued. 'She's a credit to you. I realise it must have been hard for you, alone and unsupported. If I could change that, I would do so. We have to move forward with what we've got. And what we've got is a lot compared to most. What happened on that floor half an hour ago is proof of that.'

'What happened on that floor was exactly the sort of thing I expect from you,' she spat at him. She stirred her coffee until it splashed over the sides. The ping of her teaspoon when she set it down seemed to underline the silence.

'If you have something to say, then come right out and say it,' Luca said. 'Don't play word games with me.'

Her eyes flashed blue flames of hatred at him. 'I have carpet burn,' she said on a pout.

Luca felt his lips twitch. 'Show me.'

She backed away, her eyes widening. 'Get away from me.'

He cornered her against the work top, hip to hip, heat to heat. 'Turn around,' he commanded softly.

Her chest rose and fell against his, her eyes slowly filling with moisture. She blinked rapidly but a couple of tears escaped.

Luca blotted them with the pads of his thumbs, his heart feeling another tight pinch. 'Hey,' he said softly. 'Is this about carpet burn or something else?'

She shoved him away, catching him off guard. She stalked to the living room, her arms like a barricade over her middle. 'Don't you think it's about time you left?' she said, glancing pointedly at the clock. 'I would hate for you to turn into a werewolf or something once it gets to midnight. Ten-thirty was always the cut-off point, I seem to remember.'

Luca drew in a breath as he thought about the first time he had woken up to realise what he had done while asleep. His body had let him down in a way that shamed him even now. He refused to talk about it. He couldn't stand the pity or the revulsion. It was all behind him now and he wanted to keep it that way. 'I will leave when I am happy we are clear on a couple of things,' he said. 'Firstly, do you need some help with packing before we leave the day after tomorrow? I can't help you myself as I have some last minute business ends to tie up, but I can organise for someone to help you.'

'That won't be necessary,' she said stiffly.

'The second thing is the studio arrangements,' Luca said. 'I've spoken to Rachel. She's happy to continue with the lease. It will take time for her to find another business partner. I'm not charging her rent for the first six months so she can get on her feet.'

'Why would you do that?' she asked with a guarded look.

Luca shrugged. 'It seemed the least I could do, under the circumstances.'

'It doesn't seem like a very sound business decision,' she said, still with that same suspicious angling of her gaze.

'Not all the decisions I make are motivated by making money,' he said.

He went over to where he had tossed his jacket earlier and took out a velvet ring box. He brought it back to where Bronte was standing and handed it to her. 'You will need this,' he said. 'I hope it fits. I had to guess the size.'

'You could have asked me,' Bronte said, not caring that she sounded churlish and ungrateful.

He set his mouth and turned away. 'You can smash it with a hammer if it's not to your taste.'

Bronte felt ashamed of herself as she opened the lid

of the box. The most beautiful diamond lay blinking there like a bright star in its night sky of dark blue velvet. Her throat closed over as she took it out and slipped it on her finger. It was a perfect fit. Not too small, not too big—just right. She looked up to where he was standing staring out of the window to the front garden. 'Luca?'

He turned and strode over to scoop up his jacket and keys. 'I have to go,' he said. 'I will send a car for you and Ella on Friday at ten a.m. Don't be late.'

Bronte flinched as the front door snapped shut behind him. Her heart sank as she heard his car roar off down the street, and her tears fell freely as the low growling sound slowly faded into the distance.

CHAPTER TEN

WHEN Luca arrived in a chauffeur driven car on Friday morning there were too many people about for her to deliver the apology she had spent the last two days rehearsing. By the time she had said a tearful goodbye to her mother and Rachel, Ella needed her attention. When they got to the airport Luca was busy with officialdom so it wasn't until they were on the private jet, secluded in their own quarters, that she finally found herself alone with him, apart from Ella sleeping in a cot nearby.

'Luca…' she began with a quick dart of her tongue over her lips. 'I wanted to apologise to you about the way I spoke to you when you gave me the engagement ring.'

He turned one more page of the document he was reading and she heard him release a slow breath before he lifted his head to look at her sitting opposite him. 'Forget about it,' he said and returned to his work.

She twirled the ring on her finger, her teeth gnawing at her lip as she watched him leaf through the lengthy document. The silence hummed… Well, perhaps it was really the jet that was humming as it levelled out after take-off but, all the same, Bronte felt as if a chasm had opened up between them.

'I just wanted to say I'm sorry,' she said after a long moment. 'It's a beautiful ring. It must have cost a fortune.'

He turned another page without looking up. 'It did.'

Bronte moistened her lips again and watched him for a little while. He was frowning with concentration, his mouth flat and serious and his clean-shaven jaw tight. There were lines of tiredness about his eyes, which made her wonder if he had slept at all over the last couple of nights.

'What are you reading?' she offered after another long silence.

'Nothing important.'

'Is it to do with the hotel developments in Australia?'

He closed the folder and met her eyes across the wide space between them. 'Yes,' he said. 'Now, why don't you lie back and have a sleep while Ella's down?'

Bronte twirled her ring again. 'You're angry with me.'

'Is that a statement or a question?'

'It's an observation,' she said.

He gave her a wry smile that didn't reach his eyes. 'And why would I be angry with you, do you think?'

She let out a choppy sigh. 'Because I've been an absolute cow about all this.' She waved her hand to encompass their luxurious surroundings. 'You've gone to a lot of trouble to arrange everything and I haven't thanked you once.'

'You don't have to thank me,' he said.

'But you've spent heaps on me and Ella too,' she said. 'And buying Mum that ticket. She's going to come to the wedding. I didn't think she would but she told me just as I was leaving. I don't know how to thank you for doing all that for me…for us…'

Luca put the folder on the seat next to him and, unclipping his seatbelt, stood up and came over to sit beside her. He took her hand in his and began idly stroking it with his thumb. 'The money is nothing to me, Bronte. It's not what counts in life.'

Bronte looked into his dark eyes and felt something shift in her chest. 'You really love Ella, don't you?' she asked softly.

'Now that is definitely an observation,' he said with another wry smile. 'There's no question about it. I love her more than life itself.'

Bronte felt an ache deep inside. If only he would say the same about her. How she had longed to hear those words. She looked down at their joined hands; hers looked so small inside the shelter and protection of his. His skin was so dark, so masculine with its sprinkling of black hair, while hers was so soft and smooth and creamy-white.

She felt a little quiver of awareness when she met his eyes again. Their dark depths reflected everything that had occurred between them two days ago. She could feel the rush of her blood and imagined his body doing the same. Was he remembering how it felt to be joined in out of control passion? Was he remembering the electric shock of intimate contact, the roller coaster ride of release that was as mind blowing as any illicit drug could be?

Luca took her chin between his finger and thumb, a soft tether that had an undercurrent of desire she could feel through his skin to hers. 'I have my own apology to deliver,' he said in a gravel-rough tone.

Bronte felt her face heating. 'You don't have to apologise for anything.'

'Oh, but I do,' he said in the same deep husky voice as he brushed his thumb over her bottom lip. 'I was rough with you. I could have hurt you.'

Bronte longed to slip her tongue out to touch his thumb. 'You didn't,' she said in a breathless whisper.

His thumb stilled and his eyes centred on hers. 'You mentioned something about carpet burn the other night.'

She lowered her gaze, hot colour surging into her cheeks. 'I just said that to annoy you.'

He tipped her chin up again, holding her gaze with the dark intensity of his. 'I really meant it when I said you should get some sleep,' he said. 'There's a bed through there in the curtained section next to Ella.'

'But I don't feel tired,' she said as her gaze slipped to his mouth.

His mouth turned up at the corners in a sexy smile. 'Then maybe I can think of something to occupy you until you do.'

Bronte's heart gave a little sideways movement as her eyes came back to his. 'You mean…here? In the plane?'

His eyes were glinting. 'No one will disturb us. We have this entire section to ourselves.'

She gave him a shy look. 'You really think of everything, don't you?'

He pressed a kiss to the tips of her fingers. 'Go and get ready,' he said. 'I will be with you in a minute.'

* * *

Bronte yawned and stretched a few hours later. Her body was still tingling from Luca's passionate but exquisitely tender lovemaking. She turned her head to look at him. He was lying on his back, his eyes closed and his chest rising and falling as he slept.

She smiled and softly traced a fingertip down his sternum, all the way down to his belly button. This was the longest time she had ever spent in bed with him. Seven hours, almost a complete night.

She trailed her fingers over his flat dark nipples and, as she went a little lower, she felt him flinch but his eyes remained closed. She circled his navel a couple of times, lightly, teasingly. Then she went even lower, millimetre by millimetre, watching as his abdominal muscles tightened as her caresses approached his growing erection. She took him in her hand, squeezing ever so gently, her fingers sliding down the shaft, her belly turning to liquid as he swelled even further.

He suddenly moved, rolling her on to her back in a quick movement, his body surging into hers in one slick hard thrust that sent the air right out of her lungs. She gasped in delight as he set a steady pace, her already damp body making it easy for him to gain momentum. She scored her nails down his back as the sensations rippled through her. She was climbing to the summit so quickly, all her senses spinning in the wake of his touch. His mouth captured hers, subjecting it to a sensual assault that made the hair on her head lift in pleasure.

Her body split into a thousand pieces as she came. Her mind blacked out in that moment of sheer ecstasy, every muscle, nerve and sinew twitching in the aftermath. Luca followed with his own release, a deep pumping of his body within hers, his agonised groan of pleasure sending a shiver of reaction straight down Bronte's spine.

Long minutes passed.

Bronte was content to lie in the circle of his arms, playing mind games with herself about him loving her and wanting her back in his life for good, even if Ella wasn't an issue. Her love for him had never really gone away. She had blocked it out in order to protect herself. She still had nightmares about him leaving her again. Any rejection was hard to take, but one that she had been more or less waiting for right from the start for some reason had been so much worse. It had destroyed her trust and her self-confidence had never really recovered. Telling him how she felt was out of the question. She had told him too much too soon in the past and look where that had taken her. No, this time she would play it cool. No hearts worn on the sleeve, no confessions of eternal love. No long-term promises. She would be cool and clinical about their arrangement. A marriage that would give her the security she had longed for, financial if not emotional. She had watched her mother struggle all of her life to put food on the table. At least Bronte would not have those sorts of worries to deal with. It was a compensation of sorts, but not exactly as reassuring as she would have liked.

Luca lifted his head and pressed a kiss to the end of Bronte's nose. 'Hey,' he said.

'Hey yourself,' she said back.

His eyes held hers for several beats before he spoke. 'Are you currently on the Pill?'

Bronte felt a little flutter of unease. 'Yes, but only a low dose one to control period pain.'

'If you were to fall pregnant you wouldn't get period pain, though, would you?' he said.

A small frown began to pull at her brow. 'What exactly are you saying, Luca?' she asked.

He brushed some tousled strands of her hair back from her face. It was a stalling tactic, Bronte suspected, which made her angry. Why couldn't he just touch her because he couldn't help it?

'I am saying we should maybe think about trying for another child,' he said, this time lazily curling a strand of her hair around one of his fingers. 'I missed out on the first year and two months of Ella's life. If we were to have a brother or sister for Ella it would make me feel less of that loss, I am sure. The gap between them would be ideal. If you were to fall pregnant more or less straight away, she would be out of nappies and a little more independent when the baby arrives.'

Bronte put her hands on his chest to try and push him off her. 'Let me up.'

He refused to budge, pinning her with his body, his eyes locked on hers. 'What's the problem, *cara*?' he asked.

She gave him a fulminating look. 'You've got it all planned, haven't you?'

He let her hair fall from his fingers. 'I haven't planned anything, Bronte. I am merely suggesting—'

Without the tether of her hair, this time she managed to wriggle out from under him. She scrambled to her feet and grabbed a bathrobe with his family's insignia on it, tying it about her waist with angry, jerky movements. 'I am not some stupid breeding machine,' she said through tight lips.

He reached for the matching bathrobe and slipped

it on with much less haste than Bronte had. 'You have an amazing ability to twist my words,' he said with a thread of anger stitched in his voice. 'You will be my wife in a matter of days. It is not unreasonable for me to suggest we think about having another baby some time in the future. It doesn't have to be straight away. I just think it is something we should seriously think about, especially since I missed out on all this before.'

Bronte's eyes flashed. 'It's totally unreasonable! I'm not ready to have another baby.'

He placed his hands on his hips, his legs splayed in a let's-talk-about-this pose. 'What are your main objections?' he asked.

She stared at him for a tense moment before she blew out a breath. 'How can you ask that?'

'Bronte, I want more children,' he said with an intractable set to his mouth. 'I would like to have a son.'

Bronte sent him a death glare. 'So your daughter isn't good enough? Is that it?'

His eyes rolled upwards in an impatient manner. 'There you go again, twisting my words. I love Ella. She's my whole world. I'm just saying I would like to have a son if fate or destiny or God or whatever allows it.'

'We might have several daughters,' she said with a hitch of her chin.

'Then I will love each one with all my heart.'

But what about me? Bronte silently asked. *Will you ever love me with all your heart?* 'I can see why your sister-in-law left your brother,' she said with a cynical twist to her mouth. 'Is it a Sabbatini condition upon marriage to produce an heir and a spare as soon as possible?'

He pushed his thick black hair back off his face. 'Maybe we should discuss this some other time,' he said.

'No,' Bronte said. 'Let's discuss it now. I am not going to be an incubator. I am not going to agree to bring another child into this relationship unless I am convinced it is stable and secure.'

'Our marriage will be more secure than most,' he pointed out. 'You will want for nothing. Most women would give anything to be in your position.'

Bronte folded her arms. 'Money means nothing to me, Luca. You should know that by now. It doesn't impress me.'

'I know that,' he said. 'I admire that about you. I've always admired that about you. It's the one thing that has always set you apart from all the other women I have been involved with before you came along.'

She felt the wind drop right out of her self-righteous sails. 'You say that as if there has been no one since me,' she said, looking down at the floor.

There was a short but telling silence.

Bronte slowly brought her gaze back to his. He was looking at her with an unreadable expression on his face. 'Luca?'

His slowly spreading smile was self-deprecating. 'Not quite the bed-hopping girl-in-every-port playboy profile you were expecting, is it, Bronte?'

She looked at him in confusion. 'But you were in America... Your housekeeper told me about your...your mistress...'

'There wasn't a mistress.'

Bronte wanted to believe him. Everything in her wanted to believe him but her mind just couldn't get around it, couldn't accept it. 'Then why...?' She left the question hanging in the air between them.

He rubbed a hand over his in-need-of-a-shave face, an abrasive sound that seemed louder than it should have in the silence. 'I was in America for something else. Something personal.'

Bronte continued to look at him with wide uncertain eyes. 'You didn't think you could tell me at the time?' she asked.

He gave his head a little shake. 'I told no one, not even my family.'

She drew in an uneven breath. 'I don't understand, Luca. Why did you push me away? You were so callous about it. You hurt me more than anyone, more than I thought it was possible to be hurt by another person.'

His expression became shadowed with regret. 'I realise that. I wish I could change what happened but I can't. I did what I thought was best under the circumstances.'

Bronte turned away, her arms still wrapped around her middle as if to hold her hurt and anger close. She wasn't quite ready to let it go. 'Are you going to tell me what you were doing in the US?'

It was a full thirty seconds before he answered. 'I had an operation.'

She turned back to face him. 'What sort of operation?'

Again he hesitated before he spoke. 'I had an ablation done for nocturnal epilepsy.'

Bronte's forehead wrinkled. 'You had...*epilepsy*?'

'Not the usual type, but yes,' he said, looking grim.

She continued to look at him in stupefaction. 'You had it the whole time we were together and said *nothing*?'

'What could I say?' he asked bitterly. 'Watch out in case I have a fit while I'm asleep, lose control, and knock out some of your teeth or break your nose with one of my flailing, jerking limbs? For God's sake, Bronte, I was trying to protect you. Do you know how many times I woke up to find the bedside lamp shattered or the alarm clock on the floor in pieces? I was living a nightmare each night of my life since I was twenty-seven, when I suffered what I thought was a minor head injury. I came off my mountain bike. I didn't even go to the hospital. It was a week or so later that I had my first fit. It happened in the middle of the night. I woke up...' He stopped and clawed a hand through his hair as if the memory of it was torturing him. 'I woke up and my life as I had known it had suddenly changed. I won't embarrass you with the sordid details. From that moment on, I couldn't spend the night with anyone. I daren't fall asleep until I was alone. I couldn't trust my body.'

Bronte let out a shocked breath. 'I don't understand why you didn't tell me. You could have saved us both all of this hurt and heartbreak if you had shared this with me.'

His brows narrowed the distance between his eyes. 'I did it for you, Bronte, can't you see that? I couldn't live with myself if I hurt you physically. You don't know what it was like. I lost who I was. I sometimes became irritable and bad-tempered before a fit came on. Sometimes I didn't get any notice at all. It would just happen. I felt like half a man. I was terrified the press would find out. Can you imagine what they would have done with that?'

'Luca—' Bronte moistened her lips '—I understand how awful it must have been, but you made it a thousand times worse by not telling me. If you had just explained why you were the way you were I would have loved you anyway.'

His eyes took on a hollow look. 'You don't understand what I was facing, Bronte. You can never understand. I knew the operation was an option I could take. The chance came for me to go to the States to have it done. I only had a week or so to prepare. There were risks involved, as there are with any surgery. You have to remember I watched my father become an invalid after his accident. He was completely helpless. He had to wear nappies, for God's sake. I had to spare you that. I couldn't have you tied to me in case something went wrong.'

'But it didn't,' Bronte said, still unable to let go of her hurt at being shut out at such a crucial time in his life. 'You ruined both of our lives by being so one-sided. You were only thinking about yourself, not me.'

'Damn it, I was thinking about you,' he said. 'I thought about you all the time. How I missed you. How I wanted you back, but I couldn't do it until I knew for sure I was cured.'

'You know, Luca, it's not really about what you had done in the States,' she said tightly. 'The issue is, you didn't trust me enough with what was going on in your life. I was your part-time plaything. The only intimacy we shared was physical. You weren't available emotionally then and you're not available now.'

His mouth flattened as his hand raked through his hair again. 'I couldn't offer you a future I didn't even know for sure I had.'

Bronte sent her eyes heavenwards. 'Oh, please. Give me a break, Luca. You know nothing of how relationships work, of how real love works. You wanted everything on your terms and you got it. It's your fault you missed out on Ella's first year of life, not mine.'

The sound of Ella waking in the curtained section next door brought an end to the conversation. Luca muttered something about it being his turn to see to her and strode out, brushing past Bronte's shoulder as he went.

She let out a sigh as she sat back down on the crumpled bed. She looked at the depression where Luca's head had been lying on the pillow. She picked up the pillow and hugged it to her chest, breathing in his inimitable scent that lingered on the fine Egyptian cotton

CHAPTER ELEVEN

BRONTE barely had time to shower and dress before it was announced they were beginning their descent in to the airport at Milan. Once Ella was safely strapped in her seat and sucking on a bottle of juice to protect her ears from the pressure in the cabin, Bronte had little time to speak to Luca. He was sitting in a brooding silence, his documents open again on his lap, his eyes scanning them with deep concentration.

He too had showered and changed and was now dressed in chinos and a blue open neck shirt, the light colour highlighting his tanned skin. He looked tense, however, and Bronte didn't know if it was because he was introducing his wife-to-be and his daughter to his family or because of the words they had exchanged earlier. She had thought about the operation he had said he'd had. His thick hair covered the scars but the mental scars were something she wasn't sure would ever go away. The more she thought about what he had gone through, the more she regretted how she had handled his revelation. He was a proud and very private man. No wonder he hadn't been featured in the press for the last two years. He would have done anything to keep such a personal thing away from the gossip pages.

The wall was back up between them and Bronte felt bad she might have been the one to put it there this time. She had allowed her anger and hurt to ruin everything. Maybe her touchiness was one of the reasons he hadn't told her in the first place. She had pushed and pushed him two years ago, wanting more and more from him, and he had kept closing off. It all made perfect sense now. Why he would suddenly cancel dates at the last moment, or why he would turn up on edge and tetchy, his tongue sharper than normal. A couple of days later he would be back and she had been so desperate she had capitulated as if nothing had changed. If only she had delved a little deeper. If only she had thought of reasons other than another woman, maybe none of this heartache would have happened.

She shifted in her seat and delicately cleared her throat. 'Luca?'

He kept his place on the document with his hand and looked across at her. 'Don't worry about meeting my family,' he said. 'They will accept you without question.'

She bit down on her lip. 'Actually, I wasn't worried about that... Well, maybe a little...' She took a little breath and continued, 'Are you all right... I mean... now?'

He frowned for a long moment without answering.

Bronte ran her tongue over her lips. 'The operation? The ablation? Was it a success?'

Nothing moved on his face, not a muscle, apart from those he needed to speak. 'Yes.' He paused for a nanosecond. 'Yes, it was.'

Bronte looked down at her hands. 'I wish you had

told me...' she said softly. 'At the time, I mean...but I understand why you didn't.'

It seemed a long time before he answered. 'I wish I had too, *cara*.'

Luca's older brother was at the airport gate to meet them. Bronte could see the family likeness straight away. They were both tall and dark-haired with strong uncompromising jaws and a prominent nose and deep brown intelligent eyes.

After brief introductions were made, Giorgio took her hand and leaned forward to kiss her on both cheeks. 'Welcome to the family,' he said in a beautifully cultured voice, not unlike Luca's.

'Thank you,' Bronte said and watched as Giorgio's gaze went to Ella, who was kicking her legs in the push-chair and chortling.

He bent down and smiled a white-toothed smile that made his eyes crinkle up at the corners. There was a shadow of sadness there, Bronte thought, as he took one of Ella's tiny hands in his. 'This must be my little niece Ella,' he said.

Ella smiled widely and held her arms up high. 'Up, up.'

'May I?' Giorgio addressed Bronte.

'Of course,' she said, quickly unclipping Ella's push-chair straps. 'She hates being confined in there now that she's walking.'

'Ah, a little independent miss, eh, Ella?' Giorgio said as he gathered the child in his arms.

Luca smiled cautiously as he laid a hand on his older brother's shoulder. 'How are you?'

Giorgio gave a could-mean-anything shrug. 'I am

fine. Why would I not be? She left me, not me her. It's apparently what she wants. I can stall and I am doing so, but only for so long. I am fed up with it, frankly.'

Luca's smile fell away, along with his hand. 'I'm sorry.'

'Don't be.' Giorgio's tone was curt. 'It's for the best.'

Bronte exchanged a short look with Luca. She saw the concern in his expression and grimaced in empathy. He came over and slipped an arm around her waist. She didn't move away but instead found herself nestling against his warm strength as they made their way out to where his brother had parked the car.

The drive to Luca's villa was interspersed with Giorgio pointing out various landmarks and points of interest. 'Have you been to Milano before, Bronte?' he asked.

'Just the once,' she said, chancing a quick glance at Luca, sitting silently beside his brother in the passenger seat. 'It was just a quick stopover really. I didn't do any sightseeing. There wasn't time.'

'You will have to get Luca to show you around,' Giorgio said, quickly and expertly checking the traffic before he merged into the next lane. 'Our mother will look after Ella for you. She is bursting with excitement about finding out she finally has a granddaughter. She has bought so many toys her villa looks like Hamleys in London.'

Within a few minutes Giorgio pulled into Luca's villa grounds. On the outside it was much the same as it had been two years ago, but Bronte hadn't seen inside on her one and only visit in the past. Built on four levels, it had multiple bedrooms and formal and informal rooms for entertaining. It was breathtakingly decorated inside; no expense had been spared to turn it into a villa of distinction. Priceless works of art hung from the walls, marble statues and brass and bronze figures and busts were showcased here and there. The marbled foyer and winding staircase would have been intimidating, except Luca's housekeeper—Bronte assumed it was his house-keeper—had placed various vases of late summer roses all throughout, their delicate fragrance giving the villa a welcoming atmosphere.

Bronte turned a full circle in wonder. 'It's beautiful…'

Giorgio tickled Ella under the chin before he turned to look at Bronte with a quizzical look on his face. 'Hasn't Luca brought you here before?' he asked. 'When you said you'd been to Milano, I assumed you meant for a night or two here with him.'

Bronte didn't look in Luca's direction but she could feel the weight of his gaze. 'No,' she said, keeping all trace of emotion out of her voice. 'He didn't get around to it.'

Giorgio handed a wriggling Ella back to Bronte. 'I had better leave you two to settle in before our mother and grandfather arrive,' he said.

'Aren't you joining us for dinner?' Luca asked.

Giorgio shook his head. 'No, I have a prior engage-ment.'

Luca's brows snapped together. 'You're seeing some-one?'

Giorgio's expression hardened. 'Maya is divorcing me, Luca. It wasn't my idea. It's time to move on. It's over.'

'But surely it's too early to be seen out with some-one—'

Giorgio exchanged a few rapid fire sentences in

Italian. Luca's response was clipped and the air almost crackled with tension for a few tense seconds.

Bronte was glad when Ella started to grizzle. After a tersely delivered goodbye sent in Bronte's direction Giorgio left with a closing of the front door that could almost be described as a slam.

Luca's expression was thunderous as he came over to pick up their cases.

'Is everything all right?' she asked tentatively.

He threw her a disgusted look. 'My brother is a stubborn fool.'

'I am sure it's not wise to get involved in someone else's relationship,' she said. 'They have to work it out themselves.'

He looked at her for a long moment. 'Maybe you're right,' he said on a heavy sigh.

Bronte looked around. 'Don't you have any household staff any more?'

'I wasn't expected back until the week after next,' he said. 'My mother has loaned me her housekeeper until mine gets back from leave.'

She frowned as she tucked Ella closer on her left hip. 'Is it the same one who turned me away at the door when I came to tell you about Ella?'

He gave her an unreadable look. 'No,' he said and turned and led the way upstairs.

Ella was in the wrong time zone for sleep so Bronte decided to keep her up until Luca's mother and grandfather arrived. Apart from showing her around the villa earlier, she hadn't seen much of Luca. She assumed he was answering emails or returning phone calls from his large study on the second floor.

He had shown her to the master bedroom suite and
Bronte was in there, thinking about unpacking with
Ella sitting on the floor at her feet, when there was a
soft knock at the door. A woman in her late fifties or
early sixties introduced herself as Rosa, the Sabbatini
housekeeper. She gushed over Ella, telling Bronte in
reasonably good English about her own soon-to-arrive
grandchild. Bronte liked Rosa right from the start. There
was nothing haughty or judgemental about her.

'You are a very lucky woman,' Rosa said as she expertly unpacked the first of the suitcases while Bronte
chose something to wear for the evening's dinner. 'Luca
is a good man, *sì*?'

Bronte stretched her lips into a smile as she handed
Ella another toy. 'Yes, yes, he is.'

'He loves his little *bambino*,' Rosa continued, looking
down at Ella with a smile. 'He has always loved children. Giorgio is the same.' She tut-tutted as she placed
a shirt on the to-be-ironed pile. 'Me, I don't believe in
divorce, not unless one party has been unfaithful or
violent or has an addiction problem. Marriage has to
be worked at.'

'Maybe they fell out of love,' Bronte offered.

Rosa gave her a frowning look from beneath her
brows. 'Love is like a garden. It needs nurturing even
when it changes with the seasons. Luca won't let you go
so easily. He is stubborn at times but not as bull-headed
as his older brother. And then there's Nic.' She smiled
indulgently as she folded another top. 'He's a wild one,
that one. It will take a very special woman to tame
him.'

Bronte thought about how different Luca's life was
from hers. He had a loving family, money to burn and

staff waiting on his every need. She, on the other hand, had grown up feeling the pressure of being an only child to a single mother who hadn't yet learned to untie the apron strings.

'Would you like me to press that for you?' Rosa asked, pointing at the black dress Bronte had clutched to her chest.

'Oh… No, I can do it.'

Rosa plucked it out of Bronte's grasp. 'I am here to help you, Signorina Bennett. I will take Ella with me so you can shower and dress in peace. Luca told me the nanny won't be starting work until Monday.'

Bronte blinked. 'The nanny?'

Rosa scooped up Ella off the floor and planted her firmly on one generous hip. 'He did not tell you?'

'No, he did not.'

'Ah, here he is now,' Rosa said and, smiling at Luca, left the room with Ella giggling as she tried to pull at Rosa's earring.

Bronte faced him squarely. 'What is this about a nanny?'

He closed the door of the bedroom, his expression shuttered as usual. 'You have some objection to having help with Ella?' he asked.

'Of course I do,' she said, glaring at him. 'My main one being I haven't been consulted. You keep doing everything over my head.'

'Francesca comes with very good recommendations,' he said. 'She has a lot of experience. I am sure you will get along just fine.'

'That's not the point,' Bronte said. 'Why didn't you discuss it with me?'

'What is there to discuss?' he said. 'You had your

mother on call in Australia. I thought you would need similar backup here. You are intending to teach, remember? How do you expect to do that with Ella in tow?'

Bronte crossed her arms and paced the room. 'I hate leaving Ella with anyone,' she said. 'I love teaching, don't get me wrong, it's just that I never imagined I would have to sacrifice so much of my time—the time I would rather spend with Ella.' She turned and looked at him. 'I know you feel cheated out of the first year and a bit of Ella's life but I've been cheated too. I wasn't there the day she took her first step. My mother was. I will always feel guilty about that.'

Luca came over and unpeeled her arms, sliding his hands down them so he could encircle her wrists with his fingers. 'We have both missed out due to circumstances out of our control,' he said. 'But we have the future to put what we can right.'

She looked up at him with uncertainty in her slate-blue eyes. 'It would be different if we were in love.'

Luca felt his heart flinch as if someone had struck it. He schooled his features into impassivity and dropped his hands from hers. 'I am sure we will muddle along quite nicely,' he said. 'Thankfully, love isn't a requirement for good sex.'

'Sex is hardly a good basis for marriage,' she said with heightened colour. 'What happens when the lust dies down? Will you find someone else to keep your needs met?'

'That will depend entirely on you,' he said. 'I am not a great believer in extramarital affairs. Someone always wants more than can be given. People get hurt, and not just the adults. But if you no longer want to continue a physical relationship with me then I will have to consider my options.'

She gave her head a little toss but he saw the flash of fire in her gaze as she turned away. Jealousy was always a good sign. It might not mean she loved him the way she used to do, but it meant she wasn't prepared to share him, which was a very good start.

'I'll let you know,' she said in a stiff little voice.

Luca smiled to himself. 'So you're happy to share my bed for the time being?' he asked in an even tone.

She turned back to look at him, the twin spots of colour on her cheeks still glowing red-hot. 'It amuses you that I am so weak, doesn't it?'

'I'm not amused,' he said, trying for deadpan. 'I'm delighted.'

She gave him a withering look. 'It's just lust, nothing else. I think you should know that. It's probably hormones or something.'

'Of course.'

She searched his features for a moment, her eyes narrowing slightly. 'What are you smiling about?'

'Was I smiling?' he asked with a guileless look.

'Not on the outside, but you are on the inside,' she said. 'I can see the glint in your eyes.'

Luca placed his hands on her shoulders. 'That's because I am imagining you without those clothes on with me in the shower.' He brought her up close to his body, one of his hands slipping beneath her silky dark hair, the other pressing against the small of her back. 'We have just enough time if we hurry.'

Her eyes flickered and then dropped to his mouth. 'It's hormones. Definitely hormones. I'm sure of it,' she said in a soft, breathless little voice.

'Hormones sound good to me,' Luca said and, swooping down, covered her mouth with his.

Bronte took a deep breath as Luca led her down the stairs to meet his mother and grandfather, who had just arrived. She could hear them chatting with Rosa in the *salone*, their voices full of excitement and anticipation.

Luca had Ella in his arms and his mother rushed up to him as soon as the door opened. 'Luca, *caro*,' she choked as she reached for Ella. 'She is the image of Chiara. Oh, dear God, how I have longed for this moment.'

Bronte stood to one side as Luca's grandfather cooed over Ella. She could see where Luca got his good looks from. Salvatore Sabbatini night be nudging ninety but he was still a tall man of proud bearing. He had the same air of authority about him that both Luca and Giorgio had. His hair was grey and his face a little lined but, even at that great age, he was still worth a double take.

Luca's mother too had clearly been a beauty in her day. She was small and delicately made, with salt and pepper hair that should have aged her but somehow didn't. She had beautiful skin and had a natural elegance about her.

'*Mamma, Nonno,*' Luca said, cupping Bronte's elbow. 'This is my fiancée, Bronte Bennett.'

Salvatore was the first to come over. He took Bronte's hand and, just as Giorgio had done earlier that day, leaned forward to kiss her on both cheeks. 'This is a very happy day for us,' he said in heavily accented but still perfect English. 'You have blessed us with Giovanna's first grandchild and my first great-grandchild. I have lived for this day. I cannot tell you how it makes me feel to know the bloodline will continue.'

Bronte knew her smile looked a little forced but she just couldn't help it. 'I am sorry you haven't met her until now.'

'Better than not at all,' Salvatore said.

There was a small silence.

'*Mamma,*' Luca prompted.

Giovanna Sabbatini was still holding Ella, looking very much as if she was not going to let her go. 'I am glad you finally decided to tell our son he was a father,' she said. 'But did you not think of how you were not just robbing him of all those months of her life but his family as well?'

'*Mamma—*' Luca's voice was deep and full of admonition '—this is not the time to—'

'It's all right, Luca,' Bronte said sending him a pained look. 'Your mother is absolutely right. I didn't think about anyone else at the time. If I had, it might have turned out very differently.'

Giovanna refused to be mollified. 'My oldest son is going through a very painful and, in my opinion, totally unnecessary divorce,' she said. 'That might not have happened if Luca had known about his daughter before now.'

Bronte felt her back come up. 'I hardly think it is my fault your son and his wife spilt up,' she said. 'I accept that I was wrong not to work harder at contacting Luca, but I was angry and hurt about him breaking off our relationship.'

Salvatore placed a firm but gentle fatherly hand on Bronte's shoulder. 'Forgive my daughter-in-law,' he said. 'This is an emotional time for us all. We have been through a lot with almost losing Luca two years ago and, of course, my son, his father, Giancarlo five years ago now. And before that we lost little Chiara, my grand-daughter. I am not sure if you know about her. It was a long time ago but we live with it daily. Ella is a blessing God has sent to us to help heal our pain.'

Almost losing Luca… The rest of Salvatore's words faded as those three reverberated inside Bronte's head. They had almost *lost* him? She looked at Luca, stand-ing so silently, a brooding frown stitched on his brow. She swallowed and tried to focus on what Salvatore was saying but her mind kept drifting back to those three ominous-sounding words.

Dinner was a bit of a strained affair. Bronte had no appetite and, although Luca's grandfather was charm-ing and did everything in his power to include her in the conversation, it was clear Giovanna was not going to budge. Bronte could understand it, being a mother herself. She decided to be as patient as possible and not be drawn into any comebacks she might have cause to regret later. After all, this was to be her mother-in-law, not the easiest of relationships at the best of times.

Once Luca's mother and grandfather had left and Ella was sleeping soundly in her cot, Bronte waited for Luca in the bedroom. He came in after a good hour, which made her wonder if he had been hoping she would fall asleep before he got there.

'Luca,' she said without preamble, 'I want to know what your grandfather meant about almost losing you two years ago.'

The shutters came down over his face and his mouth went into a flat line. 'My grandfather spoke out of turn,' he said. 'So did my mother. I am sorry about how she behaved. She will soften eventually. She was the same with my brother's wife Maya. Although I can't say they are all that close now.'

'Look, I recognise the mother lion thing,' she said. 'But that's not what we are discussing. What happened, Luca?'

'Nothing happened,' he said, averting his gaze. 'My grandfather exaggerated the situation.'

'You're lying.'

'You are imagining things,' he said and pulled back the covers.

'I am not getting into bed with you until you tell me what happened to you, Luca,' she said with a determined jut of her chin.

His hand dropped from the covers, his eyes locking with hers. 'You want to fight or make love?' he asked.

Bronte felt a shiver of reaction course down her spine at his challenging look. 'I don't want to fight you, Luca, I want to understand you. You keep shutting me out. You've always done it. You always keep something back of yourself.'

He drew in a breath at the same time as his hand scored a jagged pathway through his hair. 'I have never been one for wearing my heart on my sleeve,' he said. 'I am not going to change now, not for anyone.'

'Then God help us,' she said, 'for I can't see this relationship lasting more than a month or two at most.'

He clenched his hands into fists. 'Why do you have to push and push and push?' he asked. 'Why can't you just leave the past where it belongs? We both screwed up. I get that, OK? I am not blaming you. Not any more.'

'Y-you're not?' Her voice came out as a whisper.

He sighed and rubbed his hand over his face. 'No,' he finally said, holding out an arm for her. 'Come here.'

Bronte went.

CHAPTER TWELVE

LUCA wrapped his arms around her, holding her close to him and, burying his face in her hair, he pressed a kiss to the top of her head.

It seemed a decade before he spoke and, when he did, his voice sounded scratchy and uneven. 'I'm sorry you had to find out like that,' he said. 'I wanted to spare you the gory details. I like to pretend it didn't happen.'

Bronte couldn't stop the flow of tears. 'Oh, Luca, don't you see that I need to know everything because that's the only way we can get our relationship to work?'

He brushed at her tears with his thumbs. 'I didn't want to make you feel sorry for me. I couldn't bear to be pitied. How could I be sure you were back with me because you wanted to be or because you felt sorry for me?'

She swallowed a knot of dread. 'Your grandfather said—'

'He was right,' Luca said grimly. 'I had an unexpected complication. I had a bleed which put me into a coma for three weeks. No one knew how I would be when I woke up, even if I *would* wake up. Just like what had happened to my father. I couldn't bear ending up like that, sitting drooling vacantly in a chair with no recognition of all the people who most loved me. How could I do that to my family? How could I do that to you?'

Bronte could finally see now why he had acted as he had. He had been so concerned for her that he had put his own hopes and dreams aside to set her free in case something went horribly wrong. Instead of seeing what he did as selfish and ruthless, she now saw it for what it was: the most honourable, selfless thing anyone could do for someone they loved. 'That's why you let me go the way you did, wasn't it?' she asked. 'You wanted me to think you no longer had any feelings for me. It's why you never told me what you felt the whole time we were together. You always were going to let me go because you wanted me to be safe from a lifetime of caring for you if it all went wrong because you knew I would never turn my back on you.'

He met her gaze, his throat rising and falling over a tight swallow. 'It was the hardest thing I've ever had to do,' he said. 'I knew if I did it in person I would not be able to walk away from you. I was so close to telling you a couple of times about my condition but I talked myself out of it. I didn't want your pity. I didn't want to tie you down out of obligation and duty.'

She choked over the words. 'I…I would have stood by you, Luca, surely you know that?'

'That was the problem, *cara*,' he said. 'I knew you would stand by me, no matter what, but I couldn't allow you to do that. What if the worst had happened? I could have become an invalid or mentally disabled. It's happened before. The brain can't survive long periods without oxygen. Multiple seizures can cause irreparable damage. I just couldn't risk ruining your life. You had the world at your feet. You were so talented. I was sure you would end up at the London Ballet academy. I would have held you back. I had to let you go.'

Bronte put her arms tightly around his waist, her tears soaking the front of his shirt. 'I never stopped loving you, Luca,' she sobbed. 'I've been fooling myself for all this time that I hated you but really I didn't. I could never hate you.'

Luca breathed in the fragrance of her hair as he held her against him. 'I was hoping I hadn't totally destroyed what you felt for me,' he said in a gravelly voice. 'I had to wait until I was given the all-clear. I promised myself a full year without a single seizure and then I would contact you. It felt like a lifetime. I didn't realise that it *was* a lifetime: Ella's lifetime.'

Bronte looked up at him with glistening eyes. 'She loved you from the moment she met you, Luca. You don't have to worry about her not realising you weren't there for the first bit of her life. When she's old enough, we can explain. The important thing is that you're here now. You are her father. You have always been her father. I have never thought of you as anything else.'

He smiled a half smile. 'I love you, you do realise that, don't you? I have loved you from the first time I met you. You are my heart, my reason for living. I love you so much it hurts.'

Her eyes watered all over again. 'I think it's just starting to dawn on me.'

He brushed a strand of her hair off her face in a tender gesture, his dark eyes meltingly soft as they meshed with hers. 'I fell in love with you the day we met in that London bookshop. Do you remember when you bumped into me and you dropped your handbag and it scattered its contents all over the floor?'

Bronte smiled. 'That's how you got my address, wasn't it? You checked my diary before you handed it to me.'

'What was a desperate man to do?' he asked with a grin. 'I wanted to see you again. I felt an instant attraction. I had never felt anything like that before. When our fingers met when I handed you your tub of lipgloss I felt as if I was being electrocuted. My fingers were still tingling hours later.'

'Mine were too,' she said, slipping her arms up around his neck.

He bent down and planted a soft, lingering kiss to her mouth. When he finally lifted his head Bronte was looking up at him dazedly. 'I can't believe this is happening,' she said. 'I used to dream of one day seeing you again. I never thought it would really happen.'

'I am sorry things worked out the way they did,' he said. 'But I am not sure I wouldn't do things the same way again. I loved you too much to wilfully destroy your life.'

'Did you tell *anyone* about your condition?' she asked.

'Not until it was over,' he said. 'I had left a letter with my lawyer in case of an emergency. The doctors had orders to contact him if things didn't go according to plan, which, of course, he then had to do when I slipped into a coma. My family, of course, were terribly upset, as you can imagine, my mother in particular. She had already lost one child and had never got over it, as you heard downstairs. Giorgio was very good about it but Nic was pretty cut up. But I think he's more or less forgiven me by now.'

Bronte caressed his face lovingly. 'I'm so glad you told me, Luca. I was so worried about marrying you just for Ella's sake. It didn't seem right. I was frightened you might take her away from me, you know, fight for custody or something.'

A frown interrupted his features. 'I have seen the drama that my brother and sister-in-law are currently going through over their dog. Neither of them wants to compromise. I didn't want to put either of you through that. I was determined to make things work out. I just felt you needed a bit of time.'

She gave him a mock-reproachful look. 'And a little bit of pressure.'

'Well,' he said with a sheepish grin, 'a man's got to do what a man's got to do.'

She snuggled up even closer. 'Definitely,' she said on a sultry purr. 'Especially if you are serious about wanting to make a brother or sister for Ella.'

His eyes lit up. 'You mean you're ready to try for another baby?'

She smiled and wriggled against him suggestively. 'You bet I am. So how about you get on with it?'

Luca smiled and pulled down the shoestring straps of her nightgown. 'Just try and stop me, *cara*,' he said and pressed her back down on the bed, his mouth coming down on hers.

Two weeks later...

Bronte stood at the end of the aisle and looked down at Luca, standing waiting for her by the altar. The organ was playing, the congregation was smiling, the flowers and their heady scent filled the air with hope and happiness and love.

She caught her mother's eye and smiled. Ella chortled in Tina Bennett's arms and called out volubly, 'Mummy pretty, Mummy berry pretty.'

'Mummy is beautiful,' Luca said as Bronte came to stand beside him.

'Hi,' she said softly.

'Hi yourself,' he said, taking her hands in his, squeezing them gently. 'You're trembling.'

'I'm nervous.'

'Don't be, *tesore mio*,' he said. 'This is the beginning of our life together. Our life as a family.'

The priest began the poignant service and at the end there was barely a dry eye in the house. Bronte was enveloped by Luca's family as she and Luca came out of the church when it was over. Even Giorgio and Maya had seemed to put their enmity to one side so as not to spoil Luca and Bronte's special day.

Luca's mother mopped at her eyes and smiled as she pulled Bronte into a bone-crushing hug. Over the last couple of weeks she had softened towards Bronte and had spent many a happy day preparing for the wedding with her. Bronte felt that Giovanna's love for Ella more than made up for any ill feeling that had been there at their first meeting.

'Welcome to the family, Bronte,' Giovanna said. 'You have given my son so much joy. You have given me so much joy. I don't know how to thank you.'

'He's easy to love,' Bronte said, looking in Luca's direction, her breath coming out in a heartfelt sigh of happiness. 'So very easy to love.'

Giovanna smiled with maternal pride. 'Yes, he is,' she said. 'I am so glad he found you again. I don't think he would have settled for anyone else, you know. Luca's father was the same, although the death of our daughter set him off course for a while, but he finally came back to me. He knew there would be no other woman who could love him like I loved him.'

Bronte felt her heart give a little jump of excitement as Luca came back and slipped his arm around her waist.

'What family secrets is my mother letting out of the bag?' he asked playfully.

'Your mother was telling me you are just like your father,' Bronte said, exchanging a conspiratorial look with the older woman.

Luca pressed a kiss to the tip of Bronte's upturned nose. 'Did she tell you that once a Sabbatini man falls in love it is for ever?' he asked.

'She didn't need to tell me that,' Bronte said on a blissful sigh as his protective arms enfolded her. 'That's something I already knew.'

SHOCK: ONE-NIGHT HEIR

MELANIE MILBURNE

CHAPTER ONE

MAYA looked at the dipstick in shock. Her throat closed over as if a hand had locked around her neck as the two blue lines appeared.

Positive.

She sat on the edge of the bathtub, her legs shaking so much she had to clamp her knees together. Hope flickered brightly and then just as quickly waned.

It couldn't be true.

She took a deep breath and looked at the stick again. She blinked once, twice, three times but the lines were the same as before.

The doorbell suddenly rang with an incessant peal and she sprang to her feet, her heart knocking against her chest wall like a pendulum pushed by a madman. She quickly stashed the test kit in the nearest drawer beneath the twin basins and took a long slow breath to steady herself.

Gonzo was already at the door, barking joyfully in greeting, but Maya didn't need the dog's behaviour to signal to her who was at the door. No one rang the door-bell quite the same way as her soon-to-be ex-husband Giorgio Sabbatini did. He always pressed it too hard and for too long. He was summoning her and he clearly would not be taking no for an answer.

Maya fixed a deliberately cool expression on her face as she opened the door. 'G…Giorgio,' she said, hoping the catch in her voice wouldn't betray her. 'I thought you were sending one of your staff to pick up Gonzo. Isn't that the arrangement we agreed on?'

'I decided to come in person this time.' He bent down to ruffle the ecstatic dog's ears before he rose back to his full height, his tall frame towering over her. His dark brown eyes glittered with a sardonic light as they met hers. 'I am quite surprised to find you at home,' he said. 'I thought you might be out with your new Englishman lover. What was his name again? Hugh? Herbert?'

Maya bit the inside of her mouth, wishing, not for the first time, she hadn't gone on that stupid blind date set up by a friend from her yoga class. 'Howard,' she said tightly. 'And it wasn't anything like the press reported it.'

One of Giorgio's brows lifted in a cynical arc. 'So he didn't rip your clothes off in the hallway of his apartment and have his wicked way with you?'

Maya threw him a venomous look as she closed the door behind him with a snap. 'No,' she said. 'That is more your style, is it not?'

He gave her an indolent smile which made every hair on the back of her neck lift up in reaction. 'You were with me all the way, *cara*,' he said in a tone that was gravelly and rough and so deep she felt a guilty shiver of remembered pleasure cascade down her spine and bury itself in that hot secret place between her thighs.

Maya turned on her heel rather than face him with her colour so high. She still cringed in shame at how she had behaved the night of his brother's wedding. She still wasn't exactly sure what had precipitated it. Had it been the champagne or the pain of finally letting go? Break up sex, that was what it was called. It didn't mean anything, certainly not to him. He had probably bedded several women since they had separated. According to the latest press report, he was currently seeing a lingerie model based in London. Reading that had been like a dart to Maya's heart but she would rather die than reveal that to him.

She felt him come up behind her, her skin prickling all over and her nostrils flaring as she breathed in his citrus-based aftershave overlaid with his particular male smell. All her senses—the ones she had sworn would always be switched to neutral when he was around—turned to full throttle. She felt her heart give a stutter when his hands came to rest on the top of her shoulders, her breathing stopping altogether when his tall body brushed against hers from behind.

'You smell nice,' he said, bending his head so his mouth almost touched the side of her neck. 'Is that a new perfume you are wearing?'

Somehow she got her voice to work. 'Get your hands off me, Giorgio,' she said. *Before I turn around and fall into your arms and make a complete and utter fool of myself all over again.*

His hands tightened for a fraction of a second, long enough for her heart rate to go up another notch. 'Our divorce isn't final until the last of the paperwork is sorted,' he said, his breath lifting the hairs that had come loose from her makeshift ponytail. 'Maybe we can make the most of the time before the ink dries, hmm?'

Maya knew what this was about and it hurt much more than the lingerie model. It wasn't their broken marriage he was fighting for, it was his fortune. The Sabbatini family was as good as Italian royalty. When she had married Giorgio five years ago there had been no prenuptial agreement prepared. It was an unwritten, unspoken law: their marriage was meant to last, as every other Sabbatini marriage had in the past. But Maya wondered if any other Sabbatini marriage had endured the heartache theirs had and survived.

She very much doubted it.

She turned to face him, her heart tightening all over again as she looked into his inscrutable dark-as-night eyes. 'What do you want?' she asked.

His thumbs started to knead her knotted shoulders until she was sure she was going to melt into a pool at his feet. She fought the response, clamping her teeth together as she put her hands against his chest to push him away. 'Will you stop touching me, for God's sake?' she railed at him.

He captured her hands effortlessly, holding them in one of his as if they were a child's. 'It was good that night, *si*?' he said. 'I can't remember a time when it was better, can you?'

Maya swallowed unevenly. She had tried so hard not to think of that night, how wonderful it had been to make love with such abandon. No temperature or ovulation charts, no hormone injections—just good old-fashioned bed-wrecking sex, except they hadn't quite made it to the bed. But this visit: was it about a rerun of that passionate night or a truce to secure his assets?

'Giorgio…that night was a crazy, stupid mistake,' she said, not trusting herself to hold his gaze.

She pulled her hands out of his and moved away, crossing her arms over her middle. It was too soon to tell him, of course it was. It would jinx things just like before. How many times had she held up the dipstick in joy, only to have her hopes and dreams smashed like priceless porcelain on a pavement a week or two later? There were no guarantees this time would be any different. If it wasn't meant to be, at least Giorgio would be free to move on with someone else who could give him what he wanted most. They would both be free to move on. She had wasted five years of his life, not to mention her own. He was thirty-six years old. Most of his friends and colleagues had two or three children by now.

She had given him none.

Giorgio followed her into the tiny *salone*. Maya felt his gaze on her, the heat of it, the slow burn of it peeling every layer of her skin until she felt raw and exposed. She had to hold herself together. She couldn't come unstuck and get all emotional and needy in front of him. She was supposed to be over all of that now. She had worked hard at it, working out new priorities, new directions, none of which included Giorgio. Cool and in control was the only way to go with him. She had to prove to him that he no longer had any emotional or sensual power over her. She was her own person now, determined to move on with her life.

She was stronger now, much stronger.

The six-month separation had done that for her. She no longer lived in the shadow of Giorgio's money and prestige. She was making a way for herself, providing for her future by restarting her career, which she had naively cast aside in order to fit in with what Giorgio and his family had expected of her. She was quite proud of what she had achieved in the time they had been apart. She had been looking forward to starting afresh until this latest hiccup had thrown her off course. Could he see the secret she was trying to hide from him? Was there some clue on her face or in her body, even at this early stage? He seemed to be looking at her so intently, his dark gaze so piercing she felt exposed and raw, as if he could see into her soul.

'What is this I hear about you moving to London?' he asked.

She faced him with a set mouth, her shoulders pulled back in determination. 'I have an interview for a teaching position at a fee paying school. I am on the shortlist.'

A frown brought his brows together. 'Are you going to take it if it is offered to you?'

She let her arms drop by her sides in an effort to look composed. 'I don't see why not,' she said, sending him a pointed look. 'I have nothing to keep me in Italy.'

A muscle moved up and down in his jaw, as if he were chewing on something hard and distasteful. 'What about Gonzo?' he asked.

Maya felt her heart squeeze at the thought of saying

goodbye to the dog she had brought up from puppyhood. But no pets were allowed in her apartment block in London, and she knew the big ragamuffin hound would miss Giorgio too much in any case. As it was, the dog had been like a naughty child ever since she and Giorgio had separated. 'I have decided he is better off with you,' she said.

His top lip curled. 'That's quite a turnaround. You were arguing the point for weeks over who should have him. I was about to get my lawyer to file a pet custody suit.'

Maya lifted one of her shoulders in a shrug of feigned indifference. 'I am sure he will forget all about me once he moves into your newly renovated villa,' she said. 'When do you move back in, by the way?'

Giorgio raked his hand through his hair in a gesture that tugged on something deep inside Maya's chest. There were so many of his mannerisms she had found herself thinking about lately: how he rationed his smiles as if he found life not all that amusing, how his brow furrowed when he was deep in concentration, and how his eyes glinted and darkened meaningfully when he was in the mood for sex. She skirted away from that errant thought. It brought back too many erotic memories of that forbidden night.

'I'm not sure. A week or two, I think,' he said. 'The painters haven't quite finished. There was a delay with some of the fabrics for the curtains or some such thing.'

Maya didn't want to think of how she had chosen the colours and fabrics for all of those rooms in the past. She had done it with such enthusiasm and hope for the future. When she had heard he was renovating the villa, adding rooms and knocking down walls and redeveloping the garden, she had been crushed to think he obviously wanted to rid the place of every trace of her presence. It tore her apart to think of how those rooms might one day be filled with his children by some other woman. She thought of the nursery she had so lovingly decorated the first time she had fallen pregnant. After five years of dashed hopes, in the end she had not been able to even open the door.

'When do you leave?' Giorgio asked into the pulsing silence.

With an effort she met his gaze. 'Next Monday.'

'This is all rather sudden, is it not?' he asked, frowning darkly. 'I thought you had decided long ago you weren't going to go back to teaching. Or are you trying to imply to outsiders that I'm not paying you enough in our divorce settlement?'

Maya refused to rise to the bait. 'I don't care what people think, Giorgio. I want to go back to teaching because I have a brain that longs to be used. I was never cut out for the ladies-who-do-lunch set. I should never have given up my career in the first place. I don't know what on earth I was thinking.'

He continued to study her with his dark unreadable gaze. 'You seemed pretty happy with the arrangement to begin with,' he said. 'You said your career was not as important as mine. You jumped at the chance to become a full time wife.'

Maya mentally cringed at how romantically deluded

she had been back then. Although she hadn't for a moment thought he was marrying her for love, she had longed for it to happen all the same. His marrying her had more to do with tradition and expectation from his family. He had reached the age of thirty and, in the tradition of the Sabbatini blood line, he'd needed a wife and heir. Giorgio had showered her with diamonds and she had been fooled into believing in the whole fairy tale that one day they would get their happy ever after. How young and naive she had been! Just twenty-two years old, fresh out of university, she had fallen in love on her first trip abroad. It had taken her five heartbreaking years to finally grow up and realise not all fairy tales had a happy ending.

'I had stars in my eyes,' she said, knowing it would feed his opinion of her as a gold-digger but doing it anyway. 'All that money, all that fame, all those luxury hotels and villas and exotic holidays. What girl could possibly resist?'

His brows snapped together and that leaping knot of tension appeared again at the corner of his mouth. 'If you think for even a moment that you are getting half of all I own, then think again,' he bit out. 'I don't care if it takes my legal team a decade to thrash this out in court, I will not roll over for you.'

Maya raised her chin at him. It was always about money with Giorgio. She had been yet another business transaction and the thing that rankled with him was it had failed. The truth was they had both failed. She hadn't made him any happier than he had made her. Money had cushioned things for a while but she had come to see the only way to move forward was to part.

'You will only delay the divorce even further,' she said. 'I am not after much, in any case.'

Giorgio gave a snort. 'Not much? Come on, Maya. You want the villa at Bellagio. That has been in my family for seven generations. It is priceless to my family. I suppose that's why you want to take it away from us.'

Maya steeled her resolve. 'The place should have been sold years ago and you know it. We've only been there the once and you acted like a caged lion the whole time. Both of your brothers haven't been there for months and in the whole time we've been married your mother has never once gone there. For most of the year it lies empty, apart from the staff. It's such an obscene waste.'

His eyes moved away from hers, as she knew they would. He absolutely refused to discuss the tragic event that had occurred during his childhood, and every time she had tried to draw him out over his baby sister's death he put up a wall of resistance that was impenetrable. She hated the way he always locked her out. She hated the way it made her feel as if she was not entitled to know how he felt about even the simplest things. But then all he had wanted from her was a cardboard cut-out wife, a showpiece to hang off his arm and do all the things a corporate wife was supposed to do—all the things except unlock the secret pain of his heart.

He turned his back and paced back and forth, his hands clenching and unclenching by his sides. 'My mother might one day feel the need to go back to the villa,' he said. 'But, until she does, the place is not to be sold.'

Maya shifted her tongue inside her cheek, still intent on needling him. 'Are *you* planning to go there any time soon?' she asked. 'How long's it been, Giorgio? Two or three years, or is it four?'

He turned and faced her, his eyes blazing with something hot and hard and dangerous. 'Don't push it, Maya,' he said. 'You are not getting the villa. Anyway, Luca and Bronte will most probably use it now they are married. It's a perfect place for Ella to spend her childhood holidays.'

Maya felt her insides clench as she thought of the dark-haired, blue-eyed toddler Luca had introduced to his family a few weeks ago. His new wife, Bronte, a fellow Australian, had met Luca two years ago in London, but Luca had broken off the relationship before he had realised Bronte was carrying his child. Their reunion and marriage had been one of the most romantic and poignant events Maya had ever witnessed.

Being around gorgeous little Ella on the day of the wedding had been a torturous reminder of how Maya had failed to produce an heir. She wondered if that was why she had acted so stupidly and recklessly once the reception had ended. She had been so emotionally overwrought, so desperately lonely and sad at the breakdown of her own marriage that she had weakened when Giorgio had suggested a nightcap.

Going back to his room at the Sabbatini hotel in Milan where the reception was held had been her first mistake. Her second had been to let him kiss her. And her third…well, she was deeply ashamed of falling into his arms like that. She had acted like a slut and he had walked away from her when it was over as if he had paid for her services like a street worker.

'I want the villa, Giorgio,' she said, holding his diamond-hard gaze. 'I surely deserve some compensation. I could ask for a whole lot more and you know it.'

His jaw moved forward in an uncompromising manner, his eyes now darker than ink. 'I wouldn't want you to get the wrong idea here, Maya. I want this divorce just as much as you do. But the villa is not negotiable. I am not going to budge on this.'

His intransigence fuelled Maya's defiance, so too did his all too ready acceptance of the divorce. Surely, if he had ever felt anything for her, wouldn't he have fought to keep her by his side no matter what? The only reason he was dragging the chain a bit was over the settlement.

Her bitterness was like a hot flood inside her, scorching its way through her veins. 'You bastard,' she threw at him. 'You're rich beyond belief and you won't give me the only thing I want.'

'Why do you want it?' he asked. 'You're moving to London within days. What use would you have for a thirty-room villa?'

'I want to develop it,' she said with a combative toss of her head. 'It would make a fabulous hotel and health spa. It would provide a supplementary income to my teaching. It would be an investment, a great investment in fact.'

His eyes flashed like lightning. 'Are you deliberately

goading me?' he asked. '*Dio*, Maya, I've already warned you not to push me too far.'

'Why?' she tossed back at him. 'Are you worried you might show some human feelings for once? Some anger, some passion, or maybe even some vulnerability for a change?'

The air pulsed with a current of energy that made the skin on the back of Maya's neck start to tingle. His eyes were so black she could not tell where his pupils ended and his irises began. He had stopped clenching his hands as soon as he saw her eyes flick to them but she could sense the tension in him all the same. His face was carved from stone, his lips flat and tight. She wondered if he was going to close the distance between their bodies and take her in his arms the way he had done the night of his brother's wedding. They had argued just like this and then suddenly, instead of shouting at each other, they were locked in a passionate embrace. Her body quivered at the memory and when she met Giorgio's eyes she could almost swear he was recalling exactly the same shamelessly erotic moment when his mouth had crashed down on hers.

'Is that what you want, Maya?' he asked in a low and deep and silky tone as his hand snaked out and captured one of hers. 'You want me to lose control and take you just like the last time?'

Maya's body flared with heat, her wrist burning like a ring of fire where his fingers curled around it like a handcuff. 'You wouldn't dare,' she bit out.

He pulled her up against him, his body hot and hard and unmistakably male against her soft femininity. 'I dared before,' he reminded her. 'And you enjoyed every second of it.'

Shame flooded her cheeks but she put up her chin haughtily all the same. 'I'd had too much champagne to drink.'

His mouth turned up derisively. 'Is that the only way you can absolve yourself for sleeping with me again?' he asked. 'Come on, Maya, you were begging for it even before you had your first sip of champagne. I saw it in your eyes the moment you stepped into the church and looked at me.'

Maya remembered the moment all too well. That first glimpse of him standing there beside his brother after not seeing him for months had knocked her sideways. She had pointedly avoided him as much as possible prior to the wedding. The arrangement over Gonzo being picked up and dropped off by a neutral party had been at her insistence because she didn't trust herself in his company. Going into the church that day and seeing Giorgio, she had felt as if she were seeing him for the first time. All the bitterness and ill feeling had somehow vaporised, all she could see was a tall, commanding and handsome man with impossibly dark brown eyes which at that moment had been centred right on her. The message in his eyes had been as scorching as his touch was right now. 'Your imagination is getting as big as your ego,' she said. 'You think any woman who looks at you wants you.'

She pulled out of his hold and stepped away from him, tossing over her shoulder, 'You should probably take Gonzo with you now. His lead is hanging on the hall stand.'

'I am not going anywhere, Maya,' Giorgio said through gritted teeth.

Maya turned, trying to ignore the flutter of unease that passed through her belly at the dark glittering heat of his gaze as it meshed with hers. 'Giorgio...' She ran her tongue over her lips to moisten their sudden dryness. 'We've said all that needs to be said. The rest is in the hands of our lawyers.'

There was another beat or two of heavily charged silence.

'I didn't come here to discuss the divorce,' Giorgio said.

Maya ran her tongue over her parched lips, her stomach freefalling. 'You...you didn't?'

His eyes were unwavering on hers. 'I came here to issue you an invitation.'

She blinked at him in alarm. 'An...an invitation? What sort of invitation? I hope you don't mean what I think you mean because I will not for a moment agree to such an outrageous, insulting and indecent proposal.'

His sensually full lips went into a flat line again. 'Not that sort of invitation, not that it isn't a tempting thought, given what happened the last time.'

'It's over, Giorgio,' she said, reminding herself as well as him. '*We* are over.'

He held her look for two beats before he spoke. 'I know it's over, Maya. It's what we both want. It's what we both need to move on with our lives.'

Maya nodded because she didn't trust her voice to

work right then. Of course it was over. It was what she wanted. She was the one who had done the legwork to get the divorce process going. What sort of hypocrite was she to have second thoughts now? Even though those two blue lines on that dipstick were lying in that drawer upstairs didn't mean they would appear on a subsequent test. It could all be a mistake. She might have imagined the whole thing. She would need to do another test and another, just to make sure.

Giorgio pushed his hand back through his hair again, taking it off his forehead where it had tipped forward as he moved to the other side of the room. Maya noticed then how tired he looked about the eyes. Too much partying, she supposed. She could just imagine him enjoying the night life after years of being tied down in a going nowhere marriage. He had been like that before they had married and that, no doubt, would be his fall-back position.

'My grandfather's ninetieth birthday party is next weekend,' Giorgio said, facing her again. 'He wants you to be there.'

Maya tightened her mouth. 'Why then didn't he call and invite me, instead of sending you? Or why not send an invitation through the post? What's going on?'

'You know what he's like,' he said. 'He's a stubborn old fool who thinks we are throwing away a perfectly good marriage. He wanted me to ask you in person. He apparently thinks I still hold some sort of sway with you.' He gave her a wry look. 'I told you he was an old fool.'

Maya spun on her heel to pace the floor. 'I am *not*

attending any more Sabbatini family functions,' she stated firmly. 'No way. Not after the last time.'

Giorgio held up his hands. 'I promise not to touch, OK?'

She stopped mid-pace to glower at him. 'I don't hold much faith in your promises. You were barely in the door a moment ago when you put your hands on me as if you owned me.'

He gave her a crooked half smile that never failed to twist her insides. 'Put it down to force of habit or muscle memory or whatever.'

She screwed up her face in scorn. 'Muscle memory? What sort of ridiculous excuse is that? We're about to be divorced, remember? You have no right to touch me now.'

His fleeting smile disappeared and a frown pulled at his brow. 'Look, Maya, you will make an old man very happy if you agree to come. Divorce or not, he still considers you a member of the family. He will be devastated if you don't turn up.'

Maya chewed at her lip, torn between wanting to pay her respects to the only grandfather/father figure she had ever known and her reluctance to spend any further time with the one man she suspected she was not going to be able to resist if she was in too close contact with him. 'If I go it will be because *he* asked me, not you,' she said.

He jangled his keys in his pocket as if impatient to leave. *Mission accomplished*, Maya thought. He'd got what he wanted and now he was off to enjoy his freedom. She watched as he moved to the front door of her small rented villa, the words to call him back stuck like a handful of thumbtacks in her throat.

It's over.

It's what we both want.

It's over.

The words went over and over in her head like a music system stuck on replay.

'I'll pick up Gonzo the day before you leave for London,' he said as he opened the door.

'Right. Fine. OK,' Maya said, cupping her elbows to stop herself from fidgeting.

He gave her one last look, his eyes dark and unfathomable as they ran over her. 'Champagne or not, it was a great night, *cara*, wasn't it? Good note to end our relationship on.'

Maya swiftly turned her back on him, her eyes burning with unshed tears. 'Please leave…' she said, surprised her voice had come out at all, much less without cracking.

After what seemed an age, the door finally closed with a click that felt as if it had snapped her heart in two.

CHAPTER TWO

THE party for Salvatore Sabbatini was in full swing when Maya arrived the following Saturday. She had almost changed her mind about coming but knew if she didn't turn up by a certain time Giorgio would come to her place and collect her.

Right now she wanted as much distance as possible between them. Her secret was still safe and she wanted to keep it that way for as long as possible. She had conducted three more tests and they had all produced the same positive result. It was terrifyingly exciting to think she was carrying a child. Six weeks was too early to be confident it would carry to full term, but every miscarriage she'd had in the past had occurred well before the eight week mark.

'Signora Sabbatini,' one of the uniformed waiters greeted her with a tray of drinks balanced on one arm, 'would you like some champagne?'

Maya offered him a tight smile. 'Orange juice will be fine, thank you.'

Once she had taken her frosted glass, she moved through to the reception room, where a glamorous array of people were milling about to greet the guest of honour. There were Hollywood stars and high finance people, a couple of members of European royalty as well as family and close friends of Salvatore. Everyone was dressed in designer clothes and several of the women were dripping in priceless jewels.

Maya had dressed carefully for the occasion. She could play the part of haute couture-clad wife and had done so for five years. The dress she had chosen was a fuchsia pink, highlighting the natural blondness of her hair and her sun-kissed colouring from a brief holiday she had taken recently. Her heels were high, but still not high enough to bring her shoulder to shoulder to Giorgio when he appeared out of nowhere and put his hand to the small of her back.

She gave a little start and almost spilt her drink. 'What do you think you're doing sneaking up on me like that?' she said, sending him an irritated look.

'You look exquisite this evening, Maya,' he said as if she hadn't spoken. He leaned in closer and drew in a deep breath close to her neck. 'Mmm, you're wearing that new perfume again, are you not? It suits you.'

Maya scowled as she reared away from him. 'Go and mingle with your friends. Everyone will start talking if we're seen together. I don't want another press fest to deal with.'

He smiled a sinful smile, his dark eyes glinting at her. 'Let them talk. I can spend time with my soon-to-be ex-wife, can't I? Besides, we have business to discuss.'

Maya pressed her lips together. 'I haven't changed my mind about the villa. I sent the papers back to your lawyer. I am not going to let you pay me off with a lump sum. I told you what I want.'

'I know,' he said, scooping a glass of champagne off the tray of the passing waiter. He took a generous sip before he added, 'but here's the thing: I want it too.'

She looked up at him warily. 'We can't both have it, though, can we?'

His eyes locked on hers, hot and hard as steel. 'I have given it some thought. For the next twelve months I would like the villa to remain a private residence. No developments, no changes.'

She frowned. 'And after that?'

He took another sip of his champagne, his throat moving up and down slowly as he swallowed it, deliberately delaying his response, making her wait, making her feel unimportant, insignificant. 'After that, if you still want it you can buy it from my family,' he said.

Maya rolled her eyes. 'Oh, for pity's sake.'

'What's the matter, Maya?' he asked. 'I'm paying you a fortune in settlement. You'll have enough cash to buy ten villas.'

She stalked away from him. 'I don't want your stupid money.'

In an effort to move away from the interested glances aimed at her, Maya slipped out to a balcony accessed by French windows. She hadn't expected Giorgio to follow her out there but, before she could shut the doors behind her, he had stepped through them.

'Why are you being so difficult over this?' he asked, leaning back against the closed doors.

'*I* am being difficult?' she asked with an incredulous

look. 'You're the one who keeps sending legal documents the thickness of two phone books to me to sign.'

His forehead creased in a brooding frown. 'I have shareholders and investors to protect. Don't take it personally. It's just business.'

Maya put her glass of juice down on a pot stand before she dropped it. 'Oh, yes, it's always business with you. Our marriage was nothing more than a business arrangement. The only trouble was I didn't deliver the goods as promised.'

'What do you mean by that?' His voice was hard and sharp, like a flung dagger.

She dropped her gaze and let out a scratchy sigh. 'You know what I mean, Giorgio.'

A lengthy silence passed.

'I wanted it to work, Maya,' he said quietly. 'I really did, but we were both making each other miserable in the end.'

She looked up at him with a pained expression. 'You don't get it, do you?'

'What's to get?' he asked, his voice rising in frustration. 'We were married for five years, Maya. I know it wasn't easy for you. It wasn't easy for me, watching you...' He didn't finish the sentence but, moving away from the doors, lifted his glass and drained the contents.

Maya looked at his stiff spine, feeling the emotional lockout she always felt when they argued. He refused to talk about the losses they had experienced. She'd always had the feeling he had dismissed each miscarriage as nature's way of saying something was not right. She, on the other hand, had wanted to talk about each of the babies she had named as soon as they were conceived. She had wanted to talk about their stolen futures, the dreams and hopes she had had for each of them. To her, they were not a collection of damaged cells that nature had decided were best sloughed away. They had been her precious babies, each and every one of them.

Giorgio hated failure. He was a ruthlessly committed businessman who refused to tolerate defeat in any shape or form. Success drove him, as it had driven his grandfather and his late father to build the heritage that stood unrivalled in the world of luxury hotels. Giorgio had no time for life's annoying little hiccups. He wanted results and went about achieving them mercilessly if he had to. That was how Maya had ended up his wife. His father had just been injured in a terrible head-on collision and was lying in a semi-coma in hospital, not expected to live past a few weeks.

Giorgio had decided Maya would be an ideal candidate for a wife: educated, poised, young and healthy and in the prime of her reproductive life. How wrong he had been to choose her of all people, she thought bitterly. He could have done so much better, a fact some members of his family had hinted at over the last year or so. They were subtle about it, of course: an occasional comment over dinner about someone's newborn child or how one of Giorgio's school friends was now a father of twins. Each comment had been a stake through Maya's heart, worsening her sense of failure, shattering her self-confidence, destroying her hope of one day being a mother. She had failed as a Sabbatini wife. She had let the dynasty down and, until she got out of Giorgio's life, his family would continue to look upon her with pity and disappointment.

Giorgio put his glass down on the wrought iron table before he faced her. 'My grandfather is dying,' he said in a low, serious tone. 'He told me this morning. He has less than a month or two at most to live. No one else in the family knows.'

Maya felt her heart drop like a ship's anchor inside her chest. 'Oh, no...'

His throat rose and fell over a tight swallow. 'That's why he wanted all the family here tonight. He wanted tonight to be a happy celebration. He didn't want any-one's pity. He will make the announcement to family and friends in the next week or two.'

Maya could understand Salvatore's motivation in keeping tonight focused on his birthday instead of his impending demise. Pride was something she had come to recognise as a particular Sabbatini trait. Giorgio had it in buckets and barrels and spades. 'Thank you for tell-ing me,' she said softly, not quite understanding why he had. Why hadn't he told Luca and Nic, his two brothers, for instance?

His eyes were still meshed with hers. 'I want you to think about postponing your trip to London,' he said. 'Call the school and tell them you can't make the interview. Tell them you need to take compassionate leave.'

She stared at him, open-mouthed. 'I can't take leave before I've even got the job. They will give it to some-one else.'

He lifted a shoulder. 'If they do, then you weren't meant to have it. If they think you are the best one for the position they will wait until you are available.'

Maya frowned at him furiously. 'Of course they won't keep the job open for me. I'm the least experienced of the candidates. I haven't stood in front of a classroom since I was at university on teaching practice. I won't stand a chance if I don't turn up for the interview.'

'You don't need the job right at this moment, Maya,' he said. 'I have agreed on an incredibly generous allowance. If you want to work, then I am sure other jobs will come along in time.'

Maya threw him a castigating look. 'Why do you have to be so damned philosophical about everything?'

He returned her frown with a challenging arc of one brow. 'Why do you have to be so irrational and emotional?'

Maya turned away and looked out over the wintry gardens, her hands gripping the balustrade so tightly her knuckles ached. 'Is this really about your grandfather's health or an attempt to make me change my mind about the divorce?'

He didn't respond for so long she wondered if he had left her there, listening to the soft patter of the February raindrops.

'You can have your divorce, but not right now,' he said at last. 'I want my grandfather to die in peace, believing we have patched things up.'

Maya felt her heart slip like a stiletto on a slate of ice. She spun around and faced him again, her eyes wide with panic. 'You're asking me to come back and live with you as your wife?'

He held her look with enviable equanimity. 'For a month or two, that is all,' he said. 'It will make the end a lot easier for my grandfather. Our separation has upset him greatly. I had not realised how much until now.'

Maya resented the implication behind his words. 'So you're blaming *me* for his terminal illness, are you?'

His dark eyes rolled upwards in that arrogant way of his which seemed to say she was being childish and petty while he was mature and sensible. 'You are putting words into my mouth, Maya,' he said. 'My grandfather is ninety years old. It is not unexpected that he would be suffering from some sort of illness at his age. The fact that it is terminal is sad but not entirely unexpected. He has smoked rather heavily during his lifetime. He is lucky he has had as many years as he has. My father was not so blessed.'

She glared at him regardless. 'No doubt you think I have jinxed things for Salvatore or something. I announce I want a divorce and a few weeks later he is dying. I can see a pattern, even if you can't.'

A muscle twitched in the lower quadrant of his jaw. 'My father dying just a few days after we married was not your fault. It was no one's fault. It was just a tragic accident. You know that.'

'I wasn't talking about your father's death.'

His muscle moved again. 'Miscarriages are another fact of life, just like old age, Maya,' he said, barely moving his lips to speak. 'They are far more common than you think.'

Maya felt hot colour crawling beneath her skin and turned away again in case he noticed. 'If we resume living together it will only complicate and ultimately prolong our divorce,' she said after a slight pause. 'Everyone's hopes will be raised and then dashed again once we...go ahead with it in the end...'

'I realise that is something we will have to deal with,' he said. 'But, for the time being, I believe this is the best course of action.'

Maya faced him again with a lip curl of scorn. 'Why? Because it's going to give you more time to work out a way to keep your assets safe?'

He stared her down. 'You never used to be so cynical.'

She lifted her chin. 'I grew up, Giorgio. Life's repeated punches have a habit of doing that.'

He moved away to look out over the immaculate gardens as she had done moments earlier. His hands too, she noticed, were white-knuckled as he gripped not the balustrade as she had done, but the back of the wrought iron chair of the outdoor setting at least a metre away from the edge. Maya knew his fear of heights disgusted him, even though he had suffered from it since childhood. She had only found out about it by accident. He would never have told her, which said rather a lot about their relationship, she thought. He saw his fear as a weakness he had to conquer. Countless times, she had seen him fight with himself to overcome his primal reaction. His doggedness had at times both impressed her and frustrated her in equal measure. She had so often wanted to help him but he would push her away as if she had come too close, as if she would be the one to push him over the edge of the dark abyss he dreaded so much.

'I want my grandfather to die a peaceful death,' Giorgio said after a long taut silence. 'I will do anything to achieve it.'

Maya mentally ticked the box marked 'ruthless'. Giorgio would think nothing of doing whatever it took to get what he wanted, including resuming a relationship with a wife he had never loved and didn't really want now she had failed to live up to expectations, to use a particularly relevant word. He would no doubt live the lie, playing pretend while he got on with his affair with his gorgeous lingerie model.

Maya knew from experience that the press got it wrong a lot of times, but not *all* of the time. That was the thing that had plagued her the most. The 'no smoke without fire' thing had niggled at her the whole time they were married. Giorgio had always denied the occasional dalliances the press reported, but her doubts and fears had still risen to the surface like oil on water. She had waded for five years through the cloying stickiness, trying to cling to the hope that the conception and subsequent birth of a child would cement their tenuous union.

It had never happened.

She slid a hand over the flat plane of her belly, her heart giving a tight aching contraction.

It might *still* not happen...

Giorgio turned from the chair as someone came out

onto the balcony. 'Luca,' he said with a forced on-off smile. 'I didn't see you come in.'

Luca, his younger brother by two years, gave him a ready smile that lit his dark brown eyes from behind. 'We arrived late,' he said. 'Ella was a bit late having her afternoon sleep.'

He turned to Maya and bent to kiss her on both cheeks. 'It's so good you came tonight, Maya,' he said. 'Bronte will be glad of someone to talk to. She was feeling rather nervous about practising her Italian in front of everyone.'

Maya smiled shakily. 'She has no need to be,' she said. 'Everyone adores her and gorgeous little Ella.'

Luca smiled proudly. 'We have an announcement to make…' His expression faltered for a second before he continued, 'I'm sorry, this might not be the news you two want to hear, but we are expecting another baby.'

A silence thickened the air for a nanosecond.

Maya was the first to respond. 'Luca, that's truly wonderful news. I am so happy for you both. When is it due?'

'I'm not sure,' Luca said, looking a bit sheepish. 'We've only just done one of those home kit tests. It's all still a little bit unreal, to be frank.'

Tell me about it, Maya thought wryly.

Giorgio gave his brother a firm handshake, anchoring it with a grasp of Luca's forearm. 'I am very pleased for you. It will be delightful to have another niece or nephew to spoil.'

Luca appeared relieved his announcement had gone down so well. 'So,' he said, still smiling, his eyes this time full of intrigue. 'What are you two doing out here all alone?'

Another silence hovered like humidity before a storm.

Giorgio was the first to break it. 'Maya and I have an announcement of our own to make.' He put his arm around her waist and drew her into his side. 'We have decided to reconcile. There will be no divorce.'

Maya's eyes flew to his, her mouth opening but nothing coming out. The weight of his arm around her waist was like a chain, tying her to him just as effectively as his words.

Luca looked from one to the other with a spreading smile. 'That's wonderful news. Have you told *Nonno*? It will be the best birthday present for him.'

Giorgio smiled smugly. 'We are just about to do so now, aren't we, *cara*?' he said, looking down at Maya.

Maya wanted to deny it. She wanted to tell Luca his brother was a manipulating, ruthless man who would stop at nothing to keep what he wanted in his possession. But she knew if she did it would quite possibly ruin Salvatore's party. The old man was dying and Luca was right: the announcement of the reconciliation between his eldest grandson and his estranged wife would make his day.

Instead, she gave Luca a weak smile. 'It's all happened so suddenly...'

Luca grinned at his brother. 'I have to tell Bronte. She'll be so thrilled. This calls for more champagne.'

He picked up Giorgio's empty glass and then moved to where Maya had left her half-drunk orange juice. He picked it up and, after a moment, turned and looked at her quizzically. 'Not currently on the hard stuff, Maya?'

Maya felt the weight of Giorgio's gaze. 'I...I guess over the years I've got used to not drinking,' she said.

'You will have to make up for it tonight,' Luca said and, with another beaming smile, left through the French windows to find his young wife and child.

'Luca is right,' Giorgio said after what seemed an endless pause. 'This is indeed a night for celebration.'

Maya threw him a barbed glare. 'How could you lie to your own brother like that? This is a farce and you know it.'

He gave a movement of his mouth that communicated total indifference to her opinion. 'This is about making my grandfather's last weeks or months of life as comfortable and happy as possible,' he said. 'You said you wanted the villa at Bellagio.' He gave her an indomitable look and added, 'Believe me, Maya, this is the only way you are going to get it.'

CHAPTER THREE

MAYA fumed as she left the balcony with Giorgio's arm planted firmly around her waist. Even more guests had arrived and a couple of camera flashes went off. She wondered if Giorgio had primed the select members of the press present to give her no chance of denying the announcement of their reconciliation. She would look a complete and utter fool if she said anything to the contrary now. After all, she had spent the whole time so far with him out on the balcony. People had already started talking.

'Stop grinding your teeth, *mio piccolo*,' he said in an undertone as they moved through to where Salvatore was seated like a king in the main *salone*.

Maya kept her lips pressed together, her words coming out like hard pellets. 'You set this up, didn't you? You set me up so I couldn't say no. You knew I would not want to spoil your grandfather's party and you deliberately played on that.'

His arm tightened like a band of steel around her waist. It was a possessive touch but also a warning. 'Play along with it, Maya,' he said. 'Look at *Nonno*. He is enjoying himself so much. Our announcement on top of Luca and Bronte's will be the icing on the cake—literally.'

The announcement hardly needed to be made formally for as soon as they walked into the *salone* all heads turned. There were whispers and gasps, nudges and did-you-see-that looks. More camera flashes went off and then Salvatore looked directly at Giorgio and Maya and his old weathered face broke into a rapturous smile.

'Is this what I think it is, Giorgio?' he asked, tears glistening in his eyes. 'You and Maya have changed your mind about divorcing?'

Maya felt Giorgio's hand reach for hers and squeeze it gently. 'Yes, *Nonno*,' he said. 'We have called it off. We are going to work at our marriage.'

Salvatore grasped Maya's free hand and almost crushed it between both of his gnarled ones. 'Maya, you and my grandson have made me such a happy man tonight. I cannot tell you what this means to me. All my family is here around me to share this wonderful news.'

Maya could feel the bars of her gilded cage moving in on her, just as they had done for the last five years. She was trapped in a charade that went against everything she believed in. She felt such a fraud, playing to the crowd and most especially to Salvatore. She wasn't sure she could get through a night of it, let alone a few weeks. Surely someone would see it for what it was? The press were already eyeing her rather closely, she thought, or maybe that was her imagination. She had always found the intrusion of the press rather difficult to deal with. It was so different from her anonymous upbringing, when even her great-aunt had barely noticed her.

More champagne was called for and more and more cameras documented the celebration. Luca and Bronte announced their delightful news which, in Maya's mind, deserved far more attention than theirs, but it seemed everyone was intrigued by the news of the acrimonious Sabbatini divorce being called off.

Giorgio's mother greeted Maya with guarded enthusiasm. Maya understood Giovanna's caution; she had made things difficult for her son by bickering over every little detail to do with their separation, but Giovanna was gracious enough to welcome her back into the family fold. Besides, her mother-in-law was thrilled to finally be a grandmother. She doted on little Ella and, with the news of Bronte's new pregnancy, Giovanna was clearly preoccupied with the new branch of the family tree.

Nicolò, or Nic as he was more commonly called, the youngest of the Sabbatini brothers, was less accommodating. He adopted his usual sardonic expression as he approached Maya after Giorgio had gone to fetch another glass of juice for her.

'So it seems you changed your mind after reacquainting yourself with how the other half lives, eh, Maya?' he said. 'Glad you came to your senses. You weren't going to come out in front, not with Giorgio's legal team working on it.'

Maya kept her expression coolly contained, even though inside she felt furious at being reminded of how outmatched she had been right from the start. 'Hello, Nic,' she said. 'How are things with you?'

He rocked his almost empty champagne flute back and forth, his hazel eyes penetrating as they held hers. 'Fine enough,' he said.

She looked around his broad shoulders for signs of a current date. 'What? No Hollywood starlet tonight?' she asked with a mocking lift of her brows.

Nic gave her a crooked wry smile that reminded her of Giorgio in one of his rare playful moods. 'No, I didn't think *Nonno* would approve of my latest lover. He mentioned the "M" word a few moments ago. It was enough to turn me to drink.'

'You're only what…thirty-two?' she asked.

He nodded rather grimly. 'You know the Sabbatini rule. Once you turn thirty, you are meant to settle down.'

'Luca has only just done so at thirty-four,' Maya said. 'You shouldn't rush into these things. You could end up making a mistake.'

He rocked his glass again, his eyes still boring into hers. 'Like you did?'

The words hung in the air like a swinging sword.

'I don't consider my marriage to your brother to have ever been a mistake,' Maya said, wishing she really believed it. 'We just hit a rough patch, that's all.'

Giorgio came over at that moment and handed Maya a glass of juice. He must have picked up on the atmosphere, for he narrowed his gaze at his youngest brother. 'I hope you are keeping your thoughts and opinions on marriage to yourself, Nic,' he said. 'I don't want Maya upset by your teasing.'

Nic's smile was instantly charming. 'I was just

welcoming her back into the family,' he said. His expression became a little more serious as he addressed Maya directly. 'I hope it works out for you. I mean that, Maya.'

Maya wondered if he somehow sensed her insecurity. He was an out-and-out playboy—everyone knew about his wild child antics as a teenager and young adult—but the outcome of that madcap lifestyle had given him an almost intuitive sense at times. He had grown up a lot after the tragic death of his father, but it was common knowledge in the family that his mother and his grandfather in particular wanted him to settle down with a suitable wife, which was something Nic made it clear he was not prepared to do. He was a free spirit and hated being tied down. Even within the family corporation, he was the one who had been given the most flexibility. Nic was the one who travelled the world, hardly settling in one place longer than a week or two as he acquired property and oversaw the redevelopments of their hotel chain.

'Thank you, Nic,' she said. 'I aim to give it my very best shot.'

After a few more desultory exchanges with other guests and family members, Giorgio led her away to a quiet corner. He was aware of how strained she looked. Her face looked pale and he had noticed she had surreptitiously mopped at her brow a couple of times, as if she was finding it too warm. 'Don't take any notice of Nic,' he said, watching as his younger brother started chatting up a stunning redhead near the buffet table.

'Nic is Nic,' she said in a downbeat voice.

'Yes, indeed.' Giorgio sighed and looked down at Maya. 'You look tired. It's been a long night. Do you want me to take you home?'

Her fingers slipped on the glass she was holding and he took it from her before she dropped it. 'Sorry,' she said, glancing up at him self-consciously before looking away again, her teeth sinking into her bottom lip.

He studied her for a moment, wondering if he should have given her more warning about his intentions. Dropping it on her like that out on the balcony had obviously shocked her. But he was still reeling himself from his grandfather's revelation. Salvatore had always seemed so ageless to Giorgio. In spite of his weathered skin and arthritic body, his mind was sharp and he still had an active role in the corporation. Giorgio felt humbled by the trust his grandfather had shown in him by telling him first about his illness. Ever since the death of Giorgio's father, Giancarlo, Salvatore had entrusted more and more responsibility on Giorgio's shoulders. It would be very hard to say that final goodbye to the man who was not just his grandfather but his business partner and friend.

Maya too would find it hard. She had developed a special kind of relationship with Salvatore over the five years of their marriage. She had grown up in a single parent household but then tragically, when she was just ten years old, her mother had been killed in an accident. Maya had been brought up by a great-aunt who had never married and had no children of her own. Maya hadn't spoken much about her childhood. She seemed to find it painful so Giorgio mostly had avoided the topic.

He had been delighted when Maya had expressed her avid desire to have children. It was one of the things that made him so determined she was the one he should marry. When the first couple of pregnancies had ended in a miscarriage he had been upset, but out of concern for Maya he had concealed his feelings. He hadn't wanted her to think she had let him down. He knew she had blamed herself, wondering if there was something wrong with her for not being able to have a child. It was only after the fourth miscarriage had occurred that he wondered if somehow it was him that was causing the trouble. But subsequent tests had shown that he was fine, although sometimes he still worried.

And then Maya had stopped falling pregnant altogether. They had done everything they were told to do. They kept temperature charts, Maya mapped her ovulation period and they had sex when she was supposedly most fertile, but still she'd failed to conceive.

The progression to IVF was something he had not felt entirely comfortable with. It all seemed so clinical, nothing like the sex they used to have when they'd first met. Nothing like the sex they had the night of Luca and Bronte's wedding.

His body tightened as he recalled that night. He hadn't cared about anything other than having her as quickly and as passionately as he could. It had been the best sex of his life and he wanted more. He had realised that the day he had gone to her flat to invite her to the party. He had gone there thinking their one-night stand would have cooled his ardour. He had been confident he could have seen her, talked to her and even touched her without feeling a thing. He had been shocked to find out how wrong he was. Putting his hands on her shoulders had sent zapping wires of electric want through him. He wanted Maya as he wanted no other woman. How could he have forgotten how fantastic it was with her? His body had tingled for hours afterwards. He only had to look at her and his blood raced through his veins and made him rock-hard.

He was feeling it now, standing so close to her, breathing in her sexy new fragrance: flowery but spicy and exotic at the same time. The dress she was wearing brought out the glow of her skin and the platinum blond of her hair. She had left it loose this evening, the way he most liked it. Before he even realised he was doing it, he reached out and threaded his fingers through the silk of it where it lay about her shoulders.

She gave a little shudder of reaction and looked up at him. 'Do you have to do that?' she asked in an undertone.

'We are supposed to be reconciled, *cara*,' he said, taking the opportunity to brush his lips against her forehead. 'People will expect us to touch each other in public. They will imagine we will be doing much more when we are finally at home alone.'

'Where is home supposed to be now?' she asked in a soft breathless sort of voice. 'Your place or mine?'

Giorgio shifted his mouth ruefully as he straightened. 'My place, or what used to be our place, is not quite ready. I've been staying at the hotel most nights. We will have to stay at yours tonight, otherwise the press will not believe we are truly reunited.'

'You think they will follow to check up on us?' she asked with a worried frown.

He gave her a wry look. 'Surely you haven't forgotten what the press is like. Haven't they been on your tail over the last six months of our separation?'

Maya captured her lip between her teeth, thinking of all the times she'd had to get away from the intrusive eyes of the press. That ridiculous 'date' with Howard Herrington was a case in point. They had blown it right out of proportion with a photograph that looked far more intimate than it was. She had been leaning forward, trying to catch something Howard had been saying and a flashbulb had captured the moment, making it appear she was about to press a kiss close to Howard's mouth. When it appeared in the gossip pages the following day she had taken a devil-may-care approach to the fallout. There had been a photo only a week earlier of Giorgio with his model friend. It seemed fitting that Maya had started to reclaim her life, even if Howard Herrington was the worst date she had ever had.

Maya cast her eyes over the crowd. The party was in full swing now; several couples were dancing as the band played some classic dance hits. She remembered the days when she had danced in Giorgio's arms; he had swung her around and around and even though her head had been left spinning she had always gone back for more. The early days of their courtship and marriage had been so much fun, so dizzyingly exciting for a girl who had grown up with so little. There had been no parties that she could remember during her childhood, no massive family gatherings, no huge celebrations of her own or anyone else's milestones or achievements.

As soon as she had met Giorgio she had clung to him and his family, subconsciously looking for the anchor she had lacked for much of her life. She had slotted in like a small sea-tossed craft into a safe and sheltered harbour.

She had never wanted to be cast adrift.

She had done that herself.

But now the rules had been changed. She was back, but only temporarily. Giorgio wanted her to pretend things were back to normal and she could do that for a few weeks, maybe even a month or two. The chances were her pregnancy would disappear down the drain of despair, just like the others had done. All she had to do was keep it a secret until Giorgio's game of pretend was over. There was no point in getting his hopes up as well as hers, or anyone else's for that matter.

Maya's heart ached at the thought of Salvatore dying. He was such a vitally alive man. He was the last of the great patriarchs. He liked the authority his position warranted as the elder of the tribe. She had learned a lot watching the family dynamics over the past five years. The meshing of different personalities, the way each son was cast from the same mould but still so very different. Giorgio was more like his grandfather than anyone. She suspected that was why Salvatore had told him about his illness first. Salvatore knew Giorgio would have the strength to carry the rest of the family through such a difficult time. He would watch over the family finances, he would steer a steady course instead of wavering about in panic. He would grieve certainly, but in private. He would not need anyone to support him.

He never had.

Giorgio led her to say their goodbyes to his grandfather and his mother. There were more congratulatory comments, more camera flashes and an even bigger smile from Salvatore as he gripped his eldest grandson's hand in his. 'You have made me a very happy man, Giorgio. I hoped and prayed you would not give up on your marriage. I knew you would win her back once you put your mind to it.'

Maya stretched her lips into a smile as Salvatore turned his attention to her.

'Maya, you are good for my grandson. You bring out the human, more softer side of him. Don't give up on him, *mio piccolo*. You remind me of my adored wife, Maria. She was so strong, even though like you she looked so petite and fragile. Just like her, you have backbone. I knew it from the first moment I met you.'

'I hope you enjoy the rest of your party,' Maya said, leaning forward to kiss him on both cheeks. She brushed at the tears that had sprung from her eyes and added, 'I love you.'

Salvatore smiled indulgently as she stood back with Giorgio's arm looping around her waist. 'I have never doubted it,' he said. 'Now, go home with your husband and convince him of the same.'

CHAPTER FOUR

'WE CAN'T possibly live together in this small flat,' Maya said as she opened the villa door a short time later.

Gonzo was bouncing up and down, his tail going like a metronome on twelve eight time, not unlike the rate of Maya's heartbeat.

Giorgio closed the door after waving off a car that had tailed the limousine that had brought them home. He turned and scratched behind Gonzo's ears before straightening to face her. 'Why not?' he asked. 'It has a bed, does it not?'

Maya felt her stomach flip over. 'Y…yes, but only the one.'

He gave an up and down lift of his brows that sent another shockwave through her belly. 'Then we will have to share it.'

She took a step backwards, her hands going up to ward him off. 'No way,' she said. 'There is no way I am sharing my bed with you. You can sleep on the sofa.'

He glanced at the cheap sofa she had picked up in a second-hand sale in one of her staunch attempts to move away from the wealth he took for granted, having had it all of his life. His lip curled in disdain, as she knew it would. 'I wouldn't let Gonzo sleep on that,' he said. 'Anyway, how do you expect to fit the whole six foot four of me on that thing?'

Maya gave her head a little toss and began to move away. 'Not my problem.'

One of his hands captured her like a cobra striking out at its prey. One minute she was free, the next she was standing up against the hard wall of his body, his dark eyes burning like embers as they held hers. 'I think you might have missed something in our conversation earlier, Maya,' he said in a deep silky voice. 'This reconciliation of ours is not just a show for the press.'

Maya felt her eyes widen and her heart gave another uncoordinated sprint. 'What do you mean?' She swallowed a tight knot of panic in her throat. 'You surely don't want to…to…' She swallowed again when she saw the way his eyes darkened even further.

Oh, dear God, he did.

One of his hands began stroking the length of her forearm, back and forth in a mesmerising movement that was loaded with erotic sensuality. Her skin leapt at his touch, her spine went to water and her inner core contracted as if he were already driving through her hot moistness to brand her as his.

'We might as well make the most of the situation,' he said into the throbbing silence. 'What do you say? Shall we see if we can still do it like we did the night of Luca and Bronte's wedding?'

Maya tried to pull out of his hold but it was like trying to disengage from a steel trap. 'Th…this is not what I agreed to…' she said, trying to keep her voice steady and controlled. 'I thought we were just acting, you know... out in public. Not in private. Not when we're alone.'

His fingers had found her pulse at her wrist and his caress slowed to a drugging pace that made her brain turn the rational and sensible switch to irrational and impulsive. She was in danger of betraying everything she had worked so hard over the last six months to achieve: independence, confidence and immunity. She wasn't immune and that was the biggest shock of all. She had never quite got there in terms of invulnerability and quite possibly never would. He only had to look at her in that brooding all male way of his and she felt her whole body turn into a wanton needy mess.

He pulled her even closer against him, letting her feel the heat of his arousal. 'You know we could never share a flat or villa, no matter how big or small, without it coming to this,' he said in that spine-tingling gravel-rough tone he always used when he wanted sex. Not pre-planned sex, not sex with a jar or to a meticulous timetable, but sex when everything that their bodies wanted and craved was paramount.

Like at his brother's wedding.

Like now...

Maya had to scramble mentally to regain lost ground. She was in a vulnerable period of this surprise pregnancy. All the medical advice she had received in the past was no sex until the three-month mark, just to be safe. Not that she had ever got there—the three-month mark, that was. Giorgio had been so good about it— perhaps *too* good about it. It had often made her wonder if he had simply taken his needs elsewhere when she had been unavailable. Maya knew about his father's well documented affairs in the early years of his marriage to Giovanna. Of course, since his untimely death he had been enshrined as a saint but, according to what Maya had heard, he had been anything but. Was it a case of like father like son? Luca was a bit of an unknown to her, but Nic was certainly everything a playboy should be, just as Giorgio had been before they had married.

'I don't want to sleep with you, Giorgio,' Maya said with as much firmness as she could muster. It wasn't much: a bit like a Chihuahua trying to round up a herd of wildebeest, she thought.

'You know you don't mean that,' he said, his warm coffee-scented breath caressing her face just as sensually as his thumb was now doing over her leaping pulse.

'I...I do,' she said, gulping over another tight swallow.

His expression hardened, as if his blood supply had suddenly released a shot of cynicism into his veins. 'Herbert wouldn't approve of a bit of ex-sex?' he taunted.

Maya cringed all over again at how stupid she had been to use that poor lonely man as a payback for Giorgio's sexual exploits. 'Howard,' she said through gritted teeth. 'His name is Howard and I didn't sleep with him.'

Giorgio laughed but his thumb didn't stop on her wrist. 'Poor Howard. He probably didn't get much time for sleeping. Not with you in his bed.'

Maya glared at him. 'What about your lingerie

model? Did you manage to get any sleep while you were with her?'

'I did, actually,' he said, bending down to nibble at one of her ears. 'She bored me to tears.'

Maya angled her head away, arching so much she felt a pain in her back and, before she could stop it, let out a little sharp cry. 'Ow!'

Giorgio released his hold, just using his hands to keep her upright. '*Cara*, what's wrong? Did I hurt you?' he asked, frowning with dark seriousness.

She shook her head and eased out of his loose hold, rubbing at her lower back. 'It's nothing,' she said, not quite meeting his eyes. 'I think I may have overstretched myself in my yoga class.'

'Let me massage it for you,' he offered.

Oh, no, Maya thought. That would be asking for more trouble than she needed right now. 'I'm fine, really. I just need a hot bath or something.'

'Where's the bathroom?' he said. 'I'll run it for you.'

Maya looked at him with suspicion. 'What's with the loving husband routine?' she asked. 'No one's watching, Giorgio. There are no paparazzi cameras peering through the windows.' *Thank God*, she added mentally.

His mouth tightened around the edges. 'Must you always misread my motives? I am merely doing what I would do for anyone.'

Maya gave him a scornful look. 'Oh, yes, anyone you were trying to seduce into your bed, that is.'

He muttered something under his breath that sounded

very much like a very rude word but she didn't stay around to confirm it. She stalked through to the kitchen, opening and then banging the cupboard door shut as she got out a glass for water. She turned on the tap and filled the glass and, once it was full, turned and leaned back against the sink to steady her shaking legs.

Giorgio followed her into the room which, prior to this moment, had seemed of a reasonable size. Now, with him standing there within touching distance, Maya instantly downgraded it to a kitchenette.

'You sound jealous, Maya,' he said, leaning against the opposite counter, his feet crossed over at the ankles in an indolent manner.

Maya drained her glass and set it on the sink with a little clatter. 'Why should I be jealous?' she asked. 'We were officially separated for six months. We were both free agents. You could sleep with whomever you liked. So could I.'

Her answer appeared to annoy him, as that tiny hammer of tension began beating beneath the skin at the edge of his mouth. 'Exactly how many times did you see this Hugh?' he asked.

'Howard.' Maya rolled her eyes in annoyance. 'H.O.W.A.R.D. Howard.'

'You didn't answer my question.'

'And I am not going to,' she said, pushing herself away from the sink. 'Firstly, it's none of your business and, secondly, I don't want all the details of who you've been seeing, that is, of course, assuming you haven't lost count by now.'

'You, of all people, should know you can't take what is written in the press as gospel,' he said.

She gave him an ironic arch of her brows. 'Funny that you don't adhere to your own philosophy on that issue, isn't it? But then, there is always one rule for you and another one for everyone else.'

'Maya, this is getting us nowhere,' he said, uncrossing his ankles and straightening. He expelled his breath on a sigh and sent one of his hands through his hair. 'You are exhausted. You look as if a sneeze from me would send you through that wall there to the next room. Why don't you go to bed? I will make do on the sofa.'

Maya hesitated. He would not get a wink of sleep on that sofa and they both knew it. Why he was being so chivalrous about it was beyond her. The old Giorgio would have had her flat on her back by now, sending her to paradise for the second, if not the third or fourth, time. Just thinking about it brought hot colour to her cheeks. Her body was so aware of him; each time he moved, another part of her would register it and respond. How she wanted to close that small distance between them and throw herself into his arms, begging him to take her back, to love her, even if she couldn't ever provide him with an heir. But that small distance of a few cracked and faded tiles might as well have been a canyon.

'It's just for tonight,' Giorgio said. 'I don't think I could bear any longer than that in this dump. What were you thinking, renting something like this?'

Maya folded her arms and looked at him drolly. 'I am surprised you can speak so clearly with all those silver spoons sticking out of your mouth.'

He laughed again, but this time it wasn't mocking like before. It was the sort of laugh she had heard so rarely from him over the past five years. The sort of laugh that made her spine fizz, as if a fairy was tiptoeing its way over each of her vertebrae to dance amongst the tiny hairs at the back of her neck.

'Maya,' he said, his expression suddenly turning serious once more, 'I know the difference in our upbringings has always been an issue for you. I can do nothing to change that. It is just what is. You should be grateful I can provide for you. So many women suffer financially as a result of a divorce. Once our marriage is finally over you will be richer than you could ever have been as a teacher, even if you ended up at the top of the academic ladder.'

Maya felt her heart sink at the when-not-if approach he was taking to the divorce. She knew she only had herself to blame—she had been the one to instigate the separation, but still...

He closed the distance before she could move away, his hand coming down on the top of one of her shoulders before moving to the sensitive nape of her neck. 'Tomorrow we will move back into my villa,' he said. 'It doesn't matter if the curtains are not quite finished and the paint not quite dry. At least we will have more space and privacy there.'

Maya tried not to be affected by his touch but it was impossible to ignore the way her body was automatically leaning towards him like a compass point. How long before she would betray herself all over again? If he kissed her now it would be so hard to resist him. Her lips ached for the press of his. She had to bit her tongue to stop it sweeping out to deposit a layer of moisture to them in case he saw how much she wanted him to reach for her.

'What about the household staff?' she asked, thinking of the veritable droves of people who hovered about, waiting upon every need. It was yet another one of the things that had driven her crazy towards the end. The constant speculative glances at her belly and then the raised brows whenever she and Giorgio exchanged a few heated words, as any normal married couple did at times. The trouble was, they hadn't lived a normal married life. They had lived in a fish bowl—a very expensive fish bowl that, over five years, had become an oversized, overstaffed, overstocked aquarium.

Giorgio's hand dropped from her nape and he thrust it, along with his other one, into his trouser pocket. 'I have simplified my life a bit,' he said. 'I took on board what you said in one of our arguments towards the end. The villa was starting to feel more like a Sabbatini hotel than a home. I had grown up with servants so it seemed normal to me, but I can see now how you would find it intrusive. After all, you spent far more time there than me, due to my work commitments.'

Maya could barely believe her ears. She looked at him for a long moment, her forehead wrinkling as she thought about how his life would surely soon slip back into billionaire-with-everyone-at-his-beck-and-call mode.

He smiled crookedly. 'You don't believe me, do you,

cara? What's the problem? Can't you picture me doing my own cooking?'

'I can see you doing the celebrity chef thing in the kitchen,' she said. 'But, as for pushing a vacuum cleaner or a mop about the place, not to mention doing the laundry, well, no, quite frankly, I can't.'

'I haven't quite offloaded all the housework,' he said with a lingering smile. 'But Carita, my new housekeeper, only comes in twice a week and only for half a day.'

'Is she young and beautiful?' Maya asked, mentally picturing a lingerie model clone flouncing around the villa, wearing nothing but a pair of high heeled fluffy mules and carrying a pink feather duster in her perfectly manicured hand.

Giorgio took one of his hands out of his pocket and traced a barely touching caress down the curve of her cherry-red cheek, his gaze dark and intense as it held hers. 'You really are jealous, aren't you?'

Maya put up her chin but she couldn't quite bring herself to move away from his touch. 'Maybe, but then so are you. You keep harping on about Howard as if I was about to marry him as soon as our divorce is final.'

A flicker of something dark and dangerous moved behind his gaze. The ensuing silence was tense and unbroken for long pulsing seconds that to Maya felt like years.

But then, just as suddenly, it was over.

'Are you thinking of marrying again?' he asked as he stepped back from her.

'I haven't thought much about it,' she said and, taking a painful breath, added, 'What about you?'

He looked at her and then looked away again. 'There is not the same pressure on me now that Luc and Bronte have settled here with Ella and their future child. When our divorce is final I will have more time to think about what I want in terms of a relationship, or even if I want one at all.'

'So you won't be marrying for the sake of convenience next time around, I take it?' she asked with an arch look.

'It was convenient for both of us, Maya,' he said as a frown settled between his brows. 'I gave you everything I could. You wanted for nothing. I made sure of it. Our relationship ran its course. There was nothing either of us could do about it.'

You could have loved me, Maya thought. *Then maybe our relationship would have had a chance.*

Giorgio drew in a deep breath and slowly released it. 'I need to get some sleep and so do you. You wouldn't happen to have a spare toothbrush, would you? I didn't think to pack anything.'

'I think there's one in one of the bathroom basin drawers,' she said. 'There are fresh towels on the rail.'

Giorgio moved past her and went up the narrow staircase, stooping as the steps changed direction halfway up. The bathroom made him feel like a giant. He had to bend almost double to examine his reflection in the mirror. He looked every bit as tired as Maya looked, he thought. And, yes, she was right: he was every bit as jealous, if not more so. He hadn't even slept with that airheaded lingerie girl, not that she hadn't been keen. The opportunity had been there but he hadn't taken it.

He had sent her on her way and downed half a bottle of whisky instead.

He breathed out a sigh, not really wanting to think about that particular headache, and opened the drawer beneath the basin. It was filled with the usual female bathroom paraphernalia: cotton tips, tweezers, tampons, tissues and a brand new toothbrush, still in its packet.

And then his eyes zeroed in on something else…

CHAPTER FIVE

MAYA was making up the sofa as best she could with a spare blanket and a pillow when she sensed rather than heard Giorgio come in. The hairs on the back of her neck rose and even Gonzo dropped to his belly and gave a little doggy whimper, just like he did when a particularly nasty storm was approaching.

'Maya.'

She turned from smoothing out the blanket and came face to face with Giorgio's thunderous expression. Her eyes flared in panic when she saw what was in his right hand. Her heart knocked against her ribcage as if someone had shoved it from behind and her mouth went completely dry, so dry she had to brush her tongue out over her lips. 'I…You weren't supposed to find that…' *God, how awful that sounded*, she thought in anguish.

He put the positive dipstick down with careful precision on the small coffee table near the sofa. It was like laying down a challenge. It lay in the space between them accusingly, threateningly, dividing them, Maya thought, when it should have been uniting them.

'When were you going to tell me about this?' he asked with diamond-hard eyes.

She sent the tip of her tongue out again to loosen her lips enough to speak. 'I...I didn't think it was worth telling you because—'

'Because it's not mine?' He cut her off savagely.

Maya's mouth dropped open. She couldn't speak for the shockwave of hurt that smashed over her. She shuddered with it. She even felt as if she would collapse with it. Bright lights like thousands of silverfish darted in front of her eyes and she had to grasp the end of the sofa to steady herself. His reaction was something she had not expected—not even for a moment had she anticipated such a response from him. How could he think that of her? But then she recalled the way the press had handled her one date since their breakup. Of course he would automatically assume the child was not his. After all, they had been unable to conceive for years. It would be all too easy to assume someone else had got her pregnant. She bit her lip as she thought about things from Giorgio's perspective. She felt ashamed that her focus had always been on how *she* felt about not getting or staying pregnant. She hadn't really asked him what he felt about it. Had he felt less of a man? Had he felt less potent, less virile because he hadn't been able to fulfil what he saw as one of his primary roles as a husband?

Giorgio swung away and paced the room, or at least with what little space allowed for his long legs. He stopped after a moment and faced her, his expression so full of loathing Maya actually cringed. 'Were you hoping to pass it off as mine?' he asked. 'Was that what that night was all about after my brother's wedding? You know, I did think at the time how it was a little out of character for you. You were the one so insistent on a divorce and then there you were, tearing my clothes off.'

'I didn't tear your clothes off.' It wasn't much of a comeback or a defence but it was all Maya could think of at the time. 'We were both almost fully dressed apart from…you know…'

Giorgio sent her a livid glare. 'No, you didn't bother with the preliminaries. It was all about getting laid as quickly and as thoroughly as possible so you could get your insurance policy in place.'

Maya wrung her hands for the want of something better to do. 'It wasn't like that, Giorgio…'

'Damn it; what was it like?' he demanded furiously.

It was wonderful, it was just like the old times and it was spontaneous and passionate and totally unforgettable, but she couldn't tell him that. 'I never intended sleeping with you that night,' she said. 'The thought never crossed my mind.' *Liar*, her conscience prodded her. It was just as he had said the other day. She had thought of nothing else from the moment she had walked into the church and seen him standing next to his brother. It had reminded her so much of their wedding, how excited she had been, how gorgeously handsome Giorgio had looked and how she had been so proud to be his chosen wife, even if he hadn't once openly declared he loved her.

No wonder she had consumed one too many glasses of champagne at his brother's reception. No wonder she had been so unguarded when he'd suggested they go up to his room to discuss the terms of the divorce. What a silly fool she had been. He had set the scene for seduction, not her. How ironic that he had twisted things round to blame her for the consequences.

Giorgio stabbed a finger at her. 'You are a calculating little gold-digger,' he said. 'I am not the fool you take me for. How could this child possibly be mine when for two and a half years I have not been able to get you pregnant?' He changed the stabbing motion to a numerical one. '*Two and a half years*, Maya.' He underlined the words with his biting tone. 'Do you know how many times we had sex during that time?'

Maya was close to tears but pride would not allow her to give in to them. 'You are the father, Giorgio, but my advice is to enjoy it while it lasts because it might not last much longer.'

His throat moved up and down as if he was trying to swallow a boulder. 'What are you saying?'

She met his frowning gaze with her glistening one. 'I am six weeks pregnant. I have never gone past eight weeks, you know that. Most doctors say twelve weeks is the time to stop holding your breath; others say fourteen.'

Six weeks. Giorgio did the maths in his head. He wasn't the financial controller of the Sabbatini Corporation for nothing. His stomach clenched as if a cruel pair of sharp-edged tongs had snatched at his insides.

Six weeks.

One thousand and eight hours ago.

The night of Luca and Bronte's wedding, the night

when he had lost all control and taken Maya like a whore, not even bothering to make sure she got home safely. He had sent her on her way without a word. Pride had kept him silent. He hadn't wanted to beg her to stay the night, to stay another night and the night after that. But he had sent her away because that was what she had wanted. Damn it, it was what they had both wanted. They'd been desperately unhappy, sniping at each other at every turn. Sure, she was the one who'd insisted on bringing an end to their marriage, but it would only have been a matter of time when he would have got around to it.

But, if they were expecting a child, how could he possibly agree to a divorce now? He had been stalling over the divorce, making things as difficult for her as possible, not just because of what he stood to lose financially, although, as financial controller of a large corporation, he could not discount it. It was the sense of defeat he hated. He had failed to keep his marriage on track. He had failed to give her a child, the child they both desperately wanted. Their marriage had died and he hadn't been able to stop it. He had a list of excuses, which were all valid in their own way: the death of his father, the added responsibility that had put on his shoulders and then the fertility problems he and Maya had encountered. All had conspired against him to bring him to this impasse. Maya was on one side, wanting what she could get before she got out of his life for good, and he was on the other, wondering if there was anything he could have done differently.

The first thing he had to do was retract his appallingly

cruel accusation. What was he thinking, accusing her of such behaviour when she had never shown any sign of it in the past? For the whole time they were married she had been faithful, even in the face of the scurrilous rumours that from time to time circulated around him when he travelled. It was the one thing he admired about her, the way her moral code was so unlike those of many of her peers. He had been her first lover and he had never forgotten how precious that moment had been for them both.

He cleared his throat, feeling like a schoolboy instead of a thirty-six-year-old man in charge of a billion euro corporation. 'Maya,' he began, 'I don't know how to say this but I want—'

The flash of her grey eyes cut him off mid-sentence. 'I am not consenting to a paternity test. Not until after the birth, if there is one. It's too risky.'

Giorgio felt another dagger point of guilt slice at his gut. 'I am not asking for a paternity test.'

'Y…you're not?' Her wary look wounded him all over again.

'No,' he said. 'If you say the child is mine, then it is mine. The timing is spot on, in any case. And I didn't use any protection. It has to be my child.'

She turned away in disgust. 'So what you're really saying is if there was any doubt over the time frame you would be marching me off to some laboratory for a test.' She threw him a contemptuous look over her shoulder. 'God, you're such a heartless bastard, Giorgio.'

Giorgio took that direct hit because he knew he deserved it. Over the last six months of their bitter separation he had started to see a side to Maya he had not realised she had possessed. She was a lot feistier than he had accounted for previously. She had always seemed so demure, so acquiescent, and yet over the time of their drawn-out estrangement he had seen her toughen up and fight back in a way that he found strangely arousing.

'It was a shock to find the test like that,' he said. 'You know I don't like surprises. I didn't have the time to think it through.'

He pushed his hair back from his forehead, reminding himself he needed to get it cut. Maya used to do it for him once. When had she stopped? He couldn't quite remember. He used to love the feel of her fingers running through his hair as she snipped away at it. She had chatted to him as she went about her task, giggling at his dry asides until the haircut inevitably turned into something else entirely.

But that was back in the early days…

She turned around to face him but her stance was defensive. Her arms were across her middle but he couldn't stop his eyes dropping to her still flat belly. The thought of his seed growing there, their combined cells rapidly dividing, the promise of new life so fragile and yet so hopeful, he felt a tight ache in his chest. *Please let this one survive*, he prayed to the God he had neglected and ignored for most of his adult life. He wanted to reach out and lay his hand across that precious part of Maya's anatomy, to ensure his child's safety, to protect it with the promise of his love throughout its life, no matter how short or long. *Please*, he begged.

'I don't want the press to find out about this,' Maya

said. 'I don't think I could cope with everyone speculating on whether I will last the distance with this one.'

Giorgio understood what she was saying. He was used to the press, or as used to the press as anyone living in the limelight could be. He had grown up with the comments and the fabrications and the almost but not quite truths, but Maya had grown up in an entirely different world. She had been anonymous in her small suburb, and then the city of Sydney, where she had studied before travelling abroad. She had never got used to people recognising her, stopping her in the street for a comment or a photograph. Almost from the start she had shrunk in on herself, as if she wanted to hide from the world. He could see that now, when it was almost too late to change things.

Why hadn't he protected her more? Prepared her more? He had taken so much for granted: that she would slot into his high profile life as if she was born to it. By marrying her, he had cast her into a world totally foreign to her: a world of dog-eat-dog, where people took advantage of each other for financial gain, for a higher step on the social ladder. Maya had done her best to fit in, she had played the game as best she could, but it had come at a price.

Since she had left him, it had made him see his own life in retrospect. He had not had time to properly grieve the sudden loss of his father. He was still haunted by the tragic loss of his three-month-old baby sister all those years ago. Giorgio had always known the pressure to produce an heir had come from the devastating loss his parents had experienced. They had subconsciously, or perhaps even consciously, wanted to replace the tiny daughter they had lost so unexpectedly. Neither of them had returned to the villa at Bellagio since. It lay empty, as Maya had pointed out, for most of the year. No one spoke of it. It was too painful for Giorgio's mother, especially since his father had died. Giorgio knew he should have told Maya more about that time but he too had locked it away. The one time he had taken her there, at her insistence, he had felt on edge the whole time. It had been too hard to confront his feelings about the place where he had left his childhood and innocence behind.

'I will do what I can to keep the press from knowing about this for the time being,' he said. 'But it might not be something I can fully control. Have you seen a doctor yet?'

She pressed her lips together for a moment. 'No, not yet.' She looked up at him like a lost child looking for directions. 'I wasn't sure whether to believe the test or not. I thought I might wait a week or two more…you know…to be absolutely sure…'

Giorgio knew what she was waiting for and it struck him again how misguidedly he had handled things in the past. He had allowed her to think he viewed her early miscarriages as blips in nature's course, hoping that by outwardly taking a philosophical approach it would help her get over it without the added burden of his own sense of failure and loss. He knew how much she had emotionally invested in each of them. He had done the same. Why hadn't he told her how he felt? Maybe it would have helped her cope if he had shared the loss instead of pretending it was nothing to worry about. Each one of those pregnancies had had the potential to be a child.

Their child.

After seeing his parents go through the loss of his baby sister, he had closed the door on his feelings. It had been the only way he had coped. But it had left him seriously short-changed.

Maya had from the moment she had fallen pregnant been planning each child's graduation and wedding while he had said nothing. No wonder she thought him a heartless unfeeling bastard.

'You need to get it properly confirmed for a start,' he said. 'We will have to trust the doctor's confidentiality on that but I am sure that won't be a problem. You will need to rest as much as possible. Are you feeling well in yourself?'

She bit into her bottom lip again, reminding him once more of a small child abandoned by what it held most secure. 'I'm a bit nauseous but not overly so. I am tired on and off, and I have a bit of a backache, but I think that is more to do with overdoing it, as I said, at yoga.'

'I think you should stop all formal exercise until you have clearance from the doctor,' he said. 'You have to take it easy, Maya. This is the most important event in your life. We've been given a second chance. Don't do anything to compromise it.'

Her grey eyes moved out of the range of his. 'Don't fuss over me, Giorgio. It won't change anything. If I lose this baby...' she gulped as if the words had hurt as she said them '…I don't want to get my hopes up too soon…'

Giorgio came over and enveloped her in his arms. It felt so good to hold her close. She fitted into his frame like a key going into a complicated lock. He buried his head into the blond silk of her hair, breathing in the scent of gardenia and the delicate feminine fragrance that was hers alone.

He could never forget it. It had lived on his skin for months.

Six months.

'Try not to worry, *cara*,' he said, already doing the worrying for her. 'What will be will be. We have no control over this. All we can do is take the necessary precautions to ensure this pregnancy gets the best chance possible to survive.'

She raised her pain-filled eyes to his. 'And if it doesn't?'

How could he answer? He wanted what she wanted. He wanted an heir, a child of his own, with his blood flowing through its veins. He had never doubted he would get what he wanted until they had encountered all those hurdles. Like so many people, he had readily, naively assumed he would do the deed and get the results he wanted.

Life, with its twists and turns, had a way of making you re-evaluate that assumption. He took very little for granted these days. He lived from moment to moment, wondering if he would achieve the things he most wanted in life. His work fulfilled him, it challenged him enough to satisfy him, but it wasn't enough. It wasn't nearly enough. He wanted what Luca had. Luca hadn't had it easy; there was no way Giorgio could say any different. Luca had suffered, but he had come through. He had a beautiful loving wife and a gorgeous little daughter and another child on the way. What more could any man want?

It was what Giorgio wanted but, if he couldn't have it, surely that was in the lap of the gods, out of his control. That didn't sit well with him, however. He liked control. He was used to control. He controlled everything that needed controlling. He did the numbers, he aligned the figures, he knew what had to be done and he did it.

But sometimes it just wasn't enough.

'Maya,' he said, struggling to find the right words, 'if this doesn't work out, if you still want a divorce at the end, we will discuss it then and only then. We are only together now for my grandfather. The pregnancy is a bonus, a surprise package that we can only hope will eventuate into a...' again he hunted awkwardly for the right words '...a live child.'

Giorgio saw the flicker of pain pass over her features. She was measuring herself in terms of whether she could deliver the goods. He wished then that he had thought of a better way to put it.

'I need to go to bed,' she said, as if that was the end of the discussion—for her. Her chin had gone up defensively, her slim shoulders were aligned tightly and there was a fiery light in her grey eyes that warned him not to push any further.

He reached down to anchor Gonzo's collar. 'I will

take this boy out for a block or two while you settle into bed. If you need me during the night, just call me.'

She gave him a very determined look. 'I don't need you, Giorgio,' she said crisply. 'I can do this alone if I have to.'

In spite of the dog's leaping excitement at the prospect of a late night walk, Giorgio still fixed his gaze on Maya's with intractability. Hearing her say she didn't need him any more triggered something deep and primal in his blood. He would not let her leave him for a second time without a fight, baby or no baby. 'You have said this is my child, Maya,' he said. 'I am not going to walk away from my own flesh and blood. I have changed my mind. Our marriage will continue indefinitely.'

CHAPTER SIX

OR UNTIL I lose this child, just like I lost all the others, Maya thought as Giorgio strode out of the flat with the dog at his side. She couldn't see him sticking out the long years of a fruitless marriage, not unless something other than duty and obligation bound him to it.

Something like love.

She chided herself for regressing into that fairyland of hope. She had long ago given up on him feeling anything for her. Why torture herself any more when it was even more unlikely he would ever change?

She left the small *salone* and took the opportunity while Giorgio was out to prepare for bed. She quickly removed her make-up and did her usual skincare routine. She looked at the expensive lotions and potions a little ruefully. She had been tempted to toss them out with all the other things she had been entitled to as a Sabbatini wife over the years, but she hated waste, or that was the reasoning she had used when she had packed her things the day she had left.

She didn't like thinking of that awful day. She had been cowardly about it by leaving when Giorgio was in Switzerland with his team of accountants at a huge financial conference in Zurich. She hadn't thought she would have the strength to go through with it with him there in person, even though over those last few months things had become rather tense and difficult between them. They had argued a lot, bickering over the silliest things just like a live-in couple or flatmates who were thoroughly sick of each other's irritating little habits.

Maya had found it so distressing to think he was starting to hate her. She often saw him looking at her with a brooding sort of expression, as if he wasn't quite sure what to do with her.

They hadn't made love in weeks…well, it had been more like three months. The hormone injections Maya had been given as part of the IVF plan had made her moody and irritable. And then Giorgio had had to provide a sample of sperm, which she knew he found undignified, even though the doctors and staff were totally professional about it.

Sex was a chore, a duty and it had killed any feeling he might have had for her once. Not that he had ever said he loved her. It wasn't part of their relationship. She had known that and married him anyway, hoping he would gradually develop feelings for her. But Giorgio wasn't a feeling type of man. She couldn't imagine him allowing himself to be vulnerable. He held everyone at a distance.

Maya had enough friends in her life to know not all relationships worked out. Even the most secure and settled couples could be torn apart by what life dished up. She had always prided herself that she would never give up on her man. She would be the loyal, loving wife, doing everything she could to make their relationship keep its zing and passion. But in the end she had failed. She had failed because it was not just about her role in the marriage, but Giorgio's too. He had slowly but surely drifted away from her. She had felt it subtly at first and she had been gracious about it, putting it down to the tragic loss of his father and how he had so much extra responsibility as a result.

Those three weeks with Giancarlo lying in a semi-conscious state had been one of the most heartbreaking things to witness. It had been cruel to see such a strong and fit man become so weak.

Maya had tried to support her mother-in-law as best she could during that horrific and tragic time, but Giovanna had pointedly clung to her sons and Maya had felt increasingly shut out. How could a new daughter-in-law offer comfort to that depth of grief? In the end she had stayed in the background, doing what she could when she could, hoping she wasn't inadvertently making things worse.

Maya's failure to maintain a pregnancy past six weeks had at one point the following year prompted Giovanna to mention how she had delivered three healthy sons and a daughter at regular intervals, the subtext being: what the hell was wrong with Maya for not being able to do the same? Maya had put it down to her mother-in-law's ongoing grief. Giovanna rarely left the family villa and the doctor had even prescribed some antidepressant medication to see if that would help.

No one in the Sabbatini family, apart from Salvatore,

had ever spoken about the death of baby Chiara all those years ago.

Maya had learned from Salvatore how Giorgio had been the one to find his sister lying cold and lifeless in her crib. He had been only six years old.

Not much more than a baby himself, certainly far too young to cope with such a loss.

When she had tried to talk to Giorgio about it after that distressing episode with his mother, as usual, he'd refused to discuss it, other than this time to say it belonged in the past and his mother was still grieving and Maya should have more sensitivity and patience.

Maya had been stung by his blocking attitude to more intimate communication. She saw it as a sign of what was essentially wrong with their relationship. He did not confide in her. He had never confided in her. He kept things to himself; he never showed any sign of vulnerability.

Not even when he came home from Switzerland to find her note propped up on the desk in his study had he reacted as she had secretly hoped he would. He had tracked her down within a day or two and informed her he would get the paperwork regarding the separation of assets in order. He'd spoken coldly and impersonally, as if he was discussing a legal issue with a business opponent. He'd shown no anger, no emotion at all, in fact. He had left within five minutes, barely even stopping long enough to pat Gonzo.

Maya had realised then how hopeless it all was; she had been right from the beginning. They were too different, their worlds too disparate. Just like Gonzo, she was a penniless, abandoned orphan with indiscriminate breeding. Giorgio belonged to a large extended blue-blooded family where money and wealth and privilege were never questioned.

The door opened downstairs and Maya quickly slipped into her bed, pulling the covers up to her chin. She snapped off the lamp, even though she would have loved to continue reading the book she had by the bed-side. She found it almost impossible to sleep without reading for a few minutes. She closed her eyes, barely able to breathe, waiting to hear those firm foot treads on the stairs.

But there was nothing.

She didn't know whether to feel angry or grateful. But then she started to think of Giorgio trying to get com-fortable on that wretched little sofa. She could picture him crunched up like a banana folded in half; his back was probably aching by now, his long legs having gone numb from hanging over the end of the sofa arms.

She turned over and faced the wall, her eyes opening to see the silvery eye of the moon staring back at her. She lay like that for endless minutes, listening for any sound of movement downstairs.

After a while there were footsteps on the stairs but they weren't Giorgio's. There was a distinctive scratching at the door and a little doggy please-let-me-in whine.

Maya rolled on her back and groaned. She had been trying to train Gonzo to sleep on his own cushion in the laundry, but he had apparently conveniently forgotten all about his humble beginnings and now, like all the other Sabbatinis, she knew, expected to sleep on one thousand threads of Egyptian cotton every night.

She threw off the covers and padded over to the door and opened it. 'No, Gonzo,' she said sternly. 'You have to sleep downstairs.' She pointed her finger in that direction. 'Go back down. *Now.*'

More footsteps sounded on the stairs and Maya's finger went limp, along with her legs, as Giorgio appeared in nothing but his tight-fitting underwear. Her eyes feasted on him like a starved animal presented with an all-you-can-eat banquet. Tightly ridged muscle carved the contours of his abdomen, his chest was sprinkled with masculine hair, the hair that used to tickle the sensitive skin of her breasts. It narrowed down over his stomach to disappear in a tantalising trail beneath the waistband of his underwear. Strictly speaking, he wasn't fully aroused but he wasn't far off it. The bulge of his manhood was stirring even as she could feel her body responding.

How she finally dragged her eyes back up to his was nothing short of a miracle. 'I can handle this,' she said in her best teacher-like voice. 'It's not the first time he's pulled this kind of stunt on me.'

Giorgio leaned one of his broad shoulders against the door jamb, which meant Maya had to move backwards and of course Gonzo, seizing the opportunity, rapidly squeezed past and leapt up on the bed, circling a couple of times before dropping and closing his eyes with a blissful sigh.

'Now look what you've done,' Maya said hotly. 'I've

been working on him for weeks and you've undone it just like that.' She snapped her fingers for effect.

Giorgio captured her hand in mid-air and brought it to his mouth, his lips playing with her fingers in a nibble-like caress, his dark glinting eyes tethering hers. 'It seems every male you know wants to share your bed, *cara*,' he said. 'I don't blame Gonzo. The sofa is singularly the most uncomfortable piece of furniture I have ever laid eyes on, let alone my body.'

Maya wrenched her hand away. 'Gonzo is supposed to be sleeping on his dog bed in the laundry which, I might tell you, I spent a lot of money on.'

He lifted one shoulder as if in full agreement with the hound. 'Your bed looks much more inviting.'

She folded her arms and did her best to stare him down. 'If you think I am going to share it with both of you then you can think again.'

He closed the door with his foot, the clicking of the latch sounding like a pistol firing in the silence

'Wh…what are you doing?' Maya asked, backing away.

His slow-moving sexy eyes ran over her satin night-gown, relishing the way the fabric clung to her breasts in all the right places. She felt the heat of her skin go up several degrees and her heart rate escalated, making her speech breathless and jerky. 'S…stop it, Giorgio. Stop it right this instant. You know sleeping together right now is out of the question. It's too dangerous.'

He cupped the back of her head with one large con-trolling hand, his body moving just that little bit closer, close enough for her to feel the effect she was having on him. 'Who said anything about sleeping?' he said. 'Besides, we can do other things to relieve this sexual tension.'

Maya knew exactly what sort of thing he was suggesting and it made her blood sing and thrum through her veins. Pleasuring each other without penetrative sex had been something they had done in the past, in the early exciting days of their marriage when nothing had been off limits. She had not realised her body could scale the heights of pleasure it had without his body doing all the work. He had introduced her to sensual delights that had shocked her at the time, but now they were like a delicious memory she wanted to revisit.

But wait…

How dared he stir her senses up like that? She was supposed to be demonstrating how immune she was to him, even if she wasn't. It would give him too much power to know she would be his again at the sexy stroke of his tongue or one of his fingers, that he could make her convulse uncontrollably with just a few clever caresses that would leave her body tingling for hours afterwards.

'Forget it, Giorgio,' she said, affecting a bored disinterested tone. 'I'm tired. I have no interest in your bedroom games.'

He captured her hands, pulling her up against him, rubbing his aroused length against her quivering belly. 'Go on, *tesore mio*,' he said in a smouldering spine-loosening tone, 'just like you used to do in the past.'

Maya's heart fluttered like a deck of rapidly shuffled cards. She was so tempted, so very dangerously tempted.

She could almost taste his salty muskiness, she could almost feel the satin-covered steely length of him filling her mouth, and she could almost feel the shuddering quake of his body as he finally tipped over the edge...

He moved his body against her again. He was powerfully erect. She had felt that hardened length sliding back and forth inside her so many delicious times in the past, the way it caught on the most sensitive part of her if she tilted her hips just that little bit higher, how he could smash her into a million pieces of ecstasy with a soft but sure flickering caress of his fingers against her swollen need.

All she had to do was drop to her knees in front of him, peel back his underwear and swirl her tongue over him, once, twice, waiting for him to suck in his breath.

But she wasn't going to do it.

Not now.

Not like this.

Not because he had an itch he wanted scratching. That was an itch any other woman could scratch. And plenty of other women had probably done so in the time they had been apart.

Maya steeled her resolve, which took some effort considering she had none in reserve. She was running on almost empty but it was enough to put some distance between them. 'You and Gonzo can have the bed,' she said, scooping up her wrap off the end of the bedpost. 'I will take the sofa.'

'You don't have to do that, Maya,' Giorgio said, pushing a hand through the lock of his hair that kept insisting on falling over his forehead. 'The paparazzi will have given up by now. I will go back to the hotel for the rest of the night. I will see you in the morning. Have your essential things packed. I will organise for the rest to be transported over later.'

Maya watched in frozen silence as he left the bedroom. She counted each and every one of his footsteps as he went down the stairs.

After a few minutes she heard a car arrive—she assumed it was a Sabbatini staff member summoned to pick him up—and then the sound of it pulling away from the kerb and disappearing into the night.

She turned and looked at Gonzo, who was sound asleep and snoring on her bed. She gave her head a little shake and slipped in beside him, or at least as far as his solid presence would allow. It was like trying to sleep on a corkboard, she thought as the minutes slowly ticked by. She was never going to be able to sleep, she was sure of it. But, somehow, the sound of the dog's rhythmic snuffles and snores and her own emotional and physical exhaustion took over. She rolled over, curling her legs into a comma shape to allow for Gonzo, and finally went to sleep...

CHAPTER SEVEN

THE doorbell pealed just as Maya had her head hanging over the basin in the bathroom. The nausea had caught her off guard. She had never felt anything like it before. It was like being on the worst sea voyage of her life. The world of her small rented flat was not stable; it was rocking all over the place. And it wasn't just the flat, it was the smell of things that assaulted her senses and sent them into revolt. She had opened a can of food for Gonzo at his insistence and then had to bolt upstairs to deal with the consequences. Her oesophagus felt raw, as if scraped by razorblades.

The doorbell rang again, this time with Gonzo's voluble accompaniment.

Maya groaned and wiped her whitewash-coloured face on the hand towel. Her eyes were like water drip holes in snow, hollow and shadowed with exhaustion.

She clung to the banister on the way down with a deathly grip, sure she was going to drop into a faint. But somehow she managed to get to the front door and opened it, bleary-eyed and sick as she was.

'*Dio!* What the hell?' Giorgio instantly sprang into action. He took her by the upper arms, holding her steady, sending a curt command to Gonzo to back off. 'Are you sick, Maya?' he asked, his frown so tense and serious it made his head ache.

'I've got the most awful nausea,' she said weakly. 'I've been sick for the last hour. Gonzo's food set me off...'

'Right, that settles it,' he said. 'I will send someone over to pack up your things. You need to rest. I will feed Gonzo in the future. You need to concentrate on looking after this baby. The first thing that needs to happen is a doctor's appointment. Right now, as soon as I can arrange it.'

She pushed back her damp blond hair from her pale forehead. 'I don't want to be told how likely it is I'm going to lose this baby,' she said, her chin wobbling slightly. 'I don't have a great track record.'

Giorgio felt a hand clutch at his insides. 'You are not going to lose this baby, not if I can help it.'

She looked up at him with a pained expression. 'You can't control everything, Giorgio; surely you realise that by now?'

He refused to consider the possibility of failure. He set his jaw, pushing it forward indomitably. 'We have got this far, Maya,' he said. 'I know it is still early days but you are extremely nauseous. I think I read somewhere that it is a good sign of strong hormonal activity when a woman is so nauseous in the early days of pregnancy. We have to cling to that. To hope that this one will be the success we have hoped for all this time.'

She turned away from him, her shoulders slumped forward as if already preparing for defeat. 'I'm so frightened to hope,' she said in a whisper-soft voice. 'I feel like a gift has been handed to me but it's not quite in my hands. I can't help feeling it will be snatched away at the last minute if I get my hopes up.'

'You can't think like that, Maya,' he insisted. 'You have to remain positive.'

She turned and faced him. 'There are no guarantees, though, are there?' she asked. 'I know you don't like talking about it but you lost your sister when she was three months old. She was a living, breathing, interactive baby. This baby is a tiny embryo, not even independent of my body. What hope is there that we won't lose him or her in the future, just like your little sister?'

A shutter came down over his face, just like a heavy curtain over a stage. Maya knew she had overstepped the mark. She had mentioned the unmentionable. But she longed to be reassured, she longed for the confidence she lacked—that this pregnancy would be the glue that would stick their marriage back into place.

'This is an entirely different situation,' he said in a flat emotionless tone. 'We have been down this path before. It is tricky and uncertain but there are things we can cling to in hope this time around. This is a natural conception, one that occurred a long time after your previous miscarriages. This is a totally different ballgame. We did this all by ourselves: no hormone injections, no temperature charts—we just got down and did what had to be done and now we are expecting a baby. We have to go with this; we have to take it as it comes.'

She pressed her lips together, making them as white as her face. 'And if we fail?'

He gave her a look of steely determination. 'We are not going to fail, Maya, not this time.'

Maya longed for his confidence, if indeed what he was exhibiting was confidence. She had a feeling he was as worried as she was, but he was not letting on. 'Giorgio…' she began uncertainly. 'What did you feel when I lost the other babies?'

He drew in a breath and let it out in a slow uneven stream. 'I was devastated for you and for me. I know I didn't show it, but it's what I've always done in a crisis.' He paused. 'I had to be strong so you could lean on me. I didn't realise until now how wrong that approach probably was.'

'I wish I had known that's how you felt…'

'Would it have made a difference?' he asked.

Maya let her shoulders drop. 'I don't know…'

He touched her cheek with two fingers. 'I didn't want to burden you with my own sense of failure. I felt you had enough to deal with. But now I see I should have shared more with you about how it felt for me so you understood that I knew at least some of what you were feeling.'

It explained a lot, Maya thought, and yet she was still worried about his motives for keeping their marriage on track. If she failed to deliver a live child, would he still insist on their marriage continuing? And, even if she did give birth to the heir he so dearly wanted, wouldn't she then have to live with the knowledge she was the mother of a Sabbatini heir and not the love of his life, as she so dearly longed to be?

'Have you told your grandfather about this pregnancy?' she asked.

He dropped his hand from her face. 'No, but I think we should tell him as soon as possible. It would boost his spirits no end to know he might be a great-grandfather again in a few months. I only wish he could live that long to see it eventuate.'

Maya felt the pain of his statement. It was as raw for her as it was for him. She still could not quite believe the vibrant, cheeky patriarch of the family was facing imminent death. She could not imagine life without him. It would be doubly hard for Giorgio. He would be expected to carry the family through the crisis while holding the Sabbatini empire in place.

'I wish he could live that long too,' she said softly.

'We'll tell him as soon as we get back from the doctor,' he said. 'Now, do you need a hand getting ready? I have my car outside. We can go straight to the surgery.'

Maya pushed a hand through her limp hair. 'I need to have a shower...'

'Have a quick one while I call the doctor,' he said, pulling out his mobile. 'I'll get one of my staff to come and collect Gonzo and your things and take them to the villa.'

It was all happening so fast that Maya could barely keep up. Giorgio was in organising mode and he was letting nothing stand in his way. After fighting to be independent for so long, she perversely began to feel the relief of having someone take control. It made her feel protected and sheltered from having to worry about things all on her own.

The shower did much to restore her equilibrium. The worst of the nausea had abated and when she came downstairs dressed in jeans and a rollneck cashmere sweater with a trench coat draped around her shoulders in case it was still cold outside, Giorgio was already waiting for her.

He gave her a rare smile, such a small movement of his lips but it still managed to contract her heart. 'You look a lot better. Not feeling so sick now?' he asked.

She shook her head. 'No, I'm fine now.'

He held the door open for her, commanding Gonzo to sit on his cushion in the laundry instead of bolting out of the door, as clearly had been the dog's plan.

'He is getting out of control,' Giorgio said as he led Maya to his car, parked illegally in front of her flat. 'You've clearly been too soft with him.'

She sent him a resentful little glare as he activated the remote control device to unlock the car. 'He's been upset by the change in living arrangements,' she said. 'Now I can understand how children misbehave for one or both of their parents when there is a divorce. It's very unsettling having to shift between two residences all the time.'

He held open the passenger door for her. 'I wasn't the one who instigated the divorce,' he reminded her with a speaking look.

'No, but you would have got around to it sooner or later,' she said.

He didn't answer other than to close the door and

stride around to the driver's side, his expression dark and brooding.

Maya pulled down the seat belt with an angry movement of her hand. She waited until he was sitting in the driver's seat beside her before she said, 'I'm doing my best, Giorgio. I haven't deliberately spoilt Gonzo. He misses you, that's all. I didn't realise how much until we had separated.'

He looked across at her for a pulsing moment, his eyes inscrutable and impossibly dark. 'Well, he will not have to worry about that now.'

Maya tied her fingers into a knot in her lap. 'We haven't really discussed this properly,' she said. 'You said our marriage is to continue indefinitely, but that is not just up to you. I have some say in it, surely?'

He started the car with a rocket-fuel roar, putting it into gear with a savage movement of his hand. 'You, for once, Maya, will do as you are told. I am tired of being painted as the bad guy in all of this. I have done the best I could do under the circumstances. I know I am not the best husband in the world, but neither am I the worst. We've had some bad luck. Lots of people do, even worse things than we've experienced. We should both be mature enough to deal with it and move on.'

Maya clenched her teeth to stop herself from flinging an invective his way. He always made it seem as if she was the one who was being childish and petty, giving up in a pout when she should have pressed on. The nine-year age gap between them didn't help. It gave him an edge in experience that she couldn't see how she could ever make up.

'But we have nothing in common,' she said. 'I don't see how we can make our marriage work when it's already failed once.'

'We have more in common than you realise,' he said. 'We both love dogs, for instance.'

She rolled her eyes at him. 'Lots of people love dogs. It doesn't mean they would make a great life partner.'

'It's a start, Maya,' he said. 'And we're sexually compatible. You can't deny that now, can you?'

Maya turned her gaze away as she felt the stirring of her body. She quickly crossed her legs, hoping to suppress it but, if anything, it made her more aware of her need of him.

One of his hands reached across and squeezed hers. 'Just in case there are paparazzi around, put on a happy face, Maya,' he said. 'It's really important my grandfather believes this to be a genuine reconciliation.'

Maya glanced at him as he took his hand away to change gear. 'You don't feel uncomfortable about lying to him?' she asked. 'You've always been close to him. Don't you think he will see through this charade for what it is?'

He gave a little up and down movement of his shoulders. 'I don't see that I am lying to him at all,' he said. 'This is what I want right now. A divorce is out of the question.'

She frowned as she studied his expression as he focused on the traffic ahead. 'You didn't exactly beg me to return to you when I instigated proceedings, though, did you?'

He sent her a quick inscrutable glance before turning

back to the road in front. 'I knew I was making you unhappy. There seemed no point in continuing to make you miserable just to keep up appearances. Anyway, you should know me well enough by now to know it's not in my nature to beg.'

There was that damn Sabbatini pride raising its head again, Maya thought. 'So the only way to get me back was to blackmail me emotionally,' she said. 'You knew I wouldn't say no to Salvatore, so you used his illness to your advantage.'

'You make it sound as if I have engineered his illness for my own gain,' Giorgio said. 'I would give anything to keep my grandfather alive for another ten years but that is not what fate has decided.'

'All the same, this situation really works to your advantage, doesn't it?' she said. 'You get to stall a very expensive divorce for a few more weeks, if not months.'

He looked at her as if she was a small, disobedient child he was reprimanding. 'It could be years, Maya. You need to get your head around that. Sabbatinis do not take divorce lightly.'

She sent him a hot little glare. 'Do you think I care a fig for your black credit card lifestyle? Money can buy you a lot of things, but it can't buy the most valuable thing in life.'

'You seemed to enjoy what came your way,' he said with a tightening of his mouth. 'I didn't hear any complaints about the holidays and jewellery and designer wardrobe.'

'You might not have noticed but I left a lot of what you gave me behind,' she said, 'including my rings.'

'I have them in safe keeping for you,' he said. 'They are in the safe at my villa. I want you to wear them from now on.'

Maya wanted to tell him exactly where he could put his rings, but she reminded herself that this was about making Salvatore happy in the remaining weeks of his life. It wasn't the time to be scoring points with Giorgio; it was the time for a truce, so he could prepare himself and the rest of his family for the sad end of his grand-father's long and productive life.

The doctor's waiting room was almost full but Maya and Giorgio were led straight through to the doctor who had treated Maya in the past.

Dr Rossini was surprisingly optimistic about the pregnancy progressing to full-term this time around. 'You are in excellent health, Signora Sabbatini,' he said. 'You are perhaps a little underweight but that will soon change with a better diet and more rest. I will do a full blood test screen. The home test you used is very reliable so if you like we can do an intravaginal ultrasound in my examination room next door to make sure everything is as it should be, given your history.'

'Do you want me to wait outside?' Giorgio asked Maya.

Although the procedure was more invasively intimate than an abdominal ultrasound, Maya shook her head. She did not have it in herself to deny Giorgio the first glimpse of their baby and she felt in very great need of his support. 'No, please stay.'

'Come through.' Dr Rossini directed them to the room

next door. He left them for a few minutes while Maya got on the examination table, undressing her lower body and covering herself with a blanket in preparation.

She sent Giorgio a worried glance but he gave her a reassuring smile. 'Try not to worry, *cara*,' he said. 'The doctor seems pretty confident you and the baby will be fine.'

Dr Rossini came in and gloved up, talking them through the procedure, as well as pointing out the tiny embryo, which was just four centimetres long. 'You can see a tiny heartbeat just there.' He showed them on the screen. 'The C-shaped curvature is developing and those little buds there in the next few weeks will become legs and arms. Your baby looks a healthy little one so far. Congratulations.'

Maya could do nothing about the tears that rolled from her eyes as the doctor put away his equipment. Giorgio silently handed her a crisp white handkerchief, his own eyes suspiciously moist. It was too soon to hope, she kept saying to herself. She'd had early ultrasounds before and still lost the baby, but she couldn't help thinking that something felt different about this one. Was she imagining the tiny shape on the screen looked more robust than the previous ones in the first two years of their marriage?

The drive to Giorgio's villa was conducted in a silence that was tense but not antagonistic. Maya wondered what he was thinking, whether he was nervous, excited or worried or all three. She glanced at him now and again, searching for some clue to what he was feeling, but he was concentrating on the traffic, a small frown bringing his brows together over his eyes.

They arrived at the villa and Maya had to blink a couple of times as he had changed the colour scheme of the outside. Extensive work had been done in the gardens too, and he had installed an infinity pool on one of the terraces that in spring and summer enjoyed full sun.

Inside was just as transformed. Fresh curtains and festooned pelmets hung at the windows, the marbled floors were polished and the grand staircase was recarpeted in an ankle-deep runner that wound its way up like a river. The smell of fresh paint was prominent in the air but it gave the villa a new, hopeful and revitalised atmosphere.

'What do you think?' Giorgio asked as he showed her through the downstairs rooms.

'It's…it's amazing,' Maya said, turning in a full circle to take all of the changes in. 'The colours are lovely. I couldn't have done better myself. Did you employ an interior designer?'

He gave her a wry look. 'A whole team of them. I wanted to freshen up the place. I felt it needed a change.'

Maya wondered again if that had had more to do with removing every trace of her presence, but she had cause to rethink that opinion when he showed her the upstairs bedroom they used to share. He had knocked down a wall to create more space and installed a walk-in wardrobe along with a brand-new en suite bathroom that was twice the size of the one they had had before.

It had a deep bowl-like bathtub set in the middle of the room and a double headed glass shower unit in one corner. Twin basins with gilt-edged mirrors above and cupboards beneath completed the transformation.

The walk-in wardrobe off the bedroom suite was almost as big as the kitchen at her rented flat. But what was more surprising was that all of the clothes and other accessories she had left behind were hanging in neat rows or folded in the drawer section as if she had never left.

She turned from inspecting it all to look up at him. 'Why didn't you toss out all of the stuff I left behind or send it to a charity or something?'

He gave a movement of his lips that was the equivalent of a dismissive shrug, but behind his eyes a glint of triumph gleamed as he handed her the engagement and wedding rings she had left next to her departure note all those months ago. 'It's called hedging your bets,' he said. 'I took a gamble. It paid off. I had a feeling you might change your mind once you realised what you were throwing away.'

CHAPTER EIGHT

IF IT hadn't been for his grandfather's illness and the precarious state of his health, Maya would have walked out right then and there, just to prove him wrong.

'Your confidence is misplaced, Giorgio,' she said with a tart edge to her voice as she shoved the rings on her finger. 'You know I am only here now because of your grandfather and the baby, both of whom could be gone within a matter of weeks.'

His brows snapped together. 'Stop talking like that. It's almost as if you want to lose this child. You heard what the doctor said. There is no reason to be so negative. You are in good health and the baby looks healthy for its age and stage.'

She glared back at him with her arms crossed over her middle. 'Don't tell me what I can and can't say or what I can and can't feel.'

Giorgio raked a hand through his hair but it did little to restore any order to it. If anything, it made Maya want to run her hands through it as she used to do. The temptation to do so was suddenly almost too much to bear. She needed his touch for reassurance. Coming back to the villa, as changed as it was, still affected her deeply. Just a few metres down the hall was the nursery she had so excitedly prepared all those years ago. Had he stripped it until it too was unrecognisable?

She was too frightened to ask.

'Maya.' He came over to where she was standing so stiffly and placed his hands gently on the top of her shoulders. 'Forgive me,' he said gruffly. 'I am forgetting you are in the midst of a hormonal turmoil, let alone worrying about what's happened in the past. I am worried too. I am desperately worried I won't do or say the right thing, just like I did before. I am still learning how to do this. It's all new to me. This time I want things to be perfect for you and the baby. Believe me, *cara*, I don't want to upset you now. I don't want to fight with you. I want to look after you.'

She took a steadying breath as she looked into his dark gaze. 'What did you do with the nursery?' she asked.

His hands tightened for a nanosecond on her shoulders before he removed them to hang by his sides. His expression threatened to lock down as usual, but then she saw a tiny fist punching beneath the skin at the edge of his mouth, as if trying to push its way through. A war was going on within him; the effort to override his instinctive response was clearly taking a huge toll. 'I had it redecorated,' he said. 'It's a spare bedroom now.'

She disguised a quick apprehensive swallow. 'Can I see it?'

He stepped aside to hold the door open for her. 'Of course.'

Maya walked down the hall, unable to shake off the

feeling of walking back through time. She had been so excited during that first pregnancy. She had shopped and shopped, filling the villa with baby things, from teddy bears to teething rings. She had bought clothing: tiny all in one suits, booties and nappies and bibs. She had even taught herself to knit and in the evenings she would make some very odd-shaped booties until she finally got the hang of it. She had insisted on choosing and then papering the walls of the nursery herself. She had made it a project, to make the most beautiful nursery with everything ready and waiting for their precious baby.

And then she had miscarried.

The nursery had seemed to mock her with its array of baby goods each time she walked past it. After a few months she conceived again and, buoyed up with renewed hope and the optimism of youth, she had started nesting again.

By the fourth miscarriage she had learned her lesson and learned it well. She had closed the door and had never opened it since.

Opening it now was like opening a wound that had not quite healed. The sound of the handle turning felt like someone picking at the scab, pain sliced through her—the pain of loss, of disappointment, of failure and hopelessness.

The room was decorated in a duck egg blue and cream. It looked nothing like a nursery. It was just a spare bedroom, a rather beautifully appointed one with Parisian-style furniture.

'It's very…nice,' she said as the silence swirled around her. She turned and faced him, pasting a smile on her face that made her muscles ache. 'You've done a good job. No one would ever think it was once a...' she forced the word out '...a nursery.'

Giorgio reached for her and she stumbled forwards into his arms, burying her face against his chest. He cupped his hand at the back of her head, holding her to him, knowing there were no words that could take away the hurt of the past. He stood with her in the circle of his arms for several minutes, breathing in her scent, enjoying the neat fit of her body against his.

After a while she eased out of his embrace and swiped at her damp eyes with the backs of her hands. 'Sorry,' she said with a self-conscious grimace. 'It must be the hormones. I feel uncharacteristically weepy.'

He brushed the hair back from her cheek with a gentle finger. 'It's understandable,' he said. He paused for a moment before he continued, 'It was so difficult when I gave the go-ahead to redecorate that room. I felt like I was giving up on everything we had both wanted. It intensified my sense of failure.'

She tried to smile but it came out lopsided, making her seem much younger than her years. 'I hope Gonzo doesn't put his dirty paws on all the new furniture,' she said.

'I am sure he will behave himself once he is back in his old routine,' Giorgio said. 'He should be here soon, along with your things. By the way, I have dealt with the lease on your flat. I paid a couple of months extra to keep the landlord sweet about terminating the lease ahead of time. I've also sorted out the London premises you had lined up.'

'Thank you,' she said, shifting her gaze out of the range of his. 'It seems you've thought of everything.'

'It's my job to see to details, Maya,' he said. 'Now, if you are not too tired, I think it would be good to call on my grandfather and tell him our news. Do you feel up to it?'

'Of course,' she said with another not-quite-all-the-way smile.

Salvatore had not long informed the rest of the close members of his family about his prognosis.

Giovanna was weeping but seemed to collect herself once Giorgio and Maya came in. She kissed her eldest son and then turned to Maya, her greeting a little warmer than the night before. 'I am so glad you are back with my son,' she said. 'This is such a sad time but at least I can be assured now that you and Giorgio will not make things any worse by divorcing.'

Maya answered something non-committal.

Luca was looking shell-shocked but resigned and Nic was looking bored, leaning indolently against a bookcase as if he had better things to do and see, but Maya knew it was probably a mask covering what he was really feeling. More like Giorgio than he wanted to admit, Nic didn't like to show his emotions too freely.

Giorgio assembled everyone together once he made sure his grandfather was comfortable. 'Maya and I have some news,' he said. 'It's very early days and we don't want any of you to rush off and buy gifts or anything, but we have just had Maya's pregnancy confirmed.'

Giovanna's mouth fell open. '*So soon?* But you've

only spent one night back together. How can you know if it's—'

'*Mamma*...' Giorgio began sternly.

'Was it the night of my wedding?' Luca asked with a twinkle in his eye. 'I know you were putting on a reasonable show of civility for Bronte and I on our special day, but I saw you looking daggers at each other every now and again when you thought no one was looking. The air was crackling like an electric current. Everyone was commenting on it.'

Maya felt herself blushing to the roots of her hair. 'I'm sorry if it was that obvious... I hope we didn't offend you and Bronte.'

'Not at all,' Luca said, still grinning. 'If this is the outcome, I couldn't be more thrilled.'

Giorgio reached for Maya's hand and enfolded it within his. 'We are thrilled as well,' he said. 'This baby is very special to us. We have been given a second chance and this time we are not going to waste it. Whatever happens, we are staying together.'

Giovanna, to her credit, came over and hugged Maya, expressing her delight in a mixture of Italian and English. It reminded Maya of the early days, when she had felt a tentative closeness to her mother-in-law, before the death of Giancarlo and the loss of her babies had ruined everything.

Luca swept Maya up into a brotherly hug, congratulating them both, before rushing off so he could tell Bronte, who had stayed back at their villa with Ella, who was sleeping.

Nic sauntered over with a mocking smile on his face,

his green-flecked hazel eyes flicking to Maya's belly and then to his brother's face. 'Nice job,' he said. 'I knew you had it in you. Now all you have to do is keep her with you…oh, and make sure it's actually yours, as *Mamma* hinted at earlier.'

Giorgio swore at his youngest brother, his fist clenching at his side as if he was tempted to use it. 'There is no doubt in my mind this is my child,' he said through gritted teeth.

'Maya…' Salvatore's voice broke up the tense scene.

She went over to where he was sitting and took both of his outstretched hands in hers. 'Are you happy for us, Salvatore?' she asked, trying to keep her voice from cracking with emotion.

His eyes were glistening with moisture and his grip on her hands was almost crushing in his joy. 'I can now die a happy man,' he said. 'I know this baby will survive. I have prayed for this. God gives one life and takes one away. It is the order of things, *si*?'

Maya wasn't too happy with God over taking away her previous pregnancies, but she wasn't going to do or say anything to take away from the old man's faith. 'I'm very happy too,' she said. 'I still can't quite believe it. It seems like a miracle.'

'It *is* a miracle,' Salvatore said. 'And now all I have to do is see my youngest grandson settled and my life's work will be complete.'

Nic muttered something under his breath and Giorgio shot him a reproachful look.

Having grown up without siblings, it had taken Maya

a while to get used to the way the Sabbatini sons related
to each other. There was certainly a pecking order and
Luca, though strong, did not often contest the top position. Nic, on the other hand, was too like Giorgio to want
to bow down to his command just because he was the
younger by four years. They often had power struggles
that went on for days, sometimes weeks. Giorgio thought
Nic needed to grow up and take more responsibility for
his life. Nic thought Giorgio was a control freak who
needed to get a life instead of trying to control everyone
else's.

'I want champagne,' Salvatore announced. 'Not for
you, Maya, *mio piccolo*, but we must toast this baby.
Giorgio, call one of the staff to send some up.'

A few minutes later, with glasses clinking and happy
laughter ringing, it didn't seem possible that the family
had been gathered together to be told of Salvatore's illness. It was like another party. Salvatore was in his
element, enjoying the moment for what it was: the celebration of the continuation of the Sabbatini dynasty.

But, like all good parties, this one had to come to an
end. Salvatore started to look tired and pale and Giorgio
immediately swung into action. With the live-in nurse's
help, he escorted his grandfather upstairs to his bedroom
and made sure he was settled and comfortable before
he left.

'Giorgio,' Salvatore said from the bed just as Giorgio
was about to leave, 'I want you to do something for
me.'

'Anything, *Nonno*,' Giorgio said.

Salvatore took a breath that rattled inside his damaged

lungs. 'I want you to send for Jade Sommerville, my god-daughter in London. I want to say goodbye to her before it's too late.'

Giorgio frowned. The last he had heard, the wild-child daughter of his grandfather's business associate Keith Sommerville had yet again disgraced the family name by having an affair with a married man. But Salvatore had always had a soft spot for the wilful Jade. Over the years he had always made excuses for her appalling behaviour, insisting she was damaged by the desertion of her sluttish mother at a young age. Giorgio was more of the opinion that Jade was exactly like her sleep-around mother and should be left to self-destruct, just as Harriet Sommerville had done some twenty-odd years ago. 'If that is what you wish,' he said. 'I will see if I can get her to agree to fly over for a few days.'

'Thank you...' Salvatore's breathing became even more laboured and the nurse bustled over to place an oxygen mask over his face to assist his breathing.

Giorgio moved forward to help but Salvatore waved him away, mumbling through his mask, 'Leave me now, Giorgio. I will be fine. Just make sure you contact Jade for me.'

'How is he?' Maya asked when Giorgio rejoined her back downstairs in the *salone*.

'Not good,' he said grimly. 'I don't think he's got as long as the doctors have said. Perhaps they were trying to give him hope, to help him remain positive.'

Maya felt a tight hand curl around her heart. 'If only he doesn't have to suffer...I couldn't bear that...'

He trailed his finger down the under curve of her cheek. 'He has morphine on demand,' he said. 'The nurse is with him twenty-four seven. It's all we can do at this stage.'

Maya didn't move away from Giorgio's closeness. She could feel his body heat and wanted to lean into him as she had done before. How wonderful it had been to feel the warm comfort of his arms around her, to pretend, even for a moment, he cared for her. 'You are a wonderful grandson, Giorgio,' she said. 'In fact you are wonderful to all of your family. I sometimes think they rely on you too much. They expect such a lot from you.' Her gaze dropped as she bit down into her bottom lip and added, 'Maybe I expected too much of you too.'

He lifted her chin with the end of his finger, locking his gaze with hers. 'I should have given you more,' he said. 'But maybe this time it will be different. It *feels* different, *cara*. I don't know about you, but it feels completely different this time around.'

Maya searched his expression for a moment. 'You mean about the baby?'

He leaned forward and pressed a barely touching kiss to her forehead. 'I mean about everything,' he said.

'Signor Sabbatini?' A staff member appeared at the door carrying a cordless phone. 'There is a phone call for you from a relative in Rome. They want an update on your grandfather's health.'

Maya had to suppress her disappointment at being interrupted at such a time. But, even so, there was no point in forcing Giorgio to reveal his feelings, if indeed he had any regarding her. It was all so muddied now with the prospect of a baby. Of course he would feel everything was different now. He was looking forward to having an heir, especially now, with his grandfather's life drawing to an imminent close.

It was as he had said: *everything* was different now.

They left a short time later after saying goodbye to Giorgio's mother, who had lived with Salvatore since Giancarlo had died.

Once they were back at Giorgio's villa a wave of tiredness swept over Maya. He noticed immediately and insisted she go upstairs and slip into bed.

Maya suddenly realised he meant *his* bed, the bed they had once shared as husband and wife. 'Where are you planning to sleep?' she asked, looking at him suspiciously.

'Where do you think I am going to sleep?' he said. 'In my bed, of course.'

'But we…we're not supposed to sleep together,' she faltered.

'The doctor didn't say we shouldn't,' he said. 'I specifically asked him while you were getting dressed in the ultrasound room. He just said to be careful, not to be too vigorous about it.'

Maya was incensed he had discussed it without her being there but, then again, she thought she might have found it excruciatingly embarrassing if he had. 'I didn't agree to resume a physical relationship with you as if nothing has changed,' she said. 'We've been separated for months. You can't expect me to jump back into bed with you as if nothing drove me out of it in the first place.'

'You left, not me,' he said in a clipped I-am-nearing-the-end-of-my-patience tone. 'And anyway, you jumped back into it pretty quickly once you had the chance. I barely touched you that night before you were tearing at me like a wild woman.'

Maya had never slapped anyone in her life. She abhorred violence of any sort, but somehow, without her even realising she was doing it until it was too late, her hand flew through the air and connected with the side of his jaw in a stinging slap that jerked his head sideways.

She watched in silent horror as a dark red angry patch appeared on the side of his face. She put both of her hands up to her mouth, covering her gasp of shock at what she had done.

The air tightened as if someone was pulling it from opposite ends of the room.

Anger, disgust and scorn burned in Giorgio's gaze as it held hers.

Fear, shame and remorse filled Maya's eyes with tears. 'I'm sorry…' She choked over the words. 'I don't know what came over me…I'm so sorry… Did I hurt you?'

He moved a step closer, taking her still stinging hand and placing it on the side of his face, holding it there like a cold press. His eyes continued to hold hers, but they had lost their glint of anger. His mouth lifted upwards in a wry version of a smile. 'You really are surging with hormones, aren't you, *tesore mio*?' he said. 'I have never known you to strike out like that, but then I think perhaps I deserved it, *si*?'

'No, it was wrong of me.' Maya removed her hand from his face and, stepping up on tiptoe, placed her lips there instead. Her lips clung like silk to sandpaper to the stubble on his jaw. Her breath stalled as she filled her nostrils with his male scent: the grace notes of lemon on a citrus stave.

Time froze in place, as if someone had blocked the second hand of the clock from ticking any further.

Maya felt her breath hitch in her throat as it got started again, her eyelids fluttering and then closing in silent surrender as Giorgio's mouth came down and covered hers.

CHAPTER NINE

THE thing that most took Maya by surprise was how tender Giorgio's kiss was. The night of his brother's wedding, the passion had flared like a struck match. They had both hungrily fed off each other's mouths like wild animals. It had been primal and sizzling and totally out of control.

This was different.

So exquisitely, breathtakingly different.

This was slow and sensual but no less sizzling. She felt the heat come up from her toes, melting her spine along the way, pooling in a lake of need at the very core of her being.

His tongue stroked ever so softly against the seam of her mouth and she opened to him, sighing with pleasure as he slid through to meet hers, curling around it like old lovers embracing after a long absence.

He tasted so familiar and yet so dangerously new: exciting and exotic, tantalisingly male and torturously tempting. Her tongue flirted with his, any thought of not following through with this long gone now. She wanted more of his kiss, more of his touch, more of what he had given her during that night just over six weeks ago, more of what she had secretly longed for ever since.

His mouth continued its tender assault on hers as his hands moved to the small of her back, pressing her into the hardened warmth of his body. She felt his erection, that delicious reminder of the power and potency that was hers for the asking. How could she say no to this? Her body was already screaming for the release it craved. She felt it in every pore of her skin, the tightening, tingling feeling of crawling need that overruled any common sense she possessed.

His hands moved again, this time to unbutton her shirt, button by button, each deliberately slow movement of his fingers ramping up her need. She felt the brush of his fingertips in the valley of her cleavage, her skin bursting into joy at that brief contact.

She pushed up against him, a silent plea for more. He gave it, lowering his mouth to her now uncovered breast, suckling on it hotly, teasing the tight nipple with his teeth until she gasped at the sensations rushing through her like a torrent. Her breasts seemed overly sensitive and she felt her inner core responding to each and every caress of his lips and tongue. It was unlike anything she had felt before.

'You feel bigger,' he said in a low sexy voice as he moved to her other breast.

'Hormones,' she managed to croak out as he took her other breast in his mouth and sent her off on another tingling journey of delight.

His mouth came back to hers and kissed her with renewed purpose. There was an edginess about his kiss, as if his passion for her was being stoked beyond his earlier control. Maya urged him on, not caring that she might regret her actions later. This was about now, about having her needs met and meeting his.

'*Dio*,' Giorgio said, tearing his mouth away and breathing hard. 'I don't think I can do this. I might not be able to control myself. I might hurt you or the baby.'

Disappointment was like a slap with an ice-cold wet towel. 'You said the doctor said it would be all right,' she said, tying her arms around his neck to stop him pulling away.

His chest rose and fell against hers. 'Maya, I want you so badly.'

She pulled his head back down to his. 'Then have me,' she whispered against his mouth.

He lifted her in his arms as if she weighed practically nothing and carried her upstairs to the master bedroom. He laid her on the bed, dispensing of his clothes, watching with furnace-hot eyes as she did the same with hers.

He came down beside her, placing one leg over her to balance his weight, careful not to crush her, his mouth covering hers again in a kiss which stoked the fire that was burning deep inside her.

She reached between their bodies to take him in her hand, to feel that glorious silky length of him, to feel the thunder of his blood against the curl of her fingers. She began to stroke him rhythmically, the up and down sweep of her hand inciting a growl of desire from the back of his throat. She saw him suck in his ridged abdomen and secretly delighted in the feminine power she had over him.

He pushed her hand away with a grunt and began to kiss his way down her body, starting at her breasts, travelling down her sternum, lingering over the tiny pucker of her belly button, before going to the cleanly waxed heart of her. He touched the soft naked skin, his eyes gleaming with pleasure. 'I noticed how sexy you looked when we were at the doctor's,' he said. 'I thought you might have stopped waxing after we separated.'

'I got used to it like this,' she said, wriggling so his fingers kept working their magic. 'It feels fresher.'

'It's so damn sexy,' he said, bringing his mouth down to taste her.

Maya lifted her back off the bed in response. She was so close to going over the edge, every nerve was twitching and dancing, poised to let go. But he made her wait. He strung out her pleasure, leading her to the edge again and again before pulling her back before she could freefall into oblivion. In the end she was almost weeping, begging him to let her come.

Finally he gave her what she wanted, but not quite how she wanted it. He used his mouth and tongue with clever little licks and flicks that sent her into a thousand pieces of pleasure, her whole body shook and rocked with it, making her shudder with the aftershocks.

'Now it's my turn,' he said, bringing her hand back down to his erection.

'But don't you want to…?' *How silly*, she thought, to be so coy about something they had done so many times in the past. 'Don't you want to come inside me?'

He kissed her neck, nuzzling there until she squirmed as her skin tingled in response. 'Of course I do but no rough sex until we get the all-clear,' he said. 'You know exactly what speed and pressure I like.'

Maya did as he said, her belly quivering in excitement as she watched him prepare to let go. Her hand tightened around him, the slippery movements making him tense all over before he spilled over her stomach with a guttural groan of release, such an intimate act, so raw, so intensely erotic.

She lay back, looking at him, wondering if he had any idea how much she loved him. He could so easily have insisted on full on sex, but he hadn't. He had done all he could to protect their tiny baby.

The baby he wanted more than anything.

The baby he wanted more than her.

It was a painful reminder of the tenuous position she was in. He was insisting their marriage would continue, regardless of whether or not they were successful in having a child, but what sort of marriage would that be? Would he have numerous affairs, as his father had done years ago until he had finally settled down? Would she be as forgiving as Giovanna had been? Maya wasn't so sure she could handle a philandering husband. Turning a blind eye required much more strength and confidence than she possessed.

Giorgio rose from the bed and reached for his trousers.

'Where are you going?' Maya asked.

'To get you a cool drink and something to eat,' he said, sliding up his zip. 'It's been ages since we left my grandfather's place. You need to keep your nourishment up.'

It was all about the baby, Maya thought as she turned her back to stare at the wall once he had left. *Please, my precious little baby, don't die on me*, she begged as she placed a gentle hand on her abdomen. *Please, please, please...*

When Giorgio came back with a drink and some food on a tray Maya was soundly asleep. She was curled up with one of her hands tucked under her cheek, the dark fan of her eyelashes such a contrast to her platinum blond hair.

He set the tray down carefully and sat on the edge of the bed, just watching her.

Sometimes he found it hard to unravel what he felt about his wife. He had never intended to fall in love with her or anyone. For most of his life he had worked hard to keep his emotions in check. He had shut off his feelings to protect himself, just as he had done when he had found his baby sister lying cold in her cot. The shattered emotions of his parents had terrified him as a child; he had imagined he or one of his brothers would be next to die unexpectedly, or even one of his parents. It had affected him far more deeply than he had ever let on, mostly for his parents' sake. They had needed him to be strong, to be there for his younger brothers, just as he'd had to be strong when his father was injured and subsequently died. There had not been time for his own grief to surface. He'd had to see to the business side of things: to arrange the massive funeral, to transfer all the important documents into his name and so on. He had switched to automatic. He had done it so often during his life that most of the time he wasn't even aware he was doing it any more.

Emotion frightened him. The vulnerability of loving too much terrified him. Loving someone too much left you open to unthinkable pain if they were taken away from you.

He saw it in Maya, the way she let her emotions control her until there *was* no control. She was at the mercy of her feelings, tossed about and worn out by them instead of facing things rationally.

But then that was Maya, the woman he had been attracted to from the first moment he had met her. Shy, virginal, not sure of herself, a little girl lost looking for a large family to envelop and protect her.

He reached out and brushed a strand of her hair back off her cheek. She let out a tiny sigh, her lips fluttering with the movement of air, just like a child's. He looked down at where her other hand was pressed, softly and protectively against her belly.

He felt his heart give a painful squeeze and he gently laid his hand over the top of hers and silently prayed for the child they had conceived, not in love and mutual desire, but in anger and bitterness.

Giorgio hoped to God it would not suffer for his sins.

Maya woke during the night and found Giorgio lying propped up on one elbow watching her in the light of the moon that shone in from one of the windows. There was a slight frown over his eyes, making him look troubled, as if something was weighing heavily on his mind. 'I hope I didn't disturb you,' she said, running her tongue over her dust-dry lips.

He picked up some wayward strands of her hair and tucked them behind her ear. 'You didn't disturb me,' he said. 'I often have trouble sleeping.'

She shivered in delight as his long fingers brushed and then lingered against the skin of her neck once he had secured her hair. 'You work too hard,' she said huskily. 'You drive yourself all the time. When was the last time you had a day off?'

He gave a rueful movement of his lips as his fingers found another few strands of her hair to toy with. 'I have a large corporation to run, Maya,' he said. 'Especially now, with my grandfather fading so quickly.'

'But surely Luca and Nic are helping you?'

He gently coiled her hair around his index finger. 'They are a great support and both work very hard but there are some things I just have to see to myself.'

'You didn't answer my question,' she pointed out. 'When did you last have a day to yourself?'

He let her hair unravel from his finger as his eyes came back to hers. 'I will take some time off once my grandfather passes,' he answered. 'Maybe we could go somewhere together if the doctor gives the all clear to travel. It could be like a second honeymoon.'

Maya traced her fingertip over the sculptured contour of his top lip, his dark stubble catching on her soft skin. 'If we lose this baby...'

He captured her finger and tenderly kissed the end

of it, his eyes still holding hers. 'We haven't lost it so far, *cara*,' he said. 'Hang on to that hope. We have come this far. Hopefully, we can this time around have what we both want.'

As his mouth came down to cover hers, Maya said a silent prayer that somehow what he said would be true, even though she was well aware that she wanted much more than he was prepared to give.

CHAPTER TEN

OVER the coming weeks Maya saw less and less of Giorgio. Salvatore's illness had progressed to the point where he needed around the clock care. Giorgio had to divide his time between keeping the intrusive press at bay, as well as seeing to his grandfather's affairs on top of his own workload, which was considerable at the best of times. Maya began to see for the first time since they had married that the frenetic fast-paced life he lived was not perhaps his choice, but rather something he did because so many people relied on him. It made her more committed to trying to support him in the background, making sure the villa was a comfortable and quiet refuge when he came home, sometimes well after she had gone to bed.

She was still getting used to being back at the villa. It was a different environment without the crew of household workers that had worked there previously. The new sense of space gave her time to think. She was too frightened to plan too far ahead, but she was content for the time being to support Giorgio as much as she could through the difficult time of facing his grandfather's passing. She even spent long hours with Salvatore in order to give some of the other family members a break. She enjoyed sitting there with the old man, chatting to him if and when he felt up to it, or simply reading the paper to him or from one of his favourite novels.

In spite of his long absences from the villa, Giorgio still shared Maya's bed at night. She looked forward to those passionate interludes, when he would silently reach for her, gathering her into his arms and showing her a world of sultry hot delights that made her flesh hum and sing for hours afterwards. He still refused to have penetrative sex, which she found frustrating, but she was hopeful now that she had passed the danger zone of her pregnancy he would soon change his mind.

She was now close to twelve weeks pregnant. She still could barely believe it. Even seeing the baby on the follow-up ultrasound she'd had earlier that week seemed like a dream. As each day passed she felt a fraction less terrified that this too would end in despair.

That Giorgio was thrilled about the progress of her pregnancy was unmistakable, but what was less certain was what he felt about her. To be fair to him, she understood he had a lot on his mind at present, so his air of distraction at times had probably very little to do with her but more to do with the stress he was dealing with. He was gentle and solicitous towards her. No one looking in from the outside would take him for anything but a loving husband, proudly awaiting the birth of his surprise baby.

Giorgio's family showed no signs of thinking anything different. Maya and Giorgio had joined them for dinner at Giovanna's invitation only the week before.

Although, of course, everyone was feeling rather sub-
dued because of Salvatore's deterioration and because he
was too unwell to join them downstairs, the event proved
to Maya that the family took it for granted she was back
in the Sabbatini fold and was not going anywhere in a
hurry.

Bronte, Luca's lovely wife, was fast becoming a
friend. Maya had offered to help her learn Italian and
they had enjoyed a couple of sessions at the villa with
little Ella joining in with much enthusiasm. Maya had
loved being with the little toddler, who seemed to be
blossoming as each day passed. Bronte too, who was
fourteen weeks pregnant now and glowing with it, helped
Maya to feel a little less worried that things would go
wrong this time around.

The persistent and rather hideous nausea Maya was
still experiencing, Bronte assured her, was a fantastic
sign, similar to what Giorgio had said, which the doctor
too had confirmed only that afternoon when she had
gone in for a check-up.

Maya was sitting curled up with a book waiting for
Giorgio to come home when she heard the front door of
the villa open and close. Gonzo whined as if he sensed
something was wrong even before Giorgio walked into
the room.

Maya felt the book she was holding slide out of her
hands; she barely registered the little thump as it landed
on the carpeted floor at her feet. 'Giorgio?' Her voice
came out as a whisper of dread.

His eyes looked hollow as they connected with hers.

'He's gone,' he said in a flat emotionless tone. 'He died two hours ago. He went very peacefully.'

Maya felt her lip quiver and her eyes filled with tears. She scrambled to her feet and half stumbled, half fell into his arms. She wrapped her arms around him tightly, as if she could take some of the pain away from him and carry it for him. 'I'm so sorry,' she said, struggling to keep her emotions in check. 'He was such a wonderful person. He will be missed so much.'

Giorgio rested his head on the top of hers, his arms going around her to hold her close. 'Yes, he will,' he said. 'But he wanted us to move on. He didn't want us to feel sorry for him or wallow in grief. He wanted us to live life to the full, like he did.'

If only life wasn't so capricious, Maya thought. Living it to the full was fine for some people, but once you had been hit from the left-field a couple of times it made one rather cautious about living in the moment.

Giorgio put her from him after a little while, still anchoring her with his hands curled around her upper arms. 'So how are you feeling, *cara*?' he asked. 'What did the doctor say? I am sorry I couldn't come with you. Did you get my text message? I got caught up with my grandfather's palliative care doctor. I couldn't really get away in time.'

Although Maya was a little surprised by his rapid change of subject, she was starting to see it was his way of coping, to move on with life as if nothing had happened. He would grieve but he would do so in private. 'Yes, I got your message and I totally understand. It was just a check-up, in any case. Everything is fine. Dr

Rossini thinks the nausea should settle in another few weeks.'

He smiled and placed his hand on her still flat belly. 'No one would ever know you are carrying my child in there,' he said. 'How soon before you will start to show?'

'Bronte said it might not show for another month or two,' she said. 'She said she was almost five and a half months before she did with Ella.'

'I think we should make an announcement to the press once my grandfather's funeral is over,' he said. 'Look at how much attention Luca and Bronte got over their love-child and then the wedding and now a second pregnancy. It's what people want to hear. They thrive on it.'

Maya frowned at him. 'But I thought you wanted to keep the press out of this for as long as possible?'

He dropped his hands from her and moved across to the bar area. He poured some iced water in a tall glass and handed it to her before he made himself a brandy and dry. 'My grandfather wanted the Sabbatini name to be associated with growth and success, not illness and death,' he said. 'We owe it to our investors and the staff and guests in all of our hotels to remind them life goes on, business as usual. The announcement of our much anticipated child will draw attention away from the family's loss at this time.'

Maya was incensed. She hated the thought of the press hounding her, chasing her, perhaps even putting her life and that of her baby in danger as they shoved and crowded her for a photo. 'So this is all a business strategy to you, is it?' she asked.

Giorgio took a deep draught of his drink before he answered. 'You are overreacting, as usual, Maya. I am merely saying we need to stay focused on the positive, not the negative. I manage a huge global corporation. I don't want anything to have a negative impact on it and nor did my grandfather. Those were some of the last words he spoke to me.'

Maya turned away, putting her glass down with a loud thud on the coffee table. 'I will not agree to have the news of my pregnancy splashed over every paper and gossip magazine in the country, if not all over Europe, just so you can make money out of it.'

'Maya—'

She turned on him like a snarling cat. 'Don't patronise me with that I'm-the-one-in-charge tone. You know how much I hate the intrusion of the press. It's one of the reasons our marriage crumbled.'

His mouth became tight-lipped. 'The reason our marriage crumbled was because you were not mature enough to face the reality that life doesn't always go according to plan. You acted like a spoilt child who couldn't have what she wanted right when she wanted it. You stormed out of our marriage pouting all the way.'

Maya's mouth dropped open in outrage. 'You're calling *me* a spoilt child? What about you, with your private jet and Lamborghini and Ferrari, for God's sake. You know *nothing* of what it's like to struggle. All your life you've had everything handed to you on a silver family crest-embossed platter.'

He put his now empty glass down. 'I am not going to be drawn into an argument with you. You are upset over my grandfather's death. I shouldn't have even brought up the subject of the press announcement.'

Maya refused to be mollified. She folded her arms and glared at him.

Spoilt child, indeed.

Pouting all the way out of her marriage.

What the hell did he mean by that? He would have divorced her as quick as a wink if it hadn't been for what he stood to lose in a settlement.

She watched as he poured himself another drink, a double this time. He wasn't a huge drinker, which made her realise with a little jolt that he was feeling his loss rather more deeply than he was letting on. He had said *she* was upset about his grandfather's death but, as usual, he had not said anything about how he was feeling.

'Giorgio...' She curled her fingers around each other, uncertain how to progress.

'Leave it, Maya,' he said, raising his tumbler to his lips.

She waited for a beat or two. 'How is your mother taking it?' she asked.

He didn't even bother to turn around to face her to answer. His left shoulder hiked up and down in a shrug. 'She is upset, of course. It will no doubt bring back the pain of the loss of my father, but she has her family around her. Luca's with her now and Bronte and gorgeous little Ella. She will be the best distraction for *Mamma*—for all of us, actually. Nic's due to fly in tomorrow. He's in Monte Carlo, probably gambling or sleeping with some wannabe starlet or both.'

'You disapprove of his lifestyle, don't you?' Maya asked after another little pause.

Giorgio turned around and looked at her, glass in hand. 'You think I have had every privilege and certainly, compared to you, that is indeed the case, but don't for a moment think I don't appreciate or value what I have been given as a birthright. Luca had to grow up and grow up fast when he almost ruined his own and Bronte's life. Nic has yet to learn to take responsibility for his actions. But I have a feeling he is about to.'

'Oh?' she asked. 'What makes you say that?'

He gave her a grim look. 'My grandfather talked to me briefly about his will. Nic is not going to like some of the terms, let me tell you. If he doesn't toe the line within a year he will be disinherited.'

Maya flinched in shock. 'Salvatore stated *that* in his will?'

Giorgio nodded and took another generous mouthful of his drink. 'The feathers are about to fly, or at least they will when Nic finds out when the will is read. If he wants to contest it he will have a lengthy and very expensive fight on his hands. I am hoping he won't go down that path. The press will make a circus of it, for one thing. Also, it could mean trouble for the Corporation if Nic defaults.'

'I'm not used to these sorts of things,' she said. 'When my mother died she hadn't even left a will. She didn't have anything to leave in it, even if she had gone to the trouble of writing one.'

Giorgio put his glass down on the bar. 'You must have missed her when she died so suddenly. You've hardly ever talked about it.'

Maya tried not to think of that time. She hated being reminded of her lonely childhood, how much of a burden she had been made to feel by her penurious great-aunt, how much she had longed for a cuddle or a word of praise and encouragement from a woman who loathed all forms of affection and who thought words of affirmation would unnecessarily inflate a child's ego.

Maya's school days had been the worst. Watching as all the other kids had one or both parents come to assemblies or end of school prize nights. Her great-aunt had not attended a single event. Eunice Cornwell didn't believe in competition of any sort, so when Maya had taken out the Headmaster's Prize for Outstanding Academic Achievement at her Leaver's Assembly no one had been there to see it.

'It wasn't a great time in my life,' Maya said. 'My great-aunt resented having me thrust upon her. I resented being there. I left as soon as I possibly could.'

'Poor little orphaned Maya,' Giorgio said, coming over to where she was standing so stiffly. 'No wonder you were attracted to me with my big family.'

'I was attracted to you, not your family,' Maya said.

He lifted the hair off the back of her neck, sending the nerves beneath her skin into a frenzy of delight. 'Ah, yes,' he said. 'And you still are, aren't you, *tesore mio*?'

'I can hardly deny it when I am currently carrying

the evidence in my belly,' she said in a wry tone. *Long may it continue*, she tacked on silently.

His other hand went to her abdomen, pressing against it gently but possessively. 'I want to make love to you,' he said, his voice deep and sexy and irresistible. 'Now.'

Maya felt her insides flip over. That dark smouldering look in his eyes sent her heart racing and when he traced a fingertip down over the curve of her breast, even though she was still fully dressed, she felt her nipple instantly engorge with blood. 'Are you asking me or telling me?' she said in a voice that wobbled with anticipation.

His head came down, his brandy-scented breath skating over her upturned mouth. '*Do* I need to ask, *cara*?'

She gave him his answer in actions not words. She met his mouth with hers, sliding her tongue to join his in a sexy duel that got more and more heated the longer it continued. She was breathless by the time he had her locked in his arms, her dress in a pool at her feet, her breasts bare and aching for his mouth. She gasped as his lips closed over her tightly budded nipple, the pleasure so acute she felt her senses spin out of control.

The passion became an inferno, consuming everything in its path. There was no time for moving upstairs, no time for lingering over kisses and caresses or murmuring sensuous promises.

Giorgio pressed her down to the carpeted floor, his body joining hers, covering her with his weight balanced on his arms. His mouth came back to hers, taking it in another steamy assault of the senses, thrusting and probing with his tongue in a delicious and erotic mimic of what was to come.

Maya writhed with want beneath him. She wanted him naked and slick with her moisture and his inside her. She wanted to feel that hard pumping of his body she had missed so much. She became totally wanton with her need. She clawed at his clothes, popping buttons and pulling out his belt from its loops like a madwoman on a mission.

He worked on her clothes with a little more finesse, but not much. He kissed each part of her body he exposed, his lips and tongue lighting fires all along her flesh. He feasted on her breasts, sucking and pulling, swirling his tongue around each nipple, making them pucker even further.

Maya took him in her hand, relishing the turgid potency of him. He quivered and throbbed and then tugged her hand off him, pressing her back down and entering her with a stabbing thrust that sent a shockwave of rapture throughout her body.

He immediately checked himself, retreating a little in case he had gone too deep, but she dug her fingers into his buttocks and urged him even deeper. He groaned and thrust again and again, harder and faster, his breathing becoming ragged, fine beads of perspiration springing up over his flesh and hers as she too felt her control slipping in the heat and fire of the moment.

The friction was just right, catching her swollen pearl of need, the secret heart of her that responded to him so wantonly. She arched her spine and gave herself up to the orgasm as it swept her up into its vortex, swirling and tossing her about like a ragdoll. She shook and quaked with the power of it, the reverberations of her body sending Giorgio into his own powerful release. She felt every muscle in his body tense in that split second before he finally unleashed his control. The quick hard pumps of his body spilling hotly into hers made her feel another wave of pleasure, her inner core pulsing with it until she was as limbless and sated as he.

Maya lay beneath him, her heart still hammering with the thrill of having him possess her totally. She didn't want to talk and spoil the moment. She wanted to cling to this special closeness for, even though she suspected it was more physical than emotional for him, for her it was all about the feelings she had for him, and that was the way it had always been. She couldn't separate the lust from the love like other people did. Even the night of Luca's wedding, when she had fallen into bed with Giorgio, it had been less about lust and more about love.

Fate had brought them back together, fate and circumstances that meant she would have to think very carefully before she took it upon herself to walk away again.

Sabbatini men played for keeps. Losing was not in their vocabulary. Giorgio's relationship with her had nothing to do with love. It was all about pride and ownership and continuing the blue-blooded line of the family.

But that might be the one and only thing Giorgio could not control, even though Maya dearly, longingly, prayerfully wished it were.

CHAPTER ELEVEN

THE funeral for Salvatore Sabbatini was large but the service was still deeply meaningful and poignant. Salvatore had lived a good life, a long life marked along the way with a lot of success and a measure of tragedy. Outliving his son Giancarlo was something he had grieved over in his own way, and when Maya saw the PowerPoint presentation Giorgio had put together of his grandfather's life she too, along with most of the other mourners, had to wipe tears from her eyes as she witnessed the moving sweep of his life, from that of a small child to his last days, holding his much anticipated great-grandchild Ella on his knee.

The celebration of his life continued at a private function in the Sabbatini hotel. It was mostly attended by family and close friends but somehow one or two members of the press had sneaked in. While Maya was watching everyone from the sidelines she suddenly found herself face to face with a large camera lens aimed at her.

'Signora Sabbatini,' the paparazzi man said, 'is it true you are expecting a child?'

Maya was caught off guard and, after too long a pause, mumbled, 'No comment.'

'Word has it the child could be that of Howard Herrington, the man you had a brief affair with during your estrangement from your husband. Everyone knows you and your husband had issues with fertility over the past few years. Do you have anything to say about that?'

Giorgio suddenly appeared at Maya's side, his expression infuriated beyond anything she had witnessed before. 'There is absolutely no truth in those rumours,' he said. 'The child is mine; there is no doubt about it and there never has been. Now, leave, before I ask Security to escort you from the premises.'

The journalist sloped off and Giorgio took Maya's elbow and led her to one of the vacant rooms off the main function room. He closed the door and looked down at her with concern etched on his features. 'Are you all right?' he asked. 'I thought you were going to faint for a moment there.'

Maya placed a shaking hand to her forehead. 'I should have been more prepared...I felt like a stranded fish, standing there with my mouth opening and closing before I could think of something to say.'

He rubbed the side of his face with one of his hands. 'I was hoping to avoid this,' he said. 'That's why I wanted to make a proper announcement before the press got in first with their stupid speculation. It's much harder to control the rumours when they come from unknown sources.'

Maya studied his brooding expression for a moment.

'There's no doubt in your mind that this is your child, is there, Giorgio?'

'No, of course not.' He pushed his hair back where it was falling forward. 'Not now.'

'What do you mean, "not now"?' she asked. 'Has something or someone confirmed my side of the story?'

His dark eyes met hers, holding them for a beat or two before he answered. 'I ran into your date, Howard Herringbone.'

Maya didn't bother correcting him this time. 'Ran into him?' she asked with a sceptical lift of her brows. 'I can't imagine under what circumstances you would...' she put her fingers up like quotation marks '... run into him.'

'All right, I admit it,' Giorgio said after a tense pause. 'I tracked him down and paid him a visit. He confirmed that you and he had met once for a meal that was set up by a mutual friend.'

Maya was beyond anger. She stood with her blood roaring in her ears at his audacity, at his lack of trust, at his arrogance and bullheadedness. 'So you didn't believe me,' she said through tight lips. 'You could only do that when you had confirmation from another source.'

'Think about it from my side, Maya,' he said. 'It would have been the perfect payback. You left me when I failed to get you pregnant. What else was I to think when I discovered you were carrying a child?'

'I didn't just leave you because you failed to get me pregnant,' she shot back. 'I left you because our marriage was dead.'

'Even so, you didn't exactly rush to tell me,' he said. 'I only found out by chance when I opened that drawer in search of a toothbrush.'

'I was going to tell you,' she said.

His expression was cynical. 'When? Like Bronte did to Luca? When the child was over a year old?'

Maya sprang to her new friend's defence. 'That was Luca's fault, not Bronte's. He was the one who cut her from his life without a single explanation as to why. He didn't trust her enough to tell her the truth about his situation.'

'Luca is a very private person,' Giorgio said. 'He didn't even tell his own family what he was going through.'

'I don't want to get into it,' she said. 'They have sorted it out now and are so much in love; how could anyone not be happy for them?'

'I *am* happy for them,' he said. 'I just know that Luca has missed out on his child's first year of life. No one can make that up to him or to us as his family. We were all cheated of that year. I would never forgive you the way he has done Bronte if you had tried to pull that kind of stunt on me.'

Maya glared at him heatedly. 'How could I have done that when up until now I have never even stayed pregnant longer than a measly six weeks?'

The air rang with the pain of her words, filling every large and small space of the room with its presence.

He took a step towards her. 'Maya...'

She warned him off by folding her arms tightly around her body. 'Don't make this any worse than it already is,' she said. 'You forced me to come back to you to give your grandfather peace in his last days but he's gone now. I don't have to stay with you any longer. You can't force me. I could pack my bags and leave you today and there's nothing you could do to stop me.'

A flash of anger fired in his gaze like the blast of a gun. 'If you leave me this time around, Maya, you will regret it for the rest of your life. I was too easy on you the first time around. I thought you needed space; I thought we both needed it. But this time the gloves will be off. I will take my child off you as soon as it is born and don't for a moment think I couldn't or wouldn't do it.'

Maya swallowed as his hateful words began to sink in. This was no longer a fight for his money, but for his child as well. He would do anything to keep both under his control. She was immaterial to him: just another piece on the chessboard of his life, to move around as he pleased. If he loved her wouldn't he just have said so to get her to stay with him?

'You are assuming, of course, that this child will be born,' she said in a voice she barely recognised as her own: it sounded hard and bitter and full of ice-cold contempt.

'The doctor is very confident you will deliver a perfectly healthy child this time,' Giorgio said. 'I want that child, Maya. Don't make me take it off you with a long drawn out divorce and custody battle. You should know by now I will not let you win.'

She threw him a flaying look. 'I know you are ruthless and heartless when it comes to getting what you want. You are prepared to lock yourself into a loveless marriage for God knows how many years just so you don't have to give me what I want.'

'It seems to me you don't even know what you want,' he threw back. 'You said you wanted a divorce but as soon as we were thrown together for a few hours you were back in my bed. Nothing's changed, Maya. You want me. I want you.'

Maya hated that her colour was high. She felt the shame of her capitulation to him all over again. She was so weak, so wanton when it came to this man. Why couldn't she have better self-control? 'How long do you think this lust fest is going to last?' she asked.

His coal-black eyes glittered as they challenged hers. 'It's lasted pretty well so far,' he said. 'In fact, if there wasn't a crowd of people just outside this door I would take you here and now and prove it.'

Maya felt her body respond with hot wires of need. Her skin broke out in goose bumps at the mere thought of him possessing her the way he had done the night of his grandfather's death. They had made love every night since, and yet each time it had transcended the prior experience, as if her body was only now coming to full sensual maturity. She had lost so many of her inhibitions; she had enjoyed his body in every way possible.

There was a knock at the door that shattered the sensual spell like a rock on a thin glass window.

Giorgio strode over to the door and tugged it open. 'Yes?' he barked curtly.

'Oh…sorry,' Bronte, Luca's wife, said, blushing. 'I was just looking for Jade Sommerville. I saw her briefly at the funeral but I haven't seen her since. I guess she must have left early or something.'

Giorgio muttered something about not keeping a head count on every guest and how he should not be expected to and, curtly excusing himself, strode out of the room.

Bronte looked across at Maya, who was still standing with her body so stiff it looked as if she were wrapped in cling film and couldn't move. 'Are you OK, Maya?' she asked.

Maya unpeeled her arms from around her body and let out a sigh. 'Sorry about Giorgio being so rude to you just then. He's had a lot on his mind, as you can imagine.'

'I know.' Bronte's voice was softly sympathetic. 'It's such a sad time for the family. And poor Giorgio's had to do so much for so long. No wonder he's a bit tetchy with everyone. But how are you holding up?'

'I'm fine,' Maya said, shifting her gaze a little.

There was a small but telling silence.

'Look, you can tell me if it's none of my business, but I couldn't help noticing things were pretty tense with you and Giorgio just now,' Bronte said. 'Is that just because of the stress he's been under or something else?'

Maya felt her chin start to wobble but quickly got it under control. 'We are having some teething problems, but no doubt we'll sort them out in time. I haven't exactly been the best person to be around just lately. I can't quite let myself believe this baby is going to make it.'

'Oh, Maya.' Bronte came over and hugged her close. 'You poor, poor darling. I know it's hard but you have to think positively. Soon you'll be showing and then I am sure it will feel much more real to you.'

Maya pulled back from the hug after a moment. 'I know; it's just I'm not sure how to handle Giorgio. The thing is, I have never known how to handle him. I can't get close to him, at least not emotionally. He won't let me.'

Bronte frowned. 'You still love him though, don't you?'

'That's the problem,' Maya said on another heartfelt sigh. 'I love him just as much, if not more than I did before.'

'But?'

Maya's eyes met Bronte's concerned ones. 'Giorgio is incapable of love, or at least of showing it.'

Bronte frowned. 'But he must have loved you once. He married you, didn't he?'

Maya's chin wobbled again and she bit down on her lip to steady it. 'Our marriage was not a romantic match, more of an expedient one.'

Bronte's brows went up. 'What on earth do you mean?'

Maya sighed heavily. 'Giorgio and I met just before his father had the accident. I fell in love with him, but he only married me because his family expected it of him, especially once things looked so grim with his father. His goal was to get married and have an heir and I stupidly agreed to it, hoping that one day he would fall in love with me, but of course he didn't. We made each other positively miserable, especially when it became pretty clear I wasn't going to fulfil my end of the arrangement in producing an heir and a spare on schedule.'

'Oh, Maya,' Bronte said again, clearly lost for words.

'We're only back together because of Salvatore dying and, of course, the baby,' Maya went on. 'If it hadn't been for this pregnancy, we would be apart now that Salvatore is gone. Giorgio was as keen to move on with his life as I was to move on with mine.'

Bronte's expression looked pinched with pity. 'Oh, dear... You surely don't think he has someone else? You know, like a mistress or something?'

Maya thought of that svelte lingerie model and pain sliced through her like the blade of a scimitar. 'I don't know...maybe...I hope not...'

Bronte put a gentle hand on Maya's arm. 'Do you want me to have a word with Luca about it to see if he can talk to Giorgio?'

Maya shook her head. 'No, please don't involve Luca or anyone else in this. Giorgio and I have to sort it out ourselves.'

'Give it time, Maya,' Bronte advised. 'A lot of stuff has happened over a short period of time. From what I've seen, Giorgio takes on a lot of the stress for other people. I guess that comes from being the oldest brother. Once things settle down a bit he might see things differently. He certainly looks and acts like he cares about you. Luca and I were only discussing it the other day. Giorgio is so protective of you, making sure you get enough rest and don't do too much. He was absolutely furious with us for allowing you to sit with Salvatore for several hours the week before he died—you know, the day I had my doctor's appointment? He said you were only to be allowed to take short shifts. I was quite frightened of him but Luca assured me it was because he really cares about you and the baby.'

The door opened and Luca came in carrying a fractious Ella. 'Ah, here she is,' he said, winking at Bronte. 'Here's Mummy.'

'Mum Mum,' Ella wailed piteously and reached out her little arms for Bronte.

Maya felt a wave of envy go through her. How she longed for a child of her own to do exactly that, not to mention a husband as loving and devoted as Luca was to Bronte.

'This young lady needs a sleep,' Bronte said, smiling ruefully at Maya. 'Do you want to go shopping with me tomorrow? I can come and pick you up. I found this great maternity boutique. There was a pink and white top and trousers with an expandable waistline that would look fabulous on you with your gorgeous colouring.'

Maya smiled. 'I would love that. I haven't got anything planned.'

'Great,' Bronte said, cupping Ella's sleepy head against her shoulder. 'I'll pick you up about eleven, OK?'

Maya watched as Luca put a loving arm around his wife as they left the room together, the bond of their child and the new one they were expecting cementing them together in a bond that was unbreakable.

The door had barely swung shut when it opened again, roughly this time, with a stormy-looking Nic striding in, ready for some sort of showdown. 'Oh, *scusi*,' he said, pulling up short when he saw her. 'I thought you were someone else.'

'Sorry to disappoint you,' Maya said, unable to remove the tartness from her tone in time.

Nic's expression lost some of its hardness. 'Look, Maya, I know you think I belong under a rock some place but, for Giorgio's sake, can we try and get along? I'm really happy about you being back together. Giorgio needs the stable influence. He's not been the same since you left him.'

'I might not be able to give him the family he wants,' she said. 'It's still early days.'

'You're doing a great job so far,' he said, his eyes flicking to her belly and back with a green-flecked twinkle in them.

'I'm really sorry about your grandfather,' Maya said to fill the awkward little silence.

The hardness came back into Nic's face, making him look older than his thirty-two years. 'That old conniving bastard has just tried to screw up my life,' he bit out. 'But I am not going to roll over for him or for anyone.'

'You sound exactly like your brother,' she said with a touch of wryness.

'Yeah, well, I'll take that as a compliment, even though right now I swear to God I could bloody his nose for him. I just bet he put the old man up to this.'

'Up to what?' Maya asked.

'Never mind,' he said, shoving open the door. 'See you around.'

CHAPTER TWELVE

GIORGIO was silent on the drive home and Maya refused to try and nudge him out of it. She was still a little angry with him, but even angrier at herself for not having the strength to call his bluff over his threats. She could leave him before the baby was born and spend the next six months just as miserable as the six months she'd spent when she left him the first time. But, for the baby's sake and her own, she decided to stay. She was just starting to feel the bloom of pregnancy everyone always talked about, the higher level of energy, the glow of the skin and the rush of hormones that made her feel gloriously alive as a woman. It would be crazy to jeopardise all of that by living in a rented flat with Gonzo, who would no doubt lounge about mirroring her misery every day.

Besides, this had been a tumultuous and very difficult time for the Sabbatini family. They were all feeling the loss of Salvatore and it would be selfish of her to complicate things at such a raw emotional time.

And then, of course, there was the fact that she simply didn't want to miss seeing Giorgio every day. She was only just beginning to understand his character. He often showed an air of aloof indifference when something was troubling him. In the past she had taken that as cold dismissal of what was important to her, but now she could see he needed a little more time to process things before he revealed what he felt about them.

Bronte's revelation about his reaction to her sitting with Salvatore for so long had surprised her. Giorgio had made no mention of it, although she seemed to recall he had employed another nurse soon after that day. But maybe that was because the baby was his main priority. It was the only reason their marriage was continuing, after all.

But, in spite of everything, Maya didn't want him to miss seeing their baby grow inside her. Bronte had told her a couple of weeks back how hard it had been to have no one by her side, apart from her mother, when she was carrying Ella. Bronte had longed for Luca to have been there, witnessing every subtle and not so subtle change in her body, as he was doing now for this new baby.

She placed her hand on her abdomen protectively, wondering if the baby could sense how much love she had for it, how much she longed for it to grow to full term and arrive safely. If will alone could achieve such a miracle, she felt she was in with a very good chance.

'Are you feeling all right?' Giorgio asked, glancing at her. 'You're not in pain, are you?'

Maya put her hand back in her lap with her other one. 'Is it the baby you're worried about or me?' she asked, longing for reassurance.

His mouth tightened as he turned the car into the driveway. 'I have a lot of worries in my life right now and you are certainly one of them,' he said.

'Thanks,' she said. 'That makes me feel a whole lot better.'

He blew out a breath as he turned off the engine and swivelled in his seat to face her. 'I am sorry for taking a hard stand with you over this issue of divorce you keep raising. It's not that I don't believe in ending a miserably empty marriage; I just think we could make things work for us if we stick at it.'

Maya looked into his eyes, wondering if she had the courage to ask him outright what his feelings for her were now. But then she wasn't sure she would believe him if he said he did love her. How easy would it be for him to pretend so she fell in with his plans?

Celebrity divorces were ugly. They were also very public and a lot of mud could get thrown back and forth. He would want to avoid it just as much as she would.

He reached out and brushed the back of his bent knuckles along the curve of her cheek in a faineant movement that sent all her nerves dancing in delight. 'I promised my grandfather I would look after you,' he said in a husky tone. 'You were like another grandchild to him. I think he saw you as a replacement of the grand-daughter he lost.'

Maya put her hand over his, holding it to her cheek. 'You never talk of her—of Chiara,' she said softly. 'I don't think I've even seen a photo of her.'

His eyes became shadowed and he pulled his hand out from under hers. 'She would have looked just like Ella,' he said, his hands gripping the steering wheel tightly, even though the car was not in motion. 'Luca showed me some photos of when Ella was the age Chiara was when she died. It was like looking at a mirror image.'

'It must have been a terrible time for you, finding her like that,' she said, imagining the tragic scene in her head and feeling sick with anguish for him.

There was a silence that lasted only a few seconds but it felt much, much longer.

'It was,' he said, his expression darkening as if he were walking back through to that tragic day in his mind. 'I went into her room and it was so silent, so terribly, eerily silent. And then I realised she was too still, too pale, waxy, just like a doll.'

Maya swallowed against the tennis ball of emotion that clogged her throat. 'Oh, Giorgio...'

'We should go inside,' he said, swiftly changing the subject. 'You have been on your feet way too long and I too am exhausted. It's been a hell of a long week.'

Maya followed him into the villa, glad of his supportive arm around her waist, the feel of that strong band of flesh reminding her of all the passion that simmered between them, even when they were angry with each other. He had opened up to her, just a little bit, just enough for her to see how deeply he felt about things even though he gave no outward sign of it. He was obviously trying to connect with her for the sake of their baby. It clearly wasn't easy for him. She had seen the struggle played out on his face as he had spoken of finding his baby sister and she loved him all the more for it.

Once inside, Giorgio turned her into the circle of his arms. 'Why don't you go upstairs and run a bath? I will join you in a few minutes. I have some calls and emails to see to first.'

Maya felt her heart trip in excitement. Sharing a bath with Giorgio was an experience that was totally unforgettable. They hadn't done it since their reconciliation but she knew it would be every bit as thrilling as the last time they had, if not more.

She was sitting soaking luxuriously in a deep pool of warm bubbly water when he came in. He was totally, gloriously naked. She feasted her eyes on his body: his broad chest with its dusting of coarse hair, his flat brown nipples, his even flatter abdomen, and lean hips and strongly muscled thighs, and the most intensely masculine part of him rising proudly between them.

He came over and stepped into the bath, sending a wave of rippling water over her partially submerged breasts. 'How's the water?' he asked with a smouldering look.

'Getting hotter by the minute,' she said with a deliberate arch of her spine to showcase her breasts, swollen with hormones.

His eyes went straight to them, his nostrils flaring like a proud stallion. 'You become more beautiful every day,' he said, sinking into the water and spreading his legs so she was encased between them.

Maya sat up to run her hands teasingly down his hair-roughened thighs, feeling him tense in response. She held his dark gaze, mesmerising him with the sultry promise of her eyes, knowing he would be throbbing with want within seconds of her reaching for him under the water. She tiptoed her fingers up and down his legs, stopping just short of his erection. 'You like that?' she asked.

'You know exactly what I like,' he said, lying back as she came forward.

Her breasts brushed along his chest, her nipples tingling with pleasure at the friction of his hair. Belly to belly, it was the most erotic sensation, feeling his desire for her burgeoning against her, seeking entry, aching for release, twitching with the need to do so as quickly as possible.

But she wasn't going to let him until she had teased him some more. She wanted him begging and she would not stop until he did so. So far, he had dictated all the terms in their relationship. Now it was her turn, using her feminine power to remind him that they were equals, at least when it came to physical desire. Sex was another way to connect, a deeply intimate way to show how compatible they were when other things were not taking centre stage.

She pushed a finger to the middle of his sternum, making him go down further into the water. 'Down, boy,' she said in a sexy tone. 'I'm not quite finished with you yet.'

'I thought you were tired,' he said in a kind of strangled voice.

She stabbed playfully at his chest again and fluttered her eyelashes at him. '*You* said that, not me. I am not in the least bit tired. In fact, I am just warming up.'

'*Dio*,' he groaned as she bent her head to his chest and licked each of his nipples in turn.

Maya kept going, lower and lower, slowly, tantalisingly

so, stringing out the anticipation, making him quiver with each sweep and glide of her tongue and gentle playful nip of her teeth. The water was too deep for her to do what she really wanted so she deftly pulled the plug, smiling as the sound of the water gurgling away filled the pulsing silence.

Giorgio's dark brows lifted. 'Bath's over?'

She was on all fours and coming dangerously closer. 'Definitely all over.'

'So...' he snatched in a breath '...what happens next?'

She gave him a come-hither look as she stood amongst the retreating bubbles, her hands sliding down over her breasts and belly and to the naked heart of her sex. 'I think you know what comes next.'

He did and he could barely wait.

He had never seen her in quite this mood before. She was like a sultry temptress, luring him into a sex game that was unlike anything he had experienced with her before. He was ready to come, just looking at her touching herself like that.

He got to his feet and followed her to the bedroom, not even caring about the wet slap of his footsteps on the marble floor and the bubbles that trailed in their wake.

He wanted her and he wanted her now.

Urgently, passionately and endlessly.

She turned at the bed and tilted one hip in a pose that said come-and-get-me. 'What are you waiting for?' she asked.

Giorgio came down on top of her, thrusting into her

moist core, making every hair on the back of her neck quiver in response. Her tight warm body clutched at him, drawing him into her, making it impossible for him to slow things down. He was rushing headlong into a climactic release, only just managing to control himself long enough to make sure her needs were met first. He played her with his fingers, the swollen heart of her so ready for him she gasped and cried out loud with the pleasure it evoked. Within seconds she was convulsing around him, triggering his own earth-shattering response.

Her fingers worked their way up and down his spine in the aftermath, her soft little caressing movements making his body react to her all over again.

Giorgio propped himself up on his elbows and looked down at her cheeks, which were flushed with pleasure. 'You know, when the baby gets bigger we won't be able to make love like this,' he said. 'We'll have to be a little more creative.'

He saw the flicker of worry in her eyes. 'Sometimes I feel like it's not happening…that it's all a dream and someone is going to wake me up and say you're not pregnant. There is no baby.'

He brushed the damp hair away from her face. 'I know you are, *cara*, but look how well you are doing. Everyone is remarking on how wonderful you look. You are positively glowing. It won't be long now and you will feel the baby moving inside you.' He placed his hand on her belly. 'I can't wait to feel him or her kicking its little feet.'

'Bronte said it will be another few weeks before I feel the first flutters of movement,' she said.

'You will tell me the first time you feel something, won't you?' he asked.

'Of course,' she said, lowering her gaze as she traced a finger over his collarbone.

In spite of everything, Giorgio was still worried she might leave him. He had left himself wide open for a financially crippling settlement by not organising a prenuptial agreement before they married. But, with his father's accident and then his rapid decline, there hadn't been time.

He wasn't comfortable making threats about taking sole custody, but he wanted this baby and he wasn't going to allow her to take it to the other side of the world, or in fact even to England, where he couldn't see it daily and have a positive influence on its life. He was not going to join the band of divorced fathers he knew, men who hardly ever saw their children, men who spent lonely weekends and Christmases and holiday periods while their children were with their mother and her new partner.

He wanted to give this child a stable and happy childhood. His childhood had been perfect until Chiara had died. It had taken him decades to be able to think of that time in his life without flinching. His parents had become shadows of themselves; it had taken years before they came out of the abyss of grief that had consumed them. But they *had* come out. They had worked at their marriage, even in spite of his father's couple of affairs, which had seemed more a product of Giancarlo's grief than any malicious desire to inflict hurt on his already suffering wife. Giorgio's mother had forgiven him and they had moved on and, up until his death, had enjoyed a close and loving relationship.

But then Giorgio's mother had always loved his father. She had loved him in spite of her pain over the loss of their daughter; she had loved him in spite of his betrayal with other women, she had loved him right to the end, when he had closed his eyes for the last time, lying in her arms.

Giorgio was not sure what Maya felt for him but he was almost certain it wasn't love. In the beginning she had been captivated by his wealth and lifestyle and the love she had spoken of back then seemed more a star-struck variety than the real thing. After the first year, she had stopped telling him she loved him, which more or less proved her feelings had not been genuine.

He was ashamed to admit he hadn't been in love with her when he asked her to marry him. It had been a convenient marriage for him, a way to secure his future. His world had been rocked by his father's accident and he had done what had been expected of him by marrying a suitable wife to continue the proud heritage he had been born into.

It had only been recently that he had thought long and hard about his feelings for Maya. They had been changing like the seasons: warm and cool, hot and cold. The experiences they had gone through had clouded things for him. He had shied away from the overwhelming emotions Maya demonstrated at times. It was the pattern of a lifetime and it had taken her leaving him for him to see it. But he knew that without the pressure of producing an heir and fulfilling everyone else's expectations he and Maya were amazingly compatible. Not just in bed, although that was wonderful and he constantly delighted in her body and how it made him feel, but it was more than that, much more. She had been a wonderful support to him through the agonising process of his grandfather's illness. She had sat for long hours reading to Salvatore and then, when she was not with him, she was at home at the villa, making sure things were in order when Giorgio got home exhausted from trying to juggle all the things he had to do. She quietly and diligently backed him up, offering comfort when he needed it, but also maintaining her new-found independence, not allowing him to dominate her, as he had done in the past.

Maya's voice interrupted his reverie. 'Do you think we should find out the sex of the baby on the next ultrasound?'

'Do you want to know or be surprised?' Giorgio asked.

'Haven't we had enough surprises?' she asked with a wry look.

He smiled and, leaning forward, pressed a soft kiss to the middle of her forehead. 'You continually surprise me, Maya,' he said and moved his lips down the side of her face until he got to her lips.

She moistened them in preparation, her eyes flaring with reawakened need. He lowered his head slowly, inch by inch, taking his time, waiting for that betraying little murmur of pleasure she gave when his mouth finally settled on hers.

No one could kiss like Giorgio, Maya thought. Not that she'd had a truckload of experience, but enough to know that when he kissed her there was no way it could ever be described as chaste and platonic. He kissed with sultry, steamy purpose, his need erotically apparent with every thrust and glide of his tongue inside her mouth.

When he moved his mouth to rediscover her breasts her back lifted off the bed in delight. She felt her nipples tighten to twin points of pleasure as his hot moist mouth enveloped each of them in turn. His hands cupped her feminine mound, teasing her with the so-close-but-not-close-enough presence of his clever, artful fingers.

She whimpered but he kept her hungry for him, holding her in his power, as she had done just minutes before.

Just when she thought she could stand it no longer, he gently but deftly turned her over onto her stomach, coming between her spread legs from behind in the most erotic position of all. There was a primal, earthy quality to it, a raw urgency that made her blood race like rocket fuel in her veins.

He entered her in one slick possessive thrust, a dominant surge of his body that spoke of his alpha status and her feminine submission to it. It was exciting, it was enthralling, it was everything she had hoped it would be. He had her coming apart in seconds, her whole body quaking with the tremors of release, until she was sweaty and sated, her flesh singing and tingling all over.

He waited until she had finished before he emptied himself, the action of his body pumping from behind with the brush of his hips against her sensitive buttocks making her feel a ripple of reaction all over again. She heard him groan deep in the back of his throat, signalling the supreme monumental scale of his pleasure.

Did he have this level of pleasure with anyone else? she wondered. The thought was unwelcome and intrusive, like a rat suddenly appearing under the table just as important dinner guests were to arrive. She couldn't make it go away; it nibbled at the edges of her consciousness, making her ill with the thought of how Giorgio could so easily have his cake at home and any number of gateaux on the side.

But how could she know without asking, and how could she ask without revealing how much it mattered to her?

CHAPTER THIRTEEN

WHEN Maya woke the following morning she found Giorgio's side of the bed empty, which wasn't unusual since he was an early riser, but a sixth sense told her something was amiss.

She pushed back the covers and, slipping on a bathrobe, padded down the stairs. She heard him speaking on the phone from his study, which again was not unusual, even at this early hour, for he had business concerns all over the world in several different time zones. What was unusual was the way he was deliberately keeping his voice down, even though she could tell he was blisteringly angry.

He was speaking in English and it was undoubtedly to a woman.

As Maya listened her heart cramped with each word that was spoken, her fragile hopes of happiness dying an excruciatingly painful death.

'I told you never to call me on this number,' Giorgio was saying. 'Our association, as you call it, is over. I have other priorities now.'

The person on the other end of the line must have said something in return for he paused for a moment before continuing in the same harsh tone, 'I will deny each and every one of your claims. You have no evidence. Everyone will see it as nothing more than a money-making exercise on your part.'

Maya had heard enough. She slipped away and went into the kitchen, in desperate need of a glass of water to soothe her aching throat.

It was there that she saw the morning paper.

It was emblazoned with the features page headline: *Hotel Billionaire Giorgio Sabbatini Caught Out in Tell-all Exclusive by Lingerie Model Mistress.*

Maya's hand shook as she turned the pages to the section where there was a photograph of Giorgio and the lingerie model, called Talesha Barton, captured in a cosy-looking tryst in a nightclub. Talesha was everything Maya was not. She was buxom and tall, dark-haired and exotic-looking with wide almond-shaped eyes and a mouth that was impossibly full and sexy.

The tell-all story was full of saucy details of how the part-time model had met the estranged Giorgio Sabbatini and enjoyed a hot night of passion with him in a secret hideaway. 'He is an amazing lover,' the model was quoted as saying. 'He can go all night without a break. It was the best sex of my life.'

Maya swallowed against a tide of nausea and closed the paper, her whole body shaking with anger and despair and indescribable hurt.

Giorgio came into the room just as she turned from the bench. 'Maya?'

She threw the paper at him, the pages flying like sheets off a clothes line, landing all over the floor at his feet. 'You bastard,' she bit out through clenched teeth. 'You cheating, two-timing bastard.'

He frowned darkly. 'Now, wait just one damn minute,' he said, stepping over the debris of the paper on the floor. 'You surely don't think any of this rubbish is true, do you?'

Maya was close to hysteria. She could feel it bubbling up inside her; the pain and hurt and sense of betrayal was so acute it had nowhere to go but burst out of her. She felt so hurt, so crushed by his perfidy. And now it was all out in public, what he had been up to and who he had been up to it with. How would she ever hold her head up again? Would people always be looking at her and murmuring about what a naive fool she was to think he wouldn't return to his playboy form as soon as her back had been turned? How long was she to put up with this? Would there ever be a time when she would be free of this torture?

'How could you sleep with that…that…*tart*?' she asked.

His expression became stony. 'You are assuming I did actually sleep with her when you have nothing to base that on, other than what you have read in the paper. She was paid a lot of money for that fairy story and I swear to God that's all it is.'

'Oh, please.' She rolled her eyes in disdain. 'You were photographed with your arms around each other.'

'If I recall, so were you with your "date",' he returned.

Maya stiffened her shoulders. 'I told you nothing

happened. Someone took a photo that looked far more intimate than it was.'

'Likewise,' he said. 'Although I admit I did go out with her a couple of times and I considered taking it further but I decided against it. I let the press make what they wanted of it at the time. I was angry at you for leaving me so I didn't really care if you read about it at that point. Now it is different.'

'Because you want it all, don't you, Giorgio?' she said bitterly. 'You want the obedient, compliant little wife at home nurturing your children while you have your bit on the side, just like your father did.'

His jaw went rock-hard and his lips white-tipped at the corners. 'Keep my father out of this,' he said. 'My mother forgave him a long time ago for his fall from grace. It is their business, not ours. And he is no longer alive to defend himself, in any case.'

'Your mother was a fool to take him back,' Maya said. 'But maybe, like you with me, he didn't give her a choice. Did he blackmail her back into his life? Or was it the fact that she had three young sons to bring up all on her own that prevented her from leaving?'

Giorgio raked his hand through his hair. 'You have no idea what it was like for them. They lost their little girl, their much adored only daughter. It broke them. My mother grieved and grieved until she was so heavily sedated by the family doctor she couldn't function. I had to step in so many times to help look after my younger brothers, to feed them and bathe them and put them to bed when the nanny left without notice over something my mother had said in a moment of despair.' He stopped briefly to draw breath.

'My father couldn't cope. He had a hotel business to run. My grandfather and grandmother did what they could but no one could do anything to take away the pain. I lived with the fear of losing my mother, if not my father as well. I was convinced they didn't want to live any more. I had to do everything in my power to keep them strong, to keep the family together.'

Maya listened without interrupting. It seemed that each time he spoke about his baby sister he told her a little bit more of that tragic time. His gradual opening up to her helped her to understand more about his emotional distancing, the way he found excessive displays of emotion so off-putting. He'd had to be strong for everyone; he'd had to keep his emotions in check while everyone around him was falling apart.

'And then finally the cloud started to lift,' he continued. 'In an ironic way, I think it was my father's affairs that snapped my mother out of her depression. She knew she had to carry on, to do what she could to rebuild their relationship, which had been so happy before Chiara died.'

'I'm sorry,' Maya said softly. 'I didn't understand how hard it was, for you particularly. You were so young to be looking after everyone like that and feeling so responsible for them all.'

He looked at her with a grim expression on his face. 'Marriage takes a lot of work, Maya,' he said. 'Even good ones can have bad things happen to them. It is worse for people who live in the spotlight as everything we go through is reported in the press, often incorrectly.'

She eyeballed him, challenging him to tell the truth and nothing but the truth. 'Did you sleep with that model?'

It was a moment before he spoke.

A long moment.

'I am ashamed to say I fully intended to,' he answered. 'But when it came to the point of doing so I decided it wasn't the best course of action. Clearly, that ticked off Talesha Barton so her little payback was to have my reputation besmirched and my marriage put on the line for the second time.'

Relief made Maya feel giddy. She believed him because he had been honest, almost too honest. He had admitted how close he had been to having an affair, which, on reflection, she realised he'd had every right to have, considering they were officially separated at the time. 'Are you going to do anything about the story she gave to the press?' Maya asked. 'Will you ask for a retraction of it or take legal action against her or the paper?'

'I will get my legal team on to it,' he said. 'The sooner this is nipped in the bud the better. If the woman in question calls you, do not talk to her. Just hang up the phone. This is about money; it's not about anything else.'

A little bit like our marriage, Maya thought sadly.

He came over and tipped up her chin with his finger. 'I can't promise you the press won't target me again, or that some other woman I once dated before I met you won't see a chance to make money out of it and do so. All I can promise is that I will look after you and our baby, to build the family we have both always wanted.'

Maya decided to put herself out on an emotional limb. 'If I was to lose this baby, will you still want our marriage to continue?'

He frowned as if the question annoyed him. After all, it wasn't just the baby he wanted. He wanted to keep his fortune under his control and a costly divorce was hardly going to allow that.

'There are plenty of happy marriages around without children,' he said at last. 'Anyway, we have time on our side. We can have another round of IVF or even consider adoption.'

'Isn't love a prerequisite for a happy and fulfilling marriage?' she asked, stepping a little further out on that precarious emotional limb.

His eyes gave nothing away; they were dark and unfathomable. 'Like this baby, it will be a bonus if it happens,' he said. 'You claimed to love me once; perhaps you will find it possible to do so again, but maybe with a little more maturity this time.'

'You think I wasn't mature enough to know what love was back then?' Maya asked, frowning at him.

'You were blindsided, Maya,' he said. 'You said it yourself. What girl could resist the designer clothes, the holidays, the luxury villas and hotels?'

'Oh, for God's sake,' she said in frustration. 'I only said that to annoy you. I wasn't the least bit impressed by your wealth, well, maybe just a little bit in the beginning. I fell in love with you, not your money or your lifestyle. I just wanted to be with you, for who you were as a person.'

He looked at her for a heartbeat or two. 'Do you even know who that person is now?' he asked.

Maya looked into his eyes. 'I would if you would let me,' she said softly.

'I want to be the sort of person who can make you happy, Maya,' he said, touching her cheek again. 'But I am not good at showing emotion. I don't feel comfortable leaving myself open to possible hurt.'

'But don't you see you can't go through life not loving or needing anyone?' she asked. 'What sort of parent will you be if you can't show how you feel?'

'If you are suggesting that I will not love this child, then you don't know me at all,' he said. 'I would give my life for it, even now.'

'And what about me?' she dared to ask. 'Would you give your life for me?'

He took her by the upper arms and held her firmly, his eyes tethering hers with smouldering purpose. 'I have already given up my life for you, Maya,' he said. 'I have agreed to resume our failing marriage, haven't I? I could have walked away and started anew with someone else, but I didn't.'

'You know that's not what I am asking,' she said, holding his gaze as steadily as she could.

'Sometimes you ask too much, Maya,' he said, dropping his hold as if she had grown too hot to handle. 'I have things I need to see to—some business. I will be away for most of the week.'

Maya frowned. 'You're going away?'

He gave her an impatient look. 'I have a large corporation to control, Maya, you know that. My grandfather's death has intensified the workload. I have meetings in three different countries and long hours of paperwork and figures to trawl through.'

She dragged at her lip with her teeth, not sure whether she should reveal her vulnerability to him or not, but in the end she went for broke. 'But what about me?' she asked. 'I don't want to stay here by myself. Can't I come with you?'

His expression became shuttered. 'I think it is best that you stay here where you are close to the doctor you know and feel comfortable with. Dr Rossini is just minutes away if you feel worried about anything. Besides, the travelling might be too much for you. I am going to be locked away in meetings, in any case. I won't have time to spend with you.'

Maya felt hurt that he obviously didn't want her to be with him. 'Fine.' She folded her arms, not even caring that her bottom lip pushed out in a pout. 'No doubt I'll find something to do to entertain myself.'

'Maya, the press attention here is bad enough,' he said. 'But they are like jackals after a meal everywhere else. I don't want you to be harassed by them.'

'I can handle the press,' she said, glaring at the newspaper that was still lying all over the floor.

His brows moved together. 'I don't want you speaking to the press under any circumstances; do you understand?'

She raised her chin and gave him an arch look. 'Are

you worried I might sell out to them and tell the truth about how our reconciliation really came about?'

Anger flared in his dark gaze. 'If you do that you will regret it, Maya,' he said. 'I will make sure of it. You will not just be hurting me but my family as well. Do you really want to risk everything for a cheap shot at me?'

Maya held his burning gaze for as long as she could, but in the end she had to lower her eyes from his to stare at the floor. 'Of course I'm not going to speak to the press,' she said on an expelled breath. 'Surely you know me better than that.'

He tipped up her chin again with the blunt tip of his finger. He looked into her eyes for a long moment, his gaze deep and dark and inscrutable. 'Sometimes I wonder if I have ever known you,' he said ruefully. 'The real you, I mean.'

Likewise, Maya thought as his lips came down and pressed against hers.

CHAPTER FOURTEEN

MAYA had almost forgotten about her shopping date with Bronte. She suddenly heard Gonzo barking and then realised it was right on eleven o'clock.

She opened the door and Bronte immediately swept her into a tight hug. 'Are you OK?' she asked. 'Oh, my God, that awful, hideous story in the paper.' She pulled back to look at Maya. 'You didn't believe a word of it, did you?'

Maya bit her lip, uncertain of how to answer.

'Giorgio would not lie to you, Maya,' Bronte said. 'Luca told me how his brother's word is his bond. If he said he didn't sleep with that woman, then he didn't.'

'He was going to,' Maya said, feeling the hurt all over again.

Bronte looped her arm through one of Maya's. 'But he didn't and that's the main thing. There are women out there that are predators. They see rich and powerful men as prizes to be claimed. Giorgio is too smart to let himself be taken in by a trashy little gold-digger like that. Give him some credit. He wants your marriage to succeed. He wouldn't do anything to jeopardise it now.'

Maya gave her a rueful smile. 'You seem to know

him better than I do and you only just met him a couple of months ago.'

'Ah, yes, but I know Luca and he's cut from the same cloth,' Bronte said. 'Now, let's go shopping. I have left Ella with Giovanna but I don't want to tire her too much. She is still very sad over Salvatore's death. How is Giorgio taking it?'

'He hasn't said much,' Maya said, thinking of how Giorgio had acted in the week since his grandfather's death. 'It's business as usual for him. That has always been the way he handles things. I think he grieves in private, however. In fact I know he does. He's away now for the next few days.'

'Did he tell you where he was going?'

Maya shook her head. 'No, and I didn't ask. All I know is he didn't want me to go with him.'

Bronte frowned. 'Maybe he didn't want to tire you with long hours of travelling. Living out of hotels, even Sabbatini ones, can be exhausting when you are pregnant.'

Maya shrugged. 'I guess...'

Bronte touched her on the arm. 'But you really wanted to be with him, didn't you?' she asked.

Maya bit down on her lip again, this time trying not to cry. 'I just want him to love me. Is that so very much to ask?'

'How do you know he doesn't love you?' Bronte said. 'There are lots of ways of saying it, other than in words. I know the words are important—I need to hear them too—but some men are just not comfortable revealing how much they love someone. It's a guy thing.'

'Does Luca tell you he loves you?'

'Yes, but he didn't until we got back together. Be patient, Maya. A few weeks ago, you were head to head with Giorgio in an acrimonious divorce. He's not going to let you get any power over him by admitting how much he needs and loves you. You might take it upon yourself to walk away from him again. No man in his right mind would lay himself open to that happening, especially a Sabbatini. You know how impossibly proud they all are.'

Maya knew what Bronte said was right, but she still didn't have the confidence to believe that Giorgio loved her the way she longed to be loved. All she could do was hope that by sharing the bond of a living child he would one day tell her what he felt, if anything other than lust.

The shopping expedition was a great success, so much so that Bronte insisted she come back to their villa for the rest of the afternoon. The afternoon drifted into the evening and then, because Luca was also away on business just for that night, Maya decided to stay on for dinner with Bronte rather than spend the evening alone at Giorgio's villa.

One of the staff drivers took her home just before ten p.m. and, as she opened the door, she could hear Gonzo howling because the phone was ringing incessantly.

She dropped her shopping bags on the floor and, giving the dog a quick reassuring ruffle of the ears as she moved past, she snatched up the phone. 'Hello?'

'Do you have any idea of how worried I have been

about you?' Giorgio raged at her, his voice tight with anger. 'Where the hell have you been and why haven't you got your mobile with you? I've been calling it all bloody day and night.'

Maya grimaced as she remembered how she'd turned it to silent when she and Bronte had lunched in a High Street restaurant. She had forgotten to turn it back to the ringtone. 'Sorry about that,' she said. 'I went shopping with Bronte. I went back to spend the rest of the evening with her at Luca's in London. My phone was on silent.'

'Don't ever do that again,' he said. 'I thought something must have happened to the baby.'

Maya suppressed her instinctive retort and, taking a calming breath, said, 'The baby is fine. I had a lovely day. I bought my first maternity outfit.'

There was a long drawn-out silence.

Finally Giorgio broke it but his voice sounded creaky. 'What colour is it?'

'Pink and white,' Maya answered. 'I don't really need it yet, but Bronte talked me into it.'

'It's good you have her to spend time with,' he said. 'I just wish you had told me your plans ahead of time.'

'I forgot all about her offer to take me shopping,' Maya said. 'Anyway, why should I tell you where I am going when you don't tell me anything about where you are going?'

'I told you I am on a business trip.'

'You didn't tell me where.'

'I am in Prague at the moment, I will be in Lyon in France tomorrow and the day after I am going to New

York. I will be back by the weekend. There is a charity ball at the hotel on Saturday night. I would like you to accompany me, if you're feeling up to it, of course.'

Maya gave her assent and, after another little silence, said, 'Bronte and Luca are going to the villa at Bellagio this week, just for a couple of days. They invited me to come along. Would you mind? I will be back in time for the ball.'

'Of course I don't mind,' he said. 'In fact, I think it would be good for you.'

There was another silence.

'Gonzo misses you,' Maya said softly.

'I miss him too.'

'Do you miss me?' she asked, kicking herself for being so transparent.

'I miss having you in my bed,' he said in a smoky tone.

Maya felt her insides flip over with longing. 'I miss that too,' she said.

'Maya…' he began, but then paused for so long she wondered if he had changed his mind about what he was about to say.

'What?' she prompted.

'Nothing,' he said. 'Just be safe while I'm away, OK?'

'I'll be fine,' she said, squashing her disappointment that he just wouldn't say what she most wanted to hear.

Maya had fed Gonzo after their return from Bellagio with Luca and Bronte and Ella and was about to unpack her small bag when she heard Giorgio's car pull into the villa grounds. Her heart leapt at the deep throaty sound. Gonzo gave a joyful bark and bolted down the stairs. Maya followed at a more leisurely pace, not wanting to show such blatant enthusiasm until she was more certain of where she stood with him.

Giorgio looked up from patting the dog when she came down the staircase. '*Cara*,' he said, smiling, 'you are positively glowing. Did you have a good time with Luca and Bronte?'

'I had a wonderful time,' she said, lifting her face for his kiss.

She tasted of strawberries and he wanted to keep kissing her until she was beneath him, begging for the release he had been dreaming of giving her the whole time he had been away. 'I have something for you,' he said, picking up the packages he had brought in with him from the car.

Her grey eyes flicked to the bags nervously. 'But I don't need anything,' she said. 'I have too many clothes as it is.'

'It's not clothes,' he said, 'or at least not clothes for you.'

She took a step backwards when he held the first bag out for her to take. 'No,' she said. 'No, Giorgio, take it away. Take it all away.'

Giorgio frowned. 'What's the matter, Maya? It's just stuff for the baby. I bought this sweet teddy bear; let me show you.' He bent down to pull it out of the tissue wrap but by the time he'd straightened Maya had turned on her heel and stalked out of the foyer.

He picked up the bags and followed her into the *salone*, his frown tightening when he saw that she had gone out of the French windows and to the furthest edge of the balcony.

He felt the all too familiar panic seize him, the perspiration starting to pop out of his pores as he looked at her holding onto the balustrade, her ramrod-stiff back turned towards him.

'Maya, come in here and talk to me,' he commanded.

She turned and, leaning on the balustrade, sent him a challenging glare. 'Why don't you come out here and talk to me?'

He clenched his teeth together, sure he would be spitting out tooth enamel dust for weeks hence. 'Get the hell away from the edge of that balcony,' he said, the perspiration dripping down now between his shoulder blades.

She continued to challenge him with her stony expression. 'You will have to come and get me because I am not coming in until you get rid of those bags and everything in them.'

Giorgio felt like scratching his head in bewilderment. He had spent a fortune on baby goods, he had shopped when he should have been working but he had enjoyed every minute of it. He had trawled through baby wear shops instead of through the company's figures. He had bought a train set for if it was a boy and fluffy animals and dolls for if it was a girl, and he had even ordered a make-it-yourself crib set that was being delivered from the States. He couldn't wait to teach himself how to assemble it and varnish it. He couldn't wait to get started on making a nursery. He now regretted redecorating the previous one. But Maya hadn't gone in there for years and at the time he'd been glad to have it removed, as it had only reminded him of his failure.

'Maya, this is ridiculous,' he said, holding out a hand to her. 'Come inside and let's discuss this like adults.'

She shook her head indomitably. 'Get rid of the bags. Now.'

He swore viciously and spun around, snatching up the bags and taking them to one of the storage cupboards in the foyer.

He came back in, relieved beyond belief to see her now back in the *salone*, but her face was still rigid with anger. 'Do you want to tell me what's going on?' he asked.

Her grey eyes rounded with hurt. *'How can you ask that?'* she said, her chin starting to wobble.

Giorgio still didn't get it. He was trying to but her reaction didn't make any sense to him. He was trying to be a good husband. He was trying to be the sort of involved father-to-be that he knew young mothers these days wanted and needed. 'Maya, tell me what's upset you. I am not good at reading between the lines. I deal with facts and figures: concrete things, not abstract ones.'

Her eyes were filling with tears as she faced him. 'Do you have any idea of what it's like to come home to a fully prepared nursery when you've just lost the baby you longed for with all of your heart? *Do you?*'

Giorgio swallowed what felt like a coil of barbed

wire. But he didn't answer. He couldn't. The words were somehow stuck in amongst those cruel barbs, scraping his throat, tearing at him with those awful dagger-like teeth.

'Four times,' she said, holding up four slim shaking fingers. 'Four times I did exactly that. I came home to teddy bears and toys and Babygro suits and b—booties I'd knitted myself. I felt such a fool, such a failure. I felt I had jinxed the baby's future by assuming too much too soon. I am not going to make that mistake again. *Never*. Not until I hold this baby in my arms am I going to buy a single item and nor will I let anyone, most of all you, buy them for me.'

Finally Giorgio found his voice. '*Cara*, I am so sorry. I should have thought.' He swallowed and lifted his hand to rake through his hair but it was shaking so much he let it drop uselessly by his side. 'I can't believe how stupid I have been. I should have known you felt this way. I was trying to be positive but it's not what you need right now, is it? It's not what you needed before either. What you needed was someone to meet you where you are emotionally.'

She nodded on a broken sob as his arms came around her to hold her close. He held her like that for long painful minutes, his own eyes moist with burning tears of regret of how badly he had handled everything.

No wonder she hated him.

No wonder she kept threatening to leave him.

He had not shown her how deeply he felt for her, for what she had gone through, for what she was *still* going through, with the uncertainty she felt was hanging over her with this pregnancy, even though the doctor had reassured her that everything was going according to plan.

For Maya, given what she had been through, she could not allow herself to relax until she was holding that baby. It was less than twenty-five weeks until she could do so, but that was a lot of days of worrying to get through.

It was going to be a long wait, for both of them.

'Maya,' he said, holding her in the circle of his arms, his eyes meshing with hers. 'Forgive me for being so insensitive to your needs. Let me try and make it up to you. I am not sure how I can, but I am going to try.'

She gave him a weak smile but her eyes were still shadowed with sadness. 'It probably sounds so superstitious to someone like you who deals with solid evidence, but I just can't help it. I don't want anything to steal this chance of happiness from me. I have wanted to be a mother for so long. I look at Bronte and I feel so envious. I look at every woman with a child or two or three and feel like screaming with frustration that I haven't been able to do this one thing that just about everyone takes for granted.'

'We will get through this, Maya,' he said, his fingers encircling her wrists, his thumbs stroking the sensitive skin underneath.

'You are always so confident of getting what you want,' she said with a little downward turn of her mouth.

'I haven't always had everything my way,' Giorgio

said, thinking of how he'd felt the day he had found her note.

He had immediately switched off his feelings, as he did in times of stress. He had operated like an automaton, going through the motions as if the divorce was an annoying business deal he had to negotiate his way through. But on the inside he'd been screaming with frustration and injured pride. He had failed and the world was about to witness it and there had been nothing he could have done to stop it. He had cringed every time he had seen it mentioned in the press. His shipwrecked marriage had become gossip fodder, lining the pockets of unscrupulous journalists who wanted sensationalism, not the truth.

'You get your way most of the time, though,' Maya said. 'Like getting me back into your life, for instance. You weren't going to take no for an answer, were you?'

'That is true,' he said, bringing her hands up to his mouth, kissing both of them in turn. 'But then, that is where you belong, is it not?'

Maya knew there was no point in answering to the contrary. Instead, she lifted her mouth to meet the descent of his and gave herself up to the dream that, this time around, everything would work out the way she wanted it to.

CHAPTER FIFTEEN

THE charity ball was a huge affair that involved Giorgio making a speech about the work he was committed to doing for an orphanage he had set up in Africa.

Maya listened with rapt attention. She'd had no idea he had been involved in such a life-changing project for the little ones she saw on the PowerPoint presentation he had prepared.

Her heart ached for the tiny, soulful, dark-eyed infants who appeared on the screen. They had lost their parents through civil war and would have had no chance to survive if it hadn't been for the philanthropic efforts of people like Giorgio and his team of dedicated volunteers. The children were being lovingly cared for as they awaited adoption. They were being educated and had toys and clothing and special outings that would not have been possible without the enormous amount of time and commitment, not to mention money Giorgio had put in.

It made Maya feel she had been pathetically ungrateful for what she had in her life. Sure, she hadn't been able so far to have a baby, but there were literally millions of parentless infants in the world who would give anything to be loved and nurtured by someone who cared enough to give them a second glance.

She decided then and there that she would join Giorgio in his efforts to support those motherless and fatherless children; she would do anything to help them get a proper start in life.

He came back to their table and, now that the band had started its next bracket of songs, he asked her if she would like to dance.

'I would love to,' she said, slipping her hand into the warmth of his.

She went into his arms as if she had never been away, her steps falling into time with his as naturally as a professional ballroom dancer.

After a few head-spinning turns on the floor, she looked up at him with love and respect shining in her eyes. 'Why didn't you tell me about the orphan charity? I had no idea until now you were the sponsor behind it all. I had heard of it many times over the last few months, but I didn't for a moment think you were the one who had started and funded it.'

He expertly turned her away from a camera that was intent on taking a picture of them. 'I got to thinking about your childhood, how you had no one but an elderly spinster aunt to take you in when your mother died. It struck me that there are countless children in the same, if not worse circumstances. I decided if I couldn't have children of my own, I would do something for the ones who were already here but with no one to take care of them. It has been the most fulfilling enterprise of my life. Nothing compares to it. To see all those little faces light up when I fly in with gifts and toys and clothing is indescribable. I feel like a father to thousands.'

Maya was so touched she felt her eyes fill with tears. 'I feel so proud of what you have done. Can I come with you some time and meet the children?'

His hands tightened protectively. 'You, young lady, are going nowhere until this baby is born. Do you understand?'

'But Giorgio, I want to be a part of all of this,' she said. 'I need to be a part of it.'

'Then you will be a part of it, but on my terms,' he said. 'I want you to be safe for the rest of this pregnancy. I am not putting you at risk, taking you to a war-torn country with inadequate medical help.'

'If I wasn't currently pregnant, would you let me come with you?' she asked.

Giorgio frowned at her for a long moment before he finally answered. 'No, I would not.'

'But why?' she asked.

'Come on.' He took her by the hand and led her off the dance floor.

'Where are we going?' Maya asked.

'We're going home,' he said, barely pausing long enough to get their coats from the cloakroom.

Maya sat in the back of the limousine with Giorgio sitting stiffly beside her. He was looking out of the window, his fingers splayed out on his thighs, his jaw so tight it looked as if he was grinding his teeth.

'What's wrong?' she asked.

'Nothing is wrong,' he said, still with his gaze averted.

'Giorgio, I don't understand why you're so edgy all of a sudden,' she said. 'All I asked was to come with you some time in the future.'

He turned and looked at her with an intractable expression. 'It's out of the question. I absolutely forbid it.'

'It's about the baby, isn't it?' she said, resentment building inside her. 'You don't want anything to happen to the baby.'

'Of course I don't want anything to happen to the baby,' he said. 'Neither do you.'

Maya retreated into a frosty silence as their driver took them back to the villa.

Once they were back and alone at the villa, Giorgio tossed his coat over the back of the nearest sofa before he faced her. 'I know you think all I am interested in is having an heir,' he said. 'When I look back, I can see how you came to that conclusion. I haven't exactly given you any feedback of what I feel about you, apart from the obvious, of course.' His eyes flicked to the slight swell of her belly pushing against the satin of her dress.

Maya felt her heart slip sideways in her chest as his dark eyes met hers again. 'There is nothing wrong with wanting to have children,' she said. 'It's what I want too.'

He shifted his mouth in a rueful manner. 'You deserve much better than I can give you, Maya. I look at Luca and Bronte and how they are so open with their feelings for each other and I feel as if I have short-

changed you. I married you for all the wrong reasons
and then when you left me I let you go.' He rubbed at
his cleanly shaven jaw and added with a heavy frown,
'I can't believe I did that.'

Maya swallowed to clear her blocked throat. 'We were
both so unhappy, Giorgio,' she said. 'There was no point
in carrying on. You didn't love me and I didn't—'

'Don't say it,' he said before she could finish.

She frowned. 'Don't say what?'

'I don't want to hear you say you no longer loved me,'
he said, his throat rising and falling as he too swallowed
tightly. 'I don't think I can bear hearing you say that.
Not now.'

'I wasn't going to say that,' Maya said. 'I have always
loved you. I know you think I was star-struck and immature and maybe I was—immature, I mean. In fact I
am sure I was. I didn't take the time to understand you,
to listen to what you didn't say rather than to what you
did. I think you care about things a lot more than you
let on. I see the way you care for your family. You do
that out of love, not duty. I love that about you, that you
always put others' needs before your own.'

Giorgio moved to close the distance between them,
taking her hands in both of his. 'How can you still
love me even though I have let you down in so many
ways?'

Maya smiled, even though tears were falling from her
eyes. 'I think we both let each other down,' she said. 'We
didn't talk about what we were feeling. I always blamed
you for that, but I can see now how I should have been
more sensitive to what you were going through. You felt

just as disappointed and sad when I lost our babies but you covered it up to protect me, just like you do with your family. You bear the brunt of everything to protect those you love.'

He pulled her close, holding her so tightly Maya felt imprinted on his body, but it was right where she wanted to be. 'I love you, *cara*,' he said. 'I know you might not believe it, but I do. I am deeply ashamed of not loving you when I married you, but in a way it was only in marrying you that I really came to know you and how you made me feel.'

He held her from him to look down at her upturned face. 'You tried so very hard to please me. You worked much harder at our marriage than I did. I arrogantly assumed everything would go according to plan and when it didn't I felt such a failure. I couldn't make you happy, I couldn't give you a baby, I couldn't do anything to make things right. And when you wanted out I let you go when I should have fought to get you to change your mind and try again.'

'Oh, darling,' Maya said, wrapping her arms around his waist. 'We both made silly mistakes. But we're together again now.'

He stroked her face adoringly. 'Yes, but only because of a chance encounter.' He grimaced and added, 'What if I hadn't asked you to come up to my room that night after Luca and Bronte's wedding to talk about the divorce? What if you had told me to go to hell instead? We might have missed this chance. We might have wrecked both of our lives.'

Maya nestled up closer. 'I only went up to your room

because I couldn't help myself. I missed you so much. I guess that was why I kept making such a fuss about sharing Gonzo. He was the final link with you that I didn't want to let go.'

He looked serious again as he cupped her face with his hands. 'Were you really going to go to live in London?' he asked.

Maya nodded. 'I had come to the point where I thought the only way to get over you was to get away. Even without Gonzo, there were almost constant reminders in the press of what you were doing. I couldn't take it any longer.'

Giorgio dropped his hands from her face so he could hug her close again. 'Yes, well, let me tell you, you would not want to have been a fly on the wall when I saw that article about you and that Herringbone guy,' he said. 'I swore and ranted and carried on for days until no one could bear to be around me. Quite frankly, I couldn't stand to be around myself.'

Maya smiled as she leant her cheek into his chest. She didn't bother correcting him over Howard Herrington's name, she had a feeling it would never come up in conversation again. 'I would never have gone on that stupid date if I hadn't been so desperately unhappy,' she said. 'I was so jealous of you with that model.'

'Maya,' he said, holding her from him again, his expression sombre once more. 'You must believe me when I say I never had anything intimate to do with that woman. She was so vacuous and vain it made me long to be with you again. It's made me realise how wrong it was to make you give up your career. No wonder you were frustrated and bored. You're an intelligent young woman with so much to offer.'

'You didn't make me give up my career,' she said. 'I just thought that's what you and your family expected me to do.'

'I know, which amounts to the same thing,' he said. 'I want you to be fulfilled and happy, *cara*. If you want to teach, then that is fine by me. I will do whatever I can to facilitate your career; just promise not to leave me again.'

Maya smiled again as he brought her close. 'I'm not going anywhere just yet,' she said on a contented sigh. 'I'm quite happy right where I am.'

Five and a half months later...

Maya looked down at the tiny squirming, squalling bundle in her arms and felt her heart swell so much she was sure her chest would not be able to contain it. It was such a miracle to be holding her child. Although he had been in a bit of rush to get into the world, he was absolutely perfect; all his fingers and toes were in place and his little nose and that stubborn chin that looked so much like his father's made her smile every time she looked at it. He had a decent pair of lungs on him too; from the moment he was born he had not stopped letting everyone know he was here at last.

Giorgio was still wiping the tears from his eyes from watching as Maya had so bravely delivered his son into the world. He had cut the cord himself and knew he would never forget the moment when he saw that dark little head appear just before his son's wizened and bloodied body followed in a rush.

'Can you believe it?' Maya said, grinning up at him proudly.

He shook his head, still too choked up to speak; but he reached for her free hand and squeezed it tightly.

'What are we going to call him?' she said, looking back down at the baby, who had finally settled against her breast, suckling hungrily.

Giorgio cleared his throat. 'We didn't get around to discussing names,' he said. 'This poor little man hasn't got a stitch of clothing until I go out and buy some for him.'

Maya looked up at him sheepishly. 'Actually...I did buy a couple of things last week,' she said. 'Bronte took me shopping and I just couldn't resist it. She was buying stuff for Ella and her baby and I wanted to join in.'

Giorgio brushed the sweaty hair off her forehead lovingly. 'So you were a little more confident towards the end than you were letting on?'

'I was confident you would love and support me, no matter what,' she said softly.

He pressed a gentle kiss to her mouth. 'The baby is a bonus, *cara*,' he said, 'a beautiful, precious bonus to a relationship that is worth more to me than all the money in the world.'

'I love you,' she said, blinking back tears of joy.

He smiled and blotted her tears with the pads of his thumbs. 'I love you too, more than words can say. I will never stop loving you.'

The baby gave a little grizzle as he lost suction. Maya

gently eased him back in place before she looked back up at Giorgio. 'So, what do we call him?' she asked. 'Do you have any suggestions?'

Giorgio touched his finger to the tiny reddened cheek of his son. 'How about Matteo?' he said.

'Mmm, I really like that,' Maya said. 'What does it mean?'

'It means gift from God,' he said, and smiled as his gaze meshed with hers over the tiny precious bundle of their surprise baby.

THE WEDDING CHARADE

MELANIE MILBURNE

To Georgina (Georgie) Brooks: a friend, a fan
and a fabulous young woman.
This one is for you! XX

CHAPTER ONE

'THERE'S a Jade Sommerville here to see you, Signor Sabbatini,' Nic's secretary, Gina, informed him as she brought in his morning coffee. 'She said she's not going to leave the building until you agree to speak to her.'

Nic continued to look through the prime real estate properties listed on his computer screen. 'Tell her to make an appointment like everyone else,' he said, smiling to himself as he thought of Jade pacing the floor in Reception. It was just the sort of thing she would do: fly in to Rome on an impulse, demand her way no matter what, throwing her light weight around as if she had an inborn right to everything she wanted right when she wanted it.

'I think she really means it,' Gina said. 'In fact, I think—'

The door opened with a thud as it banged against the wall. 'Please leave us, Gina,' Jade said with a plastic-looking smile. 'Nic and I have some private business to discuss.'

Gina looked worriedly at Nic. 'It's all right, Gina,' he said. 'This won't take long. Hold my calls and make sure we are not interrupted under any circumstances.'

'*Sì*, Signor Sabbatini,' Gina said and left, closing the door with a soft click behind her.

Nic leaned back in his chair and surveyed the black-haired virago in front of him. Her green eyes were flashing with sparks of fury, the normally alabaster skin of her cheeks cherry-red. Her small hands were clenched into tight fists by her sides and her breasts—which he had secretly admired ever since she was sixteen—were heaving with every enraged breath she took. 'So, what brings you to my neck of the woods, Jade?' he asked with an indolent smile.

Her cat's eyes narrowed. 'You bastard!' she spat. 'I bet you put him up to it, didn't you? It's just the sort of underhand thing you would do.'

Nic raised a brow. 'I have no idea what you are talking about. Put whom up to what?'

She came over to stand in front of his desk, her hands slamming down on the leather top as she eyeballed him. 'My father is stopping my allowance,' she said. 'He's dissolved my trust fund. He's not giving me another penny. And it's all your fault.'

Nic allowed himself the luxury of the delectable view for a moment. Jade's creamy cleavage was about as close as it had ever been, apart from the night of her sixteenth birthday party. His nostrils flared as he caught a waft of the exotic fragrance she was wearing. It was an intriguing combination of jasmine and orange blossom and something else he couldn't put a name to, but it definitely suited her. He brought his gaze back to the fireworks show in hers. 'I might be guilty of many sins, Jade, but that is not one you can pin on me,' he said. 'I haven't spoken to your father in years.'

'I don't believe you,' she said, straightening from the desk.

She folded her arms across her body but if anything it gave him an even better view of those gorgeous breasts. He felt a stirring in his groin, the same rush of blood he always felt when around her. It annoyed him more than anything. He wasn't opposed to the odd one-night stand, but something about Jade made him wary of bedding her even for the short time it would take to do the deed. She oozed sensuality, but then she was known for her sleep-around ways. Only recently there had been a report in the press about her scandalous behaviour. She had allegedly lured a married man away from his wife and young family. Nic wondered how many men had enjoyed the experience of possessing her—or had *she* possessed them? She was a witch, after all: a little she-devil who liked nothing more than a full-on scene.

'Well?' she said, unfolding her arms and planting them on her slim hips in a combative manner. 'Aren't you going to say something?'

Nic picked up a gold pen off his desk and clicked it a couple of times. 'What do you want me to say?'

She blew out a breath of fury. 'Are you deliberately being obtuse? You know what we have to do. You've known it for months and months. Now we've only got one month to make up our minds, otherwise the money will be lost.'

Nic felt an all too familiar spanner of anger tighten each vertebrae of his spine at the way his late grandfather had written his will. He had spent the last few months looking for a way out of it. He had consulted legal experts but to no avail. The old man's will was iron-clad. If Nic didn't marry Jade Sommerville by May

the first, a third of the Sabbatini assets would be gone
for ever. But a month was a month and he wasn't going
to allow Jade to manipulate him into doing things her
way. If he had to marry her—and it was very likely
he would—he would do so on his terms and his terms
only.

'So,' he said, drawling the word out as he swung his
chair from side to side, his pen still clicking on-off, on-
off. 'You want me to be your husband, do you, Jade?'

She glared at him like a wildcat. 'Technically, no,'
she said. 'But I want that money. It was left to me and I
don't care if I have to jump through hoops to get it, and
no one can stop me.'

Nic smiled lazily. 'As far as I see it, *cara*, *I* am the
one who can stop you.'

She strode back to the desk but, instead of standing in
front of it, she came behind to where he was sitting. She
grasped the top of the chair next to his left shoulder and
swung him round to face her. She stood in between the
intimate bracket of his open thighs, her warm vanilla-
scented breath breezing over his face as she jabbed him
in the chest with a French-manicured finger. Nic had
never felt so turned on in his life.

'You. Will. Marry. Me. Nic Sabbatini.' She bit out
each word as if she were spitting bullets.

He curled a lip as he held the green lightning of her
gaze. 'Or else?' he said.

Her eyes flared, the thick black heavily mascara-
coated lashes almost reaching her finely arched brows.
She licked her mouth, making it glisten and shimmer,
the action of her tongue sending a rocket-fuelled charge
of blood to his pelvis.

Nic grabbed her hand before she could move away,

wrapping his fingers around her wrist until they over-lapped. 'You're going about this all wrong, Jade,' he said, pulling her farther in between his thighs. 'Why not use some of that sensual charm you're known for instead of coming at me like a cornered cat? Who knows what you might be able to talk me into doing, hmm?'

She flattened her mouth, her eyes full of disdain as they tussled with his. 'Let go of me,' she said through clenched teeth.

Nic elevated his eyebrow again. 'That's not what you were saying when you were sixteen.'

Her cheeks were like twin pools of crushed raspber-ries, which seemed strangely at odds with her cutting retort. 'You missed your chance, Italian boy. Your best friend took home the prize. He wasn't the best I've had but at least he was the first.'

Nic worked on controlling his breathing, dousing his blistering anger with the ice-cold water of common sense. She was deliberately goading him. It was what she did best. She had been doing it for as long as he had known her. She was a tart who used sex to get what she wanted.

He had done the honourable thing all those years ago, rejecting her advances, seeing them for what they were: a young, immature girl's grab for attention. He had lectured her about her behaviour but she had ignored his warning, deliberately seducing one of his closest friends to drive home her petulant point. It had destroyed his friendship with his mate and it had destroyed any respect he'd had for Jade. He had been prepared to give her a chance, but it seemed she was on the same path of destruction as her socialite mother had been before her death when Jade was a young child. 'You blame me for your father's withdrawal of your allowance, but don't you think it might have something to do with your recent affair with Richard McCormack?' he asked.

She tugged her wrist out of his hold and rubbed at it pointedly. 'That was just a stitch-up in the press,' she said. 'He made a move on me but I wasn't interested.'

Nic gave a snort. 'It seems to me you're always interested. You're every man's fantasy. The wild-child party girl who will do anything to be the centre of attention.'

She gave him an arch look in return. 'You're a fine one calling me out for being a black kettle when your pot's been stirred by more women than any other man I know.'

Nic smiled at her imperiously because he knew it would inflame her. 'Yes, I know it's hypocritical of me, but there you have it. The double standard—even in spite of enlightened times—still exists. No man wants a tart for a wife.'

She frowned at him. 'So you're going to turn your back on your inheritance?'

He gave an indifferent shrug. 'It's just money.'

Her eyes widened again. 'But it's a fortune!'

'I'm already rich,' he said, enjoying the play of emotions on her face she was clearly struggling to disguise. 'I can earn double that in a couple of years if I put my mind to it.'

Her frown deepened. 'But what about your brothers? Won't Giorgio and Luca's shares in the Corporation be put in jeopardy if yours are given to an unknown third party?'

Nic schooled his features into a blank mask. 'If it happens, it happens. It's not what I would have wished but I can't compromise my standards to fit in with an old man's whimsical fantasy.'

This time she didn't bother trying to hide her outrage. 'But this is not just about you! It's about me as well. I need that money.'

Nic leaned back in his chair again and crossed his ankles. 'So go out and get a job,' he said. 'That's what other people who haven't been born into money do. You might even enjoy it. It will certainly make a change from having your nails and hair done.'

Her gaze seared his. 'I don't want a job,' she said. 'I want that money because your grandfather—my godfather—gave it to me. He wanted me to have it. He told me before he died that he would always be there for me.'

'I agree he wanted you to have the money,' Nic said. 'He had a rather soft spot for you. God knows why, given your track record of appalling behaviour, but he did. But he also wanted to manipulate me into doing things his way and that I will not stand for.'

She pressed her lips together as she swung away to pace the carpeted floor. Nic watched her from his chair. She was agitated and rightly so. Without her father's generous allowance, she was penniless. He knew for a fact she had no savings to speak of. She lived on credit and expected her father to clear it month by month. She had never had a job in her life. She hadn't even finished school. She had been expelled from three prestigious British fee-paying schools and then dropped out altogether a week after enrolment at the fourth. She was trouble with a capital *T*.

She turned back and came to stand in front of him again, her big green eyes taking on a soulful beseeching look. 'Please, Nic,' she said in a whisper-soft voice. 'Please do this one thing for me. I beg you.'

Nic drew in a long, slightly unsteady breath. She was bewitching and dangerous in this mood. He could feel the tentacles of temptation reaching out to ensnare him. He could feel the way his resolve was melting like wax under a blast of heat.

A year of marriage.

Twelve months of living together as husband and wife in order to secure a fortune. Thank God the press so far knew nothing about the terms of the will and Nic was determined to keep it that way. That would be the ultimate in public shame if word got out that he had been led to the altar with a noose around his neck, put there by his late grandfather.

But Jade was right. It was a fortune, and while he had every confidence he could earn it in his own right, given enough time, he was deeply worried about a third party shareholder. His brothers had been good about it so far. They had not put him under any undue pressure, but Nic knew Giorgio, as the financial controller, was concerned given the ongoing economic instability across Europe.

Nic knew this was a chance to show his family and the press he was not the fool-around playboy everyone painted him as. He could make this one sacrifice to secure the Corporation's wealth and once the year was over he could get back to doing what he did best: being free from emotional entanglements. Being free to travel the world and take risks that others couldn't or wouldn't take. He thrived on it—the adrenalin and the surge of euphoric energy when a multimillion dollar deal was sealed.

He would agree to fulfil the terms of his grandfather's will but not because Jade told him to.

No one but no one told him what to do.

Nic pushed back the chair as he rose from it. 'I will have to get back to you on this,' he said. 'I have to go to Venice to check out a villa that's come on the market. I'll be away for a couple of days. I'll give you a call when I get back.'

She blinked up at him in bewilderment, as if he had given the opposite answer to what she had been expecting. But then her beautiful face quickly reassembled itself into an expression of indignation. 'You're making me *wait* for your answer?' she asked.

Nic gave her a mocking smile. 'It's called delaying gratification, *cara*,' he said. 'Hasn't anyone told you if you wait a long time for something, when you finally get it the pleasure is a thousandfold?'

'I will make you pay for this, Nic Sabbatini,' she snarled. She stalked over to where she had dropped her designer handbag earlier and, scooping it up, flung the strap over one of her slim shoulders and gave him one last gelid glare before she left. 'You see if I don't.'

CHAPTER TWO

JADE arrived at the hotel in Venice at five in the afternoon. A member of the paparazzi had told her Nic was staying there, right on the Grand Canal. She was quite pleased with her detective work. Her sources had told her Nic was in a meeting until eight this evening, and then he would be returning to the hotel for a massage before a late dinner; she hadn't been able to find out if he was planning to dine alone or with one of his legion of female admirers.

Nic was the sort of man who had always had women swooning over him. She, to her eternal shame, had once been one of them. It still riled her that he had rejected her when she was sixteen and madly in love with him. Although she knew it was really her own fault for being so wilful, she couldn't help partly blaming him for the horrid experience of her first sexual encounter, not that she had ever told anyone. Even the man who had taken her virginity had no idea of how dreadful an ordeal it had been for her. But then she was good at deception. Deception was her middle name—well, it would be if she could spell it, she thought wryly.

She smiled at the concierge at the reception desk, fluttering her lashes in the manner she had perfected over the years. '*Scusi, signor.* I am meeting my fiancé here, Signor Nicolò Sabbatini. It is to be a very big... I don't know how to say it in Italian...a big surprise?'

The concierge smiled conspiratorially. '*Sì, signorina,* I understand—a *sorpresa.* But I did not know Signor Sabbatini was engaged. There has been nothing about it in the press, I am sure.'

There will be shortly, Jade thought with a mischievous private grin. '*Sì, signor,* it is all very hush-hush. You know how the Sabbatini brothers hate the intrusion of the press.' She pulled out a photo of her and Nic that had been taken at his grandfather's funeral. It wasn't a particularly intimate one but it showed Nic with his head leaning towards her as he whispered something before the service. Luckily, the shot didn't show her face for she had been scowling at him in fury at the time. Jade smiled at the concierge as she showed him the photograph. 'As you can see, we are never left alone by the press. That is why I wanted this to be our special time together before the world gets to know. I am so appreciative of your cooperation.'

'It is my pleasure, *signorina,*' he said and, handing back the photo, passed her a regulation form to fill in. 'If you would be so kind as to give your full name and address and country of residence for our records.'

Jade felt the familiar flutter of panic build in her chest. It was like a million micro bats' wings flapping all at once. She took a steadying breath and summoned up another megawatt smile. 'I am sorry, *signor,* but I have taken out my contact lenses for the flight,' she said. 'They are packed in my luggage somewhere. I am practically blind without them and I *hate* wearing glasses. So unfashionable, don't you think? Would you be so kind as to just type my details straight into your computer?'

The concierge smiled. 'But of course, *signorina*,' he said, his fingers poised over the keys as she gave him her details.

'You are so very kind,' Jade said as he handed her a swipe key.

'Signor Sabbatini is staying on the top floor in the penthouse suite. I will have your luggage taken to the room straight away.'

'*Grazie, signor.* But there is one more thing,' she said, leaning closer. 'Would you mind contacting the masseuse who was coming at eight?' She gave him a twinkling smile. 'I will give my fiancé a massage instead. He will enjoy it so much more, *sì*?'

The concierge grinned. '*Sì, signorina.* I am sure he will.'

Jade made her way to the lift, smiling at her reflection in the brass-plated doors once they were closed. She had dressed in her best look-at-me clothes. A black and sinfully short tight-fitting dress with a daringly low neck and shoes with the sort of heels podiatrists the world over shook their heads in dismay at, and flashy jewellery that screeched inherited wealth and decadence.

Jade found the room without any trouble and immediately ordered champagne. A bit of Dutch courage wouldn't go amiss right now. She would have to go carefully, however. She had to keep her wits about her in order to bring about what she wanted. Nic would be furious, but then that was his fault for being so stubborn about this. It was all right for him with his squillions, but what was she supposed to do without her trust fund? It wasn't as if she could just 'go out and get a job' as he had so mockingly suggested. Who on earth would employ her?

She looked out of the window to the bustling tourists below. The serpentine network of the canal system and the colourful villas fringing it was exactly as the post-cards portrayed it. Even the light was the same: the pastels in the sky as the sun lowered brought out the pinks and oranges and yellows of the centuries-old buildings. She wished she had time to paint it. Her little makeshift studio back in her London flat was full to bursting with her work. Not that anyone had ever seen any of her paintings. It was her private passion. Something no one could rubbish, something no one could say was trashy and uneducated and unsophisticated.

Jade wandered over to the huge bed and tested it for comfort by pressing a hand down on the mattress. She snatched her hand away as she thought of all the women Nic had bedded on his trips. He would have lost count by now, surely? At least she could count her partners on the fingers of half a hand in spite of what the press reported of her sexual proclivities. Quite frankly, she wondered what the fuss about sex was all about. It didn't seem all that pleasurable to her to be pawed and sweated over. She could flirt and tease with the best of them and it got her what she wanted—well, most of the time.

The champagne arrived and Jade tipped the young man who brought it. She allowed herself one glass to settle her nerves. The time was dragging and she desperately wanted this to be over with so she could feel more secure. Nic had left her dangling, uncertain of whether he was going to cooperate or not. It was too risky to leave it all up to him. She had to force his hand, otherwise she would be destitute. She didn't mind pretending to be a tart at times but there was no way she was going to become one because all her other options had been destroyed.

Marrying Nic would solve everything for her. All her troubles would be over if she did what Salvatore's will stated. The lawyer had explained it all to her after the funeral last year. She had to marry Nic by the first of next month and stay married for a full year. Both partners had to remain faithful. Jade wasn't sure why her godfather had put that condition in. She didn't intend to sleep with Nic. He had spurned her in the past. What was to say he wouldn't do it again? She would find it just as shattering as she had then.

Jade was sipping at her second glass of champagne when Nic came in. His hazel eyes narrowed as he saw her sitting with her legs crossed on the bed. 'What the hell are you doing here?' he said.

'Celebrating our engagement,' she said with a demure smile as she hoisted her glass.

He stiffened as if he had been snap frozen. 'What did you say?' The words came out slowly, menacingly.

Jade took a sip from her glass, looking at him from beneath her lashes. 'The press already know about it,' she said. 'I gave them an exclusive. All they need now is a photo.'

Nic's anger was palpable. It rolled off the walls towards her, keeping her rooted to the foot of his bed. Jade fought the instinct to flee. She had been hit before. Her father had backhanded her for insolence enough times for her to know how much it hurt, but her pride would not let her show it. Instead, she gave Nic a defiantly sassy look. 'If you kick me out I will tell the press about the terms of your grandfather's will. You don't really want me to do that, do you, Nic?'

His top lip lifted in a snarl. 'You trashy, deceitful cow,' he said.

Jade let the words roll off her. 'Sticks and stones,' she said in a sing-song voice as she took another sip of champagne.

Nic strode over and snatched the glass out of her hand, spilling champagne over her lap in the process. She glared at him as she jumped up to wipe off the spillage. 'You bastard!' she said. 'This dress is brand new and now you've ruined it.'

His nostrils flared like those of an angry bull. 'Get out,' he said through tight lips. He pointed to the door with a rigid arm. 'Get out before I throw you out.'

Jade tossed her head and put her hand behind her back to unzip her damp dress. 'You put one finger on me and I'll tell even more Sabbatini secrets to the press.'

His mouth flattened to a thin line of fury. 'Do you have no principles at all?'

'Plenty,' she said, wriggling out of her dress.

His dark brows snapped together. 'What do you think you are doing?'

Jade tossed the dress on the floor, raising her chin as she stood before him in black lace bra and knickers and her come-and-get-me heels. For a brief moment she wondered if she had stepped not just out of her dress but out of her depth as well. Nic's gaze seemed to be seeing through much more than her lacy underwear. She could feel the heat of it all over her skin, inside and out. She could feel a faint stirring deep inside her, a fluttering little pulse that seemed to intensify with each throbbing second. 'I'm going to have a bath,' she said, summoning her courage and resolve. 'Then, once I am freshened up, we are going out to publicly celebrate our engagement.'

He stood there, breathing heavily, his eyes hard on hers, hatred darkening them in a way she had never seen before. 'I am not letting you get away with this, Jade,' he warned. 'You don't get to screw around with me, do you hear?'

'What a lovely choice of words,' Jade said as she sashayed over to the bathroom. 'But there will be no screwing, OK? That's not part of the deal.' She gave him a saucy little fingertip wave and closed the bathroom door, clicking the lock firmly in place.

Nic let out a breath that felt as if it had come out of a steam engine. He was beyond angry. He was livid. He was furious.

He was screwed.

Jade had set him up and he had no choice but to go along with it. He would look a hundred times a fool if the press got wind of his grandfather's machinations. If he had to marry her, he would do it but he would make sure he didn't look like a pawn being pushed around.

He clenched and unclenched his fists. He wanted to knock that bathroom door down and drag that little scheming witch out by her long black hair. He had not thought it possible to hate someone so much. Was that what his grandfather had wanted? For him to hate the very air Jade Sommerville breathed? What had he been thinking to tie them together in a mock marriage for a whole year, for God's sake? It would be torture for him. Marriage to anyone would have been bad enough. He loathed the thought of being tied down to one person for any length of time, let alone the rest of his life.

Look what had happened to his father. He had not been able to remain faithful after the death of Nic's baby sister, and it had nearly destroyed his mother. Nic had been too young to remember Chiara, but he remembered the years that followed. Both his parents had been absent emotionally, cut to the core over the death of their precious daughter. Nic had run wild for most of his childhood, trying to get the assurances he needed as a young boy that he was still a much loved member of the family. But after losing one child, his parents had lived in fear of losing another and so they had held themselves aloof. Giorgio and Luca had fared better, being that bit older, but Nic knew he had missed out on what so many children took for granted.

Being forced to marry Jade was the worst possible scenario. For one thing, there was no way she would ever stay faithful for the allotted time. No wonder she was proposing a no sex deal. He wouldn't trust her as far as he could see her.

If he could guarantee she wouldn't stray, his inheritance would be secured. But the only way to ensure that would be to sleep with her, to make the marriage a real one. To keep her so satisfied she wouldn't be tempted to play around on him.

He rubbed at his jaw as he thought about it. Bedding Jade would certainly be an unforgettable experience. The blood was already fizzing in his veins from her brazen display of flesh. She had no shame, no limits at all on her behaviour. He smiled to himself as he thought about taking her in a rough tumble of lust. The sexual tension between them had crackled for as long as he could remember. It would certainly be no punishment for him to bury himself deep inside her, to make her scream his name instead of some nameless guy she had picked up in a nightclub.

Jade came out of the bathroom a long time later with her hair piled on top of her head and some damp tendrils hanging about her face. She was wearing one of the hotel's fluffy white bathrobes. Without her make-up and high heels, she looked young and dainty, her cheeks pink-skinned from her bath. As she moved past him to access her suitcase, Nic noticed she barely came up to his shoulder in her bare feet. Her toenails were painted black. They looked stark against the porcelain white of her skin.

'What happened to my massage appointment?' he asked.

She tucked a strand of hair behind one of her small ears without looking up from her open bag. 'I cancelled it.'

'You had no right to do that,' he said. 'I was looking forward to it.'

She glanced at him as she moved with a bundle of clothes to the wardrobe. 'I can give you one if you like,' she said. She hung a skirt and top on the silk-padded hangers. 'I'm told I'm very good.'

'I am sure you are,' Nic said, watching her move back to her bag.

She held up two dresses against her chest. 'Which one do you think?'

Nic had to give himself a mental shake. She was doing it again: sideswiping him with her rapid change of demeanour. One minute the raging virago, the next a little girl playing at dress up. There would be another tantrum soon enough, he thought. 'The red one,' he said, striding over to the champagne sitting in the silver ice bucket. He poured himself a glass and sipped from it as he watched her dress.

She did it as if it were a strip show in reverse. She had slipped out of the bathrobe while he had been pouring his drink, but now she was stepping into a pair of black and red lacy French knickers that were gossamer-thin, so thin he could see the waxed clear feminine cleft of her body. His blood pounded all over again, making him uncomfortably stiff. He took another deep draught of champagne but he couldn't bear to drag his eyes away from her. She picked up a matching push-up bra. Not that she needed any mechanical help in showcasing her breasts. They were beautifully shaped, full and yet pert with rosy-red nipples. She adjusted the creamy globes behind the lace and then shook her head so her hair cascaded down over her back and shoulders.

Nic was fit to explode and he hadn't even touched her.

'Aren't you going to shower and change?' she said as she moved past him with her make-up bag.

He caught her arm on the way past, his fingers fizzing with the stun-gun effect of her warm flesh under his. He locked his eyes on her sea-glass green ones. 'How about that massage you promised?' he said.

She gave him a sultry look from beneath her lashes. 'Later,' she said. 'Dinner first. If you're a good boy I might give you a rub down when we get home.'

He tightened his hold when she made to pull away. 'Is this how you get every man to do what you want? To make them beg like starving dogs for your favours?'

She tossed her head again, making her hair swing back over her shoulders. 'You won't have to beg, Nic, because there will be no favours,' she said. 'This is going to be a paper marriage.'

Nic laughed out loud. 'Oh, come on, Jade. How long do you think that's going to last? You are a born sybarite.'

She glared at him as she tugged at his hold. 'I am not going to sleep with you.'

'Then what was the little tease routine for?' he asked.

She gave him a haughty look. 'You can look but you can't touch,' she said. 'That's the deal.'

Nic dropped her arm. 'There is something you need to learn about me, Jade,' he said. 'I choose my own sexual partners. I do the chasing. And I do not beg. Ever.'

She turned away and sat at the dressing table, opening various pots as she applied moisturiser and make-up. 'We'll see,' she said, meeting his eyes in the mirror.

Nic clenched his teeth and strode into the bathroom. *We'll see, indeed,* he thought as he turned on the shower full blast.

When Nic came out, Jade was sipping more champagne. She had her face on—the face he was used to seeing: heavy smoky eye-shadow and eyeliner, scarlet lipstick and a brush stroke of bronzing powder to highlight her model-like cheekbones. She was back in another pair of heels, even higher than the previous ones, and she had dangling earrings on that sparkled now and again behind the dark screen of her loose hair. She had a sulky look about her mouth, however, which warned him there might be another scene on its way.

He had thought through his options in the shower.

He would marry her because he didn't really have a choice, but he would dictate the terms. She thought she had manipulated him into agreeing to it but he wasn't doing it for her, but for his family.

'Before we go to dinner I want to lay down some ground rules,' he said as he reached for a fresh shirt.

She crossed her legs and swung one high-heeled foot up and down in a bored schoolgirl manner. 'Go on then, tell me what they are and I'll tell you whether I'll agree to them or not.'

Nic whipped out a tie from the wardrobe. 'You will agree to it or I won't marry you. You're the one who needs the money more than me, don't forget.'

She set her mouth in a mulish line, her eyes hardening as she held his. 'So what are your stupid little rules, then?'

'I insist that at all times and in all places you will behave with the decorum your position as a Sabbatini wife requires of you,' he said. 'You have met both of my sisters-in-law, *sì*?'

'Yes, they are very nice,' she said. 'I met Bronte briefly at your grandfather's funeral. I met Maya, Giorgio's wife, in London. She had taken the time to call on me to show me the baby since I was unable to attend the christening. Matteo is adorable.'

'Yes, he is,' Nic said. 'So why didn't you come to the christening?'

Her eyes stayed determinedly away from his, her tone dismissive. 'I had another engagement.'

'And what about Luca and Bronte's son Marco's christening?' he asked. 'It was only a month later. Did you have another engagement that day too?'

This time she looked at him directly. 'I always keep

myself busy. My social calendar is booked for months ahead.'

Nic felt his top lip curl. He could imagine her shoe-horning in party after party, nightclub after nightclub, and shallow date after shallow date. 'It was good of you to come to my grandfather's funeral,' he said with no intention of it being a compliment. She had obviously known she was going to be included in the will, for why else would she have made the effort? He knew her well enough to know she didn't do anything for anyone unless she got something out of it for herself. 'You also came to see him before he died, didn't you?'

She nodded. 'It was the least I could do. He had always been so good to me. I was just his godchild. No one takes that role all that seriously these days, but he always looked out for me.'

'Apart from the will, of course,' Nic pointed out.

'Yes, well, he must have had his reasons.'

'Why do you think he did it?' Nic asked. 'To us, I mean. It's not as if we've been the best of friends over the years.'

She gave a little shrug of her slim shoulders. 'Who knows? Maybe he thought it would be a way of bringing the two dynasties together: the Sommervilles and the Sabbatinis. It has quite a ring to it. My father no longer has a male heir so this is the next best thing. I expect they cooked it up together.'

Nic studied her for a moment. 'You were supposed to be with your brother on that skiing holiday, weren't you?'

Her eyes shifted away from his. 'I missed the flight.' She gave a little shrug, as if it was just one of those things. 'I overslept after a night out.'

'Have you ever thought of how you could have both died if you had gone on that trip?' Nic asked. 'You would have been on the slopes with him when the avalanche hit.'

She gave him a glittering glare. 'Do you mind if we get back to your stupid little rules?'

'You don't like talking about Jonathan, do you?'

'You lost your baby sister,' she said. 'Do *you* like discussing it?'

'I don't even remember it,' he said. 'I was only eighteen months old. But Jonathan was twenty, almost twenty-one, and you were just weeks off turning eighteen. It must be very clear in your memory.'

'It is and it's off-limits,' she said, looking him in the eye. 'You might think you have certain privileges as my husband-to-be but that is not one of them.'

Nic pulled his tie up to his neck and straightened it, his eyes still following every nuance on her beautiful, now ice-maiden face. She could change so quickly it was amazing. 'The second rule is I will not tolerate you playing around,' he said. 'I am prepared to give and take a little, but I am not going to be cuckolded.'

'I won't play around on you,' she said, looking at him with a cat-that-got-the-cream-and-the-canary smile. 'I'll be too busy counting my money.'

'If you don't behave yourself, there will be consequences,' Nic said. 'One false move and you will be out without a penny. It's written in the will. We both have to remain faithful, otherwise we automatically nullify the terms set down by my grandfather.'

'You will have to be *very* discreet then, won't you?' she asked with an arch look.

'You don't think I can do it, do you?'

She pulled her long black hair over one of her shoulders in a mermaid-like arrangement. 'Do what?' she said. 'Stay celibate? No, quite frankly, I don't. Who is your latest lover, by the way? Is it still the Brazilian heiress, or have you got someone else by now?'

His lips jammed together for a moment as if he was biting back a retort. 'A year without sex is a long time, Jade, for both of us. I can't see why we can't have our cake and eat it too.'

Jade rolled her eyes at his play on words. 'I want the money, not you, Nic. I thought I had made that perfectly clear.'

'You say it with your mouth but not with your eyes,' he said. 'I give it a month at the most before you have them in sync. It's all part of the game, isn't it? It's what you do to every man: make them want you so badly they forget about promises and principles.'

'I can see you think you know me inside out,' she said. 'At least there won't be any nasty surprises once we are married.'

'I am afraid we will have to have a full-on wedding with all the regalia,' he said after a short tense pause. 'I hope that is not going to be a problem for you. It's just that my family will expect it and so will the public.'

'Fine,' Jade said. 'But I am not going to wear white or a veil.'

He tilted his head at her, a smile teasing the edges of his mouth upwards. 'You're not thinking of wearing black, are you?'

Jade held his look with defiance. 'I'm not a virgin, Nic. I am not going to pretend to be something I am not.'

He frowned as if he found her statement somewhat

bewildering. 'I don't recall saying that was a requirement of this arrangement. When it comes down to it, I
am no angel myself. I probably should be ashamed to
say this but I have lost count of the lovers I have had.
You can probably still do a reasonably accurate tally.'

'Nope,' she lied, inspecting her nails. 'I've lost count
too. Ages ago.'

The silence pulsed for a beat or two.

She looked up to find him watching her with a brooding expression. 'Is there anything else?' she asked. 'Any
more tedious little rules I have to abide by?'

'No,' he said, snatching up his jacket and shrugging
himself into it. 'That will be all for now. Just leave the
press to me. I will handle the questions.'

Jade uncrossed her legs and got to her feet. 'Yes,
Master,' she said and flicked the fine chain strap of her
evening purse over her shoulder as she walked with
swaying hips over to the door.

'Careful, Jade,' he warned. 'One step out of line and
the deal's off. And don't think I wouldn't do it.'

Jade refused to let him see how unnerved she was by
his threat. He might be calling her bluff but how could
she know for sure? Of course she needed the money
much more than he did. He had plenty of his own while
she had nothing. But a year was going to change all that.
She would finally be independent of her father. She
would no longer need anyone's largesse to survive. She
schooled her features into meekness. 'I will be a good
girl, Nic, you just watch me.'

CHAPTER THREE

THEY had barely stepped outside the hotel on the Grand Canal when the paparazzi swarmed upon them. A journalist pushed a microphone towards Nic and asked, 'Signor Sabbatini, the news of your engagement and impending marriage to Ms Sommerville has taken everyone by surprise. You must have been conducting a very secret liaison. Do you have any comment to make about your romance?'

Nic smiled charmingly but Jade could tell he was grinding his teeth behind it. 'Ms Sommerville and I have been family friends for years. We finally decided to become more than friends. We are very much looking forward to our wedding next month. Now, if you'll allow us to celebrate our engagement in private, please move on.'

One of the older journalists pushed forward a microphone in Jade's direction before Nic could do anything to block it. 'Ms Sommerville, you were involved some months ago with Richard McCormack, the husband of one of your best friends. Do you think the news of your engagement to Nic Sabbatini will finally repair your relationship with Julianne McCormack?'

Jade felt the subtle tightening of Nic's fingers around

hers. 'I have no comment to make on any issue to do with my private life, apart from being very happy about my engagement to Nic. It's the best thing that's ever happened to me. I am so—'

'Excuse us.' Nic took command and led her through the crowd of tourists who had gathered.

'I thought I told you to leave the questions to me,' he said in an undertone as they weaved through the knot of people.

'Everyone will think it strange if I don't say something,' Jade argued. 'This is a momentous occasion, after all.'

He gave her a quelling look before heading for a restaurant on one of the canals.

They were led to a table in a lavishly appointed private room. Crystal chandeliers twinkled from the ceiling, plush velvet covered the chairs and hung from the windows in thick curtains in a rich shade of scarlet. There were Venetian masks on the wall, each one a work of art. The atmosphere was one of intimacy and privacy, and again Jade wondered how many women Nic had entertained here, wining and dining them before taking them back to his penthouse apartment to pleasure them. Strangely, she felt a jagged spike of jealousy poke at her and she shifted in her chair. Why would she be jealous? There would always be other women with Nic. It was the way he was made. He was not cut out for commitment and continuity in his love life. He was a playboy with a PhD in seductive charm. He could have anyone he wanted. He *had* had anyone he wanted.

The menus were placed in front of them and within minutes a bottle of champagne arrived in a silver ice bucket. Jade looked at it with wariness. She had already had one more glass than usual. Being with Nic had the same effect as alcohol. It had made her head spin to see him dressed in nothing but his black underwear back there at the hotel. She had set out to be as brazen as she could—getting dressed in front of him to show him she was just as the press reported her—but it was completely different when he had done the same to her. She had tried not to look at his carved to perfection body. She had seen plenty of male bodies on the beach or at the gym, and some of them had been downright gorgeous. But something about Nic's always made her heart race and her senses tingle in a way they never did with anyone else. It made her feel deeply unsettled. She was the one who played the cat and mouse game with men, not the other way around. She didn't like the thought of Nic having that much power over her, in fact *any* power over her.

The attentive waiter filled both of their glasses before moving away to leave them in privacy.

Nic picked up his glass and raised it to hers. 'Let's drink to our first year of marriage.'

Jade gave him an ironic glance. 'Don't you mean the *only* year of our marriage? Don't the terms of the will state we have to be married by the first of next month and stay married for exactly a year?'

He drank from his glass before he answered. 'Yes, but what if we enjoy being married to each other? What if it turns out to be more convenient than we first thought? We could make it last as long as we like.'

Jade sat back in her seat as if he had pushed her backwards with one of his strong hands against her chest. 'You can't mean that!' she gasped.

He gave her one of his white-toothed smiles. 'Only

teasing,' he said, his hazel eyes twinkling. 'Once the
year is up next May, we can both take the money and
run.'

Jade worked hard at squashing her sense of pique.
She knew his motive for marrying her was only to get
the money he felt entitled to; after all, she was doing it
for the very same reason. She could hardly blame him
for going ahead with his grandfather's stipulations. His
two older brothers had had no such conditions placed
upon them, but then Giorgio and Luca were both happily
married with children. Giorgio and Maya had separated
for a time, but had reconciled just before the old man's
death. It had been Salvatore's desire to see all of his
three grandsons settled before he died, but when he
became ill so suddenly he had obviously decided to take
matters into his own hands and make sure Nic bowed to
pressure to settle down instead of playing the field for
too much longer. Why Salvatore had chosen her as Nic's
bride was a mystery. He could not have been unaware
of the enmity between them. For the last decade they
had snarled and sniped at each other when they had to
be together at Sabbatini or Sommerville functions.

Jade knew a lot about the history of the Sabbatinis,
having been a part of their circle for so many years.
Her Australian-born father had befriended Salvatore
when he was just starting out as an accountant and, with
his Italian friend's help, his small accounting firm had
become one of the most prestigious in Europe.

Like Nic and his brothers, Jade had grown up brushing shoulders with the rich and famous. Celebrities were
not idols from afar; they were friends and acquaintances
who regularly attended the same parties and social
gatherings.

Jade's mother, Harriet, had been a London socialite herself until her untimely death from an overdose
when Jade was five. Whether it had been suicide, a
cry for help or an accident was something Jade and
her brother Jonathan had never been told. There had
always been speculation regarding Jade's parents' marriage. Throughout their childhood, it had been a case
of don't-mention-your-mother-in-your-father's-presence
by all the nannies and au pairs that had come and gone.
Whether it would upset their father because of unre-
solved grief or anger was another mystery that had never
been solved.

Jade looked at the menu and chewed her bottom lip
in concentration. She hated eating out; it was something
she usually avoided, but not for the reasons everyone assumed. It had been splashed all over the papers enough
times—how she had been admitted to a special clinic
when she was fifteen and then again at eighteen when
she had skirted with death as her weight had dropped
to a dangerously low level during the months following
Jonathan's death. She was well and truly over all that
now, but eating out still threw up the problem of how to
choose when she had no idea what was written on the
menu.

She felt Nic's gaze on her now, the weight of it like
a stone. She looked up and closed the menu. 'What are
you thinking of having?' she asked.

'The crab fettuccine to start with and maybe the veal
Marsala for mains,' he said. 'What about you?'

Jade ran her tongue over her sand-dry lips. 'Why
don't you choose for me?' she said, pushing the menu
to one side. 'You seem to know the place pretty well.
I'm not fussy.'

He cocked one of his eyebrows at her. 'No?'

'I've dealt with a lot of stuff over the years, Nic,' she said, giving him a hard look. 'I'm not going to embarrass you by dispensing with my meal in the bathroom as soon as your back is turned.'

A frown appeared between his brows. 'I wasn't suggesting any such thing,' he said. 'It was a tough time for you growing up, losing your mother so young and then your brother like that.'

Jade had perfected her back-off look over the years and yet, as she used it now, it was with shaky confidence that it would work. 'I'd rather not talk about it. They died. Life goes on.'

The waiter arrived to take their order, and when he left Nic shifted his mouth in a musing pose and continued to study her. She began to feel like a specimen under a powerful microscope. Nic always made her feel like that. He saw things that other people didn't see. His eyes were too all-seeing, too penetrating. It made her feel vulnerable and exposed—something she avoided strenuously at all times and in all places.

'Do you see much of your father?' Nic asked.

She toyed with the stem of her champagne flute, her eyes averted from his. 'Before this latest blow up, yes. He called in occasionally with his latest girlfriend,' she said tonelessly. 'The last one is only a year or two older than me. I think they might eventually marry. He wants a son—to replace Jonathan. He's been talking about it for years.'

Nic heard the pain behind the coolly delivered statement. 'You've never been close to him, have you?'

She shook her head, still not meeting his eyes. 'I think I remind him too much of my mother.'

'Do you remember her?' he asked.

Her jade-green eyes met his, instantly lighting up as if he had pressed a switch. 'She was so beautiful,' she said in a dreamy tone. She picked up her glass and twirled it gently, the bubbles rising in a series of vertical lines, each one delicately exploding on the surface. 'She was so glamorous and always smelt so divine—like honeysuckle and jasmine after a long hot day in the sun.'

She put the glass down, and ran her finger around the rim, around and around as she spoke. 'She was affectionate. She couldn't walk past Jon or me without encompassing one or both of us in a crushing hug. She used to read to me. I loved that. I could listen to her voice for hours…'

A little silence settled like dust motes in the space between them.

She gave a little sigh and picked up her glass again, twirling it before she took a tentative sip. She put it back down, her mouth pursing as if the taste of the very expensive champagne had not been to her taste. 'She loved us. She *really* loved us. I never doubted it. Not for a moment.'

Nic knew a little of the rumours surrounding Harriet Sommerville's death. There was some talk of an illicit affair that had gone wrong and Harriet had decided to end it all when the other man involved refused to leave his wife. Other rumours suggested Jade's father had not been the best husband and father he could have been at the time, but it was hard to know what was true and what had been fiction.

The press had a way of working it to their advantage: the bigger the scandal, the better the sale of the papers. Nic had experienced it himself, along with his brothers.

But there was something about Jade that intrigued him. At regular intervals over the years she appeared at all the right functions, dressed to the nines, playing to the cameras, flirting with the paparazzi, but still he wondered if anyone really knew who the real Jade Sommerville was. Not the slim, beautiful and elegantly dressed and perfectly made-up young woman who sat before him now, twirling her champagne flute without drinking any more than a sip or two, who refused to speak of her dead brother, who spoke of her father with thinly disguised disgust.

Who was she?

Who was she *really?*

Was she the woman who had broken up the marriage of her best friend, as the papers had reported?

Or was she someone else entirely?

'Losing a parent is a big deal,' Nic said to fill the cavernous silence. 'I was knocked sideways by my father's accident. Seeing him like that…' he winced as he recalled it '…one minute so vitally alive, the next in a coma.' He raked his fingers through his hair. 'It was a relief when he died. No one wanted to say it but it was true. He would have hated being left with brain damage.'

She looked up at him with empathy in her eyes. 'You are a lot like him,' she said gently. 'I suppose lots of people have said that to you before. He hated being tied down.'

Nic smiled wryly as he picked up his glass. 'My parents' marriage was an arranged one. Not a lot of people know that. My mother loved him from the start but he was not so keen on being shackled to one woman. They muddled along as best they could until Chiara came along. My father loved having a daughter. He had three sons but his daughter was everything to him.'

He put his glass down with a clunk on the table, his eyes moving away from hers. 'Losing her was like the bottom of his world falling out from under him. He felt he was being punished by God for not loving his wife and sons enough. He went through a tumultuous time. As young as you were, I am sure you heard of it: numerous affairs with shallow gold-diggers until he finally realised the only woman he could love was the mother of his still living children who had loved him the whole time.'

'Everyone reacts to grief in their own way,' she said softly.

Nic picked up his glass but not with any intention of drinking from it, more for something to do with his hands. 'I am like my father in that I do not like to be told what to do,' he said. 'He always had issues with my grandfather over that. I guess that is why Salvatore's will was written the way it was.'

'But you are doing what he wanted now and that is all that matters,' she said in the same emotionless voice. 'In a year you will be free. You will have your inheritance and you can be with whoever you want.'

'So what about you?' Nic asked, raising his glass to his lips. 'What will you do once the year is up?'

She looked down at her hardly touched champagne. 'I haven't thought that far ahead.' She looked back at him and gave him a forced-looking smile. 'I guess we will divorce amicably and get on with our lives.'

Nic wondered who she would want to spend her life with or if she wanted to settle down at all. If it hadn't been for his grandfather's machinations, at some stage she would have had to marry and to marry well. She had never worked a day in her life. She was a full-time socialite, born to it like others were born to poverty and neglect.

Until the withdrawal of her father's support, she certainly hadn't given Nic any indication that she was going to abide by the stipulations set down in the will. Nic had wanted to talk to her about it at length after the funeral, but when he had mentioned it during the service she had glared at him and then later slipped out before he could corner her. He certainly didn't see himself as qualifying for husband of the year or anything, but as long as she behaved herself he would put up with the twelve months of matrimony to secure his inheritance and thus keep his brothers' interests in the Sabbatini Corporation secure.

There were certain compensations in marrying Jade, of course. She was certainly a pleasure to look at. She had the most beautiful piercing green eyes, large and almond-shaped and darkly lashed, as thick as the silky, wavy hair that cascaded halfway down her back. With cheekbones you could ski off and a mouth that promised sensuality in every plump curve, she could have modelled if she'd put her mind to it, but for some reason had rejected an offer from a top agency when she was nineteen. Apparently she had been more than content to continue to live off her father's fortune, no doubt expecting it all to land in her lap on his demise some time in the future.

Yes, she was a gold-digger in her own way, Nic thought. She just did it a little more openly and shamelessly than most. It would be exciting having her in his bed. The more he thought of it, the more he longed to get down to it. She played it so cool but he could feel the heat of her passionate nature simmering underneath the surface. She was a born tease. She was deliberately ramping up his desire for her. She was a wildcat, a ti-gress that needed to be tamed and he would gladly be the one to do it and sooner rather than later, no matter what silly little hands-off-the-goods deals she insisted on making. He saw it for the ruse it was. She had wanted him since she was a hormone-charged sixteen-year-old and, because he had rejected her, she had played hard to get ever since.

'You do realise we will have to live together in Rome for most of the year, don't you?' he said after a pause. 'Apart from the times we travel.'

Her eyes flew to his. 'Travel? You expect me to travel with you?'

'That is what loving wives do, is it not?' he asked.

Her neatly groomed brows moved close together. 'But surely that's not necessary in our case. You're a busy man. You don't need a wife hanging off your arm in every city you travel to. Besides, I have things of my own to do.'

He hooked one brow upwards. 'Like what? Lime and vodka mornings and getting your hair and nails done?'

Her fingers tightened around her glass so hard Nic wondered if the fragile stem might crack. 'It's not that at all. I just like sleeping in my own bed.'

'Not according to what I read in the papers a few months ago,' he pointed out wryly. 'You were in and out of Richard McCormack's bed day in and day out while his wife's back was turned.'

She gave him a hateful glare. 'So you believe there is

truth in everything written about you and your brothers in the papers, do you?'

He studied her for a moment. 'Not everything, no, but you didn't deny it. You could have slapped a defamation case on the paper if there was absolutely no truth in anything that was reported.'

'I have no interest in suing anyone,' she said. 'It's not worth the bother. They would just read it as defensiveness which, in my opinion, reeks of guilt. I've always felt it better to ignore it all and hope it eventually dies down.'

'It hopefully will now that we are about to be married,' he said. 'Have you a preference for a church wedding?'

She averted her gaze. 'No preference at all.'

'Then you won't mind if we have the ceremony and honeymoon in Bellagio?' he asked.

Her eyes came back to his. 'That's where your family has a villa, isn't it?'

'Yes.' He refilled their glasses before he added, 'It's also where my baby sister died all those years ago.'

Jade picked up her glass again. 'Well, then, it seems rather fitting to conduct a dead marriage there, doesn't it?'

His hazel eyes bored into hers for a tense moment. 'Your tongue is razor-sharp this evening,' he observed. 'You are the one who insists the marriage is to be in name only.'

'I don't love you, Nic, and you don't care a fig for me,' she said. 'We're only marrying each other to access a rather large fortune. That's about as dead as a marriage can be, is it not?'

'It doesn't have to be that way,' he said. 'We can work things to the advantage of both of us.'

She rolled her eyes at him. 'I can see how your mind works, Nic. You're already straining at the leash of imposed fidelity, aren't you? I told you: have your affairs if you must but keep them private. I don't want to be made a fool of in the press.'

'Same goes,' he said, leaning forward menacingly. 'I am warning you, Jade. If I hear one whisper of a scandal of you with another man, money or no money, our marriage will be terminated immediately, irrespective of what's written in the will. I am going to have it written into the prenuptial agreement.'

'Don't you mean our marriage will be annulled rather than terminated?' she asked with an arch look.

His eyes held hers like high-beam searchlights for so long Jade felt her skin break out in tiny goosebumps of apprehension. There was a steely purpose to his expression. He was not a man to be pushed around. Somehow he had turned the tables on her. She was not the one calling the tune here now, he was, and he was not going to allow her forget it. He had made it clear he desired her but she couldn't help feeling she was just going to be a convenient fill-in while he waited for his inheritance to be secure. Although she had tried her very best to disguise her response to him, it had clearly been to no avail. But then maybe he was like a lot of men even in these more enlightened times who still thought it their right to sleep with a woman who took their fancy: an expensive dinner, an even more expensive bottle of champagne and the transaction was settled.

Jade had determined she would not allow herself to be intimate with Nic. But somehow in the last couple of hours her resolve had been challenged in a way it had never been before. She saw the heat of desire in his eyes, the way his sexy mouth tilted in a lazy smile, as if he could already taste the victory of having her mouth plundered by his so very experienced one. She shifted uncomfortably on her chair, aware of her body in a way that made her feel distinctly uneasy about her ability to be immune to his sensual power. Her breasts felt full and tingly, her legs trembling and sensitive, as if they longed to be entwined with the length and strength of his in an erotic embrace.

He reached out and unpeeled her rigid fingers from around the stem of her glass. He brought those very same fingers up to his mouth, where suddenly they loosened and trembled, as if his breath contained a magic potion that unlocked every stiff joint, making them like putty in his hold. She sat transfixed, locked in a stasis that felt so strange to her and yet totally, inexplicably irresistible. She didn't want to break the spell. His eyes were holding hers in a lockdown that was unbreakable. She couldn't look away if she wanted to. Something was drawing her to him, like a silly little unsuspecting moth heading towards a bright hot light. She was going to get burned, but it was as if she didn't care. She drew in an uneven little breath as his lips brushed against the tips of her fingers, a barely touching movement that made her instantly ache for more.

'Why are you still fighting what has always been between us, Jade?' he asked in a low husky tone.

'I don't want to complicate things, Nic,' she said in a voice that sounded like someone else's, breathy, excited, anticipatory and expectant.

'You wanted me when you were sixteen,' he reminded

her, nibbling on her fingertips again, a feather-touch of temptation—a lighted taper to her simmering need.

'I...I was young and you were—'

'Lusting after you but old enough to realise you were far too young to know what you were doing,' he said, smiling in a self-deprecating way. 'Jailbait Jade. That's what I nicknamed you. Did you know that? I daren't touch you for years after that. Not even a kiss on the cheek at any of the family gatherings. I didn't trust myself to take what had been on offer. I was seven years older than you. At twenty-three I had to be the adult, even though I wanted you like a raging fever in my blood.'

Jade pulled her hand away from his mouth, tucking it safely away in her lap. 'I wish you would stop reminding me of how stupid I was back then,' she said, her eyes downcast.

'It's still there, isn't it, Jade?' he said in a smouldering tone. 'The hint of the forbidden, the lust, the longing, the need that won't go away. I see it in your eyes; I feel it in your body. I feel it like a pulse in my flesh when you look at me. We won't last the year without consummating this marriage and you damn well know it.'

She dared to look at him then, her heart giving a little pony kick in her chest. He meant it. He wanted her and he was going to do what he could to have her. She would have to be so strong, so very strong. Falling in love with Nic was the one thing she must not do. She had done it once before and look where that had taken her. It had set her life on a completely different course. She only had herself to blame, deep down she knew that. She had wilfully thrown away her innocence to get back at Nic and it had backfired on her terribly.

'My grandfather would not have tied you up in this marriage unless he thought it was the best thing for you,' Nic said. 'He always made allowances for you, in spite of what was reported in the press. He defended you many times.'

Jade pushed the starter around her plate without getting any of it to her mouth. 'He was a good man,' she said softly, trying not to allow the mist of tears to break through. 'I have never quite understood how he and my father became such good friends. They were so very different.'

'Your father took the death of Jonathan very hard,' Nic said. 'Some people don't handle grief very well. I think my grandfather understood that, having lost his granddaughter and seeing his own son deal with it in his own way. There is no right way of doing it. We each have to find the right way to handle it—to learn to live with it.'

Jade looked up at him again. 'In my father's opinion, the wrong child died,' she said in a flat, emotionless tone that belied what she was feeling, what she had always felt.

Nic frowned, his dark brows so close together they were almost joined above the bridge of his nose. 'Surely you don't think that? It was an accident. It could have happened to anyone. There was nothing you could have done to change that. There was nothing anyone could do. I told you before: you were lucky you weren't there with him.'

Jade gave a little shrug that said so little and yet so much. She had been the one who had caused Jonathan's death. He wouldn't have gone to such a challenging ski run if she had been with him because she wasn't as confident a skier. He had always watched out for her, staying with her even though he would probably have preferred to do his own thing. She had always maintained she had missed that flight because of her partying, but it had actually been because she had not properly memorised the itinerary her father had given her and had turned up at the wrong airline counter. By the time she had run across to the right one, it had been too late because the flight had already left. The shame of her inadequacy had kept her from asking the check-in staff to book her on another flight. It had all been too much so she had simply gone home and left a message for Jon to say she had changed her mind and was going to stay home and party instead. She was dumb and stupid—a dunce, as her father had so often told her. It was all her fault Jon had died that day and she had to live with it.

'Jade?' Nic reached for her hand but she moved it away from the glass she had been reaching for.

Drinking had been one of her coping mechanisms in the early days and it hadn't worked. It had hurt her rather than healed her. 'It's all right,' she said, giving Nic a rough version of a smile. 'Life goes on. Jon wouldn't have wanted me to waste my life bemoaning the past. He died the way he lived: on the edge, with loads of adrenalin, with laughter and courage and conviction.'

'So how do you live your life?' Nic asked.

With fear, apprehension, self-loathing and a truck-load of regret, Jade thought, but didn't say. She pasted a plastic smile on her face and met Nic's dark, serious hazel eyes. 'I want to live the high life,' she said. 'I want money and lots of it. I want to never have to work, to not have to grind away at a job I loathe for the next forty-odd years and then retire to tend tomatoes and orchids or whatever it is that old people do these days.'

'Most of them spend time with their grandchildren,' he said.

Jade lifted her brows at him in a pert manner. 'Is that what you, the eternal playboy, plans to do?'

He frowned again, as if he had never given the idea much thought. 'Don't get me wrong,' he said. 'I adore my niece and two nephews. I can see the joy they bring to my brothers' and mother's lives. But I have never really envisaged a family life for myself. I travel all over the world at a moment's notice. My job in the Sabbatini Corporation requires it, especially now with Giorgio and Luca wanting to spend more time with their families. I am only home about one week in three.'

Jade felt a quake of unease pass through her. 'So you're expecting me to accompany you on *all* of those trips?'

He shifted his tongue inside his cheek, obviously giving it some thought. 'Not all, perhaps, but most. We are meant to be giving the impression of a solid and secure marriage, Jade. We can't do that if one of us is globetrotting on business and the other is lazing by the pool or heading off to the nearest health spa.'

She flashed him a vitriolic look. 'Is that what you think I do with my time?'

He picked up his glass and downed the contents before answering. 'You don't work, you don't volunteer, and you attend only the parties that suit your ends. I have no idea what you do with your time. Why don't you tell me?'

Jade thought of her canvases, back at her flat, in her makeshift studio in the small spare bedroom. How she had worked so hard to make up for her other failings. She hadn't sold anything and, like most artists, knew she might never make a decent living out of her creativity, but she secretly longed to. She longed to with a passion that was no doubt as strong as her father's drive to be the best accountant in the business. It was another one of her secrets, a passion she kept to herself in case it failed, thus proving to one and all that she was nothing but a shallow socialite with nothing to offer but a blue-blood pedigree. Like her mother, she wasn't supposed to have a brain or a goal. She was meant to be on hand with the canapés and the champagne and the convivial conversation, working the room, aiming the shining beacon on her husband's stellar achievements.

But Jade had always wanted more. The trouble was, the more she wanted, the more likely it was to be taken away from her.

Like Nic…

She pulled away from her wayward thoughts, reminding herself sternly of Nic's motivations. He only wanted what he could get out of her by keeping her as his wife for the appointed time. Within a month they would be officially married. They would be on their way to having what they wanted: the inheritance. For Nic she was a bonus thrown in for free. He had a fantasy about her that stemmed from that silly little schoolgirl crush she had subjected him to. What full-blooded man wouldn't want to revisit that hotbed of almost but not quite ripe sensuality? But what Nic didn't know was that she was not really at heart that hardened hormone-driven harlot. What would it be like for him to see her as she really was instead of how the press portrayed her? Ha! As if he would have any respect for her if she revealed all.

'I like my life,' she said, not quite meeting his eyes. 'I know it's not for everybody but it suits me.'

'You are only...what, almost twenty-six? You are in the prime of your life. Have you no desire to do something with your intellect? Perhaps do some sort of course or degree?'

She gave him a bored look. 'I hated school so I can't see myself signing up for anything academic. I haven't got the discipline for it. Jon was the brains of the family.'

'I am sure you are underselling yourself,' he said. 'I know Jonathan was brilliant but you come from the same nest. You have the same blood running through your veins. It's just a matter of finding what you enjoy and are good at doing.'

'Don't worry about me,' she said with a dismissive wave of her hand. 'I will be quite happy being a social butterfly while you are off doing what you have to do.'

'Are you even interested in what it is I do?' he asked.

Jade felt a tiny stab of guilt she couldn't quite explain. 'You do something with the Sabbatini hotel chain,' she said, suddenly feeling hopelessly inadequate. 'Aren't you the financial controller or something?'

His eyes flickered upwards as if in disbelief or frustration or perhaps a bit of both. 'That is my brother Giorgio's role. I am the property developer. I scope out new real estate for development, some for hotels and others for our family investment portfolio. I am working on projects in several countries.'

Jade thought of all those hotel rooms, all those beds and bathrooms she would have to share with him in order to keep the truth of their convenient marriage a secret. One could possibly trust a long-serving household servant to keep that sort of confidence, but not the staff in a hotel, even a luxury Sabbatini one where the staff were rigorously hand-picked. 'Have you thought about the logistics of all of this?' she asked. 'We can hardly have separate rooms everywhere we go. People are bound to speculate and talk.'

He smiled at her in that seductive way of his that made her blood bubble with excitement in her veins. 'Do you really think you won't be begging me to bed you by the time we are married, or is this all just an act to whet my appetite?'

She tightened her mouth. 'It's no act, Nic. This is a hands-off deal.'

He cocked his handsome head at her. 'Why do I get the feeling you are saying that for your benefit not mine?'

Jade felt a blush steal over her cheeks. 'I am saying it because I know what you are like. You are used to women falling over themselves to occupy your bed.'

He leaned forward, his forearms resting across the table, his eyes dark and challenging as they held hers. 'How about we make a little deal, Jade?' he suggested. 'In public I will have to touch you as any husband would touch his wife, but in private I won't lay a finger on you unless you give me the go-ahead with those seductive green eyes of yours. Not one finger, OK?'

Jade eyed him suspiciously for a long moment, her heart beating like a drum that was being played by someone not quite sure of the correct rhythm. Could she trust him to keep his word? More to the point: could she trust herself? 'O...K,' she said at last, her breath coming out a little shakily.

'Good.' He sat back and picked up the bottle of champagne and topped up both of their glasses. 'It looks like we have a deal.'

CHAPTER FOUR

THE press had gone by the time they left the restaurant. Jade quietly blew out a breath of relief as Nic walked with her back to his hotel. She worked the press when she needed to but there were times when she wished she could disappear into anonymity. The news of their impending marriage would be splashed over every paper by morning. That was well and good, for it would make Nic less likely to pull out of the arrangement. He wouldn't want to draw any attention to the terms of his grandfather's will. He had his fair share of the notorious Sabbatini pride. For a playboy such as him to be dragged kicking and screaming to the altar would be the epitome of having one's pride bludgeoned.

Nic placed a protective arm around her waist as they weaved their way through the tourist crowd. Feeling that band of muscle against her was creating enough heat to start a wildfire. She could feel the way her body responded to his closeness, the way her thighs trembled when he stood in the hotel lift beside her, not quite touching, but close enough for her to feel the hot, hard male heat of his long strong legs.

He took out his mobile and began to fiddle with the keypad. 'For some reason I don't have your mobile number in my phone,' he said, glancing sideways at her. 'I've only got your landline. What's your number?'

Jade pressed her lips together for a moment. 'Um...I don't have a mobile phone.'

His dark brows met over his eyes. 'What—did you lose it or something?'

She hesitated before answering. 'I...I had one once but then I lost it and I didn't get around to replacing it.'

He was still looking at her as if she had just landed out of time from a couple of centuries back. 'Are you *serious*?' he said. 'You really don't have a mobile?'

She shook her head as the doors of the lift opened.

'I will get you one tomorrow,' he said and pocketed his phone as he held the door back with the barrier of his arm.

Jade felt as if a butter churn had started to work on overdrive in her stomach. 'Please don't,' she said, biting her lip when he looked at her quizzically. 'I'm embarrassed to admit it but I'm really a bit of a technophobe. I only just worked out how to use the phone I had when I lost it. I don't want to have to go through all of that again.'

'Jade.' He gave her that look—the look that made her feel as if she were just about to walk in on the first day of kindergarten. 'The newer models are extremely simple to use. I will talk you through it and you'll be amazed at how easy it is. It's the same as using a computer. A little kid can do it. My niece Ella is already great at playing one of the games on my phone and she's not even three.'

She gave a vague nod of acquiescence and stepped out past him.

'What's your email address, then?' he asked once they were inside the penthouse.

Jade felt her stomach tilt in alarm. She racked her brain to think of an excuse for why she didn't have an email address. How could she possibly read an email when she couldn't even write her own name and address? 'Um...I can't tell you offhand—I've just had it changed. I was having some trouble with loads of... er...spam. The technician thought it best to change my network server. I haven't quite memorised the new address. It's a little more complicated than my last one.'

'Just shoot me an email when you get a chance and I'll add you to my contacts,' he said and handed her a business card with his contact details on it.

Jade looked down at the card. It was like Nic: distinctive and bold. The card was embossed and she ran her fingertip over it, feeling each letter through her skin, her brow furrowed in intense concentration.

'Are you learning my numbers off by heart?' he asked.

She tucked the card away in her purse, keeping her expression blank. 'I have no interest in learning anything but how to navigate myself through life to my advantage,' she said. 'Marrying you is, unfortunately, the only way of my achieving self-sufficiency.'

Nic's eyes studied her with increasing intensity and disdain. 'You are as shallow and self-serving as the press makes out, aren't you?' he said. 'You don't even bother disguising it. All you want is money and plenty of it.'

Jade gave him a fabricated smile, the sort that any hard-nosed gold-digger would use with ease. 'We are on the same mission then, aren't we, Italian boy? We both want a fortune to land into our hands and we are both prepared to sacrifice our souls to get it.'

His mouth tightened into a hard, flat line. 'Let's just hope it's worth it in the end,' he said.

'I am sure it will be,' she said, but inside she was already trembling with doubt. 'You will get your inheritance and I will finally get my independence. What more could we both want?'

His eyes seared a fire trail into hers. 'That remains to be seen, doesn't it?' he asked. He nodded towards the big bed. 'Which side do you want?'

Jade felt her eyes flicker in alarm but quickly controlled it before he could notice. 'Call housekeeping for a roll-out bed. I'll sleep on that.'

'You're joking, surely?' he said. 'We have just announced our engagement. What do you think the hotel staff will think if we insist on sleeping in separate beds?'

Jade put on her sassy face. 'They'll think we're saving ourselves for our wedding night.'

He gave an amused snort. 'You really are a chameleon, aren't you, *cara*? One minute you're the hot-blooded harlot and the next you turn into a shy virgin.'

She turned for the bathroom but he caught her by the back of her dress, pulling her into the rock-hard wall of his body, his hands coming to rest on the top of her shoulders, his chest against her shoulder blades, his pelvis pressing into her buttocks, stirring every nerve into a frenzy of awareness, making her breath stall like a faulty engine.

This was the closest she had been to him in years.

She could feel the hardened probe of his growing

erection. She could feel the hammering of his heart against her right shoulder.

Oh, dear God, she could feel her resistance crumbling. The brick wall of determination she had set up to resist him was being dismantled second by second. She was not used to feeling this out of control. She was usually the one who had all the power over men. They didn't have it over her. Not one of them.

Except this one...

Jade wondered what would happen if she turned around and pushed her mouth up to meet his. To slip her tongue in between those mocking lips of his, to show him how hard she could drive him to the very edge of control.

She wanted to.

But she didn't dare.

'You know, you really should have thought this through a little more carefully, Jade,' he said in a smouldering voice, his mouth far too close to her neck.

She felt the fine hairs on her body stand to attention, her skin lifting in a shiver. She felt the warm dancing breeze of his breath as he leaned in closer; it feathered over her skin like a fine sable brush over a canvas.

'You rushed here to Venice without thinking about how this would end tonight, didn't you, *mio piccolo*?'

Jade bit down on her lip as she felt him move against her buttocks. He was practically parting them with his swollen length. It was the most tantalising feeling, deliciously erotic and sexy. Her body felt on fire. Flames licked along her flesh. Her belly was quivering with a whirlpool of need. Her inner core was throbbing like a heavy pulse that came from deep inside her body, a place she had not even been properly aware of before.

Her breasts were prickling with sensation, her nipples tight and aching as they pushed against the fragile lace of her bra. 'You said you wouldn't touch me unless we were in public,' she said, sucking in her breath as his teeth nipped just below her earlobe.

'I said I wouldn't touch you if you didn't give me the come on,' he said. 'But you just can't help yourself, can you, *cara*?'

Jade turned and stepped away from him, sending him a defiant look. 'If you are going to break the rules from day one, then so can I. I have my contacts. I will tell them everything. I will even tell them about some of your brothers' stuff. That will go down a treat with your family, don't you think?'

He looked down at her, his jaw tight to the point of whiteness at the edges of his mouth. 'One false move, Jade, do you hear me? One false move and you'll be begging for a living off the streets, right where someone with your guttersnipe morals and behaviour belongs.'

Jade met him stare for stare, anger ballooning in her chest at his cruelly taunting words. 'You think you can control me, don't you, Italian boy?' she goaded him right on back.

His nostrils flared as he fought to control his temper. 'You can't even control yourself,' he said with a look of disgust. 'You're a spoilt brat who should have grown up a long time ago. No wonder your father cut you off without a penny. You're nothing but a prima donna who doesn't know how to behave like a woman of class and breeding.'

Jade swung her hand up towards his face but he caught it mid-swipe, holding it in a cruel grip that made tears spring to her eyes. She suddenly had the most unexpected urge to cry. She hadn't cried in years, not since Jon's funeral. She wasn't going to break down in front of Nic. She was not going to let him see how much he had hurt her. No one could hurt her. She always made sure of that. *No one*. She blinked her eyes, gritted her teeth and wrenched her arm out of his. 'I have to use the bathroom,' she bit out and stalked from the room.

When she came out after repairing the damage to her make-up, Nic was standing with a brooding expression on his face. 'I'm sorry,' he said. 'I shouldn't have spoken to you like that.'

She gave a careless shrug. She had been called far worse in the press but somehow coming from Nic the words had been so much more devastating to hear. She hoped he hadn't heard her snivelling like a baby in the bathroom. She had turned on the taps to drown out the sound, but she saw the way his hazel eyes had softened in remorse. 'Do you want me to leave?' she asked. 'I can go and stay in another hotel. No one will probably even notice.'

'No, don't do that,' he said, rubbing the back of his neck. 'You have the bed. I'll sleep on one of the sofas. There are spare pillows and blankets in the wardrobe.'

She chewed at her lip as she watched him prepare the sofa. He was going to have a terrible night's sleep on that because, as luxurious as it was, he was just too tall for it.

He was right, of course. She hadn't thought much past getting him to agree to marry her. She hadn't thought of what would come next. Her impulsive nature had got her into trouble too many times to count. When would she ever learn?

'Would you like a nightcap or something?' Nic asked once the sofa was made up.

Jade shook her head. 'No, I'll just go to bed. I'm really tired. I feel like I've been travelling all day.'

'I'll leave you to prepare for bed in peace,' he said. 'I'm going to go downstairs to use the business centre.'

Jade could see his slim laptop on the antique desk over near the window, which could mean only one thing: he wanted to avoid her. She could hardly blame him. 'Well, goodnight, then,' she said.

His eyes met hers briefly. 'Goodnight, Jade.'

She sank to the bed once he had closed the door. Her body felt so tired from her crying jag in the bathroom. She would give anything to just curl up in amongst those soft, smooth sheets and forget the world for eight hours. She looked at her half-unpacked suitcase. She looked at it for a long moment, chewing at her lip as she planned her next course of action.

She sprang off the bed and quickly gathered her things, packing them haphazardly back in the case and snapping it shut.

Nic could have his bed. She would be miles away by the time he got back to his suite. She wasn't going to spend even one night more than necessary with him.

It was far too dangerous.

Nic came back to the suite after midnight. He had a headache and a neck ache and he was still feeling a brute for the way he had spoken to Jade. She had covered it well but he knew she had gone to the bathroom to compose herself. She had been on the verge of tears. Tears he had provoked.

He couldn't remember ever seeing her cry, or at least not since her brother's funeral and even then she had kept it in until the last moment, when Jonathan's coffin was lowered into the ground. She had been hysterical and had to be sedated once they got back to the Sommerville estate. Nic had tried to offer comfort but, if anything, his presence had seemed to upset her all the more. In the end he had left early and had stayed away from her for over a year. He wasn't proud of that. He often wondered if her decline back into an eating disorder could have been averted by a little more support from those best known to her.

The suite was in darkness and he reached for the nearest lamp switch, not wanting to disturb her with a bright light suddenly coming on. The muted glow of the lamp illuminated the huge bed but it was empty. He swung his gaze to the made-up sofa but it was empty too. He drew in a sharp hiss of a breath and strode through to the bathroom but there was nothing there except a faint trace of her perfume. He came back out to the suite and raked his fingers through his hair when he saw her suitcase had gone. He checked all over the suite but she hadn't even had the decency to leave him a note. He swore in three languages and paced the floor, frustrated beyond description.

The scheming little minx had tricked him into agreeing to marry her. There was no way he could pull out of it now and she damn well knew it. The press were running with it. It had already been broadcast online and on the radio. He had already had a call from his brothers saying how pleased they were that he was doing what their grandfather had wanted. Her little staged you-hurt-my-feelings act had been convincing, so convincing he had fallen for it hook, line and sinker and outboard motor to boot. Damn the little witch!

Jade had been back at her flat twenty-four hours when Nic arrived. She winced when he put his finger on the buzzer, holding it down relentlessly, knowing she would have to answer before one of the neighbours complained about the noise. She opened the outer door for him and waited with a pounding heart for him to make his way to her flat.

His short hard knock on her door sounded like a firearm being discharged.

She opened the door with a breezy smile of greeting. 'Hi, Nic.'

He strode past her, his mouth set in a rigid line. 'Have you seen the papers?' he asked, thrusting a bundle at her.

'I don't read the papers,' Jade said, wondering if he would pick up on the irony in her tone.

'We are officially engaged,' he bit out.

She gave him a bright smile. 'Yes, I know. Isn't it exciting?'

He glowered at her darkly. 'And, since we are officially engaged,' he went on as if she hadn't spoken, 'you will at all times act like a fiancée should act. That means you will not leave my hotel or apartment or villa or wherever we might be staying without telling me where you are going. Do you hear me?'

Jade raised her chin. 'I left because I didn't want you to have a bad night's sleep. You wouldn't have slept a wink on that sofa.'

He narrowed his eyes at her. 'Don't go pretending you did anything charitable back there in Venice. You got what you wanted and left. You didn't even leave a note. What sort of disgraceful show of manners is that? I was worried sick about you.'

Jade tossed her head. 'I bet you weren't. I bet you were furious I slipped out without you knowing.'

'You're damn right I was,' he said. 'I had the press on my tail all the way back to London. I had to think of some sort of reasonable excuse for why you weren't still with me.'

'How terribly taxing for you,' she said with a roll of her eyes.

This time she actually heard him grinding his teeth. 'You really are the most uncontrollable brat I have ever met.'

'And you are the most undesirable fiancé a girl could ever want,' she threw back.

His hazel eyes flashed with green and brown flecks of hatred. 'I have organised a lawyer to come around this evening to go through the legal documents with you,' he said. 'I expect and demand your full cooperation in reading and signing them.'

Jade controlled her instinctive panic with an effort. 'I will do what is necessary to secure my inheritance but I will do nothing extra.'

'You will do as you are damn well told,' he said heatedly. 'I have decided to bring the wedding forward. I don't trust you to be out of my sight for the rest of this month. You will move to my villa in Rome as soon as it can be arranged. We will be married early next week. I have already informed my family of the change of plan.'

This time it was impossible for Jade to hide her panic.

'I...I don't want to do that...I have things to do here in London. I don't want to leave before I'm ready.'

'We do have hairdressers and nail technicians in Italy, you know,' he said with a sarcastic bite. 'We even have fashion designers.'

She sent him a fulminating glare. 'You can't have everything your own way, Nic. I know you have for most of your life, but I am not going to be pushed around by you.'

'I am sending a removal company for your things in the morning,' he said. 'The lawyer will be here in less than an hour. I have also organised a wedding planner to meet with you this evening. She will see to all details to do with the ceremony. We will travel together to Rome late tomorrow afternoon. I will send my driver to collect you. If you do not cooperate I will call the press and tell them the wedding is off.'

'You won't do that,' Jade said with not as much confidence as it sounded.

He held her gaze with steely intensity. 'Don't bet on it, Jade,' he said. 'I will do what I damn well please and you will obey without question.'

Jade picked up a cushion from the sofa and threw it at him. It missed by a mile and bounced off the wall without even making a sound as it fell impotently to the floor. 'I hate you,' she said. 'I really, *really* hate you.'

He smiled coolly as he opened the door. 'I hate you too; you have no idea how much.'

She winced as he closed the door on his exit. And for the second time in twenty-four hours she felt tears prickle and burn at her eyes.

CHAPTER FIVE

LESS than an hour later a lawyer arrived with papers in hand, just as Nic had informed her. Jade went through all the motions: politely offering coffee or tea, providing a seat at the dining table so the papers could be spread out easily, all the while hoping her façade of understanding everything would not be shown up for what it was: total ignorance.

'And if you will just sign here and here,' the lawyer said, pointing out the sections that were highlighted.

Jade scribbled her signature while inside cringing at how unsophisticated and childish it looked next to Nic's where he had signed earlier. She studied the bold strokes of his name; the confidence and assurance she always associated with him were there in every twist and turn of his pen.

Not long after the lawyer left a woman arrived, announcing herself as the wedding planner. Jade allowed herself to be swept up in the momentum of confirming all the appointments: the fitting of a dress at a designer studio once she got to Rome, a visit to the jewellers' where she would be fitted with an astonishingly expensive engagement and wedding ring ensemble that had already been chosen on her behalf, as well as a visit to a high street florist where the flowers for the church and the wedding bouquet would be chosen, ready to be flown to the church in Bellagio by private jet.

It was all done with the efficiency of clockwork but inside Jade was secretly worrying about the year ahead. She could look and dress the part of the happy bride but she was not the bride of Nic's choice.

They were both marrying under sufferance; it was a chore—it was a time line they both had to endure to get what they wanted.

Jade tried not to think of the romantic fantasies she had conjured up in the past. That was a long time ago and this was here and now. This was a cold, hard business deal, a transaction with financial rewards to be gained. It was not about love or mutual goals. It was about Nic Sabbatini inheriting what was rightfully his. She was the pathway for him to do that and he was hers. She was nothing to him but a means to an end and she would be a silly fool to think otherwise.

A courier arrived early the next morning and delivered a high-tech mobile phone to her apartment. He assured her it was already charged and ready to use. Jade signed for it and, after a long period of hesitation, she unpacked it from its packaging, not for the first time feeling all alone in the world, with no one to understand how desperately vulnerable she felt. She put it away in her handbag and got on with the rest of her packing in preparation for the move to Rome. The removal men arrived and took everything out of her flat. She hovered about as her paintings were being loaded, worried they would be damaged, but the men seemed to know what they were doing and covered everything in bubble wrap.

Nic called just before lunch to say he had to fly out of London for the rest of the week to sort out a property deal in Rio de Janeiro and she would have to go to Rome without him. 'I'm sorry about the short notice,' he said. 'But no doubt you'll have plenty to do preparing for the wedding.'

'I'm surprised you aren't insisting I accompany you,' Jade said somewhat waspishly, 'or is it because you have some unfinished business to do in the bedroom rather than the boardroom?'

'I thought you said you didn't read the gossip in the papers?' he said.

Jade ground her teeth, imagining him with the long-legged, exotic Brazilian model, having a last fling before their marriage. The trouble was, it would very probably not be his last. A man like Nic would not stay true to fake marriage vows; he would have trouble staying true to real ones.

'And I also thought you said I could do what I liked as long as I was discreet about it,' Nic added when she didn't respond.

Jade unlocked her tight jaw. 'Do what you like. I can't stop you. According to the lawyer you sent around, you've got your back well and truly covered.'

'Ah, so the prenuptial is a sticking point, is it?' Nic said.

'Do you really think I want half of everything you own?' Jade said. 'I just want what Salvatore wanted me to have.'

'Divorces can get pretty ugly, Jade,' he said. 'I am not prepared to risk all that my grandfather and father and two older brothers worked so hard for when we part company in a year's time. Don't take it personally. It's just sound business sense to protect one's assets.'

Jade knew what he said was true, and to some degree it was her own fault for encouraging his opinion of her as an empty-headed, gold-digging socialite.

'Did you get the mobile?' he asked after a tense pause. 'I tried calling you on it earlier but the message service said it was switched off. I made sure it was charged before it was delivered. Have you turned it off or something?'

Jade swallowed and looked in the direction of her handbag. 'Um...I haven't had time to answer it with all the packing I've been doing.'

'I have people organised to do that for you,' he said. 'Why are you doing it yourself?'

'I don't like strangers touching my things,' she said, turning her back on the accusing presence of her handbag.

There was another little silence.

'I probably won't see you until the day of the wedding,' he said. 'My business is taking longer than I expected. I have organised a private jet to take you to Rome. My driver will pick you up and take you to the airport. You will be driven to my villa and my housekeeper, Guilia, will help you settle in. The wedding planner will see to everything and will be in contact with you over the last-minute things. Your flat will be packed up and the keys handed back to your father. He has someone who wants to rent it as of next week.'

'Is he coming to the wedding?' Jade asked.

'Yes, he said he was looking forward to giving you away.'

Yes, well, it wouldn't be the first time, Jade thought bitterly.

Jade arrived, just as Nic had arranged, at his villa in Rome. It had been a relief to have someone see to all the travelling arrangements for once. She normally had to engage the services of a travel agent, which was always stressful as she had to memorise everything as the documents they handed to her in a file were useless. She envied everyone who could book things online. They didn't have to commit everything to memory and then worry incessantly in case they forgot a date or a time or an address. Visiting new places was an absolute nightmare for her. She had got lost so many times and felt so foolish when asking for directions, only to find she was just a street or a block away.

Rome was a place she was familiar with, so was Milan, but Bellagio was going to be a challenge; she hoped if she stayed close to the Sabbatini villa she wouldn't go far wrong. However, if Nic was really serious about taking her with him on all his trips abroad she would have to think of some way of coping. She couldn't wander around like a normal tourist, reading maps and street names. She would have to stay in the hotel and fill in the time rather than risk exposing her defect. She would rather die than have Nic know she was severely dyslexic. No one knew. It was her shameful little secret.

The housekeeper at Nic's villa was austere and un-welcoming right from the moment Jade stepped through the imposing front door. Guilia Rossetti gave Jade an up and down look that would have stripped a century of wallpaper from a wall. 'So this is Nicolò's future bride,' she said, making a guttural sound of disgust in her throat. 'He could have done much better. I read all about you. You're not worthy of the Sabbatini name. You will bring nothing but harm and shame to him and to the family, I am sure of it.'

Jade straightened her spine and stared down the dark-eyed Italian. 'If you want to keep working for my future husband, then I would advise you to keep your opinions to yourself.'

Jade pointed to the bags the driver had placed at the foot of the stairs. 'You can unpack for me and then I would like a gin and tonic brought up to my room, ready and waiting for me after my shower,' she said in a haughty tone.

The housekeeper's eyes were like black diamonds, beady and full of loathing. '*Sì, signorina,*' she said through gritted teeth and bent to snatch up the bags.

Jade tossed her hair over her shoulder and wandered through the villa. It was a glorious place, beautifully decorated with gold and marble, signalling the wealth Nic and his brothers had grown up with and most probably taken for granted, just as she had done until her supply of money had been stopped. She pushed the irritating thought aside and looked at the artwork on the walls, some of which she recognised from some of her favourite masters.

The villa was three storeys high and overlooked wonderful gardens, complete with a lap pool and jacuzzi and a tennis court. Jade walked out through a set of doors into the bright April sunshine. The water of the pool sparkled and a light breeze crinkled the surface.

The lawn was a verdant expanse of green, lush and with that delicious fresh fragrance of having just been mown. A white wisteria was hanging in a scented arras from a stone wall, the hum of bees as they collected the sweet pollen filling the air. Roses were everywhere and in every shade imaginable: pinks and whites and whites blushed with pink, deep blood-red ones, mauve and yellow and apricot. The fragrance collectively was heady and intoxicating and she breathed deeply to take it in.

She walked a little farther and sat on a stone bench overlooking a fountain that had a marble Cupid figure pouring water from a pitcher which then overflowed to the base of the fountain. It was a peaceful, tranquil sound: the gentle splashing of water over centuries-old marble. The urge to paint the scene was overwhelming but she had to restrain herself as her things were still in boxes waiting to be unpacked.

When she went back inside the housekeeper was coming down the stairs. She gave Jade a caustic look. 'I have put your things in the yellow room,' she said. 'After the honeymoon I will move them into Signor Sabbatini's suite, but not before.'

Jade suddenly decided she would sleep in Nic's bed just to annoy the housekeeper. It wouldn't matter because Nic had already told her he wouldn't be back in Rome before the wedding and would meet her at the church in Bellagio. 'I am afraid you will have to do so for I am intending to sleep in my fiancé's bed,' she said with a don't-dare-to-disobey-me air.

The housekeeper muttered something in Italian before she stalked off, her footsteps clacking with anger across the marble floor.

Jade let out a breath and walked up the grand stair-case, her footsteps muffled as they trod on the priceless stair runner held in place by solid brass bars at the back of each step.

She found Nic's room without any trouble. It was just as she had imagined it would be. It was huge, as was the bed, and it was decorated in brown and cream with a touch of black in the lamps and bedside tables, giving it an unmistakably masculine feel. The en suite bathroom was as big as her London flat's bedroom and it followed the same gold and marble theme of the rest of the villa.

The shower was refreshing but she couldn't help thinking of Nic's naked body standing right where she was standing. Her mind pictured him with the water cascading over him, over his chest and ridged abdomen, down his hair-roughened flanks and over his taut buttocks and the proud male heart of him. Her breath caught in her throat and she quickly turned off the water and reached for one of the big fluffy towels that was as big as a sheet.

When Jade came back into Nic's bedroom it was obvious the housekeeper had failed to bring her things through. She drew in an angry breath and stalked out to the landing. 'Guilia?' Her voice echoed through the villa. 'Will you come up here immediately and do as I asked you to do?'

There was no response.

Jade stormed to the yellow room and, dropping her wet towel on the floor, rummaged through the wardrobe for something to wear. She didn't bother drying her hair but left it loose to dry naturally. She didn't bother with make-up either. She never did if she wasn't expecting anyone to be around or she wasn't going out.

There was no sign of the housekeeper downstairs, although Jade did see a note propped up against the kettle. She looked at it, wondering what the housekeeper had written. The handwriting looked as if it had been done quickly and crossly, but if it was in Italian or English, she couldn't quite tell. She scrunched it into a ball and left it on the bench.

She filled in the rest of the evening by sorting some of her paints and sketchbook into a smaller bag to take with her to Bellagio. She had seen enough travel shows to know how picturesque the Italian lakes district was. It was the one part of her honeymoon—such as it was— she was looking forward to.

After a light supper of chicken and salad she had found in the fridge, she made her way back upstairs to bed. The villa was scarily empty. There was no sound apart from the ticking of an ormolu clock on a French lacquered table on the second landing.

She slipped out of her jeans and loose-fitting top, her bra and knickers adding to the pile on the floor. The sheets were smooth and cool and fresh and, within seconds of putting her head down on the feather pillows, she felt her eyelids going down as if weighted by anvils…

Jade stretched out a leg and froze. Her eyes flew open and she sat bolt upright. 'What the hell are you doing here?' she asked as Nic opened one sleepy eye from right beside her.

He propped himself up on one elbow. 'Where else would I be?' he asked. 'This is my bed.'

'I…I know but you're not supposed to be here now!' she said, pulling her legs out of the reach of his long, strong hairy ones.

He sat up in the bed, the sheet that had been covering him slipping to just below his navel. Jade saw the dark masculine hair that arrowed down beneath the sheet and her stomach did a jerky little somersault. He was as naked as she was. She could practically see the outline of his maleness.

'I came back by private jet after I got a call from my housekeeper,' he said. 'She refuses to work for me while you are in residence. What on earth did you say to her?'

Jade pushed her lips out in a pout. 'She was awful to me from the moment I stepped in the door. She refused to do what I asked and she called me horrible names.'

Nic pushed back the sheet and rose from the bed. Jade swallowed as she saw the masculine perfection of his body. He was so toned and taut, so powerfully male in every plane and contour.

He slipped on a lightweight bathrobe and tied the ends around his waist as he looked down at her in the bed. 'This has to stop, Jade. You can't act like this. Don't you understand? You have to take responsibility for your actions.'

'*My* actions?' she said indignantly. 'What about hers? She's your employee so she should have more respect. It shouldn't matter who you marry. She should accept your future bride without question or snide and insulting comments.'

'I am afraid there are times in life when you have to

earn respect,' Nic said. 'It doesn't come automatically just because of whom you are married to or how much you earn or where you were born.'

She gave him a mutinous scowl. 'I am not going to kowtow to the cleaning staff just so they'll be nice to me. I will do what I want.'

Nic grasped the end of the sheet and ripped it from the bed. He smiled at her shocked expression. She looked like an outraged virgin about to be ravaged by a devilish suitor. 'Do I have to teach you some manners myself, my naughty little wife-to-be?' he asked as he tugged her down by one ankle until she was lying between his open thighs as he stood at the end of the bed.

Her slim throat rose and fell and her breasts, which she had so brazenly flashed at him only days ago, she was now struggling to cover with her hands. Her cheeks were stained a delicate shade of pink and her eyes were wide and uncertain, their long dark lashes giving her a Bambi look that was totally captivating. 'Wh…what do you think you're doing?' she asked in a high-pitched strained sort of voice.

'I thought I might try the goods before I buy since they are right here in my bed for my pleasure,' he said, stroking his hand up the smooth length of her leg from ankle to calf. 'That was your intention, wasn't it? To get my attention? Well, you got it, baby. I am here and I am all yours.'

She tried to kick out at him but his fingers locked around her ankle. She kicked out with her other leg but he caught that slim ankle too and held it firm.

'Let me go, you arrogant bastard!' she said, struggling like a wildcat.

'Manners, Jade,' Nic said silkily. 'You will learn to speak to me with respect.'

Her face was a picture of rage, all flashing green cat's eyes and white teeth bared in a snarl. 'I'll never forgive you for this,' she said. 'If you lay even one finger on me I will scratch your damn eyes out.'

'I bet you say that to all your lovers,' he said with a mocking smile.

She fought him with a strength he didn't realise someone of her delicate frame could possess. She bucked and arched and jerked until he had to let go in case she hurt herself. She crawled away from him like a scuttling crab, scooping up the sheet he had tossed from the bed and wrapping it around herself like a shroud before she faced him with a blistering glare. 'If you think you can just do what you like when you like, you are sadly mistaken,' she said.

'Ditto, *cara*,' he said. 'It's time you learned how to behave, and if I have to teach you myself I will do it.'

Jade poked her tongue out at him.

He laughed. 'You are going to be absolute dynamite in bed. No wonder you have men following you with their tongues hanging out. I can't wait to see what fireworks we set off together.'

She gave him a cutting look. 'If you want to sleep with me you can damn well pay for it.'

'I have paid for it, Jade,' he said as he opened the door to leave. He gave her one last up and down stripping look and added, 'I paid for you with my freedom and I expect to collect on it as soon as we are officially married.'

Jade winced as the door closed on his exit. Surely he didn't mean it? He wouldn't insist on sleeping with her if she didn't want to. She bit her lip. The trouble was, she did want to.

She wanted to very much.

When Jade came downstairs the next morning Nic was swimming in the lap pool. She watched him from the windows of the breakfast room, his bronzed body carving the water like an Olympic athlete. He made her floundering efforts to stay afloat seem rather pathetic in comparison. It was another one of her failings. She had never learned to swim with any proficiency.

She turned away with a sigh and went to the kitchen. Her supper things were still on the bench where she had left them, so too was a glass Nic had obviously used to have some orange juice before his morning swim. She gave a little shrug of indifference and turned away.

Nic came in through from the doors that led to the terrace. He was naked from the waist up, a towel hanging from his lean hips. 'Is breakfast ready yet?' he asked, pushing back his wet hair with one of his hands.

Jade frowned. 'Pardon me?'

He nodded towards the breakfast room. 'Coffee and fruit to start with and then some fresh rolls,' he said. 'I'll expect you to have it ready by the time I come back from my shower.'

She opened her eyes wide. 'Are you expecting *me* to wait on you?'

'Well, it was you who caused the housekeeper to leave in a huff,' he reminded her. 'It's only fair you take over her role until I can find someone to replace her.'

Jade bristled in outrage. 'I will do no such thing. Get your own stupid breakfast.'

He eyeballed her until she felt the base of her spine

start to tingle. 'Breakfast, Jade, and step on it. I have an important meeting at my office this morning.'

She pressed her lips together, glaring at him, daring him to make her do his bidding. The air crackled with electricity as their strong wills collided. She felt the power of it, the tension escalating along with her heart rate. She was not going to be a slave to him. He was not going to order her about like some servant in his employ.

She smiled to herself as she planned her next move. She would show him just how little he could control her.

Nic came over to where she was standing. He stopped right in front of her, holding her defiant gaze with the steely determination of his. 'Do I have to repeat myself?' he asked.

Jade put on a meekly obedient face. 'It'll be ready in five minutes,' she said.

'Good girl,' he said and flicked her cheek with a gentle finger before he left the room.

Jade brewed some coffee and then sliced up some fruit and set it on a plate. She found the fresh rolls in a paper bag on the bench. She assumed someone from the bakery had delivered them earlier that morning. She carried a tray with everything on it into the breakfast room and set it out on the table that overlooked the sunny terrace.

Nic came in a few minutes later, straightening his tie. 'Nice job,' he said. 'I knew you could do it if you put your mind to it.'

'How do you have your coffee?' Jade asked, working hard at keeping her expression suitably subservient.

'White with two sugars,' he said as he sat down.

Jade put a cup down next to him and poured the coffee into it. Then she carefully spooned two teaspoons of sugar into it. She picked up the milk jug and said, 'Say when,' and then she poured the entire contents into his lap.

He leapt up from the table, his expression thunderous as he wiped at the dripping milk with a hastily grabbed napkin. 'You little bitch,' he growled at her.

Jade gave him a guileless look. 'You didn't say when.'

He tossed the sodden napkin aside and reached for her. Jade hadn't expected him to move quite so fast. Suddenly she was being held by the upper arms, his eyes blazing as they held hers.

Time stood still for the space of three rapid heartbeats.

And then with a muttered curse he swooped down and slammed his mouth down against hers.

Jade had lost count of the number of times she had been kissed. She had enjoyed some and hated others. But this was nothing like anything she had experienced before. Nic's mouth was like a flame against the soft flesh of her lips. It stoked a wildfire inside her, a raging fire that leapt and danced all over her skin. His kiss was bruising but she didn't care. She loved the taste of him, so fresh and male and commanding.

He cupped her head with his hands and deepened the kiss with an erotic thrust of his tongue. Her belly flipped as it curled around hers, flicking, stroking, teasing, conquering.

The kiss went on and on.

She tasted blood but wasn't sure if it was hers or his. She had nipped at him just as frantically as he had

nipped at her. Their teeth had even clashed at one point
in the desire to gain supremacy. It was the most breathlessly exciting sensual assault on her senses. She felt as
if she had been waiting her entire life for this moment.
It was bliss to have his mouth hard and insistent on hers,
the heated trajectory of his arousal burning like a brand
against her.

But just as suddenly as it had started it was over.

Nic stepped away from her, wiping the back of his
hand across his mouth, his breathing as ragged as hers.
'You had better make yourself scarce, young lady,' he
said. 'I am so angry with you right now I don't trust
myself to be around you.'

Jade ran her tongue over her swollen mouth, wincing
as she felt the little split in her lip. She saw him narrow
his eyes as he looked at her mouth, a flicker of remorse
passing over his expression.

'Damn it, Jade,' he said, raking his hair with one of
his hands. He stepped close again and tipped up her
face, a gentle fingertip tracing the tiny wound on her
lip. 'Does it hurt?' he asked in a gruff tone.

'No,' she said in a whisper.

He slid his hand to the nape of her neck, holding her
gaze for an endless moment. 'I'm sorry.'

'I'm sorry too.'

Nic dropped his hand from her neck and stepped
back. 'I'm afraid I haven't got time to help you clear up
here,' he said. 'I'm already running late and I have to
change.'

'What time will you be home?'

'I'll call you and let you know. I might have to fly
back to Rio. If so, I will meet you at Bellagio as previously planned.'

'Nic?'

He turned at the door. 'Yes?'

Jade twisted her hands together. 'I'm sorry about your housekeeper leaving.'

He gave her a brief crooked smile. 'Forget about it. I was thinking of firing her anyway. I think she's been filching the spirits.'

'Oh.'

'Why don't you check out the job seekers ads in the paper?' he said. 'That way you can interview all the candidates and decide who you'll get along with.'

Jade felt her chest tighten with panic. 'Oh, no, I can't do that.'

He gave her a frowning look. 'Of course you can, Jade. You just have to call them up and arrange a time to meet them.'

'But I can't read Italian.'

'You can do it online in English,' he said. 'There's a computer in my study. There are listings of all the employment agencies.'

'Can it wait until we get back from Bellagio?' she asked.

He looked at her for a long moment. 'Of course it can wait.' He walked over to the door, but then he paused with his hand on the doorknob as if a thought had suddenly occurred to him. He slowly turned and looked at her again. 'You do know how to use a computer, don't you?'

'Of course I do,' Jade said with a heavy dose of indignation. 'What do you think I am—completely brainless?'

'No, on the contrary, Jade, I think you are one of the cleverest people I have ever met. Not many people catch me off guard but you've done it not once, not twice, but three times. I wonder how many more surprises are in store for me during the next year.'

'You'll just have to wait and see, won't you?' she said with a pert look.

'I am looking forward to it,' he said and left the room.

CHAPTER SIX

As it turned out, Nic did have to fly back to Rio, or so he had said when he'd phoned on the landline later that day. Jade wondered if he was putting some space between them after The Kiss. She couldn't help thinking of it in capital letters. Her lips had tingled for hours afterwards. Her tongue kept returning to the tiny nick in her flesh, exploring it in detail. It was a constant reminder of the spontaneous combustion that had occurred between them. Nic had awakened a longing in her that would not go away. It ached and throbbed deep and low in her body, a persistent ache of emptiness she had never felt before.

She spent a couple of quiet days painting in the villa gardens before the preparations for the wedding began in full force. The flight and travelling arrangements turned out to be far easier than she had expected and the wedding planner had taken care of all the details, so all Jade had to do was turn up for her hair and make-up appointment, and finally slip into her dress and shoes.

When she finally arrived at the church in the picturesque lakeside town of Bellagio she felt as if she was acting her way through a movie role directed by Nic. Her father walked her into the church, beaming at all the guests as if he was the proudest of men. Jade went along with the façade of family togetherness but, as she walked past the front pew where her brother most likely would have been if he had still been alive, she felt a pain that was indescribable.

She looked up and saw Nic standing at the front with the priest. His hazel eyes ran over her, his lips stretched into a proud smile, she assumed for the congregation's sake. Her heart gave a little skip as his eyes darkened the closer she got. She saw his gaze go to the now healed spot on her lip. His eyes came back to hers, a silent message there that touched her so much she had to look away. She faced the front and listened as the priest began to speak.

Jade was conscious that this was the very church in which Nic's baby sister had been christened and then just three months later farewelled from this world. The wedding planner had let slip that this was the first time Nic's mother had come back to the villa since Chiara's death all those years ago. Jade wasn't sure why Nic had insisted on being married here, other than the villa was very private and the perfect place to have a honeymoon. Not that they were having a honeymoon, of course, Jade thought. It was all for the press, the pretence, the society wedding with all the trimmings. It was what everyone expected someone of Nic's breeding, and hers when it came to that, to do.

Finally the priest announced it was now time for Nic to kiss his bride and Jade felt a ripple of excitement race through her. She swallowed as he slipped a hand to the curve of her cheek, his touch and gaze as tender as any genuine groom's could be. She watched in breathless anticipation as his head lowered inch by inch until finally she felt the whisper-soft press of his lips on hers.

Again Jade was totally sideswiped at how her mouth responded to his. It was as if he had transferred some potent electrical current directly from his mouth to hers. Her lips moved beneath the gentle press of his, softly and shyly at first but then more hungrily as he deepened the kiss with a slow, smooth thrust of his tongue that took her completely by surprise. While it was nothing like the primal savagery of his previous kiss, for some reason the tenderness of this one was even more powerful and mind-blowing. She felt a shockwave of heat envelop her, and her tongue moved against his, tasting him, tasting the essential maleness of his mouth. He tasted minty, fresh and yet hot and erotic and brooding with barely leashed sensuality.

He pulled away first, smiling down at her, saying in an undertone, 'Save it for later, *cara*, for when we are naked and alone.'

Jade felt her colour rise but could do nothing but smile back as she knew the congregation was watching every move she made. She had already heard the collective *'ahh'* in response to their kiss. She silently fumed at Nic's arrogance. Did he really think she would sleep with him just because they were now married? He had probably slept with his mistress only the day before. Her anger went up a notch. No wonder he had flown straight back to Rio. He had no doubt taken advantage of his last couple of days of freedom; the freedom he claimed was the price he had paid for her.

Jade knew he would be an unforgettable lover for all the right reasons. But allowing such intimacy between them would be a disaster for her in the long run. She was increasingly worried about her feelings for him; feelings that used to be hate were morphing into something else entirely—something that was far more dangerous. She had to keep reminding herself this was a temporary marriage and any relationship between them was going to be over as soon as Nic got what he wanted: his inheritance.

The reception was held back at the villa, where a huge marquee had been set up in the gardens. Champagne flowed freely and Jade continued to play the role of blissfully happy bride—a role she found she could pull off with surprising ease, which was another worry to her—chatting with Nic's brothers and their wives and the other guests until her face ached from smiling so much.

At one point she looked across at Nic, who was cradling his baby nephew Matteo, Giorgio and Maya's son, in his arms. He was smiling at the gorgeous dark-haired baby, speaking in Italian while the baby cooed back in the universal language of young babies. Little Ella, Luca and Bronte's oldest child, was leaning against Nic's thigh, eagerly awaiting her turn for his attention. He turned and smiled at her adoringly, the words he spoke in his mother tongue obviously pleasing the little toddler, who grinned widely before saying something back in the same language with her own twist on the accent. Jade watched as he scooped Ella up in his arms, holding her high above his head, the toddler's squeals of delight filling the air.

'He'll make a fabulous father when the time comes,' Bronte said as she came over to where Jade was standing. 'He's such a natural with kids.'

Jade felt a blush flow like a tide into her cheeks. She

swept her gaze around to check for hovering members of the press before she spoke in an undertone. 'You know this is not a marriage that is going to last. We're both in it for what we can get.'

Bronte's slate-blue eyes held hers. 'I know you care for him, even if you don't like admitting it,' she said softly.

Jade bit her lip and averted her gaze, staring at the untouched champagne in her glass. 'You're mistaken, Bronte. I hate him as much as he hates me.'

'I don't believe that,' Bronte said. 'I used to think I hated Luca but it was love all along. You and Nic are made for each other. Anyone can see it. You're both so stubborn, neither of you wants to be the first one to break.'

'I can't see Nic admitting to feeling anything for anyone,' Jade said with a despondent sigh. 'He's never been one to talk of his feelings. He jumps from one woman's bed to another. I think the longest relationship he's ever had was less than a month.'

'Luca told me you used to have a crush on Nic,' Bronte said. 'Was he your first love?'

Jade turned and looked at Luca's lovely wife. No wonder he had tracked her down after he had finally sorted out his life. How he had torn himself away from her in the first place was something Jade still didn't quite understand. But they were so happy now and that was all that mattered. She envied them. She envied Giorgio and Maya too who, only moments before, had been looking at each other over by the fountain as if no one else was around. How she longed for that sort of love in her life. 'It's sort of complicated,' Jade said. 'You know what Nic's like. He's not the settling down type. This is a form of torture for him. He will want to shake off the shackles as soon as the time is up.'

'Is that what he told you?' Bronte asked, frowning slightly.

Jade looked across at Nic, who was now holding Bronte and Luca's baby boy, Marco, with Luca looking on indulgently. 'More or less,' she said, swinging her gaze back to Bronte's again. 'I'm not the right wife for him, Bronte. I don't know what Salvatore was thinking, writing his will the way he did. I could never make Nic happy. I don't have it in me to be a wife to anyone, let alone a man so restless and hard to please as him. I can't compete with supermodels and the like.'

Bronte gave her a gentle squeeze on the arm. 'I think you do yourself a very big disservice. You are one of the most beautiful women I have ever met, but not just in looks. I've seen the way you've cuddled Marco and Matteo, and I saw the way you tucked some of the flowers from your bouquet in Ella's hair. She already worships you. She thinks you're a princess. You *look* like a princess. I don't think I've ever seen a more stunning bride.'

'You're very kind,' Jade said, warming to the young woman all the more.

'I didn't get to know Salvatore very long, as you know,' Bronte said, 'but I knew enough about him to know he was no fool. If he thought the best course of action was to tie you and Nic in a marriage of convenience, then it would have been done out of love, not malice. He adored you. Luca has told me so many times of how he never had a bad word to say about you in spite of what the press reported over the years.'

Jade looked at the contents of her glass, swirling them

around, just like the thoughts in her brain. 'How do you handle it?' she asked, looking up at Bronte again. 'The press, I mean. I'm pretty used to it but every now and again it gets to me. Do you find it hard after your life in Melbourne where you were anonymous for so long?'

Bronte's eyes went to her husband's and a smile spread over her features. 'After a while you forget about the press,' she said. 'It's about you and your husband. It's about building a family unit that is so strong it can withstand the intrusion of other forces.'

She turned her gaze back to Jade's. 'I understand how people are fascinated with celebrities. I was too to some degree, but now I realise we are all just normal people trying to do our best with the limited time we've got on this earth. You have to make the most of it. But I can tell you from experience that marrying into the Sabbatini family is a wonderful thing. I have never felt so loved and accepted, even though I still haven't quite mastered the language. Do you speak Italian?'

'I can understand it more than I can speak it. I'm pretty hopeless at languages,' she said and added wryly, 'I still have trouble with English.'

'It will be expected of you,' Bronte warned. 'Maya's been giving me lessons. I'm much better than I expected but, to tell you the truth, it's really rather embarrassing to be outdone by my little daughter.'

Nic came over at that point and slung a casual arm around Jade's shoulders. 'How are you holding up, *tesore mio*?' he asked.

'My face is aching from smiling so much,' she said truthfully.

'Don't worry,' he said. 'The party is almost over.

Luca and Bronte's wedding went on for hours and hours, but then just as well, eh, Bronte?'

Bronte grinned as she looked to where Giorgio and Maya were cuddling up, no doubt remembering how they had come together for a stolen night of passion at Luca and Bronte's wedding whilst in the throes of an acrimonious divorce. 'You're not wrong there, Nic,' she said and discreetly slipped away when she heard Marco crying in the distance.

'Bronte thinks you would make a fabulous father,' Jade said, testing the waters with a bravado that had come from a few sips from a champagne glass.

Nic gave her a frowning look. 'Not me, baby girl. I like kids, I love them in fact, but I don't want any for myself. Children are hard work. They tie you down. I like my freedom too much.'

Jade felt an inexplicable ache deep inside her chest at his adamant statement. Surely she wasn't getting too attached to the loving wife role, not so soon? It was a role, an act. It wasn't for real. 'A lot of people would view that as a rather selfish stance to take,' she said, twirling her glass again for something to do with her hands.

His eyes narrowed as they centred on hers. 'Do *you* want children?' he asked.

Jade couldn't hold his gaze much longer than a second or two. 'Of course not,' she said, putting her glass down on the nearest surface. 'Having a child would totally cramp my lifestyle. You can't go clubbing with a baby, and just think what it would do to my figure.'

'So now who's the one who is being selfish?' he asked, hooking one brow upwards.

She looked up at him with a cool smile. 'I didn't say

I thought it was a selfish decision; I just said a lot of people would take that view.'

He continued to look at her with unwavering intensity, as if he was measuring her words with her expression and finding something lacking. 'So no kids for both of us,' he said, rocking back on his heels as he thrust his hands in his trouser pockets. 'At least we both know the rules from the outset. I take it you're on the Pill?'

Jade raised her brows at him. 'That is hardly any of your business, considering this is not going to be a normal marriage.'

He smiled an indolent smile that crinkled up the corners of his hazel eyes. 'Still insisting on a hands-off arrangement, *cara*?' he said. He leaned in closer, right up against the shell of her ear, his warm breath skating over her flesh, making every nerve stand to attention. 'You might want to rethink that once all these guests leave. We will be all alone. Just you and me and a document saying we are legally married.'

Jade couldn't quite suppress the whole body shiver that consumed her. She stepped backwards and, scooping up her previously abandoned glass, took a hefty sip but, as far as boosting her courage, it did nothing but remind her of how terribly vulnerable she was and had always been when it came to Nic Sabbatini and his lethally sensual charm.

Finally it was over.

Jade stood with the band of Nic's strong arm around her waist as they farewelled their guests. It was a long, slow process as everyone wanted to express their congratulations and best wishes for a happy future. Jade felt at times that her smile was so forced it would crack her face in two.

It was far easier when it was just the family taking their leave before they were flown back to Milan. They, at least, all knew the terms of Salvatore's will, but even so Jade wondered if any of them, particularly Maya and Bronte, had any idea of the way she was feeling. The ambiguity of her feelings worried her. She had been determined to get Nic to marry her so she could have the financial security she longed for, but she hadn't factored in how being with him for extended periods would affect her. She felt it now, a slight tug in her insides every time he looked at her. A twist inside her stomach, a flutter inside her heart, a breathlessness in her chest, an ache deep in her core.

Giovanna, her new mother-in-law, was tearful, but Jade knew that was more to do with having come back to the villa for the first time since baby Chiara had died all those years ago. Giovanna kissed Jade on both cheeks and welcomed her again to the family. 'I know this is not what either of you want, but do try and make the best of it, Jade. Our marriage had a rough start but I had many happy years with my Giancarlo.'

'I am sure we will make the best of things,' Jade assured her with zero confidence.

'Of all my boys, Nic is most like his father,' Giovanna said. 'He is restless, a free spirit—is that how you say it in English?'

'*Sì,* that is exactly how you say it,' Jade said.

Giovanna gave her another tight hug. 'You and Nic are more alike than you are different,' she said. 'Salvatore always said you were an angel underneath. That is just like my Nic. He has a soft core; you just have to know how to find it.'

Jade smiled wanly as the family escorted Giovanna to the waiting limousine. She was surprised at her new mother-in-law's attitude towards her. There were not many mothers who would welcome someone with Jade's reputation into the family, but then perhaps Giovanna was as eager as Salvatore had been for her youngest son to settle down, even if it wasn't to the most suitable of brides.

Nic came over to where Jade was standing, watching as the car disappeared into the distance. She felt her skin lift even though the air was still warm. She turned and faced him, forcing a stiff smile to her face. 'That seemed to go off rather well, don't you think?'

His eyes gleamed as he looked down at her. 'Everyone said the same thing: you were the most beautiful bride they have ever seen,' he said. 'I didn't tell you earlier, but you took my breath away when you stepped into the church on your father's arm.'

Jade didn't allow herself to believe he was being genuine. She knew what he wanted. He wanted to end the day in bed. He was a master at seduction and what better way than to butter her up with compliments that would melt her resolve to keep this marriage in name only. 'I think you went a little too far on the kiss in the church,' she said in a prim tone. 'A simple kiss on the lips would have sufficed. You should have shown a little more respect.'

His mouth tilted in a knowing smile. 'Feeling guilty about wanting me, Jade?'

She folded her arms across her middle. 'I do *not* want you. I just want the money this marriage will bring.'

'So you keep reminding me, but your eyes tell me something else again,' he said. 'And not just your eyes but your mouth as well. I've had trouble getting our first kiss out of my mind. You really are a little firecracker, aren't you?'

She gave a scathing little snort.

He studied her for a moment. 'Have you had anything to eat?'

She looked at him in irritation. 'Oh, please don't start on about that. I had enough from my father. Not that he was any great example, getting drunk like that and having to be practically poured into the car with his new girlfriend fussing over him as if she really gives a fig about him. She's after his money, any fool can see it, but then there's no fool like an old fool, is there?'

Nic pursed his lips for a moment. 'You don't really hate him, do you?'

She sent him a look that would have cut through marble. 'I feel nothing for him or for anyone.'

'I am quite sure that's not true,' he said. 'I saw you playing with Ella earlier. You don't hate her, do you?'

Her eyes flashed angrily. 'You seem to think you know me, Nic, but you don't. I'm not the naive, foolish, pampered little girl who hung off your every word like a lovesick puppy in the past. I've grown up. I know how to protect myself from people like you. You think you can throw a few compliments around and entice me into your bed, but I'm not that easy.'

'The press would have it otherwise,' he said with a wry look.

'The press don't always get it right,' she said. 'They interpret what they see to sell the most papers. It suits them to portray me as a home-wrecker. It fits their image of me as a tart who will bed anything in trousers. But I do have some standards. I am not interested in other people's husbands. I think that is the ultimate betrayal, to sleep with a close friend's husband.'

Nic studied her for another long moment, his thoughts flying around his head like insects trying to avoid the spurt of a poisonous spray. 'Are you saying the stuff about your affair with Richard McCormack was not true?'

She met his gaze with a challenge in her own. 'What do you think? Do you really think I am the sort of person to sleep with my best friend's husband while she was in the early stages of carrying his baby, which she subsequently lost?'

Nic raised his brows in surprise. There had been no mention of a baby in the press. He didn't know McCormack all that well personally, but they occasionally moved in the same circles. Nic had seen Richard at various functions, playing the role of the urbane businessman with consummate ease. He hadn't seemed the type to cheat on his wife, but then Jade was a temptation that would test any man's resolve. Nic felt it himself, the sensual power she had over him. Those sea-green eyes that promised so much, that lured and enticed, only to flash with hatred at the last minute. It was a cat and mouse game she was an expert at performing. But if she was innocent, then why not defend herself? She had access to top-notch lawyers. She wasn't exactly destitute, even if she had been a little overly dependent on her father's largesse up until now.

'So if you weren't McCormack's bit on the side, then who was?' he asked.

She gave him a stony-faced look. 'I have no idea.'

Nic wondered if she was lying to protect herself or someone else or whether she truly didn't know. It seemed the more time he spent with her, the less he knew about her. She had carried herself throughout the day so convincingly even he had to remind himself this was a temporary marriage, not the real thing at all. The way she had responded to his kiss, both in the church and the other day back at his villa in Rome, had revealed what a passionate woman she was under the surface of that cool don't-mess-with-me façade she customarily wore when around him. She wasn't immune to him any more than he was to her, although she insisted on denying it. Was it pride or part of the chase? He couldn't quite decide, but he was determined that he would make this marriage real, even if it took him the best part of the year to do it.

He smiled to himself as he thought of her soft full-lipped mouth around him, sucking on him, no doubt doing what she had done so many times with so many men. Oh, yes, she would come to him and come willingly. It was only a matter of time. He felt his body stirring to life, the blood rocketing through his veins as he thought of her writhing and twisting beneath him as he worked them both to the pinnacle of pleasure. A deep pool of longing started at the base of his spine and moved forwards, making him hard and ready for action.

'How about a drink to celebrate our temporary marriage?' he said, stretching an arm towards the villa.

She brushed past him with a glacial look. 'I have had my fill of celebratory drinks,' she said. 'I am going to bed.'

* * *

Nic paced the *salone* an hour or so later, wondering why he felt so restless and on edge. Actually, he did know why, it was just he didn't want to admit it. He had planned to have Jade in his bed by now and yet she had eluded him with a curt dismissal. He tossed back the contents of his glass, knowing it was probably unwise to overdo it but overdoing it anyway. What the hell was he doing spending his first night of married life—temporary as it was—alone with a brandy bottle?

He dragged a hand through his hair. This was ridiculous. He had to get a grip. Jade was not the woman he wanted to spend the rest of his life with. He didn't want to spend the rest of his life with any one woman. He wasn't like his brothers, who had settled down with their wives and children, content with their lot. He had always wanted more. More money, more excitement, more challenges.

He was unscrewing the bottle of brandy one more time when he heard a footfall on the stairs. He put the bottle back on the drinks counter and moved out to the hall. Jade was walking slowly down the stairs, step by step, her green eyes staring straight ahead, one of her hands sliding down the banister as if she was wary of falling head first.

'Jade?'

She totally ignored him. She continued on, step by soft step, her face expressionless. He blinked a couple of times, wondering if it was the brandy that had conjured her up, but no, she was still there, taking those ever so softly treading steps until she came to the base of the staircase. The nightgown she was wearing was sheer enough for him to see her slim naked form beneath it. His eyes feasted on those high perfect breasts, so full and round with those rosy-red nipples that he knew would be heaven to suckle on. He lowered his hungry gaze to the feminine cleft between her thighs and he imagined touching her there, filling her with his presence, making her feel him move inside her. It was all he could do not to go to her and pull her into his arms. He was about to take a step towards her when she looked around her with sightless eyes and sighed deeply before retracing her steps, all the way up the stairs again.

Nic watched, his throat rising and falling over a swallow as he realised she was sleepwalking. He considered waking her but then he recalled how he had read somewhere it was not the thing to do. You supposedly had to lead the person gently back to bed, to make sure they were safe.

He followed her up the stairs, keeping a few paces behind so as not to startle her. She padded back to the room she had chosen as her own. It was well away from the master suite, one of the spare rooms that in the past had been used for visitors. Half of her things were still waiting to be unpacked, in boxes and cases that littered the room. He made a mental note to get the housekeeper to sort it all out for her tomorrow. He watched as Jade moved across the room and climbed back into the bed, pulling the sheet over her body and closing her eyes as her head came to rest on the pillow.

He stood watching her in the soft glow of the landing light for so long he lost track of time. After a while she made a murmuring sound and her lips fluttered over a deep sigh as she settled down even farther onto the pillow.

Nic took a scratchy breath and stepped closer to the bed. He reached out and gently brushed a strand of her dark, silky hair back off her face. She gave another soft little murmur, something unintelligible, but somehow it made him feel as if she instinctively trusted him. It gave him a strange feeling deep inside. He was the last person she should be trusting. 'Sweet dreams, *cara*,' he said and, before he could stop himself, he bent down and pressed a light as air kiss to her creamy, velvety cheek. Her lips twitched as if she was smiling in her sleep at the light caress.

Nic moved away from the bed and, with one last long look, he turned and walked out of the room and gently closed the door behind him.

CHAPTER SEVEN

JADE woke to the sound of a knock on the door. She scrambled upright and, hauling the sheets over herself, asked who was there.

'It's me, Nic.'

She felt her heart give a funny little start. 'Um...I'm not dressed.'

'I've seen it all, Jade,' he said with amusement colouring his tone. 'You've done nothing but flaunt it at me for the last week or so.'

She glowered at the door and then stiffened when it opened and Nic stepped in as if he owned the place. The fact that he did—or at least his family did—was beside the point. 'What do you think you are doing?' she said.

He came over carrying a tray with steaming hot tea and fresh rolls and a selection of home-made preserves. 'I thought you might like breakfast in bed,' he said. 'After all, you had a pretty restless night.'

Jade frowned and angled her head at him suspiciously. 'I...I did?'

He gave a nod as he set the tray down on the bed right next to her tightly clenched thighs. 'I found you sleepwalking at about two in the morning,' he said. 'Do you do that often?'

She felt her face colour up. 'How would I know?'

'Hasn't a previous lover found you wandering about like a ghost in the past?' he asked.

Jade rolled her lips together. She looked down at the curl of steam coming from the teapot on the tray, wondering if Nic, like her father, thought there was something wrong with her, something seriously wrong as inside her head. She had walked in her sleep at regular intervals in the first few months after her mother had died. Jon had usually found her wandering around the house and had gently led her back to bed. After he had been killed she had started again, only this time her father had wanted her to see someone about it. She had seen the disgust on his face, the disappointment that his only living child was defective in some way.

'Jade?' Nic tipped her face his way with the blunt tip of his index finger.

Jade felt the pulse of heat pass from his body to hers. It was like a slow burn on her skin, making it quiver with a longing she could not explain. 'No,' she said and sent her tongue out over her bone-dry lips. 'No one has ever mentioned it. I used to sleepwalk when I was a child. I thought I had stopped ages ago but it must have been the stress of the wedding and moving and so on.'

He exchanged his finger for his thumb on her chin, using it like a soft brush over the sensitive area just below her bottom lip. 'Sometimes I get the feeling you are not the person everyone thinks you are,' he said, his eyes holding hers as his thumb continued its mesmerising action.

Jade disguised a swallow. 'Wh…what makes you say that?' she asked, annoyed at the slight catch in her voice.

His eyes were more brown than green this morning, reminding her of the shadows deep inside a forest. 'You have perfected your don't-mess-with-me-I-don't-give-a-damn air, but I think deep inside you are crying out for attention. You push everyone away but what you really want is someone to be close to, someone who understands you and accepts you as you are.'

Jade felt cornered. The tray containing the hot tea had her trapped on one side and she knew if she moved to the other it would spill and possibly burn Nic. 'I have no idea of what you are talking about,' she said, schooling her features into an expression of boredom.

He gave a slowly spreading smile and brushed the pad of his thumb over her bottom lip. It was like an electric shock as soon as his flesh touched hers; every nerve in her mouth leapt and tingled, eager for more. She wanted to send her tongue out again to taste where he had been but she fought the urge with an enormous effort. 'You play the glamorous socialite so well,' he said in a low, deep burr. 'You dress the part, you act the part, but there's something about you that doesn't quite fit.'

She tried to lift her chin but he captured it between his thumb and index finger as if he had anticipated her movement even before she had done so herself. 'Don't do that,' she said.

'You don't like it when I touch you like this?' he asked as he traced a slow-moving finger down the curve of her cheek.

Jade felt a responding quiver deep in her belly. 'I… um…n-no.'

'What about this?' he asked, leaning in and pressing a barely touching kiss to her left temple.

'N…no,' she croaked and then swallowed as he moved

to her right temple. She felt a shiver pass through her, awakening every sense inside her body.

'What about here?' he asked and kissed the edge of her mouth, not on her lips but close enough for her to feel the masculine rasp of his unshaven skin.

Heat exploded inside her, blistering heat that threatened to consume everything in its path, like her resistance and resolve, for instance. 'Don't do this to me, Nic,' she said in a breathless little voice that sounded nothing like her own. 'It will only make things so much harder in the end.'

His eyes lasered hers, holding them, searching them, as if he was looking for her soul in their depths. It seemed a very long time before he spoke. 'You're right,' he said, resettling the tray, which was threatening to slip off the bed. He stood upright and added, 'Have your breakfast. I have some work to see to, in any case.'

Jade blinked in a combination of surprise and disappointment. He could switch off his feelings just like that? She was still smouldering like hot coals while he was acting as if all of this was a game, a test to see how far he could go with her. She seethed as he strode nonchalantly out of the room. No doubt the business he had in mind had something to do with his mistress. He would probably be emailing or texting her within minutes and laughing about his loveless contract marriage and the money he stood to gain at the end of it. A year tied to a woman he had no respect for, no feelings for other than transient lust.

Jade pushed the untouched breakfast to one side as she got out of the bed. She had to remind herself that she had no choice but to put up with things as they were. She needed the money far more than Nic did. She could not survive without it. It wasn't as if she could go out and get a job. She had no skills, no qualifications and no experience.

The only thing she could do was paint, but who was going to pay her to do that when there were literally thousands of gifted art students selling their wares on the streets all over Europe? She had seen them in Milan the last time she had visited Salvatore before he'd died. A young man had sold her a beautiful watercolour of the Castillo. She had been generous to him, but how many people would do that for her? She had spent hours in galleries over the years, studying the masters and watching DVDs on their work, but none of it gave her the qualifications or indeed the confidence to feel a part of the art world. She felt like a fraud, a child dabbling in amongst gifted adults, pretending she had a chance to be like them. She didn't even have a proper studio. She had nowhere to set out her things so she could come and go as she pleased without having to pack everything up all the time.

She chewed at her lip as she looked out of the window of the villa. The lake was shimmering with the sunlight dancing on its surface in the distance. It was such a stunning view. She had been distracted by it so many times yesterday while she was supposed to be acting the role of the besotted bride. Her fingers had been twitching to get to her paints and brushes to capture the light on the water, or the way the roses in the garden hung from the terrace in a scented arras. Then there was the villa itself, so old and stately, so magnificently placed above the lake, set on five levels, with so many rooms surely there would be one she could use as a studio while they were here.

Jade quickly showered and dressed and, pulling her long hair back into a ponytail, she went on a tour of the villa. Even from her privileged background, she couldn't help being impressed by the villa's priceless artworks and sculptures. The marble floors were softened with Persian rugs and the antique furniture gave each room an old world charm that somehow was both stately and homely at the same time.

If there were any household staff around they were keeping themselves well in the background as Jade ran into no one while she was going from floor to floor and room to room.

She came to a room on the third level of the house that was clearly a nursery, but not a modern one. It was like stepping back in time as she walked through the threshold of the squeaky door. A shiver ran up her spine like a spider in a hurry as she looked about the room.

A teddy bear was leaning sideways in the cot. A jack-in-the-box was hanging over the edge of the mantelpiece where he had been released all those years ago and no one had thought to put him back inside ready for the next leap out. A doll with wide-open glassy eyes sat next to him, her pretty pink dress faded with the passage of time until it was almost but not quite white.

Over thirty years ago a baby girl called Chiara had been put to bed in that cot under the window and the next morning her oldest brother Giorgio had come in and found her lifeless.

Jade could feel the weight of grief close in on her. It was like a presence in the room. It reminded her of how her mother's room had felt when she had been told she was never coming home. Jade had gone in there repeatedly, just to check, just to see if everyone was wrong. She could still *smell* her mother's perfume. She had picked up her mother's lipstick tube and felt sure her mother would be back to reapply it as she so regularly did. Jade had felt her mother's presence as if she hadn't really been dead, but just waiting for the right time to come back. She had even dressed in her mother's clothes whenever she could until the day her father had ordered for them to be sent to a charity. It had taken years for her to accept her mother was not going to come back to her, years and years of quiet desperation until she had finally given up all hope.

Tears burned in her eyes as she went over to the cot. There was a soft pink blanket tucked in neatly, embroidered with little rosebuds. She trailed a fingertip over the fabric, wondering what that little girl would be like now if she had not died such an early tragic death. Would she be married with a baby or two of her own? Would she love her brothers as they clearly loved and supported each other? Would she have welcomed Jade to the family as graciously as everyone had, considering her tainted reputation?

'What are you doing?' Nic's voice spoke from the doorway.

Jade spun around, her heart leaping to her throat. 'I…I was just looking around…' she said lamely.

His eyes swept over the room, a mask settling over his face like a blind coming down over a window. 'This place needs to be cleaned out and redecorated. I've been telling my mother that for years.'

'Is that why you insisted on being married here?' Jade asked. 'To force her to face her grief?'

'Thirty-one years is a long time,' he said, glancing at the Tower of Pisa teddy bear before returning his gaze to hers. 'My mother never really recovered from the loss; I understand that part. No parent should lose a child; it's not the right order of things. That's why I understand what your father went through. But I felt it was time to move on. This place used to be our holiday home. I was too young to remember it, of course, but Giorgio and Luca said we spent every summer here. It seems such a waste to have it and not use it.'

'Why not sell it?'

'It's been in our family for generations,' he said. 'When Giorgio and Maya were going through their divorce she wanted to have it as part of the divorce settlement. Giorgio dug his heels in, however. There was no way any one of us would part with this place, not under any circumstances.'

Jade could see why, now she had toured most of the rooms and taken in the view from each of the windows. And then there was the fact that this was the last place their baby sister had smiled and chortled. It would be very hard to sell and move out after something as deeply personal and tragic as that. She wondered then if Nic's shallow take on life hid a deeper soul than he let on publicly. He lived life in the moment, but there was a side to him that suggested he was a lot more sensitive than most people realised. She wondered if the death of his sister had affected him more than he let on. He had been young, yes, but his parents would have been devastated by their grief. Perhaps Nic had been left to fend for himself during that tragic time. Small children picked up on even the most subtle of changes in a household, let alone something as tragic as the loss of a sibling. They could be affected in ways the experts were only just discovering now. The sense of abandonment at such a tender age could permanently change the architecture of a small child's brain. Had Nic shut off his feelings because there was no one there to listen to him, to be there for him? Who had cuddled and comforted him? His brothers would have been far too young to see to his emotional needs. Nic had been a toddler, younger than little Ella. It was so sad to think of him wandering about this huge villa with no one to take proper emotional care of him apart from nannies and servants.

'Why do you love this place so much if you were too young to even remember it?' she asked.

His expression was still shuttered. 'I am not as sentimental about it as my brothers are but I still don't think it should be left empty for most of the year.'

'How do you think your mother coped with coming back here after all this time?' she asked.

His broad shoulders rose and fell in a shrug. 'She was emotional, as you saw, but then my mother has always been that way. She coped pretty well, I think. She came up here to the nursery with Maya. Maya said she thought it was a major turning point for *Mamma*. She needed to come back, to say a proper goodbye. She didn't get the chance at the time. It all happened so suddenly. It was so different back then. There wasn't much information on Sudden Infant Death Syndrome. For years my mother blamed herself. I think she thought everyone else blamed her too.'

'Is that why you don't want to have children?' Jade asked.

His expression tightened, as if pulled inward by invisible strings. 'No, Jade, I am just selfish, like you said. I value my freedom too much. This marriage is a means to an end. Don't get any ideas of making it anything it was never meant to be.'

Jade opened her mouth to respond but, before a single word could come out, he had turned and left her with the silent ghosts of the past...

When Jade came downstairs later that evening she found Nic in the *salone*, pouring himself a drink. He turned when he heard her come in and held up the bottle he was holding. 'Would you care to join me in a drink?' he asked.

Jade agreed to have a very weak white wine spritzer and sat on the edge of one of the sumptuous sofas, holding the frosted glass in her hands once he had fixed it for her.

'So,' he said, looking down at her with a mocking smile lurking about his mouth. 'Here we are then. Our second day of marriage is almost over. Only three hundred and sixty-three to go.'

She returned his look with a little hoist of her chin. 'You're not the only one counting the days, Nic.'

'I know of a very good way to pass the time,' he said with a dark glint in his eyes.

Jade felt a frisson of excitement rush through her in spite of her determination to keep things cool and impersonal between them. All day long she had lived with the expectation of running into him while she moved about the villa and its grounds. Every corner she turned, every door she opened and every corridor she traversed, she had felt a flicker of heady expectation that at some point Nic would track her down. Why he hadn't both intrigued and irritated her. 'I am sure you are very practised in spending time in pointless liaisons,' she said.

'How is your mistress taking the news of your marriage, by the way?'

He took a deep sip of his drink before he answered. 'She was coming up to her use-by date, in any case. I have no time for clingy, needy women. They bore me senseless.'

Jade felt as if a dagger had just pinned her heart to her backbone. She would stand no chance with him if he knew even half of the needs and insecurities she had. That she even wanted a chance with him showed how vulnerable she had become. A few days ago she had hated him with a vengeance... Now she was not so sure. 'I hope you're not expecting me to take over where she left off,' she said, keeping her voice steady and controlled with an effort.

His cynical smile said it all. 'I think you know what I want, Jade. You want it too, but for some reason you are holding out on me. What do you want? More money than you are already getting?'

Her mouth tensed as she threw him a cutting look. 'Is that how you charmed all those women into your bed, by dangling huge sums of money in front of them?'

He came up close, taking her glass out of her trembling hand before she could do anything to stop him. He drew her to her feet, her body so close to his she could feel his warmth. 'Why don't I show you how I do it?' he asked as he pressed a soft feather of a kiss to the side of her mouth.

Jade could feel her body swaying towards him. She tried to counteract the urge but it was as if her body was operating independently of her reason. A shiver fluttered like soft wings beating all the way down her spine, and her breasts tightened in heightened awareness of his warm hard chest pressed against them. She felt the stirring of his erection and for a moment had to fight not to pull away. This was not some faceless man she had been flirting with, teasing and acting out to show the world how tough she was. This was Nic; this was the one man she had always wanted.

It was Nic Sabbatini, her husband for the next twelve months.

He put a hand to the small of her back and pressed her against him, his breath a caress over her lips, which were aching for his kiss. 'You are driving me crazy with those looks you keep giving me. Are you doing it deliberately to make me beg?'

Jade ran the tip of her tongue out over her lips, her eyes going to his mouth—so close, so temptingly close. 'I'm trying to be sensible about this...'

'Forget being sensible,' he growled just above her mouth. 'Nothing about this arrangement is sensible, in any case.'

Jade wasn't sure if he came down or she rose up to meet his mouth in an explosively hot kiss. She didn't really care. All she knew was her body was on fire for him as soon as their lips came into full contact. His tongue probed for entry and she gave a little gasp of longing, a space inside her stomach hollowing out as he stroked and teased her tongue into seductive play with his. His kiss was slow and sensual one minute and determined and daring the next. Jade felt the simmering of her blood as his teeth gently nipped at her bottom lip in little tease and tug bites that triggered something deeply primal inside her.

His mouth moved from hers to burn across the sensitive skin of her neck and décolletage in a slow-moving journey that made every cell of her body cry out for more. She felt the liquid honey of desire between her thighs and the aching of her tight nipples where they were pressed so firmly up against his chest. The hand that had rested in the small of her back had now moved to boldly cup her bottom; the other hand was already seeking the soft swell of her right breast. She could scarcely believe the way her body responded to his touch, even though it was through the barrier of her clothes. Tremors of reaction ricocheted through her, making her ache to be naked with him, to feel him skin on skin, hot flesh on hot flesh. She placed her arms around his neck, letting her fingers delve into the thickness of his hair, relishing in the way he felt to her touch.

'*Dio*, I want you so badly,' Nic said against her mouth. 'But then you are a witch at making men want you, are you not? A seductive little witch with a mouth of fire.'

Jade ignored his comment to concentrate on the magical feeling of being so aware of her body, so in touch with its every need. Like how wonderful it felt to have his hand move under her top to cup her through the lace of her bra. The possessive press of his palm was mind-blowing; so too was the slow but sure stroke of his thumb against her engorged nipple. For all his intentions to get her into his bed, he was certainly taking his time about it, she thought as his mouth sucked on her nipple right through the lace of her bra. If anything, it intensified the sensation of his lips and tongue, making her almost mad with longing.

She arched her head back to give him better access, her body quivering inside and out as he kissed his way back up from her breast to her mouth. His masterful tongue this time was even more determined to conquer hers. He swept every corner of her mouth, exploring her, tasting her, tempting her into a dance of desire that she suspected could only end one way. She felt the ripples of it beginning deep and low in her body, the stirring of her senses so intense she was unable to think of anything but how he made her feel.

He tore his mouth off hers, his breathing hectic and his hazel eyes dark as they meshed with hers. 'Not here. Not like this,' he said, scooping her up into his arms and carrying her out of the *salone* towards the stairs. 'I want you in bed with me where you belong.'

Jade knew she should have called a halt right there and then. It was a chance to break the spell, a moment to reorient herself, to remind herself of his motives and her shameful secret. But somehow she couldn't do it. She wanted to feel his arms around her, to feel all that it was possible to feel when you truly wanted someone and they wanted you because they felt so in tune with you physically.

The master bedroom was a suite of massive proportions but Jade was barely aware of her surroundings once Nic placed her on the big bed and came down beside her. He kissed her again, a slow searing kiss that made the blood race all over again in her veins. He had such a beautiful mouth, so firm and yet so sensually soft, as if she was the most precious fragile person he had ever kissed. He tasted so nice too, not of stale smoke and alcohol but a taste she would forever associate with him: essential maleness in its prime.

While his mouth continued to cast its spellbinding magic on hers, she felt his hands start to work on her clothes. She lifted her arms above her head as he peeled her top away. And then she raised her hips when he eased her out of her jeans, barely registering the soft thud of her shoes as they landed on the floor. She had been naked with a few men but she had never wanted to look at them the way she wanted to look at Nic. Her fingers set to work on his shirt and then, when that was cast aside, she worked on the waistband of his trousers, sliding down the zip, her breath stalling in her throat as she saw the way he had tented his underwear. She ran an experimental finger down the length of him through the fabric and watched as he quivered in response.

'Careful, *cara*,' he said in a gravelly tone. 'I want to last long enough to pleasure you.'

Her own pleasure had never been a priority before now. She had always pretended, giving her few past partners what she thought they had wanted. It had been easy and she had felt no guilt or remorse about it. But now she felt as if everything had changed. She wanted to give and receive pleasure because with Nic she knew it would be something completely different, something special, something to remember for the rest of her life once he moved on, as she was certain he would do.

Jade peeled back his underwear and stroked him again, her belly tightening in anticipation. She circled him with her fingers and saw his stomach muscles clench as she began moving up and down.

He pulled her hand away and pushed her back down on the bed. 'Later,' he said and reached for the nearest bedside drawer for a condom.

She watched as he put it on, her breath hitching in her throat as she thought of him filling her. A flicker of nervousness passed through her. What if she wasn't able to please him? That had never been an issue with anyone else. She had given them what they wanted while her mind went elsewhere. But what if Nic saw through her pretence?

It seemed ridiculous to admit it, but this felt as if she was starting all over again. Each touch of his fingers was a new experience; it had nothing to do with her wretched, sordid past—it was as if that had happened to someone else, not her. His gentle caressing of her with his clever fingers was like an act of worship; it was not in any way exploitative or crude. He was stroking her into a whirlpool of sensation she had never experienced. She could feel her body climbing a mountain so high and spectacular it took her breath away.

'You're so beautiful and feminine I want to taste you,' he said in a husky voice.

No one had ever touched her quite like this, with such reverence, such tenderness and concern for her needs. She felt the movement of his lips against her and then the soft brush stroke of his tongue, once, twice, three times and then with an increase in pace. It was so raw, so intimate and so deeply erotic she felt her body gather all its energy at one point. A delicious tension began to pull at her, making her rise on a wave that felt so precipitous she wondered if she was going to crash and burn if—or when—she fell off.

'Come for me, *cara*,' he said in between caresses. 'I want to watch you lose yourself totally in what I am doing to you.'

Jade felt a bubble of emotion come up in her chest. She was unprepared for the way she was feeling, for how her body was reacting. But then, before she could examine her emotional response any further, the pinnacle of pleasure sneaked up on her, catching her totally off guard, making her spiral into a vortex of intensely pleasurable sensations that made her mind empty of everything but what she was feeling physically.

When the waves of pleasure finally subsided she felt hot, stinging tears come to her eyes. She put a hand up to hide them, to force them back, to do anything to stop them from betraying her, but it was too late.

Nic had already propped himself up on his arms, his frowning gaze going straight to hers. 'What's going on?' he asked.

Jade bit her lip to try and stop herself from bawling like a child. 'Nothing—sorry about this...' She swiped at her streaming eyes with the back of her hand. 'I'm not used to being so emotional when...I mean during... sex...'

He blotted another trail of tears with the pad of his thumb. 'Do you want to tell me what's so different about this time?' he asked gently.

Jade pressed her trembling lips together but she had no control over the sobs that seemed to be coming up from deep inside her. There was nothing she could do to hold the rushing, gushing emotions back. She shook her head and covered her eyes with both of her hands, a choked sob escaping as she gulped, 'Sorry about this... I'll be OK in a minute...just give me a minute...'

Nic peeled her hands away from her face, his gaze serious and concerned as he looked into her eyes. '*Cara*, did I do something you didn't like? Did I hurt you in some way?'

She shook her head and bit down on her bottom lip, fighting to rein in her runaway emotions. 'No, of course you didn't hurt me—it's just that...that I've never...it's just that it's never been like that before...'

His frown made a map of lines come up on his forehead. 'Are you saying you've never had an orgasm through oral sex before?'

Jade couldn't hold his penetrating look. She lowered her gaze to his throat, where she could see a pulse beating like a drum. She took a breath that felt rough around the edges and said, 'I've never had an orgasm before. Period.'

His throat moved up and down like a piston. Seconds passed, maybe only one or two but it felt like a month of them to her. 'I'm not sure I understand,' he said, bringing her chin up so her gaze met his. 'You're not a virgin, *sì*?'

Jade gave him a pained wry look. 'No, Nic, I am not a virgin.'

He moved his mouth a couple of times, as if searching for the right words to say. 'So, what I think you're saying is sex has not always been pleasurable for you, is that it?'

She let out a heavy sigh and shook her head as she dropped back on the pillow.

He gently brushed back some tendrils of her hair off her face, his touch so soft it made Jade feel another wave of emotion rise to the surface. 'Do you want to tell me about it?' he asked.

Jade looked into his hazel eyes, so very dark and serious as they held hers. Most men would have continued on to get their measure of pleasure out of her body by now, but he had not. It surprised her, given his playboy reputation. 'Don't you want to finish this?' she asked, waving her hand to encompass their bodies lying so close to each other.

He frowned even more darkly and got off the bed,

pulling off the condom and tossing it to one side. He reached for his trousers and pulled them on and zipped them. 'I am not sure what sort of man you think I am, Jade, but there's no way I am going to make love with you unless I know everything, and I mean everything.'

Jade tugged at the top sheet and pulled it over herself to cover her nakedness. Shyness was not normally an issue with her, she had grown so used to disconnecting her mind from her body, but somehow with Nic it was different. She felt exposed in a way she had never felt with anyone else. Nic saw things she wasn't sure she wanted him to see.

'Why don't you start at the beginning?' he suggested.

She gave him a mutinous look as she hugged her knees close to her body. 'I don't have to tell you anything. I wish I hadn't told you what I did. You're making such a big deal out of it.'

'Damn it, Jade, this *is* a big deal,' he said, shoving a hand through his already mussed-up hair. 'You can't drop a bomb like that into the bedroom and expect me to carry on as if nothing's changed.'

She couldn't hold his gaze and dropped her chin to rest on the tops of her bent knees. This wasn't supposed to happen. This was too personal, too invasive. She had tried to be so strong. With any other man she would have pulled it off, but not with Nic. He was her nemesis. She had always suspected it was the case. He would totally unravel her, leaving her vulnerable and exposed.

'Tell me, Jade,' he said, his voice lowering to a gentle burr. 'Tell me why it is that with the kind of reputation you have—which, I might add, you have not in any way discouraged or taken any action to defend yourself—you have not until this point enjoyed sex fully.'

Jade slowly lifted her head off her knees. It seemed she was not going to get out of this after all. She knew Nic well enough to know he would stand there and wait for her to tell him, no matter how long it took. It was her fault for letting him get under her radar. She should have known he would be the one to see through her party-girl pretence. Shame coursed through her but she made herself meet his dark gaze. 'Do you remember the night of my sixteenth birthday when I tried to seduce you?' she asked.

He nodded grimly. 'It's not something I like to think about too much. I tried to do the right thing by you. I know I was a little hard on you. I've often thought if I had handled it better you might not have rushed off with Riccardo.'

Jade got off the bed, dragging the sheet with her as a drape. She wanted her clothes on but dressing in front of him was out of the question. She felt far too exposed as it was.

'Here,' Nic said, handing her his bathrobe from the back of the door to the en suite bathroom. 'Put this on.'

Jade slid her arms into the sleeves and tied the ends around her waist. It was far too big for her; she felt as if she were wrapped in a circus tent.

'You look like Ella playing dress-ups with her mother's clothes.'

She gave him her version of a smile: sad and wistful. 'I wish I could go back to her age and start again. Maybe I wouldn't make the same mistakes.'

His brow tightened again with a frown. 'We all

make mistakes, Jade. It's what life is about: living and learning. We can't grow until we realise where we went wrong.'

She hugged her arms close to her body. 'I should have listened to you that night,' she said, no longer able to meet his eyes. 'I should have taken on board everything you said. But I didn't. Instead, I did the very opposite. I was so rebellious, so determined to show you and everyone I could do what I wanted. But I was wrong—so terribly, terribly wrong.'

Nic felt a tremor of unease pass through his insides. This was a side to Jade he had never seen before: the vulnerable side. Gone was the tough don't-mess-with-me-I-couldn't-give-a-damn-anyway wild-child; in her place was a young woman who looked as if the world had let her down in a very bad way. He didn't say anything. He kept silent to let her continue, but he felt his throat tighten as he swallowed, as if a rough hand had grasped him by the neck and squeezed until he could hardly breathe.

She looked up at him, her forest-green eyes filled with pain. 'Sleeping with your friend is something I have always regretted. It was nothing like I thought it would be. I wanted to get back at you for rejecting me, but instead I was the one who got hurt.'

The hand around Nic's neck tightened another notch. 'Did that bastard hurt you?' he asked.

She tugged at her bottom lip with her teeth for a moment before answering. 'No, at least not by intention. You were right, Nic; I was too young to be having sex. I wasn't ready emotionally. I allowed someone I hardly knew to use my body. I was so ashamed when it was over. I cried for hours. But then, instead of learning from my mistake, I did it again. I was suddenly popular. I was the IT girl when for so long I was the one on the outside. I suppose it was a way to get attention.'

Nic momentarily closed his eyes. He opened them to find her looking into the distance, as if she were time travelling to the past. 'Jade...' he began and took a step towards her but she held up her hand like a stop sign.

'No,' she said. 'Let me get this off my chest. God knows, it's about time.' She gave a harsh-sounding laugh that contained no humour in it at all. 'For all these years I have pretended to live like a tart. I let the press portray me like that. I actively sought that sort of reputation by being in all the hip places, dressing provocatively, flirting, teasing, acting as if I was the most popular girl in town. I guess that's the way I saw myself: the cheap, shallow socialite, the reckless, uncontrollable wild-child who didn't give a damn what anyone thought about her.'

'But you do care about what people think of you, don't you, Jade?' Nic said. 'Your father, for instance. For all these years you've been acting out to get his attention, but it hasn't worked, has it?'

She gave him another world-weary twist of her lips. 'He's never quite forgiven me for not going on that holiday. If I had been with Jon he wouldn't have gone to that particular ski run. Jon was always my father's favourite. I knew that. Jon knew that, but he tried his best to compensate by being the best brother you could imagine. Without him, I was like a rudderless boat. I couldn't seem to stop from hitting the rocks. It was like I was determined to self-destruct or something.'

'You are not to blame for your brother's death,' he

said. 'There is no way you should be blamed by anyone for that, especially your father.'

'I can't turn back the clock,' Jade said sadly. 'I wish I could, not just with that holiday but everything really. I wish I had had more time with my mother. I think I would have fared better if she hadn't died when she did. She would have helped me with my—' She stopped and bit her lip again.

'Helped you with your what, Jade?' he prompted.

She met his gaze. 'Um…with my art work.'

He frowned. 'Your art work?'

Jade felt her face grow warm. 'Yes, I sort of dabble in watercolours. I'm not very good. I haven't taken any lessons or anything. It's just a hobby. Actually, I'm totally rubbish at it. I would never show anyone my stuff. It just fills in the time for me. I enjoy it, you know, the creative part of it.'

'I am sure you are being unnecessarily harsh on your talent.'

'I have no qualifications,' she said. 'Not unless you count hours, if not days, wandering around galleries and art shows. I just know what I like and what I like to paint. That's all, really. I don't even have a proper studio.'

He looked at her for a long moment. 'Would you like to have a studio of your own?'

Jade felt a frisson of creative excitement rush through her. She also felt a flutter of something deep inside her heart—a feeling of gratitude that he hadn't laughed at her or ridiculed her painting but instead was offering his support. 'Do you think I could use one of the rooms in your villa in Rome as a studio?' she asked tentatively.

'I've brought some stuff with me here but we won't be here long enough for me to set up properly.'

'Use whatever room suits you, both here and in Rome. Do you need anything? Art supplies and so on?'

'No, I have everything I need,' she said. 'I packed it all when I left London.'

He looked at her in silence for another moment or two. 'You really are full of surprises, aren't you, *cara*?' he said.

Jade felt the warm glow on her cheeks intensify and quickly lowered her eyes. 'We all have our secrets, I suppose.'

'What you see is what you get with me, I'm afraid,' he said with a wry smile. 'Shallow and selfish is what the press call me, isn't it? And, let me tell you, it's not far off the truth.'

Jade meshed her gaze with his. 'I don't believe that.'

He raised his brows at her. 'You don't?'

She shook her head. 'You are a lot deeper than you allow people to think. Sensitive too, much more sensitive than people give you credit for.'

He gave her a guarded look. 'What makes you say that?'

She kept her eyes trained on his. 'You are not like the other men I know or have known in the past. I've always felt like that about you. You stand apart from everyone.'

A flash of something moved across his features. 'Listen, Jade,' he said. 'Don't go getting any ideas about me settling down and playing happy husband for ever. This is the shallow, selfish part of me I warned you about talking here, and it's the real me. This marriage is solely to access my share of my grandfather's estate. It is not about building a future together or falling in love. Are we both clear on that?'

Jade schooled her expression into blankness, but inside she felt the pain of rejection eat away at her like sharp little teeth. It was like all those years ago, but worse somehow. She wasn't good enough for him. She was never going to be good enough for him. Telling him why she had acted the way she had had made it worse, not better. He was sympathetic and supportive and she was grateful for that, but she was fooling herself if she thought such a heart-to-heart confession was going to make him fall in love with her. He was not interested in settling down, and certainly not with someone who had acted with such impropriety for as long as he had known her.

'Jade?' He pushed up her chin with his finger.

She jerked her head away and got to her feet. 'What do you take me for, Nic?' she asked. 'I told you before, I'm not some naive schoolgirl with a crush. So we had sex, or at least you pleasured me. Thanks, by the way. It was great. Very memorable, but it doesn't mean I have feelings for you.'

He watched her for a beat or two before he responded. 'Just keep a lid on it, that's all I'm saying, Jade. I know what happens when women find a lover who finally ticks all the boxes for them. The lines get blurred. Sex for me is a physical thing. I love it, not necessarily the person I am having it with.'

Jade folded her arms across her body. 'I'm not going to fall in love with you, Nic.' *Because a part of me has already gone ahead and foolishly and irrevocably done so*, she thought in silent despair.

He walked to the bedroom door but stopped and turned around to look at her before he opened it. 'The money is not just for me,' he said. 'If I lost my share of the Sabbatini Corporation it might have put my brothers at risk of a one-third takeover. These have been pretty rough financial times in recent years. It is not sound business sense to be off your watch, even for a moment. My grandfather knew that and used it to get me to do what he wanted. He had a fantasy about you and me making a match of it, but that's all it was: a fantasy. None of this is real, Jade. It's like acting a role in a play. Our primary job is to get through this year and collect our earnings at the end.'

Jade lifted one of her finely arched brows. 'Does that mean you will no longer require my services in bed? I too can separate the act from the emotion. I've been doing it all these years. I am happy to oblige. After all, I owe you one, Italian boy.'

He frowned at her choice of words. 'Don't play the cheap tart with me, Jade. It doesn't suit you.'

She threw him a what-would-you-know look, but he had already gone.

CHAPTER EIGHT

JADE didn't bother leaving the comfort of Nic's bed, even though she was uncertain of what he expected of her now. Their relationship had stepped to a new level, but it wasn't quite where she wanted it to be. Sharing a room and a bed was not going to be enough for her. She knew it would break her heart the longer it continued, but right now she couldn't bring herself to leave the sheets that smelled of him. Her body was still tingling from the earth-shattering experience of his touch and caresses. She squeezed her thighs together, marvelling at the way her inner body still pulsed and ached for more of that delicious pleasure.

She must have drifted off to sleep for suddenly she heard the door of the bedroom open and Nic came in with a wry expression on his face. 'I thought you might have bolted to the room down the hall by now,' he said.

She sat up and hugged her knees and glared at him. 'I was seriously thinking about it.'

His mouth slanted in a smile. 'But here you are, waiting for me.'

She narrowed her eyes. 'I'm not waiting. I fell asleep.'

He moved closer to the bed, his hazel eyes dark as a shadowed swamp as they ran over her. 'Move over, *cara*.'

Jade's eyes flared, along with her desire. It was like an exotic flower opening inside her, the soft petals unfurling against the walls of her femininity, tickling her, reminding her of what it would feel like to have him there, moving intimately inside her. 'Since when am I supposed to take orders from you?' she asked with an attempt at her usual brash bravado, which somehow this time didn't quite make the grade.

Nic smiled and dropped his bathrobe. 'If you don't move I will have to move you and who knows what might happen then, hmm?'

Jade smoothed the crumpled sheets for something to do with her hands rather than putting them where she most wanted to put them. She didn't want to appear desperate and clingy and needy, but, dear God, how good it was to look at him. He smelt divine: male musk and citrus rolled up in a delicious aroma that was like an irresistible drug. His body was already responding. She tried not to look but how could she not? She ached deep inside for his body to show her what she had been missing for all this time.

Nic cupped her cheek and trained his gaze on hers. 'There you go again, giving me that look. For the last couple of hours downstairs I told myself I was going to take my time, let you feel your way with me a bit. But how am I supposed to resist you when you look at me like that?'

'How am I looking at you?' she asked, licking her lips, which were dryer than paper.

He groaned and joined her on the bed, his head

coming down as hers lifted up for his kiss. Their tongues met in a sexy duel, hot, moist and hungry. It went on and on, fuelling Jade's need with each throbbing second. She felt her body ripen in awareness, the way her breasts ached and the way her feet arched in pleasure each time he deepened the kiss. Her belly was a deep, bottomless pool of longing, her limbs like jungle vines that wrapped around him to hold him to her. Her hips were beneath the blessed weight of his, the pressure of his erection an erotic reminder of what she had yet to experience with him.

He took his mouth off hers to work his way down to her breasts, taking his time, drawing out her pleasure until she could barely think. That first suckle of his mouth on her nipple made her back come right off the bed, and her arms tightened their hold on him. He flicked his tongue back and forth and then around and around until she was like molten wax, limbless and boneless, her head spinning with the impact of such new sensations.

'You taste so divine,' he said against the cup of her shoulder as he worked his way back up to her mouth. 'Orange blossom and honeysuckle with a touch of vanilla.'

'You taste good too,' she said, surprised her voice could even function while her senses were in such overload. She stroked her tongue over his bottom lip, teasing him, waiting to see what he did.

His eyes became hooded as he gazed at her mouth, his tongue moving out over his lips to moisten them before he swooped down and covered hers. The pressure increased as his passion intensified, but Jade still felt as if he was holding back. She decided to take matters into her own hands and sent them to work on his body: touching him, exploring him in exquisite detail. He groaned under her handiwork, his breathing becoming all the more ragged the more daring she became. It was liberating for her to touch him when and how she wanted, to feel the satin of his skin, to feel the steely length of him quivering in the circle of her fingers. She kissed her way down from his mouth, all the way down his chest, dipping the tip of her tongue into the shallow pool of his belly button, watching as the ridged muscles of his abdomen contracted in anticipation of the rest of the journey.

He put a hand on the back of her head, gently grasping a handful of her hair to stop her.

Jade felt a rush of feminine power she had never felt before. This time it wasn't about privately sneering at the selfish lack of control some men had, it was about her effect on Nic and how he felt under her touch. He wasn't the sort of man to lose control. He was a playboy who had had numerous lovers before, but for some reason with her he was having trouble keeping his head. She backed off and waited for him to regulate his breathing, watching him, enjoying every flicker of emotion that passed over his face.

He brushed her mouth with his and then touched down again, lingering this time in a kiss that went on and on. His hands slid down her body and she relished the feel of his palms and fingers on her naked flesh. She didn't send her mind away; instead, she felt herself blooming under his touch. She moved against his pelvis, seeking his hardness, her body achingly empty, hot and moist and ready for him.

He touched her with his fingers, playing with her,

ramping up her need until she was writhing beneath him, breathlessly begging for him to take her to paradise as he had before.

'Please, Nic, don't make me wait any longer, please.'

He made a sound deep in his throat and reached across her for a condom. This time she took it from him and rolled it over him, watching as his body burgeoned with the need to explode. 'You are making this so hard for me to slow down,' he said against her mouth. 'I want this to be special for you. I don't want to rush you.'

She cupped his unshaven face with her hands, every nerve in her palm responding to his raspy maleness. 'I want you, Nic, like I have never wanted anyone else. I feel like I have been waiting all of my life for this moment.'

'Me too,' he said, almost too low for her to hear as he nudged against her slick entrance.

Jade felt the shockwave of delight rush like a river through her. It felt so good to have him against her sensitive flesh; the feel of his strength against her softness was pure bliss. She pushed up with her hips and he surged into her, his attempt to check himself lost as her body gripped him tightly, taking him fully. He groaned again as he was catapulted into the vortex of passion that had already swept her away on its rapid tide. She felt the ripples of pleasure roll through her body from head to foot. Tension built and built, spiralling upwards as she climbed to the summit with him in fast pursuit. Suddenly she was crying out at the sheer magnitude of it as it smashed against her like a giant wave. She was tossed about, rolled over and over until she was a limbless, mindless rag doll, limp with satiation in his arms.

She was conscious enough to feel his orgasm fire like a bullet out of a barrel. She felt his flesh pucker in goose bumps where her hands slid along his back, his skin slick with perspiration, a sexy humid heat that she wanted to bask in for ever.

Jade had never felt comfortable with the after sex chit-chat routine. She had never quite worked out what the right thing to say was when it was over, so she usually said nothing. But this was different.

Way, way different.

She wanted to cuddle up close and feel Nic's heart beating next to hers. She wanted to breathe in his scent, to commit it to memory for the time when he would no longer be in her life. She wanted to hold him within her until he grew hard again. When it came down to basics, she just didn't want it to be over.

Not yet.

Not ever.

Nic moved away and pulled the condom off but Jade noticed he was frowning.

'Is something wrong?' she asked and sat upright but then she felt what he was frowning about.

'The condom didn't do its job. There must have been a tear in it or something.'

Jade looked at him with wide eyes. 'Oh…'

He raked a hand through his hair. 'You're on the Pill, right? You said you were on the Pill. It should be fine. I don't have anything. I have regular checkups. I'm totally safe; are you?'

She didn't speak. Her mind was running ahead with the image of a baby—a gorgeous dark-haired baby. She gave herself a mental shake. Having a baby with Nic would not make him love her nor would it be right in a temporary marriage. And what sort of mother would she make, in any case?

'Jade?'

She moved away so he wouldn't see the longing in her eyes. 'Of course I'm safe,' she said, doing what she had to do with the tissues with as much dignity as the circumstances allowed. 'I've been taking the Pill since I was sixteen.'

'Fine, then,' he said, sounding immensely relieved. 'We could probably forgo condoms from now on if we both are exclusive.'

Jade kept her back turned to him. *Exclusive?* He was intending to sleep with only her for the next few months? Hope flared like a beacon in her chest but she quickly doused it.

'Can I trust you on that?' she said, finally turning to meet his gaze.

'When I give my word, I mean it,' he said. 'You should know that about me, Jade.'

The air hummed with a singing wire of escalating want.

'Come here,' Nic said, sending a shiver of reaction to her toes and back.

Jade slowly turned around, the task of getting back into her bathrobe somehow losing its importance as she met his burning gaze. 'You...you want me?'

His hands cupped her shoulders as she stepped towards him. 'I have always wanted you, Jade,' he said and brought his searing mouth down to hers.

For the next week, while they stayed at the villa, Nic took her on a sensual journey that was beyond exciting and exhilarating. He introduced her to the delights of the flesh that made her tingle all over when she thought about all they experienced together. They had made love in the shower, in the moonlight, on the deck by the pool, in the gardens with the scent of roses heavy in the air. He had been gentle but passionate with her, urging her into new and even more exciting territory, not stopping until she was blissfully satisfied before he took his own pleasure. It had made her realise how different sex was in the context of a relationship, how it intensified every touch and stroke, or at least it did for her. She could only assume Nic was unaffected, other than physically. He enjoyed sex; he was, after all, a very physically fit man in the prime of his life. He had energy to burn and she willingly partnered him in marathon sessions that left her quivering and tingling for hours afterwards. It was difficult not to think of all the other women he had pleasured before her, but then she reminded herself that she was no plaster saint and, while her experience was nothing to be proud of, she often wondered if he thought of the men she had slept with and felt any stirring of jealousy.

One of the things that had most touched her during that week was Nic's insistence on seeing some of her art work. He refused to take no for an answer, and so she found herself opening the door of the room she had commandeered on the top floor of the villa. She had unpacked the few materials she had brought with her and made a makeshift easel by using books propped up on a desk to make the most of the light. The watercolour she was working on was a scene from the villa gardens where a fountain was surrounded by clipped low-lying hedges, and in the background was the sparkling blue of the lake and the mountains beyond. It wasn't her best work and she felt uncomfortable showing him it half-done but he seemed totally entranced as he looked at it.

'You did this?' he said, turning from the painting to look at her.

Jade gave a self-conscious nod. 'I know it's not terribly professional. I haven't been to art school or anything. I'm just an amateur, as I told you.'

'May I?' Nic asked as he pointed to the little stack of unframed paintings she had brought with her.

She felt her face heating with embarrassment and silently prayed he wouldn't laugh at her paltry attempts to capture a favourite scene. 'Go ahead,' she said. 'But they're not worth anything. They're not even worth framing.'

He went through the paintings one by one, looking in detail at each brush stroke and nuance of light and colour.

Jade stood, awkwardly shifting her weight from foot to foot, feeling like the times she had waited for her father's verdict on yet another wretched school report.

'Jade, these are amazing,' Nic said, breaking through her thoughts. His eyes met hers. 'You are so talented. Why haven't you pursued this as a career? You have a gift. I'm not just saying it, you truly do. I have never seen such mastery of perspective and use of light and colour.'

Jade was stunned by his reaction. She had tried to be objective with her work but she always felt as if she could do better, that she was not good enough and never would be. She had no background in the arts; she hadn't studied art history or worked with an established artist in a mentor programme, as so many others did. She hadn't read a single textbook on technique or style because she couldn't. She had looked at the pictures, certainly, but that didn't really count for much, in her opinion. She had acted out so much during her childhood, from frustration at not being able to understand what the teachers were trying to teach her, that her behaviour had been what everyone had focused on, each school she had attended failing to recognise that her disruptive behaviour was a symptom rather than the cause. As the years went on she had felt too ashamed to tell anyone of her inability to read past a few simple words. Her dependency on her father had never been a choice, for how could she expect anyone to employ her with no literacy skills?

Nic put the paintings to one side and placed his hands on shoulders. 'Why are you hiding your talent away?' he asked. 'Why let everyone believe you are nothing but a time-wasting society heiress when you have this incredible gift?'

Jade twisted her mouth. 'It's nice of you to be so positive but I'm not exactly a gifted artist. I know nothing about art theory. I just do what I feel like at the time. Sometimes it works, sometimes it doesn't. Mostly, it doesn't.'

'*Cara*, you are being so hard on yourself,' he said. 'I just don't understand. You, of all people. You've had the money to back you to go to the art school of your choice. You have the sort of networking opportunities most struggling artists would kill for and yet you have hidden all of this away as if it's some dreadful, shameful secret. Why?'

Jade moved out from under his gently cupping hands and folded her arms across her middle, her face turned away to look out of the window to the bubbling fountain way below. 'I prefer it this way,' she said. 'When you have spent all of your life in the public's eye as I have done, it is nice to know there is at least one area you can keep private. This is mine.'

Nic frowned as he studied her. She had that keep-your-distance aura about her again, which he hadn't seen in days. He had thought he was finally breaking down some of the barriers she kept putting up. He had enjoyed seeing her relax her guard around him. He had enjoyed seeing her smile and once, when she'd laughed at something he had said, he'd felt a warm feeling spreading like hot honey deep inside his chest. It seemed as if each day he discovered something new about her. Like how her skin tasted when she had been in the sun: hot and silky and delicious. How her green eyes darkened when she looked at him when he was about to kiss her, and the way her hands felt sliding over him, over his back or chest, or the way she cupped him and stroked him until he felt as if the control he had always prided himself on was like a wisp of smoke, about to slip out of his grasp.

He was discovering things about himself too. How much he liked the way her dark, silky hair tickled his chest when she lay across him after making love, when in the past he had always preferred blondes. He liked the way her body felt as it gripped him so tightly, as if he was her first and only lover. In a way he felt as if he was. He dismissed those who had gone before as exploitative creeps who had lusted after her for all the wrong reasons. Nic liked how she continued to surprise him. He had grown increasingly bored with the women he had dated recently. They looked good and they had felt good, but he had not had an in-depth conversation with any one of them.

Jade had layers to her character that he was only starting to peel away—interesting, captivating layers that hinted at a deeply sensitive, gifted and intelligent young woman who, for some strange reason, was doing her best to keep that side of herself hidden as if she was somehow ashamed of it.

He was determined to get to know everything there was to know about his wife.

His wife.

He almost laughed out loud. His grandfather had pulled a swift one on him, that was for sure, making certain he was well and truly shackled in matrimony. But more than a week had gone by already and Nic was starting to think about how it would feel closer to the time to end it. He hadn't thought too much about that part of things before; he had simply concentrated on securing his inheritance. That had been his main priority and Jade's too, when it came to that. She had made it clear she wanted the money and, unless she decided to enter the workforce or sell some of her paintings, she was going to need every penny of it to live the life she had said she wanted to live.

Would he get so used to having her in his life that getting her out of it would prove a little too difficult?

He suppressed another laugh. Of course not! He wasn't the falling in love type. He had always lived in the fast lane. Settling down to domesticity, even with his wealth, which made his life easier than most, was out of the question. He was a freedom lover. He liked the ability to come and go as he pleased. He didn't want to answer to anyone but himself. He couldn't envisage himself any other way.

But looking at her with that faraway look on her face made him ache with need for her. How did she do it to him? It was like a magnetic force that kept luring him towards her. He had made love to her only that morning and yet his body was hardening as he thought of taking her now.

She turned from the window and saw him looking at her. Her eyes darkened and his blood began to pound. She sent the point of her tongue—the tongue that only this morning had tasted him intimately—across her lips and gave him the look—the look that he could not, in this lifetime at least, seem to resist.

'Come here,' he commanded.

She gave a little haughty lift of her chin but he saw through it for the game it was. 'Why don't *you* come here?' she said.

'I want you over here.'

She slowly walked towards him, tempting him every step of the way with her coquettish smile and gently swaying slim hips. 'And you always get what you want, don't you, Italian boy?' she said in a husky whisper as she placed both of her hands flat on his chest.

Nic smiled as her hands slid down, all the way down over his abdomen to brush against his erection. 'So far,' he said and sealed her mouth with his.

She kissed him with her whole body, wrapping her arms around his neck, her fingers lacing through his hair until he felt a shiver of anticipation course down his spine. She pushed herself against him, her pelvis exciting him as it rubbed against his. His tongue played with hers, stroking and cajoling and then stabbing and thrusting as his need for her escalated. He loved her in this mood, so playful and teasing, making him want her as much as she wanted him.

Loved her?

His mind slammed on the brakes. This wasn't about love. It was about lust. He wanted her body and that was all he wanted. And she was offering it to him in the most delightful way possible.

He cupped her breasts and heard her whimper in response. He peeled her loose-fitting top off her shoulder and kissed his way down her neck, moving aside her bra to take her nipple in his mouth. She dug her fingers into his hair and arched her spine like a cat, inciting him further. She tasted so fresh and feminine and irresistible. He wanted her so badly he felt his body straining against his clothes. But, as if she sensed his discomfort, she started to deal with it by unhooking his belt and sliding down his zip, her dancing fingers wreaking havoc on his senses.

Nic fought for control as she caressed him, slowly at first, up and down his shaft, taking her time, making each pleasurable sensation ramp up his desire. His abdomen clenched like a fist as she went to her knees in front of him, her moistened lips moving closer and closer...

'You don't have to do that,' he croaked. 'I don't expect it of you.'

She looked up at him with sultry green eyes. 'I want to do it,' she said in that same husky tone she had used earlier.

Nic swallowed as she moved closer, her pink tongue coming out to lick him like a kitten did at its first taste of milk. He felt every nerve twitch and fire, lightning-fast blood filling him to bursting point as she did it again, slower this time, long slow strokes that sent him into a tailspin of want. He couldn't speak, he couldn't even think beyond what he was feeling right at this point. Her tongue continued its sensual teasing and then she opened her mouth over him, taking him in bit by bit, sucking, pulling, withdrawing and then doing it all over again. He tried to anchor himself by holding her head with his hands, but she took that as encouragement and went harder and faster. He knew then he had no possible hope of stopping this runaway train. He came with a burst of cannon fire that sent colours exploding like fireworks in his head. He shuddered his way through it, almost folding at the knees as she milked him for every last drop of his essence.

And that was another thing that totally surprised him. It didn't feel like it had in the past. This time it felt sacred, as if something elemental had just occurred between them, something that was not so easily reversed.

Nic didn't want to think too deeply about exactly what it was. Instead, he brought her to her feet and slid his hands down her body, cupping her feminine mound, which was delightfully humid and moist with her need of him. He laid her down on the floor, removing her clothes until she was totally naked. He drank in the sight of her, the way her breasts rounded out now she was flat on her back, the way her long, slim legs had opened for him, the secret heart of her swollen and ready for his possession.

He wasn't far off it either. He was already growing hard again and couldn't wait to feel her ripples of pleasure around him. 'I can never seem to get enough of you,' he said, kissing his way down her sternum. 'I want you even straight after I have just had you.'

'I want you too,' Jade said and gasped as he slid a finger inside her.

'You're so wet for me,' he said. 'I want you to be wet for me all the time.'

Jade felt utterly shameless as he caressed her to the brink of release. She whimpered and panted as he brought her close before backing off, as if he wanted to prolong her pleasure for as long as he could. She couldn't take it any more. She wanted the precious release his body could give and begged for it without demur. 'Make me come,' she said. 'Please, Nic, make me come now.'

He removed the rest of his clothes and positioned himself over her body, flinging one leg over one of hers before he thrust into her, stronger than he had ever done before. Pleasure shot through her as he filled her to the hilt, her body wrapping around him, squeezing him, delighting in the power and potency of him as he worked them both to a tumultuous orgasm.

Jade felt every wave of pleasure in every part of her body. The aftershocks were just as pleasurable, leaving her relaxed and boneless in his arms.

'You know something?' Nic said as he propped himself up to look down at her.

She smiled coyly. 'What?'

He trailed a finger down the curve of her cheek, setting her skin alight all over again. 'If we make love in every room in this villa and my one back in Rome, the first year of our marriage will go so quickly it will be over before you know it.'

The year or our marriage or both? Jade wanted to ask but daren't. 'How many rooms are there here?' she asked instead, trying to ignore the fault line ache in her heart.

'Fifty or so, I think,' he said, sending his finger over her top lip, back and forth until it buzzed with sensation.

'And the one in Rome?' she asked, quivering as he began to nibble at her earlobe.

'Thirty or so,' he said. 'I have the perfect room in mind for your studio.'

She looked at him in surprise. 'You mean I can have another one?'

He smiled a glinting smile. 'You can have whatever you want.'

No, I can't, Jade thought sadly. *The thing I most want is way out of reach and always has been.* Nic wanted her for now. It was convenient for him, as convenient as their marriage. He didn't want her for ever.

His lips brushed hers softly. 'We should go out to dinner tonight. The press will expect us to surface by now. How about it? Do you fancy a night out?'

Jade would have much preferred a night in but sensed Nic was getting restless. He thrived on being around people and, after a week at the villa with only the skeleton staff around, he was probably going crazy for more stimulation.

'Sure,' she said with a forced smile. 'Why not?'

He gave her another quick kiss before he leapt to his feet, holding out a hand to her to help her up. 'You have the first shower while I sort out some business,' he said. 'I'll call and make a booking. Wear something sexy for me so I can fantasize about what I am going to do to you when we get home.'

Jade showered and then dressed the part of glamorous

society wife, taking extra time over her hair and make-up. The designer dress she wore was black but cut in a classic style that highlighted her figure. She arranged her hair at the back of her head in a smooth, shiny chignon and, after spraying herself with her favourite perfume, she was about to put on a pair of earrings when Nic came behind her and handed her a flat, rectangular jewellery box.

'How about you wear these?' he said.

She took the box from him and carefully opened it. Inside were an exquisite diamond pendant and a pair of droplet earrings, the sheer brilliance of them taking her breath away. She had worn plenty of expensive jewellery in the past but nothing of this phenomenal quality. It was as if three bright stars had been plucked from the night sky and laid on the black velvet just for her pleasure. 'I don't know what to say...' She looked up at him. 'Are these for me to keep or did you hire them?'

He rolled his eyes at her. 'You think I am that cheap, *cara mio*?' he asked. 'Of course I didn't hire them. I bought them for you.'

'But it's not my birthday for days and days,' she said, looking back at the glittering diamonds.

'Does it have to be a special occasion for you to be given a gift?' he asked, tipping up her chin so her eyes meshed with his.

Jade felt the magnetic pull of his gaze. All her senses began to twitch with excitement at the way he was looking at her. Her need of him made her feel more and more vulnerable. She supposed that was why she said what she did before she stopped to think about it. 'Do you buy all your lovers expensive gifts?'

His mouth tensed at the edges. 'You are my wife, Jade. It is only right that I buy you things.'

'I'm not really your wife, not in the normal way,' she said. 'Or at least not for very long.'

'Then all the more reason to get what you can out of this marriage while you can,' he said. 'Money, jewellery and memories of the best sex you've ever have. Not such a bad deal, *sì*?'

Jade wanted to call him out on that but how could she? What he said was true. She was going to take all of that and more from this marriage when it ended. But instead she smiled coolly and elegantly rose to her feet.

'Will you help me put these on?' she asked, turning her back to him.

His hands made her neck fizz with sensation as he attached the pendant, and her heart began to race as she thought of him removing it later that evening, most probably along with the rest of her clothes.

'You smell divine,' he said in a low, husky voice next to her ear. 'If we had more time I would feast on you right here and now.'

She tilted her head to one side and closed her eyes, her breath coming out as a ragged stream as he trailed a fiery pathway of kisses down to her bare shoulder. His tongue rasped along her sensitive flesh, making her shiver all over.

'Do you need help with the earrings?' he asked against her collarbone.

'I'll be fine,' she said in a scratchy voice. 'Don't… you…um…need to shower and change?'

He stepped back from her. 'I won't be long. Wait for

me downstairs, otherwise I might change my mind and drag you into the shower with me.'

Jade left the bedroom as soon as she put the earrings on because she didn't trust herself with him only metres away, naked and wet and all too irresistibly male.

CHAPTER NINE

NIC had booked them a table at the Terrazza Serbelloni at the Grand Hotel Villa Serbelloni, one of the most luxurious hotels fringing the shores of Lake Como. The restaurant overlooked the lake and, as the evening was warm and still, the water was as smooth as a sheet of glass.

They were led to their table and, once they had drinks ordered, Jade tried her best to relax. There had been no sign of the press and, while the staff had addressed Nic by name, they had retreated to the background, leaving her and Nic to contemplate the menu in peace.

She looked at the menu and chewed her lip in concentration. As usual, the words meant nothing to her. 'What are you thinking of having?' she asked after a moment.

'I think the fillet of turbot sounds good, but then again the loin of lamb is tempting,' Nic said. 'What about you?'

Jade closed the menu. 'I'll have the fish.'

He cocked his head at her. 'You're very decisive. Don't you want a bit more time? There are lots of other things to choose from. This is an award-winning restaurant.'

'No, I'm good,' she said. 'I fancy fish. It's good for the brain, or so they say.'

Nic closed the menu after a few minutes and the waiter came over and took their orders.

Once he had left, Jade asked, 'You haven't thought of developing a rival hotel here?'

'I have thought about it but Giorgio would have my guts for garters if I went ahead with it,' he said. 'It will stay in the family until all three of us come to some agreement over what should be done with it. I think Luca and Bronte will use it a fair bit. It's a great place to get away from the press.'

'I can't believe it has been empty for so long,' she said musingly. 'It's such a beautiful place. I could sit for hours just looking out at the gardens. It must take an awful lot of maintenance, even if it's not occupied very often.'

He gave her a rueful look over the top of his wine glass. 'It does and that is why I insisted on using it more. I am glad you like it. Hopefully, during this year we will get up here a few more times.'

Jade took a sip of her mineral water and then put her glass back down with careful precision to disguise the slight tremble of her hand. 'Do you think your family will be upset when we eventually divorce?' she asked.

He frowned as if he found the question annoying. 'It has nothing to do with them. It's about what we want.'

Jade already knew what he wanted; the trouble was, it wasn't the same as what she did. 'At the wedding, your mother seemed rather keen on the idea of us making a go of it,' she said. 'I didn't like to disillusion her. She thinks we will fall in love like your father eventually did with her.'

'My mother is a hopeless romantic,' he said, still frowning in irritation. 'She thinks no man is complete unless he is married with a family. When the time comes, she will have to accept the termination of our marriage just like everybody else.'

Including me, Jade thought sadly.

He looked at her with a serious expression carved into his features. 'It has to be this way, Jade. At the risk of repeating myself, you have to realise this isn't going to last.'

'How long has your longest relationship lasted?' she asked.

His frown tightened even further. 'What has that got to do with anything?'

Jade held his gaze with an effort. 'What if you still want me once the year is up?'

He shifted his mouth from side to side as he thought about it. 'We can continue our affair for as long as we like, but marriage in the long term is not an option for me. It's not that I have anything against marriage. I can see my brothers are both very happy, but it's not something I want for myself.'

Jade continued on the devil's advocate route. 'What about if you get tired of me before the year is up?'

'I can't see that happening,' he said with a glinting smile. 'You excite me, *cara*, like no other woman has done before.'

Jade felt a ripple of excitement move through her body. His eyes darkened with desire as they held hers, promising earth-shattering passion. 'Have you ever been in love?' she asked.

'No, have you?'

She looked down at her glass rather than hold his

penetrating gaze. 'I thought I was once but now I realise it was just a crush. Real love, the lasting sort, I suspect, is something else entirely.'

'So you believe in lasting love?' he asked as he picked up his wine glass again.

Jade made herself meet his eyes. 'I think it can happen, sure. I think there is probably a bit of luck involved, you know, meeting at the right time, having similar goals and values. I am sure it's hard work at times, all relationships are, but if both parties are committed and willing to go the distance, I can see it could be a very satisfying thing.'

'So once the ink is dry on our divorce papers, are you going to immediately set out to hunt down a husband and father for your children?' he asked.

Jade sent him a frowning look. 'I told you: I don't want children.'

He smiled cynically. 'So you say now at not quite twenty-six, but what will you say in five or ten years?'

'I could ask you the same question,' she quickly threw back.

'Ah, yes, but I do not have a biological clock to worry about,' he pointed out. 'I can father a child, should I choose to do so, at almost any age.'

Jade didn't like being reminded of the clock ticking inside her. She sometimes heard it late at night when she couldn't sleep. She worried about missing out on such a wondrous experience as giving birth to her very own child, but what sort of mother would *she* make? She would be as hopeless at it as she was at so many other things. It wouldn't be fair on the child to have such an inadequately prepared mother. The child would end up embarrassed and ashamed of her even before it was of school age. There were some things you could hide from adults, but children were incredibly perceptive. She had already had a couple of close calls with Julianne McCormack's children, who had picked up on her reluctance to perform certain tasks they took for granted in their mother doing for them, like reading a bedtime story.

'You have gone very quiet, Jade,' Nic said. 'What are you frowning about? Have I touched on a sensitive nerve?'

'Not at all,' she said, raising her chin. 'I guess not all women are cut out to be mothers.'

He tapped his fingers on the rim of his glass as he continued to study her. 'Has your reluctance to reproduce got something to do with your dysfunctional family?'

Jade bristled defensively. 'No, why should it? Lots of people come from broken or dysfunctional homes and they still go on to have children of their own.'

'You lost your mother so young,' he said. 'Don't you think that might be why you are so against having children in case the same happens to them? Perhaps you are worried they might go through the trauma and loss you did.'

'Why are we even having this conversation?' she asked, trying not to show how seriously rattled she was. 'It's pointless. Neither of us wants children. I don't see why I have to be cross-examined like this.'

'I am not trying to upset you, *cara*, I am simply trying to understand you,' he said. 'You are like a difficult puzzle. There are pieces you seem to be deliberately hiding from me.'

She glowered at him resentfully. 'As far as I see it, you know far more about me than anyone. But I don't see the use in becoming bosom buddies as well as sex buddies.'

The corner of his mouth lifted. 'Is that how you see us, just as sex buddies?'

'It's true, isn't it?' she said. 'We scratch each other's itch.'

'It's one hell of an itch,' he said with another glinting smile.

Jade dabbed at her mouth with her napkin. 'Would you excuse me?' she asked, pushing back her chair. 'I need to use the bathroom.'

'But of course,' he said, rising politely as she left the table.

Jade let out a breath of air when she got to the ladies' room. Her face was flushed with colour and her skin felt tight all over. She took a few minutes to gather herself. Nic was pushing on buttons she didn't want pushed. She didn't understand his motives. He was adamant their relationship was finite. Why then badger her with questions that were so deeply personal? It was unsettling to have to face such interrogation. She was so frightened she would betray herself by confessing her love for him. Making love with him made it almost impossible not to whisper the words. She had come so close so many times. He made her flesh sing and her heart ache with the weight of the love she felt for him, but telling him would make things so much worse for her. It would drive him into another woman's arms for sure.

Jade came out of the ladies' room and was halfway back to the table when a hand came down on her arm. She stopped in her tracks and looked at the man who had stalled her. Her heart gave a sickening thud in her chest and her mouth went completely dry.

'Jade,' Tim Renshaw-Heath said with a sleazy smile. 'Long time no see. What, it must be over a year now, right? How are you? Are you here with someone?'

'Yes,' she said, pulling her arm away. 'I am here with my husband.'

Tim's blond brows rose. 'Married, huh? Somehow I didn't see you as the settling-down type.'

Jade flicked her gaze to their table, but Nic was scrolling through his text messages on his phone. She tried to move away but Tim blocked her with his short but stocky frame. 'Hey, don't rush off,' he said and reached into his jacket pocket and held out a business card. 'Call me if you get sick of your husband or if he's out of town some time. I can fill in for him if you know what I mean. I'm still at the same apartment in London. Maybe this time you won't stand me up, eh?'

Jade felt sick to her stomach at his crude suggestion. She ignored the business card and gave him an icy look. 'I am not interested in betraying my marriage vows.'

His porcine eyes gleamed. 'I think I could get you to change your mind.' He fanned open his wallet in front of her face. 'Perhaps this is what I should have offered you the first time around, eh? How much, Jade? How much to sample that delectable body of yours?'

Jade hadn't heard Nic approach but she saw Tim take a step backwards as he hurriedly stuffed his wallet back into his pocket.

'If you ever insult my wife again, I will personally see to it that you never step into this or any other five-star hotel in any country in Europe,' Nic said through clenched teeth. 'Do you understand or do I need to press home my point some other, shall we say, more physical way?'

Jade put her hand on Nic's tensely muscled arm. 'Nic, no, please, it's not worth it. He's not worth it.'

'Ah, but *you* are, *cara mio*,' Nic said before turning to glare at the other man with eyes as cold and hard as green and brown flecked marbles.

Tim moved away, or slunk away was probably a more accurate description. He seemed to shrink even further in height as Nic's tall figure towered over him in an intimidating manner.

'We're leaving,' Nic said, taking her by the hand with firm fingers.

Jade didn't bother arguing. She couldn't wait to get away from the curious glances they had attracted. She felt thoroughly ashamed of her past and wished she could make it all go away. How had she been so lacking in self-esteem and self-worth to flirt with someone as boorish as Tim Renshaw-Heath? It disgusted her that she had such skeletons in her closet. It didn't matter that she hadn't slept with him or even half of the men the press had made out. The way Tim and his ilk treated her made her feel as if she had, and that, for some reason, was far worse.

Nic didn't speak until they were back at the villa. Jade glanced at him a couple of times but his mouth was set in a flat line and his eyes were still flashing with fury, his fists clenching and unclenching as if he was mentally landing a punch on the other man's face.

The door closed with a resounding echo as he slammed it once they were home. 'You should not have spoken to him,' he said through tight lips. 'You should have ignored him as if you didn't know who the hell he was and come straight back to me.'

Jade swallowed to clear her blocked throat. 'I'm sorry—I didn't see him until he put his hand on my arm. I didn't want to cause a scene in the middle of the restaurant.'

He glared at her. 'Damn it, Jade, is this how it's going to be for the next year?'

She felt her back come up. 'Aren't you being a little hypocritical here, Nic? After all, you've had numerous lovers. It's just as likely we will run into one or two or more of them while we are married, especially as you insist on me travelling with you.'

His eyes hardened as they tethered hers. 'It's not the same thing at all. My relationships had some context, some meaning, even if they were not long term.'

Jade straightened her spine. 'Just what exactly are you saying?'

His expression was dark and brooding with tension. 'I think you know what I am saying.'

'Actually, I don't,' she said, defiantly meeting his gaze. 'Why don't you spell it out for me?'

He raked a hand through his hair, his throat moving up and down over a lumpy swallow. 'I don't like the thought of you being spoken to by men like that sleaze ball back there,' he said. 'I don't like the thought of men like him treating you as if you're some sort of high street whore. You're not and you never have been.'

Jade felt tears bank up in her eyes. He was showing a depth of protection and care she could not have hoped anyone would have shown towards her, let alone him.

Nic's frown cut into his forehead. 'Why are you crying, *cara*?'

Jade brushed at her eyes. 'B...because you don't think I'm a slut...' Her voice tripped over a little sob.

He came over and enveloped her in his arms, resting his head on the top of hers. '*Mio piccolo*,' he said softly. 'Of course I don't think you are any such thing.'

She looked up at him but kept her arms wrapped around his waist. 'It's not like you think, Nic,' she said. 'I didn't sleep with Tim or even half of the men the press have reported I've been with. I let everyone think I was a tart but deep down I hate that label. I wish I could make it go away.'

He took out his handkerchief and gently blotted the tears coursing down her cheeks. 'I have things in my past I would like to forget about too—everyone does, I would imagine. The thing is to show the world you don't care. If you ever meet someone from your past, ignore them, move on without engaging in idle chit-chat. They will want to drag you down to their level but they can only do that if you let them. Hold your head high, *tesore mio*. You deserve respect. You're beautiful and talented and have a caring, gentle nature when you're not too busy pushing everyone away.'

Jade placed one of her hands on the side of his face, stroking his cleanly shaven jaw. 'I wish there were more men like you in the world, men of quality and decency.'

He gave her a rueful smile. 'You wouldn't be calling me decent if you knew what I was thinking right now.'

She smiled coyly up at him. 'What are you thinking?'

He brought her close to his growing erection, his hands warm and strong as they cupped her bottom.

'How is that for a clue?' he asked with a dangerously sexy look.

'I think I'm more or less getting the message,' she said, moving against him, delighting in the way his eyes darkened in response.

His mouth came down to meet hers in a kiss that was blisteringly hot. Jade's lips felt like fire as he plundered her mouth, his tongue sweeping against hers, calling it into a sexy duel that made all her senses sing with delight. Her whole body erupted into flames of longing, her inner core pulsing with the need to feel his hard presence moving inside her.

He scooped her effortlessly into his arms and carried her upstairs to the master suite. He laid her on the bed and then stood and stripped off his clothes, his eyes never once straying from hers.

Jade could feel her excitement building. Her blood began to speed through her veins as her eyes went to his aroused length. She licked her lips and scrambled onto her knees on the mattress, wriggling out of her dress and lacy bra and knickers and tossing them over the side of the bed. She went to undo the pendant from around her neck but Nic's hand came out and stopped her.

'No, let me make love to you wearing nothing but diamonds,' he said and kissed the valley between her breasts where the pendant hung in sparkling brilliance.

There was something decidedly decadent and yet affirming about being pleasured whilst wearing priceless jewellery, Jade decided. She felt like a princess, a person of worth instead of the trashy home-wrecking whore she had been portrayed as in the past.

Nic's mouth closed over one of her breasts, his tongue

teasing her nipple until she was arching her spine in rapture. He worked his way from her nipples to the sensitive undersides of her breasts, stroking and gently nipping with his teeth, making every atom of her being crave his final possession.

He went from her breasts over the flat plane of her belly, his tongue circling then diving into the little bowl of her belly button. Her nerves twitched and danced under the ministrations of his lips and tongue, her mind becoming vacant of everything apart from how he made her feel.

He moved lower, taking his time as he separated her tender folds. His tongue tasted her nectar, the intimate action sending sparks of electricity up and down her spine. Her toes curled, her belly flipped and flopped and her heart raced, her breathing becoming choppy as he intensified his caresses, his jungle cat-like licks making her edge closer and closer to the release she wanted so badly. Her fingers dug into his thick hair in an attempt to hold herself steady in a sea of sensation that was pitching and rocking her about like a bit of flotsam.

She cried out when the first ripples of her orgasm rolled through her, the sheer force of it as it gathered momentum making her mind go blank.

He moved back up her body, his need for her so obvious she couldn't help but reach out to stroke him, to feel the pulse of his blood as it extended him so powerfully. He groaned as she moved her hand harder and faster, and then, with another muttered imprecation, he sought her moist warmth, driving into her with a slick thrust that sent a shower of fireworks off in her brain.

He set a fast pace but she quickly caught his rhythm,

moving her pelvis in time with his, accepting each of his hard thrusts with a clutch of her inner muscles until he shouted out loud as he came. She felt the pumping action of his body, the hot spill of his life force anointing her as she lay there quivering in reaction.

His face was buried against her neck, his breathing hot and hectic against her skin. 'Am I too heavy for you?' he asked.

'No,' she said, smiling to herself as his big, strong body pinned her to the bed. She loved the weight of him; it made her feel sensuous to have her limbs entwined so intimately with his and to have his maleness encased in the secret feminine vault of her body.

He came up on his elbows and pressed a soft kiss to her mouth. 'You are beautiful, do you know that?' he said.

Jade wasn't vain. She knew she had inherited from her mother high cheekbones, a neat, slightly uptilted nose, gloriously thick long hair and unusually green eyes, but she had never truly thought of herself as beautiful be-cause she couldn't do the things she most wanted to do, the things most people took for granted. Perhaps beauty and brains didn't go together, after all, she thought. She had certainly missed out on the latter.

'Hey,' Nic said, taking her chin between his finger and thumb. 'What is that serious look for?'

Jade tried to smile but it didn't quite work. 'I was just thinking how I am going to miss this when it's over,' she said truthfully.

His brows moved together and his chest rose and fell as he let out a sigh. He rolled away and looked up at the ceiling, not speaking for a long minute. 'I know,' he finally said in a husky-sounding voice.

Jade waited for a few beats before she turned on her side to look at him. 'Will you miss me?' she said. 'I mean when we finally part company? I'll probably go back to live in London or maybe I'll go to Australia. I've always wanted to go. Have you been?'

He got off the bed and snatched up his trousers, his eyes moving away from hers. 'Yes, it's a great place to visit. I wish I'd had more time when I was there. You should go. The press wouldn't know who you were out there. You would have a chance at the fresh start you said you'd like to have.'

Jade couldn't read his expression. It was like a mask, and his voice had been curt, brusque and to the point, as if he didn't want to continue the conversation any longer than he had to. 'Nic?'

'What?' he asked, still frowning darkly as he faced her after shrugging himself back into his shirt.

She bit her lip, stung by the way he was shutting her out. 'Nothing,' she said.

'Look, Jade,' he said, scoring a rough pathway through his hair with his splayed fingers. 'You know the score. I have been totally honest with you about how far I am prepared to go. Don't go changing the rules, OK?'

She rolled her lips together and slowly lowered her gaze. 'I'm not changing the rules,' she said softly. 'I was merely saying I would miss what we've had when it's gone.'

'What do you want me to say, for God's sake?' he asked in a biting tone. 'That I will miss it too?'

She brought her gaze back to his. 'Will you?'

His eyes held hers for a throbbing second or two. 'I

haven't given it a moment's thought,' he said and, without another word, he left the room, the door closing behind him like a punctuation mark on the conversation.

CHAPTER TEN

NIC announced over breakfast the following morning that they would be returning to Rome, a decision Jade assumed meant their honeymoon was effectively over. She suspected he was putting a wall up between them, a suspicion that was confirmed as soon as they returned to his villa close to the Villa Borghese.

Although he still joined her in bed at night and made love to her as passionately as ever, he didn't engage in lengthy conversations, or even trivial ones for that matter. When he wasn't putting in long hours at his office, he spent a lot of time in his study or on the phone, conducting his business matters with the sort of focus and drive she could only envy.

A new housekeeper was appointed without any input from Jade, but thankfully the woman Nic had chosen was friendly and helpful, even effusively admiring the sketches Jade brought in each day after her treks around the city.

Jade lost track of time as she wandered through the cobbled streets and alleyways as well as the major tourist drawcards. She spent hours at The Vatican, staring up at the ceiling of the Sistine Chapel until the guards urged her on. She made sketches of The Vatican and St Paul's

Basilica and a sheltered glade in the Villa Borghese, as well as some street scenes that captured the essence of the Eternal City.

On Friday she spent the morning at the Colosseum, and then did another afternoon tour of The Vatican. And then, on a whim, she walked back to do some window shopping. She stopped outside a baby wear shop, looking at the tiny clothes with a tight ache in her heart. Her desire to be a mother seemed to increase more and more every day. It was such a no-go area with Nic. She couldn't understand why he was so adamant when he was clearly so fond of his little niece and nephews. Luca and Bronte had called in only a couple of evenings ago and again Jade had watched Nic play with Ella. He had swung her around in what Ella called a 'whizzy dizzy'. Nic had gone round and round with her in his arms until the little toddler was giggling uncontrollably. It had been such a happy family scene and Jade ached to be a part of it. Instead, she felt on the outside again, looking in, a spectator instead of a participant.

She went into the shop and picked up a little Babygro, a pink one with white polka dots. She ran her fingers over the velvet-soft fabric, wishing, hoping and dreaming for her life to be like Maya's and Bronte's. They were so deeply in love with their husbands and Giorgio and Luca were equally devoted.

Jade wasn't sure what made her look up at that point. A member of the press was standing outside the shop with his camera aimed straight at her. She put down the little suit and walked out, keeping her head down, ignoring the questions as they were fired at her.

'Are you expecting the next Sabbatini heir, *signora*?'

She moved past him and two other people who had stopped to stare.

'Is your husband pleased about the prospect of a son or daughter some time in the future?'

She skirted around another group of tourists and ducked down a side street but the journalist persisted.

'Is this a honeymoon baby?'

Jade finally managed to escape by slipping in amongst a guided tour group. Once the cameraman had gone, she walked back in the direction of Nic's villa. She was about halfway there when from inside her handbag she could hear her mobile ringing and quickly dug it out and pressed the answer button. 'Hello?'

'Jade, where are you?' Nic asked. 'I've just got home. It's after six. Why didn't you leave a note to tell me where you were?'

'I've been out sketching and then shopping,' she said, stepping out of the way of some tourists who were busily snapping their camera phones at the scenery.

'You could have at least sent me a text,' he said, sounding distinctly annoyed.

'I didn't want to bother you,' she said. 'You seem rather busy lately.'

'Feeling neglected, *cara*?'

'Not at all,' she responded tartly. 'I know you have things to do. So have I.'

'I haven't just been working on my own stuff. I have been working on setting up a meeting for you with an art gallery owner,' he said. 'He's coming at seven this evening to look at your work.'

Jade felt her skin break out in a sweat. 'Why? I told you it's mostly rubbish. I don't want anyone to see it, let alone a gallery owner. I can just imagine what he's going to say. I'll be mortified.'

'He will give an unbiased opinion,' Nic said. 'You have no need to get into a state about it. Constructive feedback is important, in any case.'

'I don't appreciate you interfering with my private life,' she said as she walked briskly back the other way along the footpath, her agitation rising with every step.

'Jade, you are being childish about this. And of course I have the right to interfere in your private life. I am your husband.'

'Only for the next eleven months,' she said with cutting emphasis.

There was a silence that lasted only a couple of seconds but, even so, it seemed more than a little menacing.

'I will see you when you get back,' he said in a clipped tone. 'The art guy will be here in less than an hour. Don't be late.'

'Don't tell me what to do,' Jade shot back but he had already rung off.

When Jade got back to the villa after taking a lengthy detour, which included a coffee to fill in the time, Nic was fuming. He threw open the door as she came in, his eyes blazing with anger. 'Do you have any idea of what you might have just thrown away?' he asked. 'Clyde Prentham waited over an hour for you. He's an extremely busy man and he made a special effort to be here to meet you. He left just a few minutes ago.'

Jade tossed her head and stalked past but he captured

her by the arm and turned her to face him. 'Let me go,' she said, glaring at him.

'Jade,' he said, this time lowering his voice. 'You seem to want to deliberately sabotage any chance at a career.'

She tugged on his hold but his fingers were like a manacle of steel. 'You don't understand,' she said, terrifyingly close to tears. 'I don't want to have my work analysed and judged and laughed at.'

Nic frowned and slowly loosened his grip to more of a caress on her arm. 'Why are you so worried about what people think of your art when you don't give a toss for what they think about you as a person? You seem to have it the wrong way about, *cara*. You let people say hideous things about you in the press without defending yourself and yet you hide your amazing talent as if it is something you are embarrassed about.'

Jade blinked back the blur of tears that were banking at the back of her eyes. 'I bet your art guy didn't say I was amazingly talented.' She brushed at her eyes with her free hand. 'I bet he thought you dragging him here was a complete and utter waste of time.'

'Actually, he was very impressed,' Nic said, stroking her wrist with his thumb.

She looked up at him with a guarded look. 'You're just saying that...'

He sent his eyes upwards in a frustrated roll. 'Why do you doubt yourself so much? Of course he was impressed. He said you have a very special way with colour and light. He couldn't believe you hadn't had tuition of any sort. You have natural talent, Jade. He wants to show some of your work, a limited space in a general exhibition to start with to get a feel for the market. He thinks you could have your own exhibition eventually.'

Jade thought of all that would entail. The business side of things would be her downfall. She would end up looking a fool, not even able to read through a contract or write her own biography for promotional purposes. She would be mocked in the press—the illiterate artist who could paint but not write down her own address.

'Why are you chewing at your lip like that?' Nic asked, brushing her savaged lip with his thumb.

'I can't do it, Nic,' she said. 'Please don't make me.'

'*Cara*, no one is making you do anything you don't want. If you don't feel ready to put your stuff out there, then that is your decision. It's just that I thought you would be interested in having something to fall back on should you need it in the future.'

She sent him a pointed look. 'Don't you mean when our marriage comes to an end and I've spent all the money? That's what you think, isn't it? That I'm going to spend all the money your grandfather left me and have nothing to show for it.'

His frown deepened across his forehead. 'I don't think that at all. I just don't believe you will be content with all that money unless you have a purpose for your life. Art is meant to be seen and appreciated. I don't understand why you won't take this chance to show the world you are not the shallow socialite everyone thinks you are.'

Jade turned away, not sure she could keep her emotions in check with his penetrating gaze focused on her. 'Let me think about it,' she said, knowing full well what her decision would be.

There was a small silence.

'You won't budge on this, will you?' he said.

She let out a tiny sigh and slowly turned around. 'My art is the one thing I can keep private,' she said. 'Like you and your brothers, I have lived my whole life in the public eye. This is one area I can keep to myself. It's an outlet for me. I do it because I love it, not because I have a deadline or a contract or an exhibition looming. I just love it.'

Nic gave her a crooked smile. 'You constantly surprise me, do you know that?'

Jade bit her lip again. 'I appreciate what you were trying to do for me, Nic, I really do. I'm just not ready to take that step.'

He slowly nodded, as if he finally accepted her position. 'So, tell me about your shopping trip,' he said. 'Did you buy anything?'

Jade felt her colour blast like an open furnace on her cheeks. 'Um…no…I didn't.'

'Any paparazzi lurking around?'

She had to look away, her gaze going to the gardens outside. 'They're pretty hard to avoid,' she said. 'You know how it is.'

'Yes, I do indeed,' he said, coming up behind her to place his hands on her shoulders.

Jade felt her whole body shiver in reaction. She automatically leant backwards, seeking his hard warmth. He brought his mouth down to the sensitive skin of her neck, just beneath the thick curtain of her hair, his teeth nibbling at her playfully, sending every nerve into a madcap frenzy.

'You always taste so delicious,' he murmured against her neck. 'I can't keep my hands or my mouth off you.'

'Maybe after eleven months you won't feel quite

the same way,' Jade said, desperately looking for reassurance.

Nic turned her around in one movement, his eyes dark and frowning. 'Why do you have to keep on about that?' he asked. 'You know the terms. We stay in this marriage until we get what we both want. That's the deal. You signed on it, Jade. You read the contract. It's in black and white with your signature at the bottom of it.'

Jade moved out of his hold, cupping her elbows with her palms. 'Don't you ever think about anything else but money?' she asked. 'You drive yourself so hard in business, but what for? Who are you going to give it to when you leave this earth?'

He looked at her for a tense moment before turning away to rub at a knot of tension at the back of his neck. 'I haven't any plans to leave this earth for the next sixty-odd years if I am lucky.'

'You can't know what life will have in store for you,' she said. 'No one can.'

'I realise that, Jade, but you have to be sensible about this. This was never about the long term. We both agreed on that. When this is over, I want my life to continue the way it always has.'

'But what if it can't?' she asked. 'What if this year changes everything?'

He frowned at her. 'What do you mean?'

'What if that's what your grandfather wanted to communicate to you by tying things up the way he did?' she asked. 'You can't have life the way you want it, Nic. It doesn't work out that way. Sometimes things happen that change everything and you can't change it back.'

He cocked his head at a wary angle. 'What sort of things are we talking about here?'

She bit her lip and looked away. 'Nothing specific.'

'Jade?' He turned her with one hand, forcing her chin up to meet his gaze. 'What is going on?'

Her green eyes flickered with something but then she lowered her gaze. 'I'm just tired,' she said.

Nic brushed his thumb across her cheek. 'I can see that. You look pale and you have dark smudges under your eyes. Why don't you go to bed and I'll sleep in one of the spare rooms tonight?'

She looked at him with a nervous flicker of her gaze. 'You don't have to do that...'

He pressed a soft kiss to the little frown in between her finely arched brows. 'Oh, but I do, *cara mio*,' he said softly. 'Otherwise I will keep you up all hours pleasuring you because I can't stop myself.'

She gave him a small movement of her lips that wasn't quite a smile. 'Well, goodnight, then,' she said and stepped away.

Nic caught her hand on the way past, closing his fingers around hers for a fleeting moment. He felt the tingles all the way up his arm, the flow of his blood increasing its pace as her fingers moved against his. But then her hand slipped out of his and she was gone, her soft footsteps fading into the distance.

He stood staring at the space where she had been for a long moment, a frown pulling at his forehead as he pictured their final goodbye in eleven months' time. His stomach felt wrapped in barbed wire as he imagined that parting scene: the final handover of money, the polite goodbyes and 'thanks for the memories' routine. Why had his grandfather locked them together like this when it would only cause grief and pain when it ended?

It doesn't have to end...

Nic shook his head as if to get rid of the errant thought. Of course it had to end. Jade had the right to her own life—a life with someone who could give her the things she wanted. She believed in lasting love and she deserved it. No one deserved it more. She said she didn't want children but he wasn't sure if she was being truthful on that. He had seen her with his nephews and niece, the way her face lit up and her smile bloomed like an exotic and rare flower.

He thought about her vulnerability. She pretended to be so tough but inside she was like a frightened little girl. Who would be around to protect her if he wasn't? If they divorced as planned she would be even more vulnerable. She would be such an easy target for some creep after her money. She had a naivety about her that, in spite of her street-smart past, had never really gone away.

Letting her go was not going to be easy. He had not expected their time together to be so intensely satisfying. He ached for her and couldn't imagine how this need he felt so constantly was going to ever fade.

Maybe it wouldn't...

He frowned until his forehead hurt. It had to fade. It always did. He had never fallen in love. Love was not an emotion he trusted. Sure, he loved his family and would put his life on the line for any one of them, but romantic love was something that came and went. It was unreliable and transient. He had no intention of allowing himself to be sucked into the fantasy of happily ever after, although he had to admit that in some cases, such as his brothers' lives, it actually was a reality and not a fantasy at all.

He gave a cynical laugh but it caught on something deep in his chest.

Maybe there was hope for him after all.

CHAPTER ELEVEN

WHEN Jade woke up the next morning Nic was standing by the bedside with a newspaper in his hand. 'What is the meaning of this?' he asked, thrusting it at her.

Jade frowned as she pushed her tousled hair out of her eyes. She glanced at the paper before returning her eyes to his glittering ones. 'You know I can't read Italian,' she said. 'Why don't you read it to me?'

'Here's an English paper,' he said, pushing another paper towards her. 'It says much the same thing.'

She looked at a photograph of her in the baby wear shop the day before. She couldn't read the caption but the photo told the story: she was holding the pink with polka dots Babygro, looking down at it with a dreamy, wistful look on her face.

'Well?'

Jade looked at him. 'It's not what you think.'

'Then why don't you tell me what it is?' His voice contained a thread of steel.

She decided to be honest with him. 'Nic, I can't go on like this. I have to be honest with you.'

'Is this another one of your attention-seeking tricks?' He stabbed a finger at the paper. 'To tell the press you were pregnant before you even told me?'

Jade looked at him in shock. *'Is that what it says?'*

His frown deepened. 'What, you're not pregnant?'

'No, of course not,' she said. 'How could you think that? I told you I was on the Pill. I wouldn't deliberately try and trap you like that.'

Nic dropped the paper and rubbed a hand over his unshaven face. 'I'm sorry, Jade,' he said. 'Just like everyone else, I immediately jumped to the wrong conclusion.'

'It's OK.'

'No, it's not OK,' he said. 'I'm the one who should know better. I know you. I should not have judged you so quickly.'

'You don't really know me, Nic,' Jade said softly. 'You don't know me at all.'

'How can you say that?' he asked. 'Of course I know you.'

'Do you know what I want most in the world?' she asked.

His expression faltered for a moment. 'You want to be loved,' he said. 'I know that you want to be loved and accepted for who you are.'

'Do you love and accept me as I am?'

His throat moved up and down over a rough swallow. 'I care about you, Jade,' he said in a gruff tone. 'I admit I didn't at first. I was annoyed that we were forced to marry. I couldn't think of anyone I wanted to marry less. But I have come to see how wrong I was about you. You are a very special person. So talented, so beautiful and so damned sensual I can't keep my hands off you.'

He cares for me, Jade thought with a mental curl of her lip. What a pathetic word that was. People cared for their goldfish and pot plants, for God's sake. It didn't mean they would give anything to be with them. It didn't mean they felt achingly empty when they were away from them. It didn't mean they couldn't imagine life without them in it. She felt all that and more for Nic. Surely she deserved to be loved, not just cared about.

'*Cara?*' He stroked a gentle thumb across her cheek. 'We're good together. You know we are. We care about each other. That is a good thing, *sì*?'

'How do you know what I feel about you?' Jade asked. 'I might still hate you for all you know.'

His thumb moved to stroke across her bottom lip. 'If you do, you have a delightful way of showing it.'

Jade pulled away from his tempting touch. 'Nic, I want some space…to think about things.'

He frowned darkly. 'Things? What things?'

She chewed at her lip where his thumb had set off the nerves into a tingling frenzy. 'The news thing…the false report about a pregnancy? Well, I've kind of changed my mind about babies and…things…'

Nic's frown intensified until his brows met over his eyes. 'Are you saying you *want* to have a baby?' he asked.

Jade held her breath for a moment before she answered. 'I know this is not what you want. And I know it's not really fair to spring it on you, so that's why I want some time to think about what happens after this year is over. I need time, Nic. Please, just let me go back to London for a few days. I can't think straight when I'm with you.'

'*Cara*, I can't think straight when I'm with you either but do you really have to go to London?' he asked. 'It'll be wet and cold, for one thing.'

Jade steeled her resolve. 'Just a few days, OK? Just until my birthday. I want to see Julianne McCormack.

I want her to know I didn't betray our friendship. I need to do that face to face. I should have done that right at the start. At least now she knows we are married maybe she'll listen to me.'

He scraped a hand through his hair. 'I'll book you a room in our London hotel. But I want to join you in a couple of days, got that? I am not having you out of my sight any longer than that.'

'Because you don't trust me?' Jade asked.

He gave her a long and serious look before he brushed the back of his knuckles down the curve of her cheek. 'Because I will miss you, *mio piccolo*,' he said.

London was as cold and wet as Nic had warned but Jade had too much on her mind to notice. She called on Julianne at home, taking a very big chance on whether she would let her in, but surprisingly she did. It was an emotional meeting for both of them. Julianne had found out only a few days before that her husband was conducting an affair with a woman from his office. A compromising text message had come up on Richard's phone, which resulted in Julianne confronting him about how he had used Jade to shield his perfidious behaviour.

Jade explained why she hadn't defended herself, confessing for the first time to anyone about her severe dyslexia. Julianne was wonderfully supportive, which made Jade wonder if she should exhibit the same courage and come clean with Nic. It would be a brave step but she couldn't see how their relationship had any chance of moving forward unless he knew everything there was to know about her.

He had phoned her several times a day and each day—along with a dozen red roses—he had sent her a present. A string of pearls with matching earrings arrived first, then there was a dress from one of her favourite designers, and on the third day a bracelet encrusted with shimmering diamonds. There was a card with the bracelet but Jade could only make out his name. She ran her fingertip over and over it, wondering if he was missing her as much as he said he would. She was certainly missing him. The huge bed felt so empty at night without his long, lean limbs reaching for hers.

When Nic called soon after the bracelet arrived Jade thanked him. 'It's beautiful, Nic,' she said. 'But you shouldn't be spending so much money on me.'

'Did you get my card?' he asked.

She rolled her lips together and looked across to where she had propped it up against the latest vase of roses. 'Yes...'

'Did you read it?' he asked after a slight pause.

Jade wanted to tell him then but she couldn't bear to do it over the phone. She wanted to see his face, to make sure he wouldn't mock or ridicule her. 'I was too distracted by the diamonds,' she said in an airy tone.

There was another pause before he said, 'I will get to the hotel about six this evening. I have a meeting in the afternoon but I shouldn't be late.'

'OK,' she said. 'See you then.'

Just before Nic was due to arrive at the hotel, Jade's father called by to drop in an early birthday present. The timing couldn't have been worse, but then she had come to expect that from her father. Keith Sommerville was two drinks down and reaching for his third when Nic arrived at the penthouse.

Jade got up from the sofa and went over to greet him. 'Hi,' she said, twisting her hands in front of her awkwardly. 'My father dropped by when he heard I was in London. I hope you don't mind.'

Nic brushed his mouth against hers, once, twice and then on the third time held her mouth with his in a lingering kiss that made every cell in her body swell with longing. 'Of course I don't mind,' he said. He looked up and smiled politely at Keith. 'How are you, Mr Sommerville?'

'You'd better call me Keith now that you're my son-in-law,' he said, raising his glass of Scotch. 'Cheers.'

Nic put an arm around Jade's waist and led her back to the sofa, taking the seat beside her. It was hard to tell if the tension in her slim body was from her father's presence or his. Nic desperately hoped it wasn't his. He had spent a torturous few days missing her, aching for her each night, dreading the thought of her announcing she wanted to end their marriage. He couldn't bear the thought of spending the rest of his life without her. He was a fool for not recognising how he felt until she had gone but when had he ever recognised emotion? He had always run from it. He had done it for so long it had become automatic. He had hardly been conscious of how he compartmentalised his life until Jade had come along and unpicked the lock to his heart.

'So,' Keith said as he leaned forward to refill his glass, 'when are you two going to give me a grandchild for real? I saw that article in the press. I was looking forward to becoming a grandfather. You'd better get on with it. Jade's not getting any younger.'

Nic felt Jade cringe as she bent her head to her glass.

'All in good time, Keith,' Nic said. 'We're still on our honeymoon.'

'I hope the first one's a boy,' Keith said. 'Every man wants a son to carry on the family name and the business.'

Nic reached for Jade's hand and gave it a gentle squeeze. 'I will be thrilled, no matter what sex any child of ours is,' he said. 'And, as to carrying on the business, that is up to our daughter if we have one. It will be her decision, not ours.'

Jade's father harrumphed and reached for his fresh Scotch and drained it. 'Well, thanks for the drink but I must love you and leave you,' he said and got to his feet.

'It was nice of you to make the time to see Jade,' Nic said, still holding Jade's stiff little hand in his.

'Well, I can't make it for her actual birthday,' he said. 'I have a golf day with my firm. But Jade doesn't mind, do you, Jade? As long as she's got her present, that's the main thing, eh?'

'Thanks for the book voucher, Dad,' Jade said in a tight voice. 'I am sure it will come in very useful.'

Nic waited until Jade's father had left their penthouse before he turned her in his arms. 'Are you OK?' he asked.

She gave him a been-there-done-that-a-million-times look. 'At least he didn't embarrass me by getting completely drunk, but I'd say he's well on his way.'

Nic frowned and brought her hand up to his chest. 'He doesn't deserve a daughter as gorgeous and talented as you.'

She looked at his shirt front rather than his eyes. 'Thank you for saying that.'

He tipped up her face. 'I mean it, *cara*. You are one

of the most unique people I have ever met. I discover more and more about you every day.'

She lowered her gaze and began to fiddle with one of the buttons on his shirt. 'Nic, there's something you should know about me. Something I should have told you right from the start.'

Nic clasped both of her hands. 'I know about your reading problem,' he said.

She looked up at him in wide-eyed blinking surprise. 'You...you do?'

He nodded. 'I didn't cotton on at first. It took me a while to realise why you never responded to my text messages and never sent any of your own, and why you always asked me what I was going to order in restaurants before you made your own choice. You had already told me you never read the papers, but I couldn't work out why you were so surprised about what was written in that false report. I put it down to the fact you just hadn't had time to read it for yourself. But it wasn't until I was on my way here this evening that I finally realised why you hadn't read it.'

Jade moistened her suddenly dry mouth. 'How did you work it out?'

He smiled at her tenderly. 'You said you didn't read the card that came with the bracelet because you were distracted by the diamonds but that's not true, is it?'

She felt her cheeks heat up. 'No...'

He cupped her face in his hands. 'Do you want to know what I wrote in that card?' he asked.

She looked at him with tears shining in her eyes. 'I'm a bit frightened to ask...'

His eyes softened even further as he gazed into hers. 'I told you I loved you, that I have loved you for most of my life. I can't think of a time when I didn't love you and want to protect you. Those feelings have always been there but I have covered them up. I've done it since I was a child, I guess because I don't like being at the mercy of other people's emotions, let alone my own. It made me feel too vulnerable.'

Jade choked back a sob. 'I can't believe you love me when I'm so…so stupid.'

Nic frowned and tightened his hold on her hands. 'You are not to say that about yourself. Never, do you hear me?'

'But I caused Jon's death,' she said, struggling not to cry. 'I forgot the details of the flight. I couldn't read the itinerary my father gave me. I was so good at covering it up. I was too proud, too stubbornly proud to ask for help. I'm so ashamed…'

Nic held her close, his heart aching for all she had suffered. '*Cara*, you are not to blame yourself. It was up to the adults around you to have you properly helped and they didn't do it. I wish I had known earlier. That's why I was so surprised when you acted as if nothing had changed this afternoon when I called you. I couldn't see why you wouldn't have read the card, diamonds or no diamonds. It was only when your father was here that I finally realised. I saw the look on your face when you thanked him for the book voucher. He still doesn't have a clue, does he?'

She shook her head. 'I've always been too frightened to say anything. He puts such a high value on academic achievement. He's always at me to better myself; that's why I get book vouchers every year even though I've never read a book in my life.'

Nic held her from him to look down at her lovingly.

'That's why you've never held down a job. It's why you refuse to show your art work. It's why you married me even though you didn't want to because you so desperately needed the money, wasn't it?'

Jade had to bite the inside of her cheek to stop herself from crying. 'I feel ashamed that I only wanted to marry you for the money. I was so determined not to fall in love with you again like I did when I was sixteen. But I couldn't seem to stop myself. Everything you said, everything you did, every time you kissed or touched me made me realise how much I loved you.'

'*Tesore mio,*' he said with a catch in his voice. 'I will help you learn to read if you will help me to be a better person. I am ashamed of how shallowly I have lived my life up until now. I have sought my own goals with no thought to anyone else. Now all I can think about is you and our future. You have done that, Jade. You have changed me, just as my grandfather knew you would.'

She smiled at him as his arms wrapped securely around her. 'Do you think he suspected this might happen? That we would fall in love eventually?'

'I am sure of it,' Nic said. 'We were always bickering at family gatherings, remember? The love-hate thing is a dead giveaway.'

Jade looked at his shirt button again. 'The night of my party—I wish it had been you instead of him. I've always regretted it. You have no idea how much.'

He cupped the back of her head and held her close against his chest. 'Do not talk of it, *cara*,' he said. 'I wish I hadn't spoken to you so harshly. Perhaps if I had been less heavy-handed in how I handled that it might never have happened. I blame myself. I should have protected you but I was too damned focused on keeping my distance in case I overstepped the mark. You were so young—so young and innocent.'

She looked up at him again. 'I feel like that young girl when I am with you,' she said. 'You make me feel as if the past hasn't happened.'

'As far as I am concerned, it hasn't,' he said, holding her close. 'It is the future we have to concentrate on now. And I think it's going to be a bright one, don't you?'

Jade smiled. 'I think it's going to be an absolutely brilliant one,' she said as his mouth came down and covered hers.

Six months later...

The exhibition was a stunning success. Every painting had a 'Sold' sticker on it and Nic was smiling from ear to ear as yet another camera aimed its lens at his beautiful pregnant wife. Jade was glowing as she had never glowed before. He could still not believe how excited he was about the prospect of becoming a father in three months' time. Each night he placed his hand on Jade's growing belly, feeling the outline of little heels and elbows that would one day be in his arms to love and protect.

Giorgio and Maya came to stand beside him. They were arm in arm, Maya's own glow another giveaway, although nothing so far had been announced in the press. 'You must be so proud of her, Nic,' Giorgio said, smiling.

'I am,' Nic said, feeling his chest swell as he looked at his gorgeous wife.

Luca and Bronte were hugging Jade in turn, making Nic feel all the more proud of how she had become such a treasured part of his family. His mother was constantly boasting of how Jade had tamed her wildest son, turning him into a devoted family man just like his older brothers.

Jade looked at him from across the gallery, her radiant smile making her green eyes dance with happiness. He went over to her and wrapped a gentle and protective arm around her expanding waist. 'You're not getting too tired being on your feet all this time, are you?' he asked.

'Not yet,' she said, snuggling in close. 'Did you see what the reviewer wrote in the exhibition pamphlet?'

He smiled indulgently. 'Why don't you read it to me, *cara*?'

Jade flicked it open and, following the words with her finger, read each one out carefully. '"Jade Sabbatini is a fresh new talent in the art world. Her stun...stun...stunning collection entitled *In Love with Rome* has drawn inter...international interest."' She grinned up at him. 'Are you proud of me, darling?'

Nic pulled her close, resting his head on the top of her silky one, the words catching in his throat as he spoke. 'Unbelievably proud, *mio piccolo*. You constantly amaze me. I am the luckiest man in the world to have you as my wife.'

Jade looped her arms around his neck, the bump of their baby joining them as one. 'I love you, Nic Sabbatini,' she said. 'I really, *really* love you.'

'You know something, *cara*?' Nic smiled as the paparazzi hustled closer to capture the moment. 'I really, *really* love you too.'

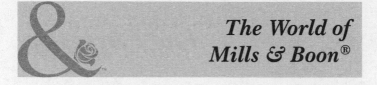

The World of Mills & Boon®

There's a Mills & Boon® series that's perfect for you. We publish ten series and, with new titles every month, you never have to wait long for your favourite to come along.

Scorching hot, sexy reads
4 new stories every month

By Request

Relive the romance with the best of the best
9 new stories every month

Romance to melt the heart every time
12 new stories every month

Desire

Passionate and dramatic love stories
8 new stories every month

Visit us Online

Try something new with our Book Club offer
www.millsandboon.co.uk/freebookoffer

What will you treat yourself to next?

*Ignite your imagination,
step into the past...*
6 new stories every month

INTRIGUE...

Breathtaking romantic suspense
Up to 8 new stories every month

Medical Romance

*Captivating medical drama –
with heart*
6 new stories every month

MODERN™

*International affairs,
seduction & passion guaranteed*
9 new stories every month

n o c t u r n e™

*Deliciously wicked
paranormal romance*
Up to 4 new stories every month

RIVA™

*Live life to the full –
give in to temptation*
3 new stories every month available
exclusively via our Book Club

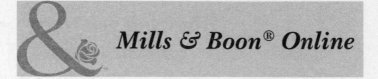